'Do you know how old I am, R—Rogan?'

'What? Of course I know how old you are. Twenty-five. And I know how old I am too. Thirty-six, in case you've forgotten,' he snarled, almost sarcastically. He'd sensed she was off-balance and what she wanted to discuss with him was, doubtless, even more so. 'What does that matter to the point?'

Jassie breathed deep and fixed her attention on their hands gripped so tightly their knuckles had whitened. This was her moment, her only chance. She might as well just spit it out as her brother, Philip would have said.

'I'm never going to marry but—but I—confound it, Rogan, I just have to know—just once—what it's like to—to make love—no, I'm not asking that—I know the mechanics but I want to know how it *feels* to— you know—*lie* with a man!' He never blinked and her own gaze danced across his face, desperately searching for a reaction, an emotion. Anything but the impression of horror that looked out of his eyes! She swallowed. 'There is no one else I can ask. No one else I would want to ask—'

By JEN YATES_{NZ}

Other books in 'Lords of the Matrix Club' series:
Bk.2. The Perfect Duchess
Bk.3. The Virgin Widow
Bk.4. Her Dark Lord

Contemporary Romance set in New Zealand
A Deal with the Devil
Fallen Angel
Token Bay

Anthology of Short Erotic Romance

NEWSLETTER
To join my email list and receive a free Prequel and Sequel to this series send
an email to Jen YatesNZ at

jenyatesnz@mail.com

The Earl of Windermere
Takes a Wife

'Lords of the Matrix Club' Series. Bk. 1.

An Erotic Romance set in the Regency Era.

JEN YATES_{NZ}

Gyneva Publishing

New Zealand

The Earl of Windermere Takes a Wife
Author Name: Jen YatesNZ
Publisher: Gyneva Books, New Zealand
Genre: Historical Romance set in Regency Era.
Copyright Notice: Copyright© 2016 by Jen Yates
Cover Design: by Tamian Wood twca0005 via
romancenovelcovers.com

Disclaimer
This is a work of fiction. The characters and events in this book are the creation of the author, and resemblance to persons, whether living or dead, is strictly coincidental. Towns and places are used as settings and have no relation to any event or actual happening outside the author's imagination.

For my husband.
Your patience, support and encouragement is without price.

The Earl of Windermere
Takes a Wife

CHAPTER ONE

May 1815

Rogan was home! Her heart was going to burst through the walls of her chest.

That dancing organ leapt right up into the base of her throat as she watched his tall broad-shouldered form urging the black stallion over the rails from Windermere. In and out of her home for as long as she could remember, he was as close as family, and his mother, Lady Olwynne, had long played the maternal role in her life. The image of him, six foot tall, broad and solidly muscular with black, Byron-cut hair, dark blue eyes, harshly squared jaw and deeply cleft chin was ever vivid in her mind. There were weeks when that remembered image was all she had but when he was home she knew he would seek her out, believed he needed her presence in his life just as surely as she needed his.

Knew that while he'd vetoed marriage and they'd never talked of it since her sixteenth birthday, he was not indifferent to her as a woman. It was this knowledge that had long simmered in her breast until she could no longer contain it.

She'd made a life-defining decision after his last visit and here he was home again. So today—

Dear God, she wouldn't think on what she'd decided or she'd be unable to go through with it.

Forcing the aching excitement back down into her belly, Jassie schooled her features into the ladylike, friendly smile of welcome she always showed him, when what she really wanted to do was throw herself onto his lap, grab that gorgeously scowling visage and kiss the harshly sculpted lips until he—

Botheration! Now she'd have to work harder at containing her smile, her love, her need—

'Good morning, Jassie,' he said, as he reined in the black to where she waited by the tree. The deep rich tones of his voice and the warm smile in his eyes were balm to her very soul. Her whole being wanted to sigh with relief at the sight of him, at the slow but guarded sweep of his gaze from the crown of her head to the tips of her boots. As if he was—reassuring himself it was really she.

'Good morning, Rogan. I'm so glad you're home at last,' she answered, darting her own swift glance over the whole of his person to be assured he'd returned unharmed. She only had a vague understanding of what he did when he vanished, sometimes for weeks at a time. Once he'd returned with his arm in a sling, claiming to have badly sprained it by falling off his horse. His mother, Lady Olwynne, had been of the opinion it was more in the nature of a wound of some sort, but he had never changed his story. 'When you leave I am never easy until you return. Lady O worries too, I know.'

Thick lashes drooped over the deep blue of his eyes so she could not read his true thoughts.

'I am here,' he said simply. 'And as always, so are you. A most refreshing sight. Is that a new habit?'

'How clever of you to notice! It's the exact same color as my old one!'

The slight scowl left his face and for just a moment the old, sunny Rogue from her childhood grinned down at her.

'But it's styled quite differently. A more military look. Very becoming.'

She allowed her hungry gaze to drink in the magnificence of him in buckskin trousers, midnight blue coat, and curly brimmed beaver sitting low on the broad brow, shadowing his beautiful eyes to a deep navy blue.

She could drown in those eyes if only he would allow her.

Her breath hitched in her chest as she briefly considered the momentous proposition she intended to put to the Earl of Windermere today. She'd planned the scenario right down to where she wanted to be standing when she uttered words no self-respecting single gentlewoman would ever speak to a man. To that end she must contain her unravelling emotions and try to keep her mind on other things until after they'd completed their ride.

'Where are we headed today?'

'Upper Farm. Harte has some new-fangled cropping notions he wants to discuss.'

'Wonderful,' Jassie instantly responded. 'I can already taste Mrs. Harte's scones with quince jelly and fresh cream.'

With a touch of her knees Chester leapt forward, Raven close on his heels. It was a glorious day for a gallop. Raked with nerves at the thought of her plans for later, Jassie needed a distraction and concentrating on keeping her seat on the flying red horse was just the distraction she loved best of all.

She intended to request they ride home via the standing stone on Neave Tor—which would tell Rogan there was something serious afoot.

They'd developed the habit of riding to Neave Tor when there were weighty issues to be discussed and resting on one of the huge flattish stones lying about the foot of the strange, rough monolith that had stood on the Tor for centuries. It was the only possible place for such a potentially life altering discussion.

Meantime she would just enjoy the balmy morning and the delight of the Earl of Windermere at her side and leave the possible joyous outcome of her daring proposition in the lap of the Gods. She was equally prepared to face the consequence, whichever way Rogan chose to step.

She was, she told herself firmly.

'Which way home?' Rogan asked two hours later as they rode down the lane from Upper Farm.

'By way of Neave Tor,' Jassinda answered, flustered that she was unable to look at him when she said it. Nevertheless she was aware of his sudden intense scrutiny and forced herself to ride without saying anything further. He could read her too easily.

'Well?'

She couldn't help but glance his way then. It was as difficult as she'd known it would be to maintain an innocent expression while he regarded her with that puzzled frown that always made her want to grab his face and kiss him until the worry lines went away.

'Well what?'

'Are you going to give me a hint of what you want to discuss?'

'So you can line up your arguments to shoot me down?'

Thankfully she managed to waggle her eyebrows to give the impression it was nothing to angst over.

'Mmm. Something like that.'

'No.—About Mrs. Harte's request to find a position for young Lucy; you know Jensen is not that much younger than the Countess and though she tries to hide it her arthritis causes her considerable grief. A young pair of hands and legs to fetch and carry would greatly relieve her, I think. Your mother is quite demanding, as you know, much as we love her.'

Rogan rolled his eyes, but allowed himself to be diverted from pressuring her to reveal the topic she wanted to discuss with him at Neave Tor.

'If you think she would suit perhaps you could sort it out with Mother and Jensen? I'm—'

'—you're totally out of your depth dealing with domestic issues. You need a wife.' The last four words had popped out of her mouth before she'd really thought about what she was saying. She snapped her betraying lips shut, then sucked in a breath and added, 'Of course I'll handle it for you.'

A pained expression flashed in the cobalt depths of his eyes but it was gone before she'd really been sure she'd seen it and he grinned lazily at her.

'I don't need a wife. I have you. I consider myself well blessed in my friendship with you.'

Jassie hoped the smile she pasted on her face for him was sweet enough to conceal the real state of her emotions.

'As am I,' she concurred. 'Race you to the Tor.'

Further conversation was impossible but nothing could stem the torrent of her thoughts.

On the night of her sixteenth birthday, she'd carefully secured a private moment alone with him, determined to experience her first kiss with the only man she'd ever wanted anywhere near her person. He'd gone to great pains—after he'd fulfilled her dearest wish way beyond her maidenly dreams—to make her understand he would never marry and she must not set her sights on him if she thought to find herself a husband in the near future. He'd never offered a reason as to why and the bleak, bitter visage he'd worn while warning her had deterred her from ever venturing to ask.

Could she still make her request in the face of this latest avowal that he didn't need a wife? Could she ask for what she wanted without suggesting marriage? He'd never explained why he didn't want a wife. Was it marriage per se he objected to, or was it what marriage involved—in the bedroom? It wasn't actually marriage she'd be asking for. Would he think her beyond the pale? Be surprised? Angry?

Impatient with the intensity of her desire to anticipate his responses and feelings, Jassie, lowered her head and concentrated on the ride. Of course he arrived first. He always did. Chester, disadvantaged by the uneven weight of the sidesaddle was no match for the more superior height and strength of Raven. It would be a different story if she were riding astride as she often liked to, she thought, trying desperately to still the wild hammering of her heart as he waited to lift her down as soon as she pulled Chester to a standstill.

His hands were hard and warm at her waist and gone all too quickly as he reached for Chester's reins and dropped them over his head, leaving him to graze and snort with Raven. Hoping he would not feel the nervous tremor of her fingers, she laid her gloved hand on the arm he offered and together they climbed the last steep rise to the base of the looming stone monolith. Several other long flat stones lay about the hilltop and were suited for sitting and surveying the rolling green of the downs as they fell away right down to the distant valley where Brantleigh Manor nestled in peaceful rusticity. A rise in the landscape concealed Windermere Abbey from sightseers at this point.

As always, Rogan removed his jacket and spread it over the lichen covered stone before assisting her to settle comfortably. Then instead of taking his seat beside her as he usually did he stood with one foot on the stone, arms braced across his knee and levelled her with that unwavering midnight blue stare.

Jassie blinked then looked away from the intensity she saw in Rogan's gaze. She fussed with the arrangement of her moss green velvet riding habit, her mind racing with panic—more like excitement.

What was he thinking? Would the next few minutes produce her heart's deepest desire? When she looked up again her attention was caught by the straining muscles of his thigh encased in taut buckskin and her heart rate increased from frantic to frenzied. What would that thigh look like—naked? Don't think about it or you'll hyperventilate.

Jassie concentrated on slowly removing her gloves and setting them on the rock beside her while she scrabbled in her mind trying to remember how she had intended to start this conversation. Because she had gone over it and over it until she'd had it clear exactly what she'd say. Now not a word of what she'd so carefully devised would come to her. Her mind was a blank—except for the startling vision of a naked and muscular male thigh stretched out on her bed for her exclusive perusal and touch.

Lord, she was going to make a mull of this if she didn't pull herself together. And she'd probably never dredge up the courage to broach the subject again.

Breath shuddered into her lungs.

The large dusty leather boot thudded to the ground and suddenly Rogan was kneeling before her, cradling her restless hands between his large ones. The side of her brain that wasn't entirely stultified by panic, noted how beautifully masculine and strong those hands were and longed to know how they'd feel, gliding over her skin, on her breasts—

She dragged in another shuddering breath.

'Jassie! What the hell is bothering you? Are you in some sort of trouble? Do you need money? This is me, Rogan bloody Wyldefell, not the Grim Reaper come to haul you off! Tell me how I can help.'

'It's—it's not so bad you need to swear,' she muttered, making no attempt to retrieve her hands as a proper lady should. But she couldn't really consider there was anything ladylike about her if she was going to carry through with the proposition she intended to put to him, could she?

She closed her hands around his, savoring the moment of close connection and finally allowed herself to look straight into the deep blue of his eyes darkened with concern and let him see—whatever he would—in hers. When he blinked and drew back a little, she knew he'd seen enough to shock.

Breathe, Jassie, breathe, she ordered herself as the healthy tan leached from his angular cheeks and his eyes changed from dark blue to the silvery shade of—horror?

'What do you want?' he whispered.

Oh God!

'Do you know how old I am, R—Rogan?'

'What? Of course I know how old you are. Twenty-five. And I know how old I am too. Thirty-six, in case you've forgotten,' he snarled, almost sarcastically. He'd sensed she was off-balance and what she wanted to discuss with him was, doubtless, even more so. 'What does that matter to the point?'

Jassie breathed deep and fixed her attention on their hands gripped so tightly their knuckles had whitened. This was her moment, her only chance. She might as well just spit it out as her brother, Philip would have said.

'I'm never going to marry but—but I—confound it, Rogan, I just have to know—just once—what it's like to—to make love—no, I'm not asking that—I know the mechanics but I want to know how it *feels* to—you know—*lie* with a man!' He never blinked and her own gaze danced across his face, desperately searching for a reaction, an emotion. Anything but the impression of horror that looked out of his eyes! She swallowed. 'There is no one else I can ask. No one else I would want to ask—'

Breathing no longer a priority, Jassie wrenched her hands from his and jumped to a spot about three feet away and stared blindly down at Brantleigh Manor, lying like a toy model in the shimmering distance.

Then she closed her eyes and focused on the pain flowering in her chest and spreading to her belly. What had she done?

'I'm sorry. Forget I said anything. It never occurred to me you would be horrified by the thought of—of—making—having s—making l—love to me,' she finished in a rush.

There was still no sound from behind her and she hurried into speech again to fill the awful silence that was something she usually treasured about the Tor.

'I th—thought men—um—didn't mind. That—that any w—woman would do. I'm so sorry. You will now think me the most l—loose of—of d—demi reps! P—please forget I ever mentioned anything!'

What was he doing? She dared a glance back over her shoulder and wished she had a stiletto to stab her own heart.

Still on his knee, he'd turned his head to watch her. The skin along his cheekbones had gone a pale pasty yellow, his jaw hung open and the most peculiar expression filled his eyes. Anguish? Horror? Terror?

Anger? Or a ghastly potpourri of all the above? She'd done this to him, given him such an abhorrence of her he'd never speak to her again, let alone anything else her foolish heart—and body—had been thinking of! The unimaginable had happened and she'd lost the most precious friendship she would ever have.

She'd assured herself she could live with the outcome whatever it was. She'd lied.

A violent sob wanted to burst out of her chest and she could not have stayed a second longer if the devil himself had threatened her with eternal purgatory for moving.

Grabbing a handful of her riding skirt, she fled the few yards down to where the horses were placidly grazing. She snatched Chester's reins up over his head, threw herself at the saddle with a desperation that despite the heavy encumbrance of her riding habit, enabled her to get her leg almost over the pommel.

Startled between one wrench of the sweet grass and the next, the horse leapt sideways, threatening to toss her in a very humiliating heap on her backside. Recognizing his attacker was his beloved mistress he settled with a sudden shudder of his whole body, legs bunching, poised for take-off.

With her weight all to one side, the girth began to slip and to her terror she knew she was going to end up under Chester's belly and nothing would hold him then. Her only hope of deliverance was to throw her body from the saddle again and away from Chester's deadly hooves.

Matching thought to action she closed her eyes and launched—into a warm, solid obstacle, closer and more forgiving than the hard earth was ever going to be. Arms clasped about her like a vice and Rogan took the total impact of her momentum and staggered to the ground, rolling their bodies so that in one second she was clutched desperately against his chest and the next his whole length pressed intimately down against hers. Another roll and she was above him again and they had fetched up in a shallow crater in the ground.

Their lungs bellowed, pounding their chests against one another as their wide-eyed stares locked together.

'Christ, Jassie! What the fuck did you think you were doing, woman?' he yelled suddenly.

She blinked, swallowed, closed her eyes, opened them again and tried to tell herself he hadn't just said what she thought he had. He might have been her mentor in many manly pursuits but he and Philip had rarely sullied her much younger and very feminine ears with the rough cant she knew gentlemen shared among themselves. And it was entirely her own fault he'd lost control to the extent he had now. Her blood must be so confused, rushing in and out of her cheeks like a demented storm tide, it was a wonder there was enough to drive her stampeding heart. She should roll off Rogan, put distance between their bodies, try and restore some semblance of propriety to the situation.

'Propriety!' her brain mocked. 'You abandoned that the moment you decided on this brazen-faced plan of action.'

Deciding propriety well-lost in the circumstances she simply dropped her head to his massive, heaving chest and let her arms slide in ugly desperation around the powerful masculinity of his neck. She knew her desperation was ugly—and obvious—but if she were never to have the opportunity to be this close to the temptation of his body again, and the universe had seen fit to gift her with this one luscious moment in time, she would steal every second of it Rogan would allow her, seconds he did not appear to be about to curtail any time soon.

Oh blessed be!

Speech was not an option. It would take all her strength and concentration to restore anything approaching a normal breathing pattern, as much because of where she now found herself as for what had transpired before her spectacular mode of arrival there.

'Are you—all right?'

His voice was a rumbling vibration against her forehead.

She managed to nod and ask, 'You?'

'I think so,' he answered slowly, his voice husking and the brutal grip of his hands softening across the small of her back.

Just when she thought she might regain the ability to breathe, those same hands lowered and opened against the swell of her buttocks before beginning a slow, sensuous glide, into the hollow of her back where the fingers splayed, sliding under her riding jacket, fanning her waist and raking hungrily up her straining rib cage.

She'd never hated her corset more. How could she get those hands beneath her clothes, exploring her skin? Her moan was involuntary, a rasping ache of need rippling through her, shimmying her heated feminine softness against the hard masculine torso. Her fingers pressed into the warmth of his neck and she began to wonder if she'd ever be able to prize them away.

Why couldn't her mind shut down and just let her body revel in the realization of her deepest, most secret desires? Why must thoughts still bombard her with distraction? Not the least of which was how far short her maidenly memory or imagination had fallen from the reality of how it would feel to finally be in Rogan's arms again—however she'd managed to arrive there.

Ever since her sixteenth birthday she'd wanted to feel again the wonder of his lips, his tongue dancing intimately with hers, deep in the cavern of her mouth. He would come to his senses any moment and toss her unceremoniously on her backside, just as instinctively as Chester would have. *Her* senses demanded she grasp every experience she possibly could before that moment arrived. Tightening her grip round his neck she dragged her body over his, achingly aware of a hard ridge behind his trousers pressing up into the fork of her thighs. Instinctively her hips bucked a little, wanting more. Her breasts sliding roughly over his chest were aching so badly she wondered if they might have been bruised in the fall. But that worry went the way of all other rational thought when her mouth came level with his.

He'd lost his hat in his crazy rescue of her person and now her fingers threaded hungrily through the short black silken curls that had called to her hands for years. For just a second she was distracted by the glow in the deep blue eyes that seemed to pulse in rhythm with her breathing, with the regular thrusting of her breasts against his still heaving chest.

Sanity had not claimed him yet. She lowered her mouth—and his opened to welcome her! Her last thought before abandoning herself to the heated seduction of that mouth was, sanity was greatly over-rated.

Her fingers dragged down the smooth shaven planes of his cheeks to grip his jaw and hold his face for her ravaging mouth. Somewhere in the fog of her brain she was aware she'd lost all semblance of anything ladylike and was at the mercy of the love, the hunger, the lust she'd carried deep in her being for this man for as long as she'd been aware of such things.

The hot chiseled lips that had starred in her dreams for years were at last exactly where she'd longed for them to be, drinking her in, suckling hungrily, devouring her every breath which she gave willingly into his keeping. His tongue danced along the edge of her teeth, seeking entrance, demanding more. Instinctively her mouth opened and suddenly his hands were at the back of her head and there was no pulling back even in the unlikely event she would want to.

She wanted to climb inside him, to take him inside of herself, meld their two beings into one perfect entity from here until eternity. Her desires tried to make themselves known through passionate mewling whimpers in the back of her throat and then his hands, those two fiery brands holding her head, stroked back down her torso to grip her buttocks and pull her hips hard against the solid ridge in his trousers. Finally there were no words, no thoughts in her mind, just an all-consuming fire that had been smoldering, simmering, threatening to combust for so long no other tinder was needed. Her hips pumped against him, eliciting a deep groan from his chest that maddened her still further.

This was what she'd wanted, what she'd been asking for, and now for whatever miraculous reason, it was hers. Nothing could keep her hands from him now. With desperate fingers she ripped the already loosened neck cloth undone, exposing the violent pulse at the base of his manly throat.

Hers—for now.

Her mouth settled there, suckling deeply at the vulnerable spot while her fingers worked with feverish intent at the stud fasteners of his shirt. One by one they slid from the fabric, abandoned the moment they'd succumbed.

'Rogan!' she whispered, more to herself than him. 'I—oh—I have so longed—'

Words failed her again for her fingertips had discovered the pure masculine textures of his body beneath the shirt; hot skin, taut over straining muscle, and a soft dark mat of fine curly hair. Where her fingers led her mouth instinctively followed, kissing, licking, suckling with noisy delight. Impatient hands spread the shirt wide exposing the full extent of his broad muscular chest with dark, flat nipples offering a challenge she never thought of resisting.

At least she had some idea what to do, having had the freedom of the very extensive libraries at both Brantleigh Manor and Windermere Abbey all her adult life. If she'd been thinking at all she'd have thanked whoever had thought to provision the topmost shelves, at the Abbey in particular, with some very explicit tomes. No one, not even Philip had known she'd found those, let alone Rogan.

With a soft moan of deep satisfaction she closed her lips over Rogan's hard left nipple, sucked deeply and nibbled with her teeth, eliciting a harsh groan from him that excited her almost beyond bearing. He was as lost to desire as she was. He was not going to stop her! The knowledge was a heady burst of excitement, sparking her every nerve ending with wildfire.

Her breasts felt as if they were straining free of her corset, her mouth was a furnace of insatiability and her whole lower body was about to burst into flame at any moment.

This was what she'd wanted, knew had been missing from her life. Would she ever be able to go on if this was all she would ever have? That thought was enough to spark another explosion through her bloodstream.

Her mouth slid across his chest to pull deeply at his right nipple and Rogan gripped the back of her head, clearly indicating his appreciation. Then his hands were dragging restlessly down her body again. A cool breeze whispered across the back of her thighs, quickly warmed by large, heated palms sliding upwards under her skirt and over her tingling flesh to curve over her buttocks.

As she lifted her mouth back to his with a hissed, 'Yessss!' one hand slid right round under her hip, finding the soft mass of curls at her mound. She tried to raise her lower body a little to ease his access but the other hand clasping her buttock held her firm. Nevertheless, his seeking fingers slid deep, unerringly finding where her desire wept for him. More encouraging groans were driven from her throat.

'Please—oh Rogan—please!'

A deep, almost animalistic growl, rumbled up from his belly and between one breath and the next that didn't seem to know whether it wanted to flow in or out, she was on her back beneath him, riding skirts rucked up to her waist, all her woman's secrets open to him. Gripping her flailing arms he thrust them above her head and held her wrists down with one hand while ripping open the fall of his trousers with the other. His huge swollen cock sprang free and just for a breath Jassie felt doubt, and words quivered on her lips.

Then his fingers were back between her desire soaked folds sending streaks of lightning straight to her womb, and her body over-rode her mind. Unable to move her hands to grasp any part of him, she bucked her hips upwards in a desperate plea for the ultimate connection.

'Please,' she begged again, her head threshing helplessly against the harsh, wind-dried grass of the Tor.

His mouth was a taut, grim slash; a small scar beneath his left eye gleamed oddly white and a strange fire glittered in his eyes. Jassie had the sudden disconcerting thought he was no longer aware of who lay beneath him; he was lost in the power of his need and the instinct to mate, maybe even to—punish?

Harsh, guttural sounds emanated from his throat and she could only hope they were the sounds of a man in the throes of passion for if they were not—it sounded almost as if he'd called her some very ugly names. But she was helpless against the strength of him and the desperate surging need within her.

And then he thrust, hard and deep, and a wild yelp of pain ripped from her throat at the tearing, intensely burning power of his possession. A deep moan of satisfaction was his only response as he held himself deep in her body for several seconds before he began to withdraw. In those few seconds Jassie realized the pain had subsided and she didn't want him to leave her body. But then, to her great relief, he thrust again, and again, over and over, his eyes closed, his body hammering into hers with the power of a battering ram and his fingers still manacled about her wrists—and yet—now the pain was gone she welcomed him. Her brain was sizzling, lyrical, with the wild realization, at last—she *knew*.

Knew how it was to be loved by a man. Knew herself capable of bringing the man she loved, *this man*, beyond the limits of his own formidable control.

Something was building within her, some awesome pinnacle she was striving to conquer, the peak of which promised a spectacular boon she could not begin to imagine. Just when it seemed she might reach out, claw her way to this crowning glory, Rogan's whole body stiffened above her, his penis buried deep, surely as deep as the mouth of her womb, and with a harsh, long-drawn out, rending groan, he gradually collapsed down over her, relinquishing his punishing grip on her wrists.

His eyes opened, glowing like molten silver in his head and then the strange glitter faded and Jassie saw the moment when he came back to her, really saw her. Anger, black, ugly and bitter, flashed before he closed his eyes and with an ugly oath he rolled off her to lie with his hand across his eyes as if trying to block out the sight of her.

As if he hated her. As if he really had called her a 'fucking whore'. What had she done? In her selfishness—somehow she'd hurt him.

Stunned by the crazy wildness of it, the ache within her that wanted to cry for something lost, or maybe never found, she lay as he left her, arms still above her head as if she could no longer pull them down, her lower body exposed like some abandoned trollop, and fought to drag air into her lungs and stop the tears that suddenly burned at the backs of her eyes. Succeeding desperately with the first and failing miserably with the second she finally moved with the thought of touching his shoulder, comforting him, telling him it was all right, it was her fault and she'd never bother him about this stuff again, when he rolled even further way from her and slammed his fist into the hard ground with a jarring force that must have been exceedingly painful. But the words he shouted with the force of bullets from a gun, ugly curses she'd never heard him use before today, held her from touching him.

Instead she began to push agitatedly at her skirts with one hand while attempting to wipe tears from her cheeks with the other. *Why* was he so angry? What awful darkness filled his soul? For she knew she had glimpsed the dark pit of despair in his eyes. Did he hate her so much for bringing him to the point he could not refuse her?

Gradually he became still, face buried against his arm where it lay on the ground and the only sounds on the Tor were the soft whisper of the wind about the standing stone and the trill of a skylark far above them.

'Jassie, Jassie—damn it! Damn it all to hell.' The words came to her in a harsh, almost broken whisper then he rolled back and folded her limp body in his arms and held her close against his chest. His whole being trembled. 'How can you ever forgive me?'

His lips pressed hotly against her forehead, then his cheek rested gently against hers and she imagined the dampness on her skin was as much from his tears as hers.

Dear God, where did they go from here?

When his mouth found hers again, it was gentle, caressing, seeking. His tongue moved tentatively in search of hers and she surrendered to the sweetness of it with a sigh of intense relief. Perhaps all was not lost. The large heated hand that had driven her to such heights only moments before closed gently over the swell of her breast. Then with a groan of frustration he swiftly unfastened her jacket and shirt to ease her aching flesh above the confines of her corset. Her brain was fit to explode with the delight of it and then he bent his head to hers, delving deep into her mouth with his tongue until she moaned and writhed with need.

'I know—I know,' he growled, lifting his mouth from hers and allowing their breaths to mingle. 'I promise—I will—control myself this time.'

His head lowered again to the breast he cupped and held for his hungry lips to savor, pulling and suckling with exquisite tenderness. Once again her body seemed to have a mind of its own, bucking and jerking up towards his mouth, wanting—wanting—more. Trailing kisses across the valley between her breasts he lavished the same attention on her other nipple and the fire in her belly magnified.

'Rogan,' she begged. 'Please—'

'Don't!' he said sharply. 'Don't beg. It's all right. I'll not leave you wanting this time. But—don't—beg.'

His hand found her thigh, cool from its exposure to the air, and rubbed gently upwards, leaving a restless heat in its wake. Strong masculine fingers found that place that still ached for him, slid into the searing inner heat of her—and out—and in again.

Suddenly the peak she'd strained for with such futility earlier was within her grasp, and she hissed through her clenching teeth.

'Yesss!—Oh God, Rogan! Oh—oh—'

As she screamed her release to the heavens with total abandon he increased the speed and depth of his hand until she was convulsed in one long cry of total ecstasy.

She dragged desperately at his hips, trying to haul his body over hers.

'Rogan-I-want-you!' she cried.

His body as immovable as the rocks above them, he absorbed her screams with his mouth and continued to pump his hand until her cries became whimpers and faded at last to tiny bubbling sobs. Gently he drew her skirts down over her trembling legs and folded her into his chest with her face buried against the thundering pulse in his neck. Jassie could do no more than cling to his warmth and strength. It was safer than whatever would come next.

CHAPTER TWO

He was the lowest, ugliest cur in the pack. Jassie was wrapped in his arms and he could not force himself to release her as a gentleman would. He should never have allowed himself to touch her in the first place. She had trusted him with her body, her innocence, her virginity and what had he done with that momentous gift? He'd raped her. Sure, a purist might argue she'd been willing, even importunate, but the fact remained Rogan Master-of-Control Wyldefell, aristocratic bloody Earl of Windermere, had lost all semblance of self-command and taken her with the finesse of a stag in the rut.

Everything he'd feared of himself had come to pass. He'd captured her wrists so she had no chance of fighting against his superior strength and body weight and forced his way into her body with never a thought for her untried, uninitiated state.

In short he had betrayed her in the worst possible way—this woman who had loved him so well and so long. She deserved better. So much better. He'd known that from the start and had told her so when she was sixteen and just coming into her power as a woman. It would have been so easy to take what she'd offered then and sully her with what he'd already become. But he'd prided himself on still being the gentleman he'd been raised as—in all the ways left to him. He'd been damaged beyond repair when it came to the intimacies between a man and a woman and he'd vowed never to subject her to that, no matter how his soul had hungered for her. He'd known every time he'd come home to Neave, drawn irresistibly as a fish to the lure, he'd risked—this.

There was only one way this could ever be put right. They would marry and he would install her at the Abbey—where she should have been from the day she was old enough to wed.

And then?

Then he'd give her the key to her bedroom door with instructions to keep it locked at all times—and offer himself for every damned courier mission to the Continent he could possibly undertake.

Today—all things considered—he'd been remarkably restrained with her. What would happen when he could have her behind closed doors—to which *he* had the key—when she would be at the mercy of his hideous obsession to punish all women for the sins of the one who had forever distorted and stolen his innocent joy in the act of love.

The cold damp of the ground began to seep through his buckskins and he wondered how long they'd lain there, wrapped tightly together as if seeking assurance one from the other what they'd done wouldn't change anything about their world—or hiding from what must be faced now.

Grimly Rogan sat up, pulled a limp, heavy-eyed Jassie upright beside him and busied himself working her beautiful, rosy breasts back into her corset and tying the strings of her chemise. It didn't look like she was capable of doing it for herself, as if she might even be suffering from shock. Well, he could blasted well do it. It would prove, to himself at least, he could touch her without turning into some wild ravening beast. He could, goddammit he could, he told himself through gritted teeth, as his fingers sank into the softness of her flesh, tucking the taut little nipples back behind the boned stuff of her corset. Jassinda Carlisle could very well be the death of him, he thought as he helped her to her feet and buttoned her shirt and jacket.

Suddenly aware of cold air at his crotch, he tidied his own clothes while Jassie, eyes glowing like soft golden gems, watched his every movement as if she'd never seen a man—well, hell, of course she'd never seen a man buttoning his shirt and falls before. It seemed his own wits had gone begging.

Respectable once again, his gaze was drawn back to hers. Dear God, she was temptation personified. Her hair had come loose from its careful arrangement and was an unraveled tangle down her back. He'd never seen her disheveled, at least not since she'd been a tomboy kid still in the schoolroom, and the sight almost undid all the good intentions induced by his shame and guilt. Gently he turned her as it seemed she'd completely lost her senses. God, had the shock of what he'd done cast her completely out of her mind? He dragged his fingers through the riot of golden curls, retrieving whatever pins were still tangled in it, twisted the mass back into some semblance of a bun and secured it with the pins as best he could. Hopefully anyone seeing her would think she'd simply been for a wild ride across the Downs.

Or maybe, considering the state of her clothing, she'd taken a spill off her horse. Where the hell was her hat, the jaunty military-styled shako that had looked so elegant atop her perfect coiffure when he'd met her this morning? Where was his own?

He began casting about the hillside when he was stopped by her low, husky voice saying, 'Thank you, Rogan. You'd make some woman a wonderful maid.'

He finally allowed himself to look into her eyes and guilt stabbed painfully into his gut. Such love shone from her countenance, he could only think of running his heart through with a dagger. He had done nothing to earn that look, nothing to earn any regard from her except hatred or at the very least, disdain. She should be calling him every vile thing she could lay her tongue to. Instead, she looked at him as if—as if—he'd planted the standing stone on the Tor—just for her.

Damnation! He was the lowliest varlet who had no right even breathing the same air. But the wrong had been committed and there was only one way of putting it right.

'We will marry. Saturday a fortnight from now. I'll ride back to London tomorrow and get the special license.'

The sated kitten look lasted all of two seconds after he'd made his grand statement and then in the blink of an eye he was facing a feral, hissing she-cat.

'Oh-no-we-won't-Windermere!' Each measured word was accompanied by a flash of fire from blazing topaz eyes and her use of his formal name said more than enough about the sudden change of her mood. 'You'll not turn that table on me now so afterwards you can accuse me of trapping you into a marriage you didn't want.—I *know* you have vowed never to marry. That is not what I was asking for.—I love you too well and value our friendship too deeply to allow you to make that sacrifice.'

'If you'd truly valued our friendship you'd never have—', he began but hearing the ugly snarl in his voice clamped his mouth shut and tried for a deep breath to calm the fury beating through his blood; fury directed not at the perfect, innocent being standing before him but at a woman from his youth whose every treacherous feature was carved across his soul in shame.

'I wished to *know*! Only you could ever have redeemed that wish for me, Rogan, for not only did I wish to know, but I wished to know it *with you*. It is something I've been desiring and considering asking you for some time now, not some ill-considered whim of the moment!'

'What if you are with child?' he ground out.

Her whole being sobered a little as she considered him and when she spoke again, it was in a quiet, gentle tone that vibrated across the chords of his heart with a terrifying temptation.

'It would be my greatest joy to bear your child, Rogan.'

The picture of her, belly swollen with his seed, engulfed his mind, undermining his resolve. She would have him on his knees begging before too long. That he couldn't allow. She must be protected from him just as she must be protected from the vicious tattling dames of the ton.

'You stupid damned wench! You're ruined! Did you consider that in your *ill*-considering? And if you are pregnant—because at this very moment you could be!—you will never be received in polite society again. Certainly not in London and not even here in what stands for polite society in Neave!' he yelled.

The crack of her hand against his cheek was loud in the quiet of the hilltop and for a moment they both stood as if turned to stone, as rigid and unmoving as the great monolith itself. The chasm between them yawning at his feet was not to be borne. She had been his lifeline, his only reason for living for so many years. If he could not see her, talk to her whenever he returned to the Abbey there would be no reason to continue with his life. Knowing she lived, would be pleased to see him when he returned, would listen and smile and laugh and touch his blackened heart with light was all he lived for. He could not lose that. He would not.

And he'd not abandon her to the viciousness of society. It would be like tossing an innocent ewe lamb to a pack of wolves.

Blindly he reached for her, pulled her close against his heart and pressed her face to his neck where he could feel her skin against his. She was the embodiment of his every dream and longing, all he craved but could never possess, for in possessing it he would sully that which was bright and perfect. But he couldn't live entirely without her in his life, had never been able to.

'I cannot leave you to the mercy of the wolves, Jassie-my-love. Let me do this one pure and honorable thing I can. Let me marry you and settle you into the Abbey where you rightfully belong as my Countess. Let me protect you. Then if there is a child he will be the rightful heir to the Windermere land and titles, not growing up with the hated stigma of illegitimacy. You would not want that for your child—our child.' He could hardly keep his voice steady, so filled was he with yearning for the realization of a dream he'd long believed impossible. 'I will not take no for an answer.'

He gripped her shoulders and held her a little away from him to see what was in her eyes now, but she hung her head and there were fresh tears on her cheeks.

'No one else would do to show you what is between a husband and a wife and yet—you do not wish to marry me?'

'More than anything but—not like this. It is not what *you* want.'

Her voice held the sulky undertones he remembered from the day Philip had blasted her out for sneaking his pistols out to shoot targets in the woods behind Brantleigh. She'd been thirteen and more responsibility than her poor young brother had wanted or known what to do with. They'd both been sick to their stomachs considering what might have occurred when a thirteen year old lass with no notion of fear was alone with a pair of dueling pistols.

No more sick than he felt now, considering the outcome of this day that had begun with such innocent promise.

'We should never have done what we did. More than that, I should not have allowed it to happen *how* it did. It was little short of rape. You might have some small inkling now of *how I am,* why I've been so careful to eschew marriage all these years.'

'What do you mean?'

He considered the innocence of her gaze. Dear God, pray she did not believe that was how the act of love should be consummated. Then again, what else did she know?

'I was rough, totally lacking in consideration, or caring. A lady should not be subjected to such bestiality. It will not happen again. I vow to you.'

A light went out in her eyes, leaving her countenance shuttered and devoid of animation.

'Very well,' she said, starting to cast about for her hat which had rolled further down the hill. She slipped from his grasp and picked up the shako, which looked very much as if Chester had put his large hoof right in the center of it.

'Oh! How unfortunate!' she cried in an utterly false voice. 'My hat blew off and Chester trampled it. Guess I'll never wear it again.—I'd appreciate a leg up, Windermere,' she called over her shoulder as she caught up Chester's reins.

Rogan found his own hat lying upside down just beyond the crater where innocence had been tarnished and he'd acted in such a way as to negate the most solemn vow he'd ever made, jammed it on his head and strode down the hill to where Jassie waited by her horse. Clearly she was set to show the world and his worthless self, nothing of any note had occurred here today.

She raised her foot for his hand. He ignored it, straightening the saddle and reaching for the girth to tighten it a few notches. Then he came upright and confronted her, holding her gaze with the fierceness of his scowl.

'We go nowhere until you agree to be my wife.'

Snapping her head back, she fixed him with eyes bright and hard like shards of amber glass.

'I agree to be your wife,' she snapped.

'Saturday a fortnight from now.'

'I've agreed. Isn't that enough?'

'No. Saturday a fortnight from now.'

'Very *well*! Saturday a fortnight from now. *Now* put me on this horse, Windermere, so I can go home.'

'Wait.' He tested the tension of the girth, tightened it a notch, then without another word he cupped her raised boot with his hands and lifted her into the saddle.

She was gone the moment her foot was in the stirrup. Rogan climbed back up to the fallen stone to watch her crazed flight, all the way down the broad flank of Neave Tor and across the rich bottom lands dotted with oaks and yews. He couldn't relax his vigil until she disappeared behind the stable buildings at Brantleigh.

'So,' he muttered, dragging on his jacket and throwing himself down on the rock where she'd sat to deliver her startling request, 'The Earl of Windermere takes a wife.'

He picked up the neatly aligned pair of riding gloves Jassie had laid there earlier and ran them restlessly through his hands.

How was he to keep himself away from her? What would become of them if he could not? She was everything that was bright, innocent and beautiful in his world. How could he prevent his husbandly attentions from changing that?

Dobbie, Brantleigh Manor's head groom was old enough to be Jassie's grandfather. He took one look at the lathered horse and his mistress's unusually disheveled state and his bushy brows came together in a way that had made her giggle as a child, but which today only added to her agitation.

'What happened, Miss Jassie?' he growled. 'Are ye hurt? Not like ye to blow yer horse—or take a tumble. Ye should be takin' young Jem with ye, not ridin' alone. Aren't I al'ays tellin' ye?'

'I wasn't alone,' Jassie snapped before thinking. 'Lord Windermere was with me.'

It wasn't until Dobbie's brows bristled again that she realized what she'd revealed, and what that said about the state of her mind. If he rode with her, Rogan always saw her back to Brantleigh and often stayed for luncheon. Even less would Dobbie understand his neglect to do so if she had actually taken a tumble.

The old man's chest began to swell and his ancient jowls worked in his growing agitation. Jassie could almost see him wondering how much he could get away with saying with regard to such neglect on the part of the Earl.

'Don't start, Dobbie. We had a slight difference of opinion. None of it was the Earl's fault. He's probably sulking on Neave Tor—where I left him.'

'Sounds more nor like a Banbury tale to me,' Dobbie began muttering.

'Are you doubting my word, Dobbie?'

'Nay, Miss Jassie,' he muttered. 'Wouldn't think on it.'

Jassie turned away from the darkened look that settled on the old man's weathered features and ran her hand down Chester's flanks, trying to hang on to her temper and not feel shame for her sharp words to her old retainer.

'I'm sorry, Dobbie. Please give Chester a good rub down and a special treat. He's carried me well today.'

She couldn't have the old man thinking ill of the loyal animal either, whatever that meant he now thought of her.

Then turning on her heel before he could question her more, she hurried across the stable yard, through the kitchen gardens and in through the back of the house.

In the back hallway she ran into the housekeeper, Mrs. Jolly, who, like Dobbie, had been at Brantleigh Manor since before its current mistress was born and had no qualms about tutting with horror at said mistress's sadly disarrayed state.

'Miss Jassie! What happened to you? You look as if—'

Not wanting to get into any details with her doughty housekeeper, Jassie interrupted her shocked questioning and, adopting a very rare haughty tone, said, 'Nothing that can't be tidied up Mrs. Jolly. I'm fine and I'd be grateful if you would order a bath sent up immediately and—perhaps you could send Tilly to find Mrs. Lyndon and ask her to attend me in my rooms please.'

Mrs. Jolly gave her young mistress a narrow look, pursed her lips and hurried off in the direction of the kitchen, muttering, 'Yes, Miss Jassie, I'll see to it straight away.'

As soon as the housekeeper disappeared round the corner of the hallway Jassie grabbed up her skirts and took to her heels, pounding up the back staircase as if fire licked at the soles of her boots. The day was only falling from one disaster to the next. Not only had she ruined her friendship with Windermere and given him a terrible abhorrence for her, but she'd also given the two most loyal and long-serving members of her staff at Brantleigh cause to be certain something more than a tumble had occurred that morning. They'd always watched out for her. Lord knew, she couldn't expect that to stop just because she'd done something she'd rather they didn't know about.

Her flight didn't slow until she reached her room at the far end of the east wing, threw herself through the door, across the thick and colorful Aubusson carpet to the deeply stuffed wing chair by the window. Sinking into its familiar comfort, she finally let her emotions wash over her. First to suffer for it was the flattened shako she still clutched in her hand. It flew across the room in the general direction of the fireplace and landed squarely in the empty grate. Next she attacked her boots, struggling, kicking and swearing in a rare unladylike fashion until she managed to tear them off and send them flying after the hat. As the second one landed with a satisfying thunk, the door opened a crack and Francine Lyndon peered cautiously around it.

'Is it safe to enter?' she asked. 'Are you all right, Jassie? Mrs. Jolly seemed to think you'd had a fall, or maybe something 'more dastardly'! She said you definitely weren't yourself. What on earth has happened since this morning? Maybe you should listen to Dobbie and take young Jem with you instead of traipsing all over the shire on that huge great horse on your own.'

Jassie flopped back into the chair, closed her eyes and exhaled deeply, before saying in a relatively even voice, 'It's safe to come in, Fran. Chester only looks huge to you because you're terrified of any animal taller than a beagle and when have you ever known me to fall off that horse—or Chester to let me? I wasn't alone. I was riding with Lord bloody Windermere.'

'Jassie! Oh my God. I've never heard you use such a word before and well, if you didn't have a fall then—you look as if you—you've—been—'

'Raped,' Jassie finished for her. 'That's what he called it too.'

'R-raped? You? And—the Earl?' The door shut with a slam and Francine was instantly on her knees at Jassie's side. 'Jassie, he wouldn't! I mean, he's never even touched you. It's what you've always been complaining about. You're not making sense.'

Francine's voice trailed off into uncertainty and she tentatively closed her hand over Jassie's where they kept fisting in her lap.

Jassie turned her gaze on the carefully manicured wilderness of Brantleigh Manor's front garden, a riot of color, textures, shapes and energies created by her grandmother and lovingly tended by the garden staff ever since. None of it registered. All she could see was a pair of deep blue eyes filled with horror, anger, bitterness and something disturbingly like fear. She was agonizingly afraid nothing would ever erase the memory.

'Of course he didn't. I instigated it. We are to marry on Saturday a fortnight hence.'

It was the first time she'd ever seen Francine truly shocked.

'But you said—he'd never—he'd vowed—'

'Yes.'

She ground her teeth in an effort to hold in the tirade that wanted to pour out of her.

Francine stared at her accusingly and then asked in an oddly censuring tone, 'Jassie, what have you done?'

Heat rushing into her cheeks, Jassie turned to stare once more out the window while fighting to bring the explosion that threatened within her, under control. Francine was her companion and a very close friend and she'd alienated enough people today. She was not going to add Francine to their number.

Letting her breath sigh out between her lips and striving to keep emotion out of her voice, she said, 'I've done the most dreadful thing, Fran. I've—quite selfishly—achieved my deepest desire and thereby lost a most valued friend.'

Jassie turned her head to stare into Fran's summer blue eyes that were shadowed with concern. Tears burnt at the back of her own eyes and she bit hard on her lips in an effort to stem the flow. She might never stop if once she began to cry.

Francine levered herself up and drew another chair to Jassie's side. Taking Jassie's restless fingers in hers once again, she said, 'Tell me all.'

Jassie swallowed, considered Fran's solemn countenance and managed to dredge up a smile for this best of friends. Francine understood heartache and grief. She'd suffered more than her fair share. There was nothing she couldn't tell her, nothing they wouldn't share with each other. The story dropped from her lips and became easier in the telling with each revealing word. She'd reached the point of her ignominious flight down Neave Tor when the arrival of the footman with the bath finally halted the flow.

When her maid, Ruby, offered her services, Jassie dismissed her saying Mrs. Lyndon would attend her.

As soon as the servants were gone, Jassie stood up and began unbuttoning her jacket, still unable to let go of her miserable story.

'When he told me we'd marry I thought I'd die. His face was a mask of—lord, I don't know what, Fran! He'd become someone I'd never seen before.'

She tossed the jacket onto the chest at the foot of the bed and began on her shirt buttons, so recently refastened by Rogan's large hands. That memory had her squeezing her eyes shut and gritting her teeth. His touch had been so precious, so wanted. And none of what had transpired between them had lessened the soul deep yearning to feel it again.

'So you see,' she muttered when her heart stopped gasping in her chest like a starveling bird, 'I will finally become Lady Windermere as I've always dreamed I would—and Windermere hates me.'

The shirt fell on top of the jacket and she turned her back to a silent Francine so she could loosen the ties of her corset. Her voice would scarcely work but she had to ask.

'It wasn't rape, was it, Fran?'

'Not if you welcomed it, Jassie,' Francine answered quietly.

Peeling the corset from her body and clad only in her chemise, she turned to face Francine.

'Thanks dear friend. I can manage now.—What's the time?'

'Almost half after two.'

Jassie felt her eyes widen with shock.

'Truly?'

Where had the morning gone? Oh stupid question!

'Would you like a tray sent up?' Francine asked as she turned to the door. 'You missed luncheon.'

Jassie shook her head.

'I don't think I could eat anything. Maybe just a cup of tea. And then I think I just want to be alone, Fran. Do you mind?'

Francine crossed back to hug Jassie.

'Whatever you need, Jass. You know that.—When you need me just ring. I have such an easy life with you. You totally spoil me. God knows how I'd have coped as companion to some high-nosed old biddy who just really requires a willing doormat. Always supposing I could have found one willing to hire the widow of a man killed in a duel for cheating at cards! Oh!'

She stopped. Her eyes filled with horror and her face drained of color.

'Will you—once you're married—you won't need a—'

Jassie snapped out of her mental fug and cut in.

'Don't even say it, Fran. I will need you more than ever. Who will talk sense into me when I'm up in the boughs over Windermere? Who will talk nonsense to me when I'm in the black pit of despair—which I can't help feeling is waiting to swallow me up.—You know, I have the most dreadful feeling Windermere intends to dump me at the Abbey and disappear, honor taken care of. *What* is he so afraid of? For I'm sure fear was his over-riding emotion and what he said—'did I now have an inkling of *how he was*'. What did he mean? He certainly wasn't *afraid* to *take* me. Quite the opposite, I would have said.—Like a dam bursting,' she ended in a mumble.

'But *how* he took you *is* the problem, Jass! No real gentleman would have attacked you like that—as if you were no more than a doxy in a brothel! Especially not when he *knew* you were a virgin. *And he knew it. That's* what he was trying to tell you.'

'It wasn't meant to be like that?' Jassie asked in a small voice. 'But it was terribly—exciting, Fran. How—how should it have been?'

'Like it was later, when he came to his senses again—slow, gentle, *loving*.—I say again, Windermere *knew* that, was probably absolutely appalled at what he'd done.—What do you really know of Windermere, Jass?'

'Huh? I've known him all my life! He claims he was once allowed to hold me when I was a very tiny baby and—I grinned at him and he's been my slave ever since!'

'So why, when you grew up, didn't he marry you? I've always wondered. You two were made for each other. You're together every day when he's at the Abbey. He'd have to be daft not to know your feelings. You've never made any secret of them. And contrary to what you might think he is not unmoved either. It's in his eyes when he watches you—especially when you're with other men. It would have been interesting to see what he did if you'd ever encouraged any of them.'

'Then why, why, *why?*'

'Only Windermere can answer that, Jass,' Fran murmured, finally leaving the room, eyes dark and troubled.

At the closing of the door Jassie stripped off her chemise and stood before the mirror of the tall mahogany armoire, staring at the evidence of her passage to womanhood. Twenty-five and no longer a virgin— finally. Almost involuntarily her fingers crept across her skin to caress the dried smears of blood on her thighs—thighs that had cradled Rogan's, her womanly portal that had welcomed his manhood, his joining of them as one being. There had been pain; sharp and intense though brief. But she found she could scarcely recall it now, having been obliterated by what came after. She tried harder to recall the piercing sensation that had made her cry out, for the moment was precious in that it was a necessary precursor to all that followed.

And what followed had felt so right, so blessed—until she remembered the look in his eyes and then his words. 'I'm so sorry. It should not have been like that.'

And those other ugly words she'd tried to tell herself he hadn't uttered.

How should it have been? The words were a wail in her head. Wasn't that how it was supposed to be, each totally lost to the ecstasy of being joined as one with the other? Jassie wasn't sure how it could have been better. Admittedly she was ignorant—this once being her only experience. The books she'd read were mostly about the mechanics and variations rather than what either partner should be experiencing emotionally.

But when she thought of his hand manacled over her wrists as if he'd never let her go and his body pounding into hers as if he'd lost all control, had simply been overcome, finally, by what he felt for her— what she'd always, deep down, *known* he felt for her—she simply wanted to hug herself with bliss.

So why, *why* didn't Rogan feel that same euphoria in the aftermath she did?

And was Fran right? Did she *really* know the Earl of Windermere? By far the greater proportion of his time was spent in London or fulfilling his secret courier missions onto the Continent for the War Office. She had little or no idea of the circles he moved in, who he really was.

Practically raised by Rogan's mother after the death of her father when she was ten, she'd had her first season in London when she was eighteen. She now knew his secret service career began that year of 1808, when Napoleon Bonaparte had usurped the Spanish throne in favor of his brother, Joseph. British Forces, led by Lt. General Sir Arthur Wellesley had stepped in to drive the French from Spanish soil. They were becoming far too powerful, having overrun a large part of the European Continent and as such constituted a grave threat to Britain.

Windermere had definitely played least-in-sight during that season and the ones that followed. He'd rarely appeared at any events she attended except those he couldn't refuse if he was in London, such as her come-out ball and any affairs his mother, Lady Olwynne Windermere, had organized as Jassie's sponsor into society. His father had died in March of 1809 while delivering an impassioned speech about the cost of the war against the Bonaparte in the House of Lords, effectively curtailing Jassie's second season before it had truly begun.

She'd gone to London for the seasons of 1811 and 1812 and stayed with Lady Augusta Parmenter, Lord Windermere's great aunt. But after that first season he'd put in an appearance at very few events, principally those organized by Lady Augusta or close friends. Even so he'd only ever danced once with her at each of these occasions and had conspicuously avoided ever dancing a waltz. Although, she'd taken comfort from the fact he stood up with no one else and always left right after their dance.

Where had he gone thereafter? Why was he never seen at any other society events? He'd said he found them dull, couldn't stand the way the society mamas and their whey-faced daughters stalked his aristocratic eligibility. He wasn't looking for a wife so why would he parade through the marriage mart as if he were?

She'd accepted his answer back then, but was there another, more sinister reason for that vow of eternal bachelorhood?

Jassie caressed the dried smears on her thighs one more time, wishing wistfully there was some way she could preserve them, like pressed petals in a book. With a sigh she stepped into the waiting bath and considered what advantage she might take of the greater freedom of the married state to discover more of the hidden life of the Earl of Windermere.

Rising and breakfasting early next morning as she always did, Jassie took Chester out for a wild gallop across the Downs in the opposite direction to Neave Tor. She wasn't sure yet whether she would ever visit that place again. She'd dressed accordingly in buckskin riding trousers as she often did when riding alone on Brantleigh land, and young Jem rode at her heels, a sop to Dobbie for her curt behavior of yesterday; a buffer between herself and Windermere should he put off his return to London and ride out to try and intercept her instead; and a greatly appreciated treat for Dobbie's horse-mad grandson whom he was training as a groom. But no matter how hard and how fast they raced, into the wind or away from it, she could not outrun the travail of her thoughts, the leaden feeling of guilt lying heavy in her stomach as if she'd ingested a huge cannonball.

What pain had she caused the man who held her heart, by forcing him to take the only honorable course of insisting she become his wife? What did this breaking of his vow portend for him?

For them?

It wasn't until she sat down to luncheon, bathed and dressed in a sunny yellow silk day gown trimmed with emerald braid at neckline and hem and tied with the same colored ribbon beneath her breasts, that Willis, the round-cheeked Brantleigh Manor butler, handed her a folded note stamped with the Windermere seal and the pair of riding gloves she'd left on Neave Tor.

'This came from the Abbey this morning, Miss Jassie,' he said, his eyes twinkling as they always did, as if he shared whatever secret was in the air on any given day.

'Thank you, Willis.'

Jassie's heart thumped violently against her ribcage as she laid the gloves on the table then let her fingers close over the expensive piece of heavy, hand-pressed paper embossed with the Windermere crest, hoping she'd kept her voice even and shown no undue emotion to the elderly servant.

'That will be all. Mrs. Lyndon and I will serve ourselves.'

With a nod, Willis backed out of the room and Jassie wondered what the gossip had been in the servant's hall after yesterday's debacle. Her fingers clenched on the letter, crunching it into her palm. What did Rogan have to say today? Was he perhaps, crying off? How would she feel if he did? What a coil! For no matter the depth of her guilt she desperately hoped he had not. Being ruined and ostracized by society held no terror so bad as that which attacked her at the thought of Rogan ostracizing her.

'Are you going to read it before you destroy it?' Francine asked.

'What if—what if he wants to cry off?'

'You'll let him,' Francine responded promptly; firmly but gently. 'But I'd be very disappointed in Windermere if that were the case.'

Jassie bit down on her lip, breathed deeply, broke open the seal and quickly scanned the contents in Rogan's familiar bold scrawl. It was impossible to keep the outrage from her expression when she looked up at Francine.

'What does he say to put that scowl on your face,' she asked, eyes widening in trepidation.

'There is no salutation. — *'I have spoken with Mr. Worth, the vicar, this morning and the wedding is set for 3pm in Windermere Chapel on Saturday May 20th. Please order the event as you wish. Mama will make out our list of guests.*

As soon as I have sent Raoul off with this, I ride for London. I will acquire the special license and send it to you by courier for safe-keeping.

I will also put a notice in the London Times. Windermere Abbey will be ready for you to move your things over by Friday 19th. Mama is ecstatic. She is expecting you will call. You might try for a happy countenance when you visit. She indicated this was all she'd been waiting for, to see you settled—as Lady Windermere. She also has a selection of rings from the Abbey vaults for you to choose from. My fancy is the topaz.

Until we meet at the altar,

Windermere.'

'Well, that about covers everything. I wonder how long I am to be served cold shoulder. Bodes well for a happy marriage, don't you think?—Oh Fran, how am I to act for Lady O as if—as if all is as fine as fivepence when it so definitely is not! She's not one to be fobbed off with gammon. Never has been.'

Jassie closed her mouth with a snap before a great wail of despair issued from it.

'Are you thinking Windermere actor enough to fool her? Don't you think she knows her son quite well? Mothers do, you know. Why not confide in her Ladyship? She has always struck me as a very wise woman.'

'Windermere is the Inscrutable of Inscrutables. I would never play poker against him—and he's had years of practice at bamboozling his mother.'

'Being inscrutable wouldn't convince Lady Windermere her son was happy.'

'She probably wouldn't see that as any different from normal.'

'I think you underestimate the Countess, Jassie. She might be ailing in her body but her brain is still as sharp as ever.'

Jassie sighed.

'You're right of course—and she knows me just as well as she knows Windermere. And I'm just now realizing what a lot there is to do—since it doesn't appear his Lordship is about to allow anything to stand in the way of his honor, not even a vow he made goodness knows how many years ago! Certainly before I was sixteen! I guess I'd better start with informing the staff so they don't have another reason to feel slighted. And then I will go over and visit with Lady O. It would look rather shabby if I didn't.'

Francine nodded.

'And since you really don't need me for any of that, shall I start making a list of people locally who should be informed and invited? Then we could start writing the invitations this evening.'

'Thank you, Fran. You're so sensible and I'm anything but at the moment. That sounds like an excellent plan.'

An hour later Windermere's very staunch and upright butler, Melton, welcomed Jassie into the vaulted entry hall at the Abbey. Bowing low, he accepted her gloves and pelisse, arranging them carefully on the ancient and monstrous oak hall stand, which Jassie privately thought had stood in that exact spot since the place had been inhabited by monks back in medieval times. The Abbey and everything within it was as familiar to her as Brantleigh Manor. Usually she stopped to admire the ancient piece of furniture, stroke the time-blackened wood and wonder at all it had seen. Today she scarcely registered its presence.

'I would like to offer my congratulations on your betrothal to His Lordship, Miss Jassinda. It is the best news heard within these walls for many a day.'

'Thank you, Melton,' she managed to respond, forcing her mouth to curve in a smile she hoped would convey the delight Melton would be expecting her to show. 'Is Her Ladyship receiving?'

A hint of a grave smile softened the butler's rigid features and he inclined his head towards the sunny parlor where the Countess could usually be found when downstairs.

'I believe she's been expecting you ever since Lord Windermere told her your news this morning.'

'Oh! Then I'd best not keep her waiting any longer. I'll see myself in, Melton.'

'Very well, Miss Jassinda.'

He bowed and disappeared through a side door.

Jassie hurried down the east passage from the Great Hall and knocked briefly on the parlor door before entering.

'Jassie! At last!'

Her Ladyship's voice, the strongest thing about her, rang across the sunny room with such delight Jassie came to a momentary halt just inside the door. Her heart was pounding, her mind racing with panic. All she wanted to do as she came to the woman who'd been the only true mother she'd ever had, was burst into tears and have those well-loved arms hold her, soothe her, and that strong, no-nonsense voice tell her all would be well. But how could she give in to her misery in the face of such intense joy as shone across the room at her from eyes, which today, were as blazing blue as her son's?

It had been so long since Rogan's mother had had anything to smile about, much less fill her being with such pure joy she came swiftly and easily to her feet with her arms outstretched.

'You see! I am renewed. Come here, child.'

And Jassie went. *Come here, child,* three words from childhood Lady O had made their special bond. She put her own arms around the thin shoulders and clung tightly, reveling in the warmth and love of the older woman's embrace. Unable to utter a word, Jassie gently eased the Countess back into the comfortable support of the cushioned wing chair and dropped to kneel at her feet, burying her face in the soft rug Jensen immediately replaced over the frail knees.

But it was hopeless. Jassie could no longer stem the tears that had been lying in wait ever since she'd received Windermere's note at luncheon. She scarcely registered the soft closing of the door as Jensen left them alone, so deeply aware was she of the loving warmth emanating from the fragile hand caressing the back of her head.

At last Jassie sat back inelegantly on her bottom on the carpet, crossed her legs under her skirts and tried to wipe the tears from her face with her hands. Something as mundane as putting a handkerchief in her pocket had not figured in her things to do today. A small square of linen dangled before her and she took it gratefully, wiping at her eyes and blowing her nose.

'Am I the only one who is *happy* about this betrothal, Jassie?'

All the fire had gone out of her Ladyship's voice and it was inclined to quaver.

But even to make this special lady happy, Jassie could not lie.

'P-possibly,' she whispered, head bowed with the weight of her misery.

The silence eventually forced her to look up to see the Countess with her head leaning back against the chair and her eyes closed tight, as if in pain.

Jassie leapt to her knees again and took the motionless, blue-veined hands in hers.

'Lady O! Are you all right?'

'I am, Jassie,' she murmured, neither moving her head nor opening her eyes, though her hands gripped Jassie's with a surprising strength. 'I've been waiting so long for this day. I told myself it would be a day of such—blessedness—when it came. It is hard to let go of the dream and face the reality. When Rogan left me this morning—he looked like he was going to his own hanging. Now you come—and appear to be in no better case. You are what he needs. Your love could heal what ails him, if only he would let it.—Jassie,' she said with sudden urgency in her voice and finally opening her eyes, 'do you *know* what ails my son?'

Jassie worried Lady Windermere didn't seem to have the energy left to lift her head from the chair back, as if the supreme, joy-driven effort of standing to embrace her future daughter-in-law had used up her store of animation for the moment. But her gaze was steady, imploring, and Jassie hated that even in this she could not offer relief.

Helplessly she shook her head.

After a moment of consideration, the Countess said, 'It was while he was at Oxford. The second year, I think. He changed—quite terribly—between one visit home and the next. But no matter what angle I took, I could never get him to talk about it. Eventually he lost patience with me and said—said there was absolutely nothing wrong and if I didn't stop questioning him about it he simply would not come home again. My heart broke for him that day and I've never figured out how to repair it. He used to be so open and sharing. We talked of everything. You know yourself I'll not turn away from any subject my children need to discuss with me. But since that day he's shared nothing with me that didn't concern my needs or the running of Windermere.

'I was hoping maybe he shared more with you. I took comfort in the fact he could never wait to seek you out when he came home, hoped at least with you, he shared the inner workings of his heart. For you love him, sweetheart, do you not? You've never tried to hide that from him. He has to know and I thought, even though he is so hard to read these days, he loved you too. I have clung to the belief you would be his salvation from whatever bitterness stalks his soul.'

Jassie sniffled and blew her nose again.

Suddenly, Lady Windermere lifted her head and sat upright, fixing Jassie with her intense blue gaze.

'What do you think, Jass? What do you *think* may be wrong? You must have some *thoughts* on the matter.'

Jassie closed her eyes, savored a deep breath and clenched her hands in her lap, the piece of linen a sodden ball between her palms. The Countess had never spoken more true. There was nothing Jassie could not discuss with her and in this she knew herself deeply blessed. But what if her surmises only added to a mother's deep pain? As the question formed, the answer came hard on its heels. What deeper pain could there be than knowing a child suffered yet not understand the cause or how one might begin to ease that suffering?

'I think—after yesterday—I finally have an inkling.'

'Will you share it with me?'

'I think—I should just tell you what happened. It was all my doing and maybe you won't think so well of me when I've told it. But I have to believe you know more of the—of what goes on between men and women than I do and perhaps you can make sense of it.' Jassie fell silent, twisting the wet hanky in her fingers. 'I don't know where to start,' she mumbled at last.

'The beginning's always a good place,' Lady Windermere observed with a wry smile, reminding Jassie so much of Rogan that her heart skipped in her chest.

She forced a small smile in response, then said, 'I guess that would really be at my sixteenth birthday. I was so determined to have my first kiss that night and that it would be from Rogan. I've never wanted to kiss any other man. I tricked him into following me out onto the terrace and once out of direct sight of the French doors I—grabbed his jacket lapels and demanded he give me my first kiss. A birthday boon, I called it. I didn't wait for him to decide in his stuffy way it was inappropriate or some such fustian. I just reached right in and kissed him!'

The memory, as vivid as ever, filled her mind. The surprise of the warmth and firm yet soft texture of his lips; the subtle scent of citrus and spice and—man; the painful belt of her heart against her chest as his tongue caressed her lips and invaded her mouth the moment she opened for him; the knowledge, as sure now as it had been then, he felt what she did; the grip of his fingers on her skull; the pressure of his lower body against hers and the ecstatic belief she was about to discover the whole meaning of life. Nor would she ever forget the bereaved feeling when he pulled back, released her and stared at her as if he'd lost his senses and simply couldn't believe it. Then he'd delivered the words that had crushed her heart and sealed her doom to spinsterhood.

'What did he do?' the Countess prompted.

Jassie blinked and looked up at her, momentarily disoriented. She sighed.

'He kissed me back. For just a moment I believed all my naive girlish dreams were about to become reality. Then he let me go as if— as if I'd burned him and he became so stern, so—remote and *then*—he looked right into my eyes and said, 'That behavior with any other man could get you into trouble, Jassinda. Promise me you'll never do such a thing again!' I was so angry! I never even *wanted* to do it with another man! And then—*then* he said, 'Don't set your sights on me to become your knight in shining armor. I'm not husband material and I shall never marry. There are better men out there for you, Jassinda Carlisle.' He stormed off to the end of the terrace, down the steps into the darkness and disappeared round the end of the house. I didn't see him again that night—nor for a long time afterward.'

'So that's why you suddenly developed a sick headache and abandoned your own party! I thought you must have drunk a little more wine than you were supposed to!'

Jassie nodded miserably.

'When you were sixteen Rogan would have been twenty-seven. I can understand he might have thought himself too old for you but— why would he vow not to marry?' the Countess murmured thoughtfully. 'Whatever the trauma, it happened before that. Rather confirms my belief it was while he was at Oxford. Something sexual, I'm thinking now. Could I be right, Jassie?'

Jerked out of her thoughts, she looked up at the older woman and felt the flood of color burning in her cheeks.

'What haven't you told me, sweetheart?'

'About yesterday. It's much worse. I'm almost certain you will not even want me for a daughter-in-law when I tell you about yesterday!'

A loud chuckle escaped the Lady Windermere's thin lips, startling Jassie.

'Good heavens, child, there is nothing, absolutely *nothing* you could admit to that would cause that.—I was young once. I've felt the burn of desire, the bitterness of rejection. Windermere, Rogan's father, was not an easy catch, you know! But I was determined to have him. Like you, I wanted no one else! And in the end it was worth it. Marriage was as wonderful as I'd dreamed it would be. I was very happy with my Jonathan.' A dreamy smile lit the blue eyes and for a moment Jassie felt as if she looked into a star-filled summer night and had no trouble at all picturing the Countess as a beautiful young woman in the flush of youthful love. 'So tell me about yesterday. I can easily determine it had to be something quite scandalous to pin Rogan to his honor.'

'I'm twenty-five!' Jassie wailed suddenly. 'How long was I supposed to wait? Until we are both old and wrinkled and past caring! I wanted to know! I so longed to know—just once—,' she stammered then covered her burning face with her hands.

'So you seduced him?'

'Oh God,' Jassie sighed, dragging her hands down her face. 'Not really. I said—pretty much what I've just said to you. We were on Neave Tor. It's where we always go to discuss important things. He— he just stared at me as if my words had turned him to stone. His eyes went this terrible silvery color and—I don't know what was going through his head but definitely rejection, anger, maybe even fear or horror. It was so awful I just dived at Chester and tried to mount at the run and of course he jumped sideways. I might have managed it even then but my weight pulled the saddle down. I was sliding under Chester's belly and I panicked and leapt for the ground and—Rogan caught me and we fell together and rolled several times. When we stopped he was beneath me, yelling and—swearing. I think I went a little crazy because finally I was exactly where I'd wanted to be and he—he—well, he couldn't disguise that he wanted it too.

'Then—we both went a little crazy and I—we—oh! I can't say it! Suffice it to say nothing could have stopped us at that point but somewhere along the way he changed. He wasn't the Rogan I knew. He became—I don't know—kind of maddened, like I was someone who must be punished. When—after—he was so angry. I've never seen him like that, never want to again either. He—hit the ground with his fist. I'm inclined to think he would have liked to hit me! Then he asked me to forgive him and there was more—like he was trying to make it up to me. He said we should never have done what we did. That it was more or less—rape—and—now I should have some idea of why he'd avoided marriage all these years.

'When I asked what he meant, he said he was rough and lacking in consideration, or caring and—a lady shouldn't be subjected to such— such bestiality. He vowed it wouldn't happen again!—Then he insisted we marry, wouldn't let me leave Neave Tor until I agreed. He looked so fierce, so remote, untouchable and a little frightening. It wasn't what I'd been asking for. I didn't want to trap him into marriage. I *knew* his feelings about that, after all!'

Suddenly she was scrambling to her knees and wrapping her arms around the Countess and sobbing. 'I deserve to burn in hell for being so wicked but—dear God—I love him so much—'

There were long moments when her sobs were the only sounds in the room and the stroking of the Countess's hands in her hair her deepest comfort. Then at last Jassie plopped back to the floor and sat in a dejected heap.

'Now he has ridden off to London and according to the note he sent this morning he won't be back till the day of the wedding, which *he* has organized with the vicar for Saturday 20th. *I* get to organize everything else. How can I organize a wedding when I know it's the last thing he wants?'

'Easily, sweetheart,' the Countess said bracingly. 'You have Jensen and I and your lovely Francine to help you and it will be perfect. We'll accept nothing less.—And I'll send for Augusta and Sheri. Would you like that?'

Jassie nodded. Even though there was only five years difference in their age, Lady Augusta Parmenter was Lady Windermere's aunt as well as her closest friend and she'd willingly sponsored Jassie's third and fourth seasons in London, along with her own daughter, Lady Sherida Dearing. Already friends, the two young women had become even closer. With Sheri and Fran to help, she would manage somehow.

'This is the best outcome, Jassie. Trust me. This way, you'll be able to work on Windermere without trying to preserve your good name and propriety and all that nonsense. In marriage you have all the advantage. You're a woman—and *he* is only a man, at the mercy of his deepest instinct to mate. I have to say I'm greatly relieved by what you've told me for I'd even wondered if his problem was he preferred men to women. But I don't believe that's it. Thank goodness. So within marriage you're free to seduce him any way you will. But you must consider, if you entice him into your bed, will it be what you want after all? Do you have any idea of what you're facing, what darkness festers in Windermere's soul?'

Jassie spread her hands in surrender.

'I love him, Lady O. We've been the closest of friends all my life. That has to count for something. I believe he loves me, if he'd only let himself acknowledge it.—Knowing you're here, that you care and understand, that I could talk to you if it all gets too much, is deeply—fortifying,' she said, finally finding a smile to lift her spirits. 'Windermere doesn't know what he's getting into.'

'That's the Sassy Jassie I know!' the Countess chortled. 'He used to call you that quite often when you were small. It used to fire you up and he loved to tease you. He said once it made your eyes sparkle like champagne diamonds. It seems so long ago since he was that carefree young man, a little reckless, a little daring, always laughing and teasing. And so deeply caring. That young man is still in there, Jassie, deeply hidden behind layers of darkness. Your love can find him, bring him out again. I know it can.'

Jassie sat staring up at the Countess, while the words echoed in her mind, restoring the dream that had seemed so crushed and pointless only moments before.

Scrambling to her feet she leant in and kissed the frail, dry cheek.

'You are an angel. Why could I not come to that understanding for myself? I'm finally going to realize my deepest desire, marriage to Rogan. However it's come about is immaterial. What it becomes is up to me. I love him enough for both of us and I intend to have the happiest marriage possible. Thank you, Lady O. Now we have a wedding to plan.'

Lady Windermere smiled beatifically and Jassie settled into Jensen's chair at her side.

'I think we should start,' the Countess suggested, 'by sending for Augusta and Sheri. I think Augusta is feeling quite hipped with you two. For all her efforts on behalf of you both she never got either of you married. She will be delighted about this even though it was nothing she did that brought it about—and for me, because she knows how I've worried about Windermere.'

'I'd be delighted if Sheri can come. She and Fran can be my bridesmaids.'

'And Augusta could help with the organization. She is so good at that. I'll write to them immediately and then you'll see, Jassie, all will simply fall into place for the perfect wedding.'

She wished she could believe the same for the marriage. Jassie smiled at Lady Windermere, though inwardly her heart still quaked.

By stopping to change horses at regular intervals Rogan made it to London before dark. His body should've been exhausted but his head would not let him rest. Stopping at Windermere House in Berkeley Square long enough to bathe and change and have his town coach brought round, he headed down Berkeley Street to Piccadilly where they joined the crush of evening traffic heading to the theatres and clubs.

Amidst the roil of his thoughts one thing was clear. Since marriage was inevitable he must search out Wolverton. Dominic Beresford, Duke of Wolverton, his second cousin, had been the third in the close-knit trio of his boyhood. They and Philip Carlisle had been kindred spirits. None of them had expected to inherit titles. Rogue's brother Quentin would inherit Windermere, Philip's father didn't have a title and Wolverton was the third son of the tenth Duke of Wolverton. All three faced the need to find some other means of supporting themselves. They'd learned early to deflect the disparagements of those more fortunate, and learned young how to fight back to back in a tight circle.

Philip's death at the Battle of Vitoria had cut to the heart of them both, effectively strengthening the bond they shared. He needed to find Wolverton and ask him to stand at his side on his wedding day. It would be painful for Dominic, he knew, for his friend loved Jassie almost as well as he did himself.

Dom had recently returned from a trip to America and it was possible he'd left for his vast estates in Norfolk or Kent already, to ascertain all was in order before returning to the capital for the Season, but he'd check out the Clubs first. He struck a blank at White's and had to talk hard and fast to slide out of making the fourth at a high stakes table in the card room. Lord Marston thought he'd seen Wolverton at Brooks' earlier, so Rogan stepped out into the street and walked along to the smaller club on the corner of St James Street.

If Wolverton wasn't there he'd have to call at his house in Bruton Street. In fact he was wondering whether he shouldn't have simply done that when he spotted his quarry leaning back in his chair at a table in Brooks', cynically observing a lively altercation between two gentlemen obviously far gone in their cups. At his approach, Wolverton rose lithely to his feet, the cynical amusement dying from his eyes and the scar down his cheek flexing as he clenched his jaw. Rogan guessed his own expression was the cause but he just didn't seem able to ease the grimness radiating outwards from deep in his gut.

'You looking for me, Rogue?'

'I am.'

'Excuse me gentlemen.'

'Windermere! Haven't seen you f'r ages. Come 'n' join us, man!'

Rogan managed the semblance of a grin and replied, 'Thanks, Ogilvie, but I need a word with Wolverton. Some other time maybe.'

'What? You 'fusin' to drink with us, Windermere?' Ogilvie's friend, Chumsley, slurred, rising belligerently out of his seat.

'Stubble it, Chum,' the Duke snapped. 'You should probably get him out of here, Ogilvie. He's beyond reasoning.—Come on, Windermere. Time for a change of scene, I think.'

Rogan led the way back out onto St. James Street then stopped to face Wolverton.

'I didn't mean to drag you away.'

Dominic rubbed a hand ruefully down his face.

'If I stay I'll only end up dagger's drawn with Chum. He's got some bee in his bonnet about Wellesley being made a Duke. Lord knows why. Apart from the fact it's last year's news, we'd be dancing to the Frenchie's drum if it weren't for Arthur. I've had enough to drink. I don't seem to have the stomach for it I once did. And Chum ceased to be entertaining about half an hour ago. What's the problem?'

'I'd rather not discuss it here on the street, Dom. How about my place? I've got my coach here. Where's yours?'

'I came with Chum and Ogilvie. Your coach, your place, is fine.'

Rogan led the way to where Hobbs was waiting with the equipage across the street. Both remained silent until they were settled in Rogan's study, each cradling a crystal tumbler, Rogan's filled with whisky and Dom's with brandy, and the two decanters on the table between them.

Dominic raised his glass.

'So what's got you looking so Friday-faced?'

Rogan couldn't find the will to raise his in response. In fact, if he raised it at all it would be to dash it into the fireplace.

'I'd like you to stand up with me when I marry Jassie on May 20th at Windermere Abbey.'

He didn't want to see what his disclosure would do to Wolverton, but neither of them needed the gossip that would ensue if someone else stood at his side. They and Philip had been known as a tight trio since their school days and with Philip gone it would look dashed peculiar if he asked anyone else. But the harsh curse accompanying the clatter of Dominic's glass as he thumped it down on the table drew Rogan's gaze.

The scar of the sabre cut on his cheek was a livid white slash down the darker hue of his skin and his eyes glittered with some intense emotion. Rogan had no trouble working out what it was.

'Why? Why now?' Wolverton's mouth snapped on the words as if he would bite them through. 'All these years you've said nothing. All these years she's waited. You've loved her—since forever. We all knew that and yet—you never offered. You know she turned me down? Twice?'

Rogan nodded and lowered his gaze, unable to confront the pain in his friend's eyes.

'Of course I know. You made damned sure I wasn't going to offer before you did.'

'Do you know why she refused me?'

'No—but I guess I'm—about to hear it.'

'Damn right you are! She wasn't averse to me. We could've had a very satisfactory marriage on all levels—but even though I proved to her she could respond to me—she said while you lived she'd never give up hope. It wouldn't be fair—to any of us—she said.'

His face clenched, clearly expressing the pain induced by the memory.

And Rogan flinched at the thought of Wolverton kissing Jassie, touching her. Damn it all to hell. He downed a gulp of whisky and savored the burn of it down his gullet, taking the edge off the vision in his head.

Jassie in Wolverton's arms.

He leaned his head back against the chair, closed his eyes and ground his teeth.

'Why?' Wolverton snapped again.

Downing the rest of the whisky in his glass, Rogan placed it on the table then gripped the arms of his chair to steady himself. Jassie had got sick of waiting but he'd not betray her by telling Wolverton that.

'I compromised her and—'

Wolverton almost came up out of his chair at that admission, but then he sat back, clenching his fists and glaring at Rogan from eyes gone as dark as smoldering charcoal.

'Again,' he ground out, '*why*, after all this time?'

'That's between Jassie and me.'

A slight flush touched Dominic's cheeks then he subsided, taking several deep breaths.

'So why do you look as if you're being forced to put your head in the hangman's noose?'

Because that was exactly how he felt. How could he explain to Dominic without revealing the depth of his depravity; without losing the one friend left whose regard mattered? But he had to tell him something. He owed him that, if only because Wolverton cared so deeply for Jassie.

'I'm not the man she needs—not the man she believes me to be. I— can never be that man again.'

'What the devil are you talking about, Windermere? You're the only man she's ever wanted!'

Rogan felt his heart thudding in his breast, painfully telling him he could lose Wolverton's regard anyway if he couldn't give him more of a reason than that. But God help him, he could not.

Dominic sat forward in his chair, and fixed Rogan with a piercing glare.

'Does this have anything to do with what really drives you to seek the kind of release offered by the Matrix Club?'

The words propelled Rogan out of his chair and across the room to stare blindly out of the window into the moonless night. His fists clenched and unclenched at his sides and imprudent rage boiled in his chest. He knew it was a wonder Dominic hadn't called him on it long since, but it didn't mean he was any more ready to admit to the truth of what he was, what he'd become. They were both members of the exclusive club founded by their older cousin, Ajax Beresford, Earl of Knightsborough, to cater for members of the ton whose sexual needs were considered outside the norm. For years they'd pretended their membership was based on nothing more than a need for light-hearted entertainment that nevertheless allowed certain boundaries to be pushed, and perhaps, as a show of family solidarity with Ajax, a.k.a. the Knight.

'Do-you-or-do-you-not-stand-up-with-me-at-the-altar?'

Dominic came and stood at his side to stare as sightlessly into the darkness beyond the window.

'Do you have any idea what you're asking of me?' he muttered.

'Yes. But the gossip would be untenable if I asked anyone else.'

Silence stretched between them, heavy with emotion too deep to be expressed by either. The weight of Wolverton's hand landed on his shoulder.

'We always pledged there was nothing we couldn't ask of one another. Yes, Rogue, I'll stand with you at the altar when you make those most sacred of vows to Jassie, *but-you-had-better-be-the-best-bloody-husband-to-her-you-can-possibly-be.*'

Rogan's whole body jerked as if Dominic had struck him. Needing to put space between them, he lurched over to the mantelpiece and kicked the brass fire fender hard enough to cause acute pain—had he been able to feel any kind of physical pain at all. But nothing could penetrate the emotional agony that filled his heart when he thought of being married to Jassie.

'I will be no sort of husband to her. I'm marrying her. That's all.'

Suddenly Dominic's hand was back on his person, but there was nothing conciliatory or gentle in his touch now. Gripping a fistful of Rogan's collar, Dominic swung him about so they stood toe to toe, nose to nose.

'What in damnation do you mean by that?'

'That I'll *wed* her because honor demands it,' Rogan snarled, glaring back into Dominic's molten eyes.

Before either of them could blink Dominic flung Rogan from him and he landed untidily across the arms of the chair where he'd been sitting earlier, his foot flying out and toppling the table, crystal and alcohol spraying across the carpet.

For several minutes the only sound in the room was the hiss and crackle of the dying fire in the grate and two sets of heavy breathing. Then slowly, Rogan unfolded his body from the chair and reached for the bell to summon Deacon.

They stood, one either side of the room while Deacon moved, silently and po-faced, about the business of sweeping up the glass, sponging the alcohol off the carpet and stoking up the fire.

'Will that be all, my Lord?'

'Two more bottles and two more glasses, if you would? Thanks, Deacon.'

'Certainly, my Lord.'

Neither moved nor spoke until Deacon silently closed the door for the second time, then Rogan returned to his chair and motioned Dominic to the other, before he lifted the bottle to fill Dom's glass.

'D'you think that's wise?' Dominic asked, one eyebrow raised as he watched Rogan pour.

'I won't retaliate, Dom, and gentleman that you are, you wouldn't fight me if I refused to defend myself. Although we'd probably both feel better for a round or two.'

Once he'd poured his own whisky, he raised his glass to Dominic, his gaze fixed and steady, and said, 'To Jassie.'

Slowly Dominic reached out and took up the other glass, touched it to Rogan's and repeated, 'To Jassie.' With a flick of his wrist he tossed the contents down his throat and thumped the glass down on the table.

'So, are you going to tell me what the hell goes on with you, Rogue? How can you even think of marrying that woman and not being a husband to her? You do realize what you're risking, don't you? And I don't mean any disrespect to Jassie because I know where her heart lies. But there are bastards out there—like me—who would give a great deal to be where you are—married to her.'

'Damn it, Dom! Stop trying to rile me! We will be married. The last thing I want is for Jassie to be the butt of any more gossip than I've already caused her. And that aside, I should not be marrying anyone. Ever.—And no, I won't tell you what goes on with me. I can't.'

'Bloody hell, Windermere, you can be an ornery cuss when you set your mind to it!'

She was marrying Rogan today.

Unable to sleep, Jassie had been sitting in her bedroom window-seat wrapped in a heavy quilt for hours. Or so it seemed. The moment the sun began to brighten the eastern sky over Neave Village she scrambled out of the warm cocoon, threw on a shirt and riding breeches, pulled on a warm jacket, then twisted her hair and bunched it up under a close-fitting cap. Boots in hand she slipped down the service stairs so as not to awaken the house and quietly unbolted the door into the back garden. Sitting on a rustic seat against the red brick wall of the Manor, she pulled on her boots before starting down the path to the stables.

The sun wasn't truly up yet but it was light enough to see and already the blackbirds were singing in the orchard. Regardless, Jassie was too restless to stay still a moment longer. If Dobbie and Jem were still abed she'd saddle Chester herself. It wouldn't be the first time and she wouldn't have to endure Dobbie's disapproving frown at her attire and the saddle she intended to use today. A lady-like canter was not what she needed this morning. Only a wild ride over the downs would settle the incipient panic threatening to overwhelm her. She needed distraction, action, something that required all her focus.

And that kind of ride demanded the safety of riding astride. There might be a part of her that would like to run and never stop or simply find some excuse to put off this wedding but she wasn't so desperate as to risk breaking her neck.

There was still no one around when she led Chester out of the stable, threw herself into the saddle and headed in the direction of the Windermere Downs. There was nowhere quite so satisfying to ride as across the exposed tops. Chester, sensing in the moment his mistress mounted a wild ride was the order of the day, shivered with excitement. Jassie patted his neck and settled him with soothing words. When they were clear of the Manor grounds she gave the big red horse his head. They rode in a huge circle coming back along the ridge to the east of the Abbey from which point Neave Tor stood, eerily silhouetted against the morning sky.

The desire to revisit the Tor surprised Jassie. Until this moment she hadn't thought she'd ever again want to revisit the monument to her deepest humiliation, but she didn't question it, realizing subconsciously it was where she'd been headed from the start. Chester picked his way down into the Neave Valley and they trotted more sedately along the banks of the brook then up the eastern slopes of the Tor. An eerie wind whistled about the standing stone and Chester eyed it warily as Jassie slid from the saddle.

'God knows why, Chester,' she said, dropping his reins and stroking his neck, 'but I want to be here for a while.'

Climbing the last few yards to the top, she settled on the flat rock and gazed down the long valley to Brantleigh then across to the hill hiding the Abbey from sight. Had Rogan come home last night? Or was he planning to arrive at the last minute? She hadn't waited by the willow for him this morning, or any morning this last week.

What would she do if he failed to turn up at all? She propped her elbows on her knees and her chin on her hands and tried to envision where he was at this very moment, the first hours of their wedding day. Was he already at Windermere, still asleep in the huge and ancient oak tester bed, his manly nakedness between crisp linen sheets? Or was he on the road, riding up from London, his hat jammed tight on his head and his big body lying low along his horse? He was a superb horseman. The vision was easily formed.

Just as easy as it was to visualize him on his back in the grassy crater with her on top of him, their mouths locked together and his large, warm hands on her naked buttocks. Suddenly Jassie was on her feet, unable to sit still for the heat rushing through her entire body and pooling almost painfully in that place Rogan had initiated just two weeks ago. Walking down the hill to the crater, she dropped to her haunches and laid her head on her arms across her knees. The pictures flowed through her mind and then she stopped them and backed up.

To the moment he had forgotten himself in his desire for her. Right after he'd asked if she was all right. His hands had shaped her then, learning her as if—they'd finally come home. Oh the glory of those few moments when he'd been hers, their hearts and bodies in tune. She'd swear they were. So what had changed and when? Scrolling the memories forward in her mind again she sought the moment when something changed and he'd become a stranger with rough words and hands, and a demanding body with no thought for hers, but to dominate and punish.

It was when his fingers had found that inner center of all her desire and she'd lost her mind and begged—though she'd little enough idea of what she was really begging for at that point. Then he'd gripped her wrists as if he'd thought she might try to fight him off—and given her what she'd been begging for—only it was way more than she'd ever imagined.

And even if it wasn't what he'd told her it should have been, it was—curiously, persistently exciting.

If he couldn't give her the kind of loving he seemed to believe she deserved, could she accept what he could give? With a heavy sigh she had to admit the answer to that riven question was unknown. Given that Windermere had been so adamant about not marrying, Jassie had to presume there was much more to know that he'd suppressed.

Whatever the outcome, they would be married today.

Rising, she climbed back up to the standing stone and embraced it, arms spread wide and cheek pressed to the cool, weather-worn surface. Always if she stood thus, her body was energized by a faint, humming vibration that seemed to touch every molecule of her being, shake it, re-vitalize it, and re-align it within her skin. She smiled and the energy seemed to take the smile and magnify it throughout her being.

When she finally turned from the stone to gaze back down the valley, she stood with feet apart, planted firmly on the earth and with her hands crossed reverently over her heart. Facing in the direction of the Abbey and with eyes raised to the heavens, she said in a clear, ringing voice, 'I love Windermere and he loves me! Together we'll find great happiness. Thank you God.'

Feeling lighter than she'd felt in years, Jassie hurried down to where Chester grazed quietly, gathered up the reins and led him up by one of the flat stones to use as a mounting block. Setting one foot into the stirrup, she lifted herself into the saddle and said, 'Take me home Chester. Today I intend to be so beautiful Windermere will not even think about crying off or that he once vowed never to marry. I intend to make that man so happy he will wonder why he wasted so many years! Home, Chester!'

He was going to be late for this damned wedding, which wasn't what he'd intended when he'd set out to be so busy he'd not be back at the Abbey until the morning of the 20th. He hadn't wanted to face his mother and the questions she'd not be able to contain; or run into Jassie before they met at the chapel. He'd determined to allow no chance for either of them to think about the reality of what they were doing. Honor demanded he marry her and so he would. It had to be the lesser of two evils.

Surely.

He would make her understand their lives would be separate—as they always had been. She had to accept he couldn't be alone with her. Knowing she was his, to do with as he wished according to law, was more damnation than he needed. He might have honor ingrained deep enough to insist on the marriage, but he was deadly uncertain if honor went deep enough to keep him out of Jassie's bed should they spend too much time together under the same roof; or keep him from taking her in the only way his body seemed to understand.

His hands still remembered the feel of the soft satiny skin of her buttocks and the wet heat of her desire for him. The pleading, desperate need shining in her eyes as she'd forced herself to ask him to show her how it could be, haunted him.

The sensation of her fine-boned wrists manacled by his grip and her startled cry of pain when he'd taken her like the beast he'd become, tormented his every waking moment. God, he hated how he was! If he ever came face to face with the bitch who'd made him this way he'd probably kill her. There could be no greater torment than loving and wanting Jassie as he did and knowing he couldn't allow himself to have her.

And he just couldn't trust himself to resist her. Their ill-starred tryst on Neave Tor had proved that.

His secretary, Barton Matthews who was also a cousin, and Wolverton, rode at his back. Wolverton, his face more grimly piratical than ever, had never once harked back to their conversation of the night Rogan had asked for his support. Nor had he stinted on that support in any way.

And Bart's skills as a secretary were invaluable but those were only a small part of the talents he brought to his position in Windermere's household. Rogan could never have found a better nor more loyal man to watch his back. Younger by five years, Bart could have been Rogan's brother, so alike were they—and had often been mistaken as such. It was probably his most valuable asset. While Rogan was following his deadly profession on the continent, he could also be seen riding in his well-known neck-or-nothing style through the Park on Raven, his shiny black stallion. Those rides were always undertaken during less fashionable hours when Bart was unlikely to be accosted by any of Rogan's aristocratic acquaintances and put to a scrutiny too close to be safe.

But the trademark Windermere neck-or-nothing style and magnificent black stallion would be seen and remembered if it ever became necessary to deny his presence anywhere than in London. He'd never been an habitué of the fashionable ton balls and soirées so his absence from these elite social events was not noticed.

His latest foray into Paris had been fraught with danger and setback. His contacts were edgy and elusive, having to keep moving ahead of Fouché's agents, who were vicious and determined in the service of their restored and revered Emperor. He wouldn't be surprised if some of them didn't believe the poxy Little General could walk on water.

Sweat popped out on his forehead when he allowed himself to think on how close he'd been to discovery in that stinking alley in the bowels of the city. Glad he'd dressed in the filthy tattered clothing of a homeless vagrant, he'd hunkered down in a garbage strewn doorway as if half dead from cold and starvation and listened with a pounding heart to the brutal searching of the tenement a couple of doors down. He'd left that building not moments before, in possession of some very damning information about the strength and disposition of Napoleon's troops. Lying still had been the hardest thing he'd ever had to do. There was no point to wondering what had become of poor Boucher, but Rogan doubted he'd be able to find his erstwhile accomplice in Paris again.

Just when Europe was beginning to breathe easy, Bonaparte had escaped from the Isle of Elba and returned triumphantly to Paris with an army of a hundred thousand men at his back. The powers of the Seventh Coalition, Austria, Prussia, Russia and Great Britain, had declared him an outlaw and each had agreed to commit 150,000 men to finally rid Europe of his constant quest for power. Accurate information on Bonaparte's plans, and the strength and movement of his troops, was vital to Field Marshal the Duke of Wellington, cantoned with his troops near Brussels, to ensure Europe was cleansed of the Napoleonic scourge forever.

Holed up in a nondescript cottage on the outskirts of Paris with another contact, Rogan had memorized the information in the coded message and destroyed the original.

His unusually retentive memory was what had got him into the secret courier business all those years ago when he was in his early twenties, a second son with no immediate prospect of becoming the Earl but who'd already known he could never marry. If he were to die an honorable death in service to King and country then he wouldn't have lived in vain. That he'd survived his many forays into enemy territory only showed what a devious and cunning devil he'd become, certainly not attributes a woman looked for in her husband.

He glanced over his shoulder to encounter Bart's devilish grin. The man loved nothing better than a wild ride, as did his huge bay, Mayfair.

'I can see the turrets of the Abbey,' Bart yelled.

Rogan punched his fist in the air and spurred Raven into a last burst of energy. The beautiful animal never failed him. They would arrive a mere fifteen minutes late. Wolverton's dark countenance never changed but he urged the big grey he rode into a final burst of speed.

Rogan had only managed to get back to England late yesterday morning and by the time he'd ridden up from Portsmouth and finally satisfied his superiors at his de-briefing at the War Office, it was near midnight. He'd decided to abandon his original plan to ride down last night, electing to catch up on sleep and start early in the morning. They'd left London before dawn and should have made the twenty-eight mile ride in plenty of time.

But Suleiman, Dominic's mount, had thrown a shoe outside of Pleat Village and they'd had to cool their heels for a couple of hours while the village blacksmith sobered up enough to make the valuable horse roadworthy again. Dominic had wanted them to ride on without him, but Rogan was damned if he was going to stand before the bloody altar and promise himself to Jassie without Wolverton at his side.

Truth to tell, he wasn't sure he wouldn't turn round and ride straight back to London if Dom and Bart weren't riding with him.

They thundered up the long Elm Drive, across the front of the Abbey, over the lawns bordering the ancient cloisters, thereby ensuring a peel of aggravation from old Peabody the gardener, and right up to the doors of the chapel.

She was poised on the steps of the ancient arched stone portico of the historic Cistercian Chapel, a stunning vision in cerulean blue satin and champagne lace over a wide hooped underskirt of silk in the same color as the lace, a style her mother might well have worn. He'd never seen her more regal, nor more beautiful. His heart stuttered in his chest and for a moment he could only sit in the saddle and stare at her.

Little Jassie all grown up. God, he wished Philip was here to see her and for one horrific moment he was choked with emotion. For all she was. For all he couldn't give her. Goddammit, he had to pull himself together!

Then he noticed the rhythmic rise and fall of one section of the shimmering lace hem of the silken underskirt. One small foot was tapping with annoyance. His beautiful Jassie was in a snit, and rightly so. He was the one who'd insisted they marry and he was the one who was late. Giving himself no further time to consider, he leapt from the saddle, dropped Raven's reins, and strode across the neatly raked cinder path to where she stood, a vision of loveliness if it weren't for the scowl on her face. He stripped off hat and riding gloves, scarcely registering Bart taking possession of them.

Reaching for her hand he bent low over it and said, 'I humbly beg your pardon, Jass. We would've been here in plenty of time but Wolverton's horse threw a shoe outside of Pleat Village and more time was lost in sobering up the blacksmith. I'm sorry.'

He looked up and noticed her eyes were suspiciously bright and knew himself the lowest of dogs. He could easily have been back in London two days before he had returned, but had felt the need to stay out of England and thereby away from the temptation of Jassie, for as long as he could.

He leaned in and kissed her cheek.

'You look beautiful,' he murmured. 'How did you manage such a beautiful gown at such short notice?'

'It was my mother's.'

The frost in her voice could have taken chips off his ears and belied the hint of tears he'd seen in her eyes.

'Ah—it looks delightful on you.' Then crooking his elbow, he said, 'Shall we?'

'Actually,' she said, tilting her chin and firming her mouth, 'I was just about to leave. I've changed my mind.'

'That was never an option, Jassie.' He stared her down until her lashes drooped, then gripped her fingers and laid them firmly on his sleeve. 'You have the license?'

'The vicar has it.'

'And the ring?'

'Francine has it.'

There was a distinct sulky tone to her voice.

'Is there anything else to be done before I walk you up that aisle?'

'A bath and a change of clothing?' she snapped, suddenly glaring at him, arching her eyebrows in haughty disdain and wrinkling her nose.

God! She would slay him where he stood. Her eyes were now sparking with anger, her perfectly bowed mouth looked as if she'd been chewing at her lips in anxiety and he wanted nothing more than to kiss her senseless right where she stood, before God and whoever she and his mother had seen fit to invite to this farcical event.

Deeply conscious of Wolverton glowering at his back and probably feeling everything he himself was, he said, 'Too late for that, Jass. Let's not keep everyone waiting any longer. Mama will be getting anxious.'

He didn't think it would be a good time to tell her it was simplest if he stayed just as he was, since he intended to leave again as soon as the last of their guests left.

'Lady Sherida and Mrs. Lyndon are your attendants?'

'Yes.'

'Good. Dom and Bart are attending me. Will they walk up the aisle in front of us?'

Jassie nodded and he had to look away for she was biting her lip, just as he imagined she'd been doing for the last quarter hour at least.

Wolverton gravely offered his arm to Lady Sherida Dearing, his eyes briefly sweeping her ice-blonde perfection and Bart stepped forward and held out a hand to Francine, smiling his appreciation of Jassie's companion. Mrs. Francine Lyndon was a comely widow the same age as Jassie, with a sad scandal in her past. Rogan had always thought her a little stand-offish and aware of her consequence as the widow of a Lord though she didn't use the title. But today she merely handed Jassie the exquisite posy of bluebells and forget-me-nots she'd been holding, before slanting his handsome rake of a cousin an almost shy smile and touched her fingers delicately to his sleeve. The two couples set off through the portico, and into the intimate little chapel, which along with the cloisters, was all that was left of the ancient church that had stood on this site. The third Earl of Windermere had restored the small building and every Wyldefell since had been married within its hallowed walls.

'Our turn,' he muttered, swallowing air and facing the door.

Jassie's whole body stiffened and he thought she was going to baulk but after a moment's hesitation, she took a firmer grip on the posy of blue that matched her gown and stepped forward.

The chapel was full. Extra chairs must have been brought from the Abbey. Servants from both houses filled the back rows, then local gentry and persons of status in the community. In the front row, his mother sat with Jensen to one side of her and Aunt Augusta on the other. Bart's sisters, Elizabeth and Marion were next with his Aunt Miranda and Uncle James on the end of the old pew.

Dominic and Bart stood to the right and Lady Sherida and Mrs. Lyndon to the left of the altar, leaving the space in the center for himself and Jassie. As they stopped before the Reverend Worth, who was beaming down at them as if the marriage was his own personal triumph, Rogan became aware Jassie was trembling. The forget-me-nots in her posy were dancing. In fact he could feel the whole of her body shivering against his. She was right to be afraid, he thought suddenly, taking the flowers from her and handing them to Lady Sherida before they slid from her grasp. Then, even though something inside him was snapping with anger at what Jassie had set in motion with her wicked request on Neave Tor, he slipped his arm round her waist and let her lean against his body for support.

It was embarrassing enough he'd arrived late and walked up the aisle in his rumpled and dusty riding attire without the bride falling into a faint at his feet. There was doubtless already gossip about the indecent haste with which the thing was being done.

There wasn't enough air in the little chapel. The panic she'd managed to allay with her wild dawn ride and the moments of communion on Neave Tor came crashing back, almost suffocating her. An insidious trembling started in her knees and by the time they reached the altar and Reverend Worth, who appeared to be trying to light the whole chapel with his smile, her entire body was shivering as if with ague.

Where had the buoyancy gone, the certainty with which she'd ridden home from Neave Tor? She'd clung to her determination to be happy through her long soak in the bath, through a late breakfast with Fran and Sheri during which she'd talked of the decision she'd made on the Tor—to be happy. Buoyancy had stayed with her while Ruby labored to put her hair up in the bouffant style laced with ropes of pearls her mother would probably have worn with the dress at the end of the last century.

Even during the short carriage ride from Brantleigh Manor to Windermere Abbey she'd managed to keep up a constant bright commentary on the abundant blossom on the trees and the fields starred with jonquils and daffodils. They'd timed their arrival so all the guests would be seated in the chapel and Rogan would already be waiting for her.

He wasn't.

Jensen, Lady Windermere's companion stood stoically on the steps instead with the intelligence that the Earl had not yet arrived but nor had any word come to say he'd been delayed so they were still expecting him at any moment. Cold energy had shivered down her spine, chilling the whole of her body.

Where was Rogan? What had happened? Jassie knew his honor would not allow him to stand her up at this late point, but she couldn't help fearing for his safety. Where had he been during these last two weeks? News from the Continent suggested a major battle was soon to be engaged in the vicinity of Brussels and the Duke of Wellington was encamped there with his forces in preparation. Had Rogan been on another mission? He hadn't mentioned it, which would be unusual, for he normally let her know if he was to be out of the country. She'd probably forfeited that consideration through her brazen actions on Neave Tor but—surely—he wouldn't leave her just waiting at the chapel with no word?

She had to believe he would arrive soon.

Or should she just abandon the whole dreadful mess and return to Brantleigh Manor? For the next several minutes she alternated between staying and going, Fran and Sheri taking turns to talk sensibly and quietly, reminding her of Windermere's deep sense of honor and respect for her. Jassie had almost scoffed at that. She'd lost his respect. All she had to fall back on was her belief in his honor.

Dammit, this was intolerable. She couldn't continue to stand here like an uninvited guest at a masquerade ball. Though she wished she had the mask to shield her emotions from curious eyes. She was painfully aware every head in the chapel was turned to the door, watching, waiting—it was too much. She'd waited long enough.

She turned to snap her decision to her companions only to see Fran gazing beyond and silently pointing.

When Jassie turned to see three riders galloping up the Elm Drive, every crazy jumbled emotion she'd been suppressing, rushed into her throat. Away across the other side of the grounds the riders disappeared behind the Abbey and Jassie gave thanks, thinking she'd have a few moments to collect her shattered wits while they left their horses at the stables and walked the length of the vast Abbey structure to reach the chapel. But she was shocked from her momentary calm by the thud of hooves straight across the velvet lawns at this end of the Abbey and the sight of Raven, closely followed by Mayfair and a large grey bearing none other than the Duke of Wolverton, curvetting to a halt on the cinder pathway almost at the door of the chapel.

The Duke, whose hand in marriage she'd almost accepted in her second season, sat tall and grimly piratical, at Windermere's back, the wicked scar down his cheek vivid in the sunlight. As if it wasn't enough she knew he suffered as much for her refusal as she'd suffered over Windermere. Would nothing lighten the heaviness of this day?

Then everything stilled, faded from her consciousness except the man, boots and buckskins mud-spattered and dusty, sitting the heaving black stallion and staring at her as if turned to stone. It was only a second's reaction, just time enough to forget her fright for his safety and for cold anger to surface instead, and then he leapt from the saddle, becoming all urbanity as he bent over her hand and apologized.

She'd been a total mess of opposing sensations then. Fiery hot and icy cold; straight-backed to the point of rigidity and yet her stomach had felt like nothing so much as a bowl of quivering calf's foot jelly; and while love wanted to burst from every pore of her body, anger had rushed from her head to her toes like a bolt of lightning.

No wonder at all that by the time she reached the altar on Windermere's arm she was a trembling mess on the verge of collapse.

In his inimitable way he knew. Why did it surprise her? They'd always been totally attuned emotionally. Numbly she released the posy to him to pass to Sheri and settled with relief against the warm strength of his body as his arm slipped round her waist.

It would be all right. *They* would be all right. They had to be.

When it came time to make her first response Rogan had to squeeze her waist and she managed to squeak out, 'I do' loud enough to satisfy the vicar at least. The rest would forever be a hazy blur; the only memory retained that of the pressure of his arm at her waist. He had touched her many times over the years, apart from that one memorable kiss at sixteen, but always since that night they'd been brief courtesies or gallantries such as a woman might expect from any man.

His arm never left her waist during the entire ceremony nor even as they turned to face the congregation and stoop for the Countess's blessing. It remained as they walked back down the aisle as husband and wife, the Earl and Countess of Windermere, greeting their guests with wide smiles pinned to their faces. He never even removed it as they walked through the ancient cloisters and back towards the east door of the Abbey.

'Where are we headed?'

Startled out of her swirling inner world of shimmering joy, desperate hope, and leaden terror, Jassie came to a faltering halt.

'Oh—I forgot—you don't know what we've arranged, do you?'

He shook his head and a faint smile twitched his lips. Lord, she wanted to reach up and kiss him—properly. Not a tense little peck at her lips as he'd offered her in the chapel, but a kiss such as he'd given her on Neave Tor. A nervous giggle wanted to erupt out of her when she thought where that had led. Probably better left as it was.

'We've arranged for a meal to be served in the Great Hall. It's more in the nature of a cold collation since I wanted all the staff to be able to attend the—the service. I hope that meets with your approval, my Lord.'

He stiffened a little and the arm at her waist seemed to clench. Tilting his head in acquiescence, and in a tone bordering on frosty, he said, 'Anything you've arranged meets with my approval—just so long as you haven't arranged for dancing half the night. The sooner these free-loaders and penny-gawpers disappear the better.'

A slight flush touched his cheek as Jassie lifted her shocked eyes to his and then she turned back to find they were at the threshold of the east door.

'Better give them something to gawp at,' he muttered fiercely and on the instant Jassie found herself swept off her feet, one strong arm at her back and the other beneath her knees causing her skirts to billow upwards. Before she'd had time to squawk the smallest protest, he'd lifted her clear over the doorstep and deposited her on her feet in the narrow flagged hallway of the east wing. Cheeks hot, but determined not to scold, for in truth the moment had been straight from her dreams, she kept her face averted while settling her petticoats.

'Bravo!' Bart's voice rumbled from behind them and then Jassie heard him ask Fran, 'Can I lift *you* over the threshold like that, Mrs. Lyndon?'

Jassie couldn't resist a glance back as Fran responded firmly in the negative. Her friend's cheeks were flushed and her eyes smiling nevertheless. Sheri's head was down and she was giving every impression of being totally detached from the tall, glowering Duke whose arm supported her elegantly gloved fingers.

Francine at least looked alive. How long had it been, she wondered, since a man had teased Francine and made her feel like an attractive woman? Far too long, Jassie decided, wondering whether, if now they were to spend a lot more time under the same roof, something might be nurtured between her friend and Barton Matthews.

And Wolverton? Perhaps she could try and find him a wife, a woman who could take his mind off the love he thought he'd lost with her. Could Sheri be that woman? Was she trying to hide an attraction to the scowling Duke? Probably not. Sheri never allowed herself to be attracted to any man.

And truly, Jassie rebuked herself, she'd be best advised to just concentrate on nurturing what should be the natural outcome of marriage between herself and Rogan before she set her sights on any further match-making.

'We should wait for Lady O to catch up. I looked out mother's old sedan chair for her and the footmen are carrying it. I'd like her to lead the procession into the Great Hall. The meal is not going to pass any faster if we charge ahead like we can't wait for it to be over.'

'That's how it's supposed to look,' Rogan muttered and Jassie stole a glance at his taut profile. Of course his eagerness was all for show. He was the quintessential illusionist. Appearing to be something he wasn't in order to slip into enemy territory to gain the information he'd been sent after, was as natural to him as breathing. She would do well to remember that while he was lulling her into a false sense of anticipation with his lover-like attentions.

At least she felt as if she was back in control of her senses and not about to slide ignominiously into a dead faint. But she'd reveled in the feel of his arm at her waist and so he needn't know she felt perfectly capable of standing without his support. To that end she emitted a soft sigh and leant against his shoulder. Carefully hiding the smile that wanted to transform into a satisfied smirk, she welcomed his arm back at her waist and then held her skirts back so the footmen could move through with the Countess—now more properly styled the Dowager Countess.

'I like your mode of travel, Mama,' Windermere said with a chuckle. 'Why hadn't we thought of that before?'

'I don't know, Windermere, but I'm very grateful to *your wife* for thinking of it.'

Her eyes twinkled up at her son and Jassie sighed as she watched his own smile falter and his struggle to reinstate it to his mother's satisfaction.

'Lead on,' he muttered. 'You're to be the advance guard, I'm told.'

The tedious meal over at last, Jassie rose to lead the ladies to the Blue Salon and leave the gentlemen to their port. A quick glance round the famous room with its Angelica Kauffman painted ceiling depicting scenes from a Greek mythological tale, assured Jassie all was as she'd ordered. Tea was set out on the heavy ormolu side tables, presided over by her own Mrs. Jolly with Jassie's maid, Ruby, at her elbow. The familiar faces were so welcome Jassie had to swallow back a gulp of emotion. It was rather an indictment of what a country mouse she'd become when she felt happier in the company of her household staff than with those of her own social standing.

Mrs. Worth, the vicar's wife, peered censoriously over her lorgnette at the giddy Miss Landon's and their bright younger friend, Lady Gillian Meredith, who were gasping and chattering incessantly about the wonders of finally being inside Windermere Abbey's renowned Blue Salon. Their mothers stood a little beyond, no less cat-eyed than their daughters but slightly more circumspect with it. Jassie realized there'd been no society events at Windermere since the death of Rogan's older brother, Quentin Wyldefell, eight years ago. He and two friends, after a night of deep drinking, had made an ill-conceived wager as to who could beat the current speed record for a curricle and four from London to Newmarket.

Quentin's curricle had locked wheels with that of Lord Alfred Mowbray, who, it was said, was trying to cut him off. Both vehicles were overturned and Quentin died on the side of the road. Lord Mowbray had lived, though rumor had it, it would've been kinder for all concerned if he hadn't. The scandal of that night's work and the loss of two of society's most eligible bachelors had rocked the ton and stolen the laughter from the family at Windermere Abbey.

She glanced over to where Jensen was settling Rogan's mother beside Aunt Gussy and Lady Allerton-Smythe from Neave Manor. Her new mother-in-law was pale and looked tired, but there was a smile in her eyes Jassie hadn't seen in many years.

Lady O had put aside her grief to sponsor Jassie's debut into London Society in 1808. But the death of Rogan's father, the 7th Earl, in March the following year was the final blow to the Countess's health. Windermere Abbey had been a place of retirement ever since.

Concerned the day had over-strained the older woman's meagre resources of strength, Jassie settled herself on a chair at the Dowager's side.

'Would you not prefer to retire and have Lucy bring your tea?'

The faded blue eyes took on a militant sparkle.

'I do not intend to miss one minute of this miraculous day, *daughter*.—Do you have any conception of what joy that brings me? To finally have a daughter? And that *she* is *you* whom I've always thought of as a daughter anyway—I just can't find the words to express it,' she finished, squeezing Jassie's hand.

Jassie found she was still feeling somewhat fragile. Tears threatened and she leant down to kiss her mother-in-law's cheek.

'And I could not be more blessed in having you for a mother-in-law,' she whispered back and they shared a conspiratorial smile.

Fran appeared before her with a cup of tea and Jassie took it gratefully, and set about applying herself to being the gracious hostess and chatting with each of her guests as the afternoon darkened towards evening. A commotion at the doors of the Salon heralded the arrival of the men. Leading the charge was Rogan, still clad in the riding attire he'd first arrived in. Hair in a state of casual disarray and his neck cloth loose as if he'd been tugging at it, his eyes glittered with an emotion Jassie was hard put to read, but was very afraid was similar to that silvery look of horror that had overtaken him on Neave Tor.

Was the battle for her marriage to begin so soon?

Distraction from that panicked thought came in the form of the Duke, similarly attired to Windermere though suavely elegant as always. Immediately taking her hand in his he bent his dark head to place a heated kiss on her fingertips.

'I've come to take my leave of you, Lady Windermere,' he said, his deep voice oddly constrained. He looked briefly into her eyes, searching, silently saying things that could never be said.

Before Jassie had gathered the wits to respond, he said, 'Be happy.'

Dropping her hand, he stepped back, said a few words of farewell to the Dowager, shared a punishing handshake and a piercing stare with Rogan, and strode from the room.

While her racing mind tried to process the meaning of the strangely tense, but brief, interlude, Rogan stepped to her side and then there was no room in her mind or any other part of her for anything but her husband.

Wouldn't these people ever go home? What didn't they understand about a wedding night? The usual thing would be for the bride and groom to slip away and leave other family members to continue as hosts but his mother was beyond exhausted, her eyes hollow and shadowed.

Feeling an absolute charlatan, Rogan made one of his lightning shifts into character, that of an anticipatory, bride-hungry groom, and addressed the room.

'Well, ladies, I do believe your gentlemen have come to fetch you home. My *wife* and I have other business to conduct this night and I'm sure my Lady Mother is craving her bed, but is loath to seek it while there is one more drop of pleasure to be wrung from this day.'

'I say, Windermere, are you throwing us out? That's a bit boorish, ain't it?' rumbled Sir Gresham Landon with a leering grin.

'Absolutely old chap, and I make no apologies! Bart, don't we have a whip somewhere hereabouts you can crack?' Rogan demanded of his cousin and in the general laughter everyone began taking their leave.

Rogan took up a stance by his mother's chair and drew Jassie into the circle of his left arm, leaving his right free for shaking hands with the gentlemen and bowing over those of the ladies. A few more smiles, a few more polite words, a loving goodnight for his mother and then he'd take Jassie upstairs and—abandon her.

Damn it all to hell! For a split second he actually wished he had the guts to slit his own throat.

As the last guest vanished through the salon door to be ushered down the front steps with grave efficiency by Melton, Rogan turned to his mother, relieved to find he was still capable of a genuine smile.

'Goodnight Mama,' he said gently, bending to kiss her forehead.

She caught at his hand with her frail fingers before he could back away and drew him back to her.

'You've made me truly happy this day, Windermere. I pray the same may be said of you.'

Damn this lovely fragile woman who loved him unconditionally and saw through every disguise he could ever hope to try and hide behind. He could lie to her but she'd know and somehow on this night of all nights, he couldn't.

'Our happiness is in God's hands, Mama,' he said, pressing his lips briefly to her fingertips. 'Sleep well.'

He could see she wished to respond to that but he immediately turned away and called for the footmen to carry his mother along the candle-lit corridors to her rooms in the ground floor west wing. She glanced back over her shoulder as her chair passed through the salon doors, her eyes troubled and filled with messages he knew he didn't want to think about. She'd understand if he could tell her but how did a man go about telling his mother he'd been abused by a woman to such an extent that when he had any other woman beneath him begging for sexual favors he transmuted into some kind of avenging demon, bent on bondage and punishment? How could he tell her there was no guarantee he wouldn't use Jassie in this way, making her pay for the sins of another committed long ago? Why could he never let go of the humiliation, the bitterness, the anger, the need to punish?

Jassie was tugging at his hand.

'Rogan! Are you all right?' she whispered and he looked around to find Lady Sherida and Mrs. Lyndon watching him from the doorway.

'Of course,' he snapped. 'Let's get you upstairs.'

She shot him a startled look and he realized he'd been so distracted by his bitter thoughts he'd forgotten to censor his words.

'Where are you going?'

'Upstairs with you,' he growled immediately and pulled her from the room before his lifelong habit of honesty with Jassie kicked in and he added, '*and then I'm leaving.*'

Jassie knew Rogan wasn't being honest with her but she was totally unprepared for him to usher her into the suite of rooms they should henceforth share as husband and wife and then to announce he was leaving immediately for London and did not know when he'd be back. The shock of his bald, toneless announcement temporarily stole her soul. For a long moment it seemed as if all thought, feeling—*spirit*— had left her body then into the vacuum left behind rushed an anger so intense it seared through her veins and roared in her ears.

Hooped skirt swinging violently, she leapt across the room before he could move, placed her back against the door and let him see the seething cauldron of emotion in her eyes.

'Oh-no-you-don't-Windermere! I never took you for a coward, but if you walk out that door I have no choice but to think you one now! Or have I given you such a disgust of me you can't stand the thought of sullying your hands with my body? Is that it, *my Lord*?'

Her voice had risen from a low, ugly snarl to a loud hectoring growl, but Jassie was beyond caring how she sounded. This confrontation was long overdue.

A muscle twitched violently along his jaw and his fists clenched at his sides.

'No, that's not it.'

He ground his teeth on the words and Jassie felt each one to the pit of her stomach.

'Then *why*? I know you desire me. I've already proved that. What do I have to do to break through your bone-headed stubbornness, tie you to my bed?'

Rogan Wyldefell, her dearest friend since the day she was born, vanished. In his place stood a deadly, dark-eyed stranger with grimly clenched jaw. A stranger who moved so fast she never even thought to avoid him. In violent silence he gripped her arm, and twisted her round to face the door. His left arm pinned her at the neck, pressing her face hard against the wooden panels of the door. A harsh slicing sound and the terrifying sensation of cold steel against her backbone was followed by the clatter of a knife to the floor swiftly followed by her mother's beautiful gown and every item she'd worn under it.

Had he gone mad? Terror froze her tongue as he swung her across the room and thrust her face down on the bed, holding her there with his knee in the small of her back.

'Rogan!' the word was barely a whisper. It felt as if she'd never be able to unlock her throat again.

Once more he seemed to have forgotten who she was. She certainly didn't know this madman. What was he doing now? Her mind felt near to exploding through her skull. When he suddenly reached the length of her body, gripped her flailing wrists and bound them together with his neck cloth, she tried to fight, to scratch, to yell obscenities at him, anything to bring him to his senses. But Windermere had learned street-fighting in a dirty school, the dark alleys and filthy slums of almost every major European city. An untrained woman had no chance. Swiftly she was hauled up onto the mound of pillows at the head of the bed and the other end of the cloth secured to the headboard. He rolled her to her back and surveyed his handiwork with an ugly smile that stole all the light from his eyes.

Painfully aware all she wore were cream stockings and pale satin slippers, Jassie was incapable of forming a thought, let alone speaking. Her mouth seemed to be frozen in a silent gasp.

When he came at her with his handkerchief in his hands she opened her mouth wider to scream. He stopped it with his hand, then before she could angle her teeth to bite, he deftly wrapped the cloth across her mouth and twisted the ends behind her head, turning her roughly to knot it tightly before shoving her back into the pillows.

A strange rough sound emanated from his throat and then he bent his head and began devouring her breasts in an assault that instantly sent her blood from freezing to boiling point. She uttered a wild incoherent cry, muffled by the gag. He sucked harder until she was writhing and moaning then bit sharply, first one breast then the other until she screamed helplessly against the gag.

It was all happening so fast, the sensations firing like rockets in her brain, Jassie couldn't make sense of any of it. Even the pain seemed too fantastical to be real. Suddenly he rolled her onto her stomach, shoved her up the bed so her face was thrust among the pillows. Grabbing some, he shoved them under her hips, pushed her knees high and wide until she was shamefully exposed to him. Then without warning his hand crashed across her backside in a hard open slap.

She yelped into the pillows and tried to roll away from him but he pushed her back as she'd been and held her down with a hand on her back while he thrashed her as she'd never been thrashed in her life. Dear God, where was this going to end? Somewhere amid the pain Jassie felt a terrible excitement build and threaten inside her but it was kept at bay by the ugly names he was calling her, words she'd never heard before but knew she should never be subjected to. So this was what he'd been trying to protect her from!

But even as the thought formed it was cleansed from her mind by a rush of violent ecstasy from some impossibly deep place in her belly that spread and engulfed her whole being until she was screaming into the pillows and begging, begging, 'Rogan please, Rogan please.'

Over and over.

And finally he was there behind her on the bed, thrusting into her even harder and deeper than he had on Neave Tor and for a few moments out of time her crazy body exulted; at last he had given himself to her. At last the real Rogan Wyldefell, Earl of Windermere was truly her husband. His shout of release and the final violent thrust of his body was a symphony playing in her heart.

'I love you, Rogan,' she sobbed. She could not have stopped the words if he'd held a sword to her throat. Even muffled he could not but interpret what she was trying to say.

His body went momentarily rigid above her then he leapt off the bed leaving her once again exposed and humiliated. She rolled off the pillows, hands still tied above her head and tears dribbling down her cheeks, and lay watching him as he rebuttoned his falls with stiff uncoordinated movements. When he looked up at her his eyes were that strange shade of silver horror she'd first noted on Neave Tor and his mouth a trenchant dark slash in a stark white face.

'Don't-ever-threaten-to-restrain-me-or-I'll-not-be-responsible-for-my-actions.'

He untied the cravat from the bed and her hands, taking care not to touch her, it seemed. Wrapping it twice round his neck and shoving the ends inside his jacket, he picked up the knife and stowed it back down his boot then strode for the door.

He left without another word, the door slamming behind him and she lay staring at it as his boots clattered into silence down the back stairs.

CHAPTER FIVE

Blood roaring in his head, Rogan took the stairs at a headlong pace, uncaring whether he fell and broke his cursed neck.

'What the fuck? What the fuck? What the fuck?'

No other thought would form in his head. Exiting onto a path at the back of the Abbey, the cool night air struck his heated face, threatening the return of sanity. Desperate to outrun anything approaching normality, whereby he'd have to confront the horror of his actions, he strode down the path to the stables as if Fouché or one of his minions dogged his heels. He deserved to be thrown to them like the cowardly dog he was.

Bart's voice came out of the darkness shrouding the stable entrance.

'That took longer than you said it would. Get the better of you, did she?'

A step closer and Rogan could see his cousin leaning nonchalantly against the doorway. His grin was a white slash in the shadows. Without conscious thought, Rogan's fist connected with the gleaming white teeth, smacking the dark head back against the wall with a satisfying thunk of bone on wood.

Before the gratification reached his brain Bart's fist flew out of the darkness, connected with his chin and slammed him on his backside in the dust.

He sat for a moment, rubbing his smarting chin and wondering why, when his brain was frozen in the desire for revenge and punishment, he forgot the power and accuracy of Bart's left hook.

'Fuck! Fuck! Fuck it all to hell!' he ground out, feeling as if each word tore out a piece of his intestines. He stood up, faced his cousin and said, 'You want more of that? I'm in the mood to go a round or two and I'm just ugly-minded enough to slam you into oblivion and enjoy every moment of it.'

Bart pushed himself away from the wall he'd been leaning against, planted his feet barely twelve inches away from Rogan's and clenched his fists at his side.

'What the hell is wrong with you, Windermere?' he thundered. 'First of all you're adamant you don't intend to bed your brand new bride— and God knows, I'd happily bed her for you if you've got a problem. She's a damn prime article, not some spotty-faced chit!—And then, you've been with her long enough to bed her when you said you'd only be as long as it took to see her upstairs. *Then,*' he continued, stopping only to suck in air, 'you come at me out of the night like a blasted Myrmidon, eyes blazing and fists swinging like a battering ram! Did she turn the tables on you? Tell you where to stick your randy prick because she's worried about where it's been? Or is it the opposite? You only married her to save her from a scandal of another man's making? For, let's face it, Windermere, if you'd *wanted* to marry Jassinda Carlisle, you'd have done it years ago. She's as near an ape leader now as makes no difference.'

He drew breath again and waited, as if expecting Rogan to interrupt. Every word twisted and stabbed at Rogan's guts as if his belly writhed with snakes. But he couldn't speak to stop the flow; knew he deserved every vilifying word Bart was moved to shove down his throat. Slowly he came to his feet but when it became obvious he couldn't get a word through his clenched jaws, Bart continued.

'That's the gossip in town, in case you're wondering! Been spreading like wildfire since you put the notice in the Times. Probably the only reason a bet hasn't been written in the book at White's is because they can't figure who the cur is who could've got Jassinda Carlisle pregnant if it wasn't you!'

Rogan's fist left his side again before he knew it. He would close Bart's filthy mouth and satisfy his own urge for violence at the same time. Bart smacked him back on his arse again. Having a healthy respect for Windermere's title and status as his employer, his cousin didn't usually release the full power of his swing against him, but Rogan had to admit tonight was exceptional. He wouldn't pull his punches either, if he was Bart.

His cousin now stood over him, rocking on his heels, fists ready.

'Come on, Windermere. Get up if you want to fight. I'm not averse.'

Rogan stayed where he was, pulled up his knees and laid his head on his crossed arms.

'Fuck! Fuck! Fuck!' was all he could say.

Sanity had returned. Tonight he'd managed to alienate almost everyone who mattered to him. There was only his mother left. How long before his ugliness gave her a disgust of him too?

'I'm just a mongrel dog, Bart! I'm sorry. If you were to ask Jassie, I've no doubt she'd agree. I've just proved I was right to avoid marrying her all those years. Years through which her loyalty could never have been in doubt—yet still she wanted—still she cared. Well, I guess I've taken care of that now.'

Bart hunkered down before him, grabbed his hair and yanked his head up.

'What did you do to her?' he asked, horror making his voice harsh.

Rogan stared up into Bart's eyes. He knew they were hazel. It was the main disparity in their appearance. But in the shadows of night they just glowed like black coals.

'I tied her up, thrashed her as if she were some hardened miscreant, then I raped her. Now you know why I didn't want to marry her.'

Bart's mouth dropped open then snapped shut. But he didn't question as to whether Rogan was jesting or not.

'No I bloody don't!' he snarled. 'Jassie Carlisle is the most—lady-like—lady I know! Why would you use her like that? For Christ's sake, Windermere, what the devil is wrong with you!'

'I'm damned, damned, damned,' Rogan groaned, jerking his hair out of Bart's grip.

Bart dropped to his backside in the dust before him, as if disbelief had stolen the stiffening from his legs. After a long, glaring silence, he said, 'All right, *Cousin*, here's the deal. You're going to tell me exactly what is going on with you and you'd better have a damned good reason to treat a beautiful, genteel woman like Jassie Carlisle in that way—or I ride out of here tonight and you're on your own—*after* I've punched you senseless! I can't work for an asshole like *that.*—*Why?*—That's what I want to know, because the man I've always believed you to be could not have done what you just said you did.'

Seeing Bart bristling with horror at this glimpse into his dark, secret world, Rogan wondered if he *could* break away from his deeply ingrained habit of silence. Could he expose that ugly, inner darkness; explain to his cousin, and very good friend, what he'd become—and how? What would Bart's reaction be then?

Could he begin to imagine his life without Bart—as well as without Jassie? For marriage notwithstanding, he'd definitely lost Jassie. There were few women who would accept the treatment he'd dished out unless they were being paid for it—or played on the perverted fringe of society which was the only place he socialized these days.

Dragging his hand over his face he realized it was starting to stubble with beard, another inconsideration he'd visited on Jassie. He struggled to his feet.

'Let's ride, Bart. We're sitting in the dirt like a couple of gypsy brats. I'll talk as we go.'

'I'll have your oath on that, Windermere, or I'm not moving.'

'My oath, is it? When did you start mistrusting my word?' Rogan growled.

'Since you became someone I never met before.'

He couldn't argue with that.

'You have my oath,' he said tersely. 'Are the horses ready? Where are Buckton and the others?'

'I sent them back to the Abbey. Miss Jassie, that is, her Ladyship, has done the staff proud, Buckton tells me, with their own celebration in the servants' hall. So I sent them off to enjoy the first celebration seen at Windermere in a long time.—The horses are ready.'

Rogan winced at the unspoken inference nothing good had happened for the Windermere staff until Jassie had had the right to order it, then silently turned into the stable where a single lantern offered a feeble light, to lead out Raven.

About to ask after his cloak, hat and gloves, Bart handed them to him. He dragged them on, mounted up and headed down the Elm Drive, Bart close on his heels.

No word passed between them as they negotiated the cold, dark tunnel beneath the ancient trees. But when they exited through the stone gate pillars and had given Marsh, the gate-keeper, leave to return to the celebrations at the servants' hall, Bart settled down into his saddle and said, 'Now Cousin, let's have it.'

Gazing briefly up at the stars twinkling serenely above, wishing that somehow he could borrow some of that serenity, Rogan focused on the road ahead between Raven's ears and began.

'I always knew I'd marry Jassie one day. At least from the time she was five and splattered the two of us with a rotten bird's egg because she was too impatient to listen to my instructions on how to blow it.' His voice softened, sounded a bit soppy even to his own ears. But it was a precious memory. 'The damn thing was so bad that in short order we were both casting up our accounts and Carlisle was rolling on the grass, laughing like a drainpipe. I cleaned myself up as best I could—and her—and then I just sat there with her small, precious self draped against my chest while we waited to see if our stomachs had settled. Carlisle kept exploding into chortles of unholy glee.

'Something changed in the dynamics between us three that day. Until then it had always been him and me agin her. Christ, she was only a baby! Eleven years younger than us, five to our sixteen and she used to follow us round like a damned pet rat—and so I often told her. Especially after her mother died when she was not yet six. But it was like we'd forged an unbreakable bond over that rotten bloody egg. That day I knew she was to be mine. Though truth to tell, I'd loved her since the day her nurse placed this tiny bundle—no bigger than a rat—in my eleven year old arms—and she bloody looked at me and grinned like—like I was the reason she'd been born. My heart has been in her keeping ever since. I just had to wait for her to grow up.'

Rogan fell silent, thinking about the years waiting for Jassie to grow from the full-blown tom-boy she'd been even at five. Quite often over those years he and Philip had forgotten she wasn't a younger brother to be taught all the things young men taught their younger male siblings.

And then she'd started to change and the hints of the beautiful young woman she would become began to appear. It was then his mother had become more assertive in preventing them from carting Jassie everywhere they went about the estates and often well beyond.

She'd sulked and fought against the lady-like strictures the Countess had imposed. By the time she'd begun to truly blossom into womanhood he'd lost the right to even think of taking her to wife when she was ready.

'You loved her,' Bart declared. 'You do still. It's quite obvious. So that's only the beginning of the story.'

Rogan sighed. Sometimes he felt so *old.*

'Yeah.'

His mind went off at a tangent again, dredging up image after image of Jassie; at ten, dressed in black at her father's funeral, her small cold hands clenched firmly round his and Philip's. His mother had tried to veto her attendance, but Philip had made his first decision as her guardian and decreed if she wished to make her farewells to their father as he was able to, then she should. At thirteen, wearing trousers and riding astride the new dappled mare Philip had bought for her, hair in pigtails as she galloped between them over the Downs, her eyes and cheeks glowing with excitement. At sixteen, suddenly confident of her womanliness as displayed in the beautiful cream muslin empire line gown tied under her enticingly rounded breasts with golden yellow ribbon. He should not have touched her then, but had been unable to forego what she so sweetly and innocently offered. He'd learnt to keep his distance since that night—

'I'm waiting, Windermere,' Bart snarled.

'Yeah,' he muttered again. 'Damn it! You don't know what you ask, Matthews.'

Bart's chin tilted forward belligerently. They rarely used the formal address. They were cousins. Rogan didn't care. He wasn't feeling particularly chummy with his cousin right at this moment.

'I've never revealed this to anyone and if I ever hear so much as a whisper of it—from any quarter—*I* will punch *you* senseless. In fact I'll probably *kill* you.'

'You have my silence.'

Rogan didn't question it. There was no one more arrow-straight than his secretary.

'I boarded in the house of a professor when I went to university. His young wife was every twenty-year-old's wet dream.'

His nostrils flared with the outrage he felt as the image of Adelaide Barratt floated before his eyes, all creamy curves, titian-colored hair, and sultry green, feline eyes.

'And you were easy prey.'

'I was.' Rogan ground his teeth on the admission. 'Trouble was she wasn't satisfied just to be thoroughly pleasured in the normal way and began harassing me to let her introduce me to–some deviant stuff. Dammit! I was a stupid, horny young bastard and never in my life had I thought to turn down sexual favors. But I wasn't into the kind of diversions she was talking about—and so I told her. I was stupid enough to think I could control the situation and still get my regular grind which was all I thought about at that age.'

Bart's derisive snort brought him out of the story for a moment.

'You were just a randy young prick!'

'And you weren't?' Rogan bit back defensively.

'Of course I was, but I'd grown up in a tougher school than you. Sometimes wealth and position are not all that advantageous.'

Rogan grimaced into the darkness and considered Bart's wisdom. For it was true, he might have fared better had he not learnt to think of himself as privileged and deserving of every consideration, especially from the lower class comely women who were available to him and not shy about showing it.

'So what did the bitch do to you?'

A sigh rasped through Rogan's whole being. How many times had he wished he could go back and undo the events of that night, create a different scenario with a different outcome? Behave, perhaps, as the man his parents had raised him to be instead of some muff-hungry idiot who thought his every sexual need should be assuaged—on demand.

'At a guess I'd say she doped my ale at dinner then she slipped me a note to say she'd visit my room as soon as her husband left the house. The last thing I remember before waking up gagged and with my wrists bound and secured to the head board, was that I was unconscionably tired. I was already well aroused when I came to but I'm reasonably certain it was pain that woke me. I think she bit my balls. They felt bruised and tender for days after—though that could have been because of what followed.'

'Hell!' Bart muttered involuntarily and Rogan smiled grimly into the dark. That kind of pain had that kind of effect on any man.

The horses had long since slowed to a walk and neither of them thought to change the pace. There was no panic to be back in London after all. Neither Lord Hadleigh nor his cousin, Knightsborough who was his immediate superior at the Ministry, was expecting him back in the capital until the end of the week. Both knew he was being married today. He wasn't the only experienced courier they had to call on.

'Windermere?'

Bart's voice had softened, even gone a little wary.

'Yeah?'

'You don't have to tell me any more—if you'd rather not.'

Rogan rode for a time in silence, eyes raised to the star-bright heavens. There was a soft illumination in the east. The moon was about to crest the horizon. That would make travelling easier. He looked back at Bart.

'Thanks.—But—you know—I think, I do need to tell you a little of it, just so you understand. Maybe it's just time I told someone instead of trying to hold it all in, hold myself together. I don't think that's working anymore.'

'You're probably right. Go on then,' Bart said.

'She used a small deadly dagger to get me where she wanted me, threatened to castrate me. She used stuff on me which at that point I had no experience of. A cock ring, nipple clamps, a butt plug and a flogger.'

Bart's face had taken on a strange green tinge in the moonlight.

'It's a wonder I didn't tear the headboard from the bed. But the beds in all our rooms were very sturdy and I guess that was the reason why. In my still fuzzy opium-induced state, I reasoned maybe if I just let her have her way she'd set me free—and *then* I'd make her sorry she'd messed with me.—You ever used a cock ring?'

'Couple of times,' Bart admitted with an embarrassed grin.

Rogan found he couldn't respond in kind. There was nothing remotely funny about what that bitch had put him through.

'She then set about arousing me in every deviant way known to *woman*! It could have been torturing. Bloody bitch! She knew there is something—addictive—about that kind of sexual animalism; she showed me the guilty pleasure of extreme pain; she showed me no matter how such acts disgust a man he has to admit in his deepest secret mind he enjoys them on some level; and she showed me a side of myself I've never been able to reconcile with.

'Eventually I was able to turn the tables on her. Treated her in every foul way I could imagine. I actually thought I'd succeeded in humiliating her at least as much as she'd humiliated me. She'd finally slumped, silent and inert so I removed the gag. The first words out of her mouth were, 'God, Wyldefell, you were magnificent!' Before I could digest the fact she'd loved every damned minute of it, had in fact got everything from me she'd originally wanted, she offered to bring Carlisle in to fuck my arse while it was so stretched and sensitive. Said I'd love that too. I—'

His whole body shuddered and his head dropped to his chest, lost in the horror of that moment.

'She'd corrupted Carlisle too?'

'So it would seem. The ugly truth of that was, I was consumed with a terrifying mixture of excitement and revulsion at the thought of what she'd suggested. I learned to hate myself that day.—So I gagged her again and flogged her until there were welts on her arse and then—aahh, never mind.—Finally I shoved her out of my room, and threatened her with death if she came anywhere near me again.'

When he drifted off into a silent pensiveness, Bart asked, 'Did you ever talk to Carlisle about it?'

Rogan shook his head.

'God no! I was too bloody ashamed. And if she'd put him through anything like what she put me through he likely didn't want to talk about it either. But I left that house as soon as I was able to make other arrangements and Philip readily agreed to come with me. Guess that said enough.'

'I have a little understanding of what you mean by feeling ashamed. I've been bloody uncomfortable in my breeches the whole time you've been talking. Makes me as sick as you think you are.—I can see why that all might have given you a taste for bondage and punishment.'

'I don't have a taste for it,' Rogan snarled. 'Whatever it was she unleashed in me that night takes over. It's like some other bastard moves into my skin and I'm compelled to—somehow—succeed in punishing the bitch. She forever ruined me for the beautiful lady-like loving Jassie should've been able to look forward to. Bondage and punishment have become my modus operandi. My satisfaction now must be taken within brothels or under the secrecy of certain fringe groups of society.'

Like the Matrix Club, but he didn't mention that. It was the kind of place a man found on his own if he had the need. And he was pretty certain Bart was as straight in that way as he was in every other.

Bart waited for several moments in silence, allowing Rogan time to find some inner peace before asking, 'What will you do now? Might I suggest you ride back to the Abbey and tell Jassie what you've just told me? If there is anyone who can help you in this mess, I'd say Jassie Carlisle—Lady Windermere—is it.'

Rogan slowly turned his head and stared at Bart.

'Have you lost your fucking mind?' he whispered at last. 'I-will-never-return-to-Windermere. Jassie now has the protection of my name—whether she carries my child or not. And I will ride to London, take the most hazardous assignment Hadleigh can offer me and hope I do the honorable thing and get myself killed in the line of duty. That way Jassie will be safe from me. Because now I've finally had the love that is Jassie, regardless I've defiled it beyond redemption, I-want-it-again. If I'm anywhere in her vicinity she won't be safe from me.'

'Have you asked her whether she wants to be safe from you? Have you told her *any* of what you've just told me? Or have you made an arbitrary decision about how your two lives are to be played out regardless of what she might wish? At least return and talk to her—'

'Have you heard anything I just said?' Rogan yelled, finally once again as deeply out of control as he'd been with Jassie.

'Nothing that made sense—' Bart began.

'Damn you to hell!' Rogan tightened his grip on the reins, dug his heels into Raven's belly with a suddenness that startled the horse into rearing in surprise, then man and horse settled and started for London at a crazy breakneck speed, leaving Bart to mutter and curse in their wake.

Dear God! Jassie lay staring at the door in glassy-eyed horror, her trembling fingers fumbling desperately at the knot of the gag. She wanted to yell after Rogan, demand he stay, ask him to explain, tell him again that she loved him—enough—for both of them. Her mouth was as dry as parchment and her throat, strained from the stifled screaming, seemed swollen shut. As she finally ripped the spittle-soaked linen from her mouth, the distant slam of a door downstairs was followed by the kind of silence that was thick enough to taste—and it tasted of acid and horror.

Who was that man who'd bound, thrashed and—taken her—as if he held her in the deepest hatred? That man was not her Rogan. What would she become if she ever lost faith in that truth? Slowly she rolled her aching body into a ball, wrapped her arms tightly about her midriff and let her tears soak silently into the pillows—because in some twisted place deep inside her she knew if that was the only way Rogan could make love to her she still wanted it, still wanted him.

It seemed she'd been lying staring into the darkness for hours, her body aching and trembling, when she heard the eerie echo of horse hooves in the stillness of the night and crawled off the bed. Dragging the quilt with her and wrapping it round her shoulders, she knelt in the window seat and watched as two horses and their riders, ghostly figures in the night shadows, moved away from the Abbey and were swallowed up by the black maw of the Elm Drive. Her hand reached for the window to shove it wide and yell for Windermere to come back to her, but again she saw the silvery horror searing her from his eyes and her hand dropped. She had to think.

And she had to give him time to think. For surely, when he did, he'd know they couldn't leave their marriage like this. With fists pressed to her mouth to quiet her sobbing she stared longingly at the spot where her husband of a few hours had disappeared into utter darkness. It wasn't until exhaustion claimed her and she fell off the window seat to land on her already bruised backside on the hard floor she finally crawled back into her bed and tried to find the oblivion of sleep.

That she'd eventually succeeded was proved by the fact when next she opened her eyes the sun was high in the sky and the bracket clock on the side table showed it was almost twelve. For a moment Jassie stared blankly at the timepiece wondering why it had stopped just before midnight and then the musical chimes rang out and she realized it hadn't stopped at all.

Why hadn't Ruby woken her? The answer to that question flooded her brain with the whole disastrous mess of yesterday's events: Windermere arriving late for their marriage and having no time to change from his dusty riding attire or to tidy himself in any way and thus he'd stayed through the entire ceremony and interminable meal afterwards; his rather rude disposal of their guests and the crazy excitement that had exploded in her stomach because she'd thought he was finally as impatient as she was for them to be alone together; his terrible pronouncement he intended to leave immediately for London and the awful scene that had followed her rabid protest.

Falling back onto her pillows she tried to block the memories from her mind. All she could seem to think about was what everyone would say when they realized Windermere had gone back to London. That he was not, as they were obviously all fondly thinking, lost to the world in the arms of his brand new bride. Slowly she sat up and hid her face in her hands, feeling like nothing so much as abandoning herself to her misery and hiding under the bedclothes for the rest of her life.

I never knew you for a coward, Jassie Carlisle, she berated herself. You've achieved a dream you've carried in your heart for years. You are now Lady Windermere, Rogan's wife. If the dream doesn't look like the picture you've carried with you for so long, are you going to accept that? Let the dream die? There is no one who can fix this but yourself. And surely Rogan cares deeply enough about you to want to change it? You have to believe in that.

So, Jassie *Wyldefell, Lady Windermere*, are you going to lie here and wallow in your cowardly misery or get up and face the world and slay the dragons that so clearly have Rogan by the throat—or some other body part entirely?

She flung herself out of bed, pulled on a russet colored silk peignoir, tugged the bell to summon Ruby and slumped on the chair before her duchess and stared critically at her reflection in the mirror. She looked like a—loose woman—after a night of utter debauchery. Wild color spotted her pale cheeks beneath puffy, bloodshot eyes and her hair was a tangle of loose pins and pearl rope, having no resemblance to the beautiful arrangement Ruby had wrought for her yesterday.

There was a light tap on the door but instead of entering with a blithe good morning as she'd always done, Ruby waited for Jassie to bid her enter, clearly thinking it possible the Earl would still be with her.

When she entered in response to Jassie's call, Ruby's eyes darted quickly round the room before flickering back to scan Jassie's mirrored face with obvious concern.

'Would you like me to order your bath, Miss Jassi—my Lady?' Ruby asked, unable to mask her confusion at the absence of the Earl—or any sign he'd even shared the bridal bed with his new wife.

'Yes Ruby—and a cup of tea please.'

The maid left again, her face deeply troubled. So it starts, Jassie thought. By the time she returns with my tea the whole staff will probably know the bridegroom is conspicuously absent.

Ruby returned a few minutes later with a tea tray and closely followed by the footmen with the bath and buckets of water. As soon as they were gone she turned, her face a mask of rigid forbearance and began removing pins and pearls from her mistress's hair. As she helped Jassie out of her peignoir and into the bath, as she had on countless occasions over the years, she gasped in horror.

Startled, Jassie stopped with one foot balanced at the edge of the bath.

'What?'

'You—your—I *knew* something wasn't right! Your buttocks are bruised, Miss—my Lady! And I'll swear that's the imprint of a man's hand!' The maid's voice ended on a trembling note. Then she rallied herself, to ask almost fearfully, 'Are you all right, M—my Lady?'

Jassie turned her naked backside to the mirror and stared in silent fascination at the dark bruises, one in particular definitely in the shape of Windermere's hand. No use trying to claim she'd fallen on the steps then. She dragged in a shuddering breath.

'What do you think, Ruby? Do you think I'm all right? And please stop with the 'my Lady' stuff! I know I'll have to get used to it in public, but when it's just us can you please call me Miss Jassie like you always have?'

She wouldn't cry, she wouldn't! But Ruby couldn't contain her outrage for her young mistress and snatched up the peignoir from the chair where she'd only just placed it, wrapped it around Jassie's shoulders and pulled her into her plump arms.

'Oh, Miss Jassie,' she whispered, pressing Jassie's face against her neck. 'I never would've believed that of Lord Windermere if I hadn't seen it for myself! Why, if I could get my hands on him—'

'Hush Ruby,' Jassie murmured, slipping her arms round her horrified maid and letting the tears fall down her cheeks. 'He didn't know what he was doing. There is something dreadfully wrong with Windermere and I mean to get to the bottom of it. You know he's resisted asking me for marriage all these years and wouldn't have now if I hadn't forced the issue. I've only myself to blame. But I love him so much and somehow I have to believe that love is enough to heal whatever ails my husband.'

'But Miss Jassie—'

Jassie pulled away from the maid's comforting arms, dropped the robe and stepped into the bath.

'You are not to say a word of this to anyone, Ruby.'

'But—'

'Not a word!' Jassie said fiercely. 'I'll not have one whisper of this going beyond this room! I'll most likely discuss it with Lady O—for she's not unaware something ails her son. But do not mention anything to any member of the staff or anyone else. This is something for Windermere and myself to resolve—or not.'

The last two words slipped past her lips in little more than a whisper. She couldn't bear to think Windermere would deny them any chance to at least discuss what lay between them. He was her dearest friend, her deepest confidant. Always had been. There was nothing they'd not been able to discuss with one another in the past. Why should this be any different?

She laid her head back against the tub, closed her eyes and concentrated on breathing deeply through her nose.

'Miss Jassie, where is the Earl?'

'In London by now I would imagine, Ruby, judging by the way he stormed out of here last night.'

'Oh Miss,' the maid whispered sadly.

'It's all right, Ruby. Just hand me the soap. I'll be done here in a few minutes and you can come back and help me dress.'

'Shall I put out the primrose morning dress for you, Miss Jassie?'

'I rather fancy the deeper color of the marigold gown today. I think it says more about how I'm feeling. Primrose represents eternal love and that feels somewhat uncertain this morning. Marigold on the other hand represents pain and grief, which is much more in tune with my feelings.'

With the gown in place, Ruby handed her a light spencer to cover her shoulders against the cool spring air.

Jassie tugged it into place then asked, 'Ruby? Would you mind folding my gown away?' She waved a hand to where the beautiful wedding gown lay in a sordid heap against the wall. 'Maybe someday we'll be able to create something from all the material in it.'

As Ruby lifted the pile of cloth, the under-gown, corset and chemise fell away and the maid instantly realized how they'd been removed. Her eyes were almost bulging from their sockets and words she was struggling not to speak trembled on her lips.

Jassie just shook her head.

'Don't say anything, Ruby. Just take it out of my sight, please.— And remember, not a word to anyone. Much as I'd miss you, I'll let you go in a heartbeat if I find you've not obeyed me in this.'

The maid's dark head bobbed then she said, 'Of course you have my word, Miss Jassie. None shall hear aught about any of this from me. You can be sure of that.'

She turned to the door of the dressing room, her mouth pinched tight and a deep frown on her brow.

'Thankyou Ruby,' Jassie murmured after her. 'And please would you ask Mrs. Lyndon to attend me here?'

Ruby bobbed her head and hurried from the room and when she returned, Fran arrived soon after, waiting silently until Jassie dismissed the maid. Once they were alone, Jassie allowed her eyes to meet Fran's in the mirror. Suddenly Fran was at her side.

'Jassie? What's wrong? Where's Windermere?'

Slowly Jassie rose from the stool and turned to face her friend.

'Oh Fran, what am I going to do?' She started to lower her face to her hands, then threw her head back and gritted her teeth. She would not cry again. 'I—I think I should go and talk with Lady O. Come with me please. I'll tell you everything when we get there.'

Never needing to be told anything twice, Fran hurried to open the door and stand back for Jassie to lead the way.

The Dowager, for such she was now, was seated at her dressing table, a warm shawl about her thin shoulders while Lucy drew a brush rhythmically through her soft white hair. Her deep blue eyes fixed directly on her new daughter-in-law as she opened the door. Caught in a moment of panic, Jassie's legs trembled alarmingly beneath her and there was nothing to support her except the door handle, to which she clung in desperation.

Lord knows what the older woman saw in her face for she immediately struggled to come upright and go to Jassie's assistance. Francine, seeing Lady O's alarm, swiftly slid an arm round Jassie's waist and ushered her across the room to a chair by the window.

Struck silent, the Dowager watched for several seconds before quietly asking Lucy to leave them. As soon as she was gone the older woman pushed herself slowly upright and crossed the room to drop into the other chair in the window embrasure, while Fran knelt at Jassie's side and began gently massaging her frozen fingers.

'What's wrong, Jassie? Where's Rogan?' Lady Windermere asked, her voice thready with apprehension.

'He's likely in London by now,' Jassie whispered. 'He left—not long after—after we went up last night.'

Her face suddenly deathly white, the Dowager struggled to her feet and stood on shaking legs, gripping the arms of her chair. Her blue eyes blazed with a fury Jassie had never seen her display before.

'Windermere did what?' she snapped, albeit in a raspy whisper.

Fran leapt to the Dowager's side to hold her steady.

'I'm sorry,' Jassie whispered, closing her eyes and biting her lip hard to contain her emotions. 'I—I—'

Helplessly she dropped her face into her hands. She really thought she had more strength than this, but the Dowager's distress was more than she could bear.

Accepting Fran's arm, the frail woman dropped back into her chair but her eyes continued to blaze like blue fires in her head.

'Windermere will answer to me for this.'

'No, Lady O, no!' Jassie whispered. 'It's—I need to talk to you—'

Lady Windermere snapped her mouth shut and sat for a moment breathing deeply to calm herself. Patting Fran's hand to let her know she could go back to Jassie's side, she smoothed the folds of her dressing robe over her knees then clasped her hands tightly in her lap.

'Jassie, from now on I insist you call me 'Mama'. I've waited so long for you to become my daughter, and regardless of the actions of my *infamous son*, you are now that.—Won't you bring your chair over here so I can hold your hands and maybe we can help each other through this.'

Francine helped Jassie get settled at the Dowager's side, then asked, 'Would you like me to leave you alone, Jass?'

'Lord no! Why would you think that? We've never had any secrets from one another and I won't start now. I need all the help I can get—

and so does R—Rogan. Bring another chair here, Fran,' Jassie said, indicating her other side and impatiently brushing the tears from her face.

When they were settled, the Dowager took Jassie's hands firmly between her own bird-like ones and said, 'Now explain why Windermere is not with you, if you please, child.'

Jassie looked down at their clasped hands then gently began massaging Lady O's delicate skin. This would be as painful for Rogan's mother as it was for his wife. She hated to hurt a woman who'd given her every consideration a mother would have, the woman who'd been the feminine strength and guidance she'd fallen back on all her life.

Fran's arm settled across Jassie's tense shoulders as Lady O continued speaking from her other side.

'We all understand there's some sort of problem, Jassie, so there's no point in being embarrassed to speak of what happened. We have long known something is not right with Windermere and I'm guessing you now know a lot more than you did. So just spill it and we can start to piece together a plan for handling it.'

Fran squeezed her shoulder in agreement.

Jassie closed her eyes tightly for a moment then whispered fiercely, 'Thank goodness I have you two. I know I could handle it on my own—somehow—but with your support I feel so much stronger.—I cried for ages after he left me last night and then of course I couldn't sleep. I remember hearing a blackbird and thinking 'dear God it's morning' and then I must've fallen asleep after all.'

'What did he *do*, Jassie? What did my son *do*?'

'Oh Lady O—'

'Mama.'

'M—Mama, I don't want to cause you pain.'

'Jassie, I need to know what ails my son. He is all I have left of my family. If there is anything I can do to help him—and you—find happiness, then please show me where I have to start.'

Jassie nodded, swallowed, retrieved her hands and gripped them firmly together in her lap. She was likely to fracture the Dowager's bird-like bones without realizing, given the intensity of her emotions.

'When we went upstairs to our rooms last night he was quite grimly silent—though he was in every way polite, giving me his arm and ensuring I didn't trip over my gown. But as soon as we got to our rooms he stopped just inside the door and released my arm. When I turned to see why, he just stared at the floor and stated in this dreadful, dead kind of voice he was leaving immediately for London and couldn't say when he'd be back. I thought at first he was joking, but he looked too—awful—for that. As soon as I registered he meant every word I became insensibly angry and rushed to stand against the door so he would have to physically manhandle me if he wanted to leave.

'I was beyond thinking. All I knew was finally, *finally,* he was my husband and he intended to abandon me on our wedding night and ride back to London!—Oooh, I wanted to scratch and kick and punch! I still do! I have never felt so out of control. I called him a coward and asked—oh God—I asked if I had to tie him to the bed to get him to make love to me.'

Jassie hid her face in her hands to hide the wild tide of fire in her cheeks. Fran's firm fingers caressed her shoulders and Lady Windermere asked quietly, 'And what did Rogan say to that?'

She couldn't look up; she couldn't watch his mother's face when she told her of her son's actions. But she knew she couldn't withhold the information either.

With her head bowed she said, 'It was terrible. It was like—the Rogan I knew just disappeared and in his place stood this terrifying stranger. His eyes seemed to lose all color, turned a horrific burning silver. It happened that day up at the Tor too. Everything else about him became—dreadfully dark. Then—almost before I could blink—he slammed me against the door and sliced through the back of all my clothes with a knife he must have had in his boot. I felt the cold of steel running down my spine and—I thought—Oh God, I thought he meant to kill me. I tried to speak, to call to him but he didn't seem to hear. I don't know. In one stunning movement he wrenched the clothes from me onto the floor and threw me on the bed. He tied my wrists with his neck cloth, gagged me with his handkerchief and then—then—he thrashed me like I'd done something—dreadfully iniquitous and—Oh, I can't say the rest! Suffice it to say he did consummate the marriage.

'When it was over he—just rose up, tidied his clothes, untied me and then he said, 'Don't-ever-threaten-to-restrain-me-or-I-will-not-be-responsible-for-my-actions' in a rough, angry kind of voice I've never heard R—Rogan use.'

She sat, face covered for several minutes, then raised her tear-blurred eyes to Lady O. 'And you know, the worst, most heart-breaking thing about it all is I love him still. I know I should be horrified, hate him, denounce him as a—an abuser of women. But I can't. I'm not sure what kind of perverted person that makes me—but I just can't stop loving him!'

'Your love is not a terrible thing, child,' the Dowager said, gently stroking Jassie's hair. 'Your love is the most precious asset in all of this. Your love is a miracle and it's my son's only hope, like we said before. Dry your tears, daughter, and let us consider what might be done. It's clear he understands this about himself and it's why he has so long held off asking for your hand in marriage. Obviously he never intended to. I, at any rate, Jassie, am deeply grateful you had the strength of character and the depth of love to force the issue. But it cannot be left like this. We must formulate a plan. And if all else fails I'll confront my son, demanding he explain himself and let you help him.'

'Oh Lady—Mama! Please don't tell him I've told you any of this. He'd be so mortified!'

'And are you not mortified, my child?' the Dowager demanded. 'Why should you carry the burden all on your own? If he will not confront and deal with his own issues then I will take a mother's prerogative and confront them for him!'

'You must not upset yourself,' Jassie begged. 'You're not well enough—'

'Psshaw!' Lady Windermere exploded inelegantly. 'If I was going to die I would've gone with my dear Jonathan. Not a day has passed since his death when I haven't longed to be with him. That I'm still here means there's still work for me to do. I'm not without resources, you know, Jassie. I might appear to be helpless and just waiting my time out here in the peace and rustic seclusion of the Abbey, but I still have several friends in London I keep in touch with. And Augusta returns there today.—Let us have lunch and—let it be known Windermere was called back to London urgently—something to do with the war effort. That will still the wagging tongues for there's not a true Englishman anywhere who doesn't want to see a victorious end to this dreadful war.'

Jassie felt her eyes widen.

'You know of that?' she whispered.

'It's my body that's weak, not my mind,' the Dowager asserted astringently. 'It's not hard to work out when you consider his way of playing least in sight for days, even weeks, at a time and then fobbing one off with vague and nonsensical notions of where he's been. Too bad if he doesn't want his involvement generally known. T'would be infinitely worse to expose any hint of why he really left you to return to London before the ink was dry on the marriage lines!—Does anyone else know anything? Ruby?'

'Ruby saw the marks on my—rear end when she was helping with my bath. I'm afraid there is a bruise that is the unmistakable imprint of Windermere's hand. I th—threatened her with dismissal should she mention anything to anybody. I trust Ruby.'

There was a gasp of outrage from Fran, but Jassie patted her knee to calm her.

The Dowager was not so easily subdued however.

'Windermere bruised you?' she whispered, her eyes wide with horror.

'T'is only a bruise, Mama. It will heal.'

A huff of disgust escaped the Dowager then she said, 'We'll talk again this evening before dinner. But for now perhaps Fran can help repair the ravages of your face and we'll try to act as nothing other than disappointed Windermere was called away so urgently. It should be enough to explain your lowered spirits. It's fortunate Gussy and Sheri are planning to leave straight after luncheon as they still have some engagements in London they are promised for. They are the most likely to sense something is wrong. Do you think you can hold up through luncheon, daughter?'

'I'll try.'

Days had never passed so slowly. She decided to reinstate the afternoon reading, writing and figuring lessons for children of the staff on both estates, which had been put on hold until after the wedding. Though her heart wasn't really in it and her mind had a distressing tendency to wander off in search of Windermere, she knew it was better to keep occupied.

Unable to ride, she spent the first few mornings walking with Francine or practicing the archery they were both quite adept at. But it didn't seem to matter what she did, she was constantly consumed by a restless energy that kept her on edge, feeling there was something more she should be doing. Staying tamely at Windermere Abbey waiting for Rogan to remember his obligations and return was an agonizing strain on her nerves. Especially when she was reasonably certain he had no intention of returning at all.

Exasperated with the treadmill of her mind continually worrying at the problem of her marriage, Jassie climbed out of bed at sunrise on Wednesday morning. She needed to ride, had been fretting for the freedom and the mental release it always gave her. The bruising on her behind should have healed enough to handle it and if not—she'd just endure. She needed the wildness, maybe the luxury of screaming in the wind, high on the Downs where no one could hear. The walls of the Abbey were suffocating her.

Clad in buckskin trousers and with boots in hand, she ran down the service stairs, only stopping at the outer door to pull on her footwear. The grounds of the Abbey were more extensive than those of Brantleigh Manor but just as familiar. It was only a matter of minutes and she was letting herself into the dimness of the stable. Her own carriage horses were stabled here now along with the beautiful team of blacks who pulled the Windermere travelling coach. They whuffled a greeting and shuffled about in their stalls, but Jassie knew the stomping she heard would be coming from Chester's stall. The big red was not used to going so long without being ridden.

'Morning Miss—um—my Lady.'

Jem hurried down the aisle of horses towards her.

'Morning, Jem. I think Chester has missed me.'

Jem grinned his toothy smile and said, 'Yep. He's right antsy. I'll get him ready for you, my Lady.'

He disappeared into the stall and led the big red horse out and Jassie patted his nose and offered him an apple from the flat of her hand.

'There Chester, I'm sorry. But we'll have a really good run today to make up for it.'

'You want I sh'd ride with you, my Lady?' Jem asked hopefully. 'He could be a bit frisky.'

'No thanks, Jem. We'll be fine. My Chester is the best mannered horse I've ever known.'

As soon as they were clear of the Abbey Home Park, Jassie nudged Chester with her heels and finally they were flying up the hillside and across the tops, the wind whipping at her cheeks and grabbing at her small riding top hat, which was firmly anchored to her head with a length of gold silk. Somehow she had to outride this deep-seated sense of edgy frustration before it drove her to do something ill-considered and foolish.

Francine was seated in Jassie's private sitting room quietly reading when Jassie returned from riding.

'You had a good long ride. You must've been feeling—comfortable in the saddle?'

Fran's delicate brows rose enquiringly and a concerned smile curved her lips as Jassie strode into the room.

'I just needed to ride—regardless! Lord, Fran! I hate this inaction, the uncertainty. I can't get past feeling angry with Windermere and I think it's time I went up to London and bearded the monster in his den! This waiting about for him to come to his senses is intolerable. What am I supposed to do? Say? People will start calling again soon. It's going to look very odd he's not here. I'm married but a few days—to avoid a scandal—and what am I facing? Scandal like I believe Windermere hasn't even stopped to think about!'

Jassie threw herself inelegantly down on a delicate chaise longue by the window and pulled off her hat.

'He certainly hasn't given any thought to your position, Jassie. It would seem he has his own agenda in all of this,' Fran agreed in her quiet way.

'Yes! To abandon me here like unwanted baggage while he—what *do* you suppose he does in London, Fran? For he's not always sneaking about the Continent. I've not been able to discover he has any kind of rakish reputation.'

Jassie stared out beyond the Abbey gardens to the wooded hills hiding Brantleigh Manor from view. Homesickness tugged at her heart. It was only her consideration for Lady Windermere and her own reputation that prevented her packing up all her belongings and returning there. And if something didn't change soon she still could, scandal be damned!

'Forbidden discussion coming up, Fran,' Jassie muttered, turning back to watch as her friend marked the place in her book and set it aside.

Her blue eyes lightened as she settled back on her chair and said, 'Oooh, we haven't had one of those since—well, at least since yesterday! I'm feeling quite staid and proper which is not entertaining at all!'

'Oh you!' Jassie laughed and waved a hand at her. Then solemnity overtook her as she fixed her gaze on Fran's. 'Do you think Windermere has a secret sexual life? Do you remember the lewd tales Lady Lara Oswald used to tell us after lights-out at Mrs. Rabone's? If she was to be believed, most *gentlemen* live a life in the city no woman would consider in the least *gentlemanly*! She even hinted there were Clubs and

Societies for certain—proclivities like—like bondage and sp— spanking. I've not thought of her in all these years but, you know, I'm now wishing I'd asked her a few more questions. Problem was, back then I had no idea what questions to ask nor any real need to know. Now I have a bit more of an idea but I'm kind of afraid what I might learn.'

Fran's gaze had turned solemn.

'Jass, you're going to make yourself ill worrying over Windermere,' she said.

Jassie knew Fran was trying to divert her but she was tired of the restless tangle of her thoughts and needed to air them, needed to try and find some answers. Fran's experience of life in general and gentlemen in particular was a lot broader than Jassie's own. She was a fount of astonishing salacious facts when Jassie was able to get her to open up. She'd been married after all, to a Lord who'd turned out to be nothing more than a juddering rake and a card sharp. This last had cost him his life in a duel, leaving his wife mired in scandal and poverty. These days she never used the title, preferring to hide behind the anonymity of plain Mrs. Lyndon.

'No I'm not, Fran. But I can't sit still here much longer. Who do you know in London that would know about the kind of circles Windermere might move in? Or be able to find out?'

Fran's mouth quirked.

'Lady Lara has been in London since she married the ancient Lord Riddley, who quite conveniently died a couple of years back leaving her very well off and able to follow her salacious interests under a rather false cloak of respectability. Though I doubt it would do your reputation much good to be known as her friend or even acquaintance. Nor would I vouch for her discretion. Her love of gossip has only amplified since we were at school together. But I rather think she may actually move in the circles you're referring to.

'But Madame Lady Bouvier understands about discretion. She might be able to help. She could certainly help with your education, should you want to know more about what you are trying to deal with, Jass.'

'*Madame Lady* Bouvier?'

'Mmm. She's a Madame *and* a Lady in her own right.'

'Madame as in—owner of a—a brothel?' Jassie felt incredibly naive. 'How do you come to know such a person?'

A flush of color stained Fran's ivory cheeks.

'I probably would've ended up working for her if you hadn't rescued me,' Fran said tightly, lowering her eyes to her hands. 'Abingdon didn't leave me with many choices. The scandal of his cheating and being killed in a duel precluded me from the usual genteel occupations of companion or governess. It's only because you are the good friend you are and willing to tilt your nose at the vindictive society tabbies, I'm not plying my trade under the auspices of Madame Lady Bouvier. She'd have snapped me up in a trice. I'd been married—to a well-known rake, which she was pleased to tell me was an absolute asset in that occupation! I was still young and very comely. And I had a title. That last is an essential requirement to working at Bouvier's. It is very exclusive, all her 'gels' being titled and all the clients also must be titled and wealthy. A plain Mr. or Sir could never gain entry and even a Lord has to be known to possess an income of at least £20,000 a year.— Remember Addy Walsingham?'

Jassie's face lit up.

'Lady Adeline? Oh I do. She was your very good friend at Mrs. Rabone's, wasn't she? Where is—No! Never say—'

'I'm afraid so,' Fran murmured. 'It was such a shame. Her father gambled everything away then committed suicide and her mother couldn't face the poverty and the shame and took an overdose of laudanum. It was hushed up to a degree but Addy said she couldn't face trying to make a life for herself with that scandal hanging over her head. Not to mention she really wasn't cut out to be a governess. She says her life is not so bad. Madame Bouvier runs a very tight shop. The patrons must abide by her laws regardless of who they are or how rich they are. So Addy feels quite—safe there.'

Fran looked up at Jassie from beneath her brows.

'Actually—truth to tell, I think she enjoys it. She also might have some advice on how to—handle—Windermere.'

'Should I ever get so lucky as to actually—handle—Windermere,' Jassie growled.

'Jass!'

Fran tried to sound shocked but ended on a bubble of laughter.

A knock on the door was followed by Ruby and a footman bearing their breakfast trays of poached eggs on toast which Jassie had ordered as she'd passed the kitchens on her way up the back stairs. The Dowager never came downstairs until late in the morning and often not until luncheon so it had seemed pointless for the staff to go to the unnecessary effort of laying a full breakfast in the dining room for just the two of them.

Besides, it was quicker and easier this way and as soon as they'd finished eating they could head down to the old tilt yard at the back of the Abbey if it was fine, or practice their sword play in the Abbot's refectory which was now only used for balls and large social occasions. It was something Jassie had inveigled Philip into teaching her and Fran had been delighted with the opportunity to learn from Jassie. It kept them both fit and agile—and satisfied the rebel lurking within both their breasts.

Once Ruby and the footman had left, Jassie picked up her knife and fork then leant back in her chair to stare at Francine.

'Fran, do you think Madame Lady Bouvier *would* talk to me? Well more like—teach—me?'

'*Teach you*!' Fran squawked, almost choking on the first mouthful of her breakfast. 'Teach you what?'

'H—How to please a man like—Windermere?'

Eyes wide with horror, Fran said, 'Jass, you should find out what kind of man Windermere really is before you—um—try to get any closer to him. It may be when he goes into that sort of animalistic state he gets into,—he could hurt you. Seriously.'

Jassie shook her head.

'Windermere wouldn't hurt me, Fran. He might not be prepared to admit it, but he loves me. Always has. That much I do know about him.'

'I think you need to be a little more patient. Wait and see what Windermere does next. He's a gentleman and an intelligent man. He'll work out pretty soon you cannot conduct a marriage in this— scandalous fashion.'

'Patience!' Jassie muttered fiercely. 'I ran out of that commodity weeks ago. That's the cause of this whole awful mess!'

Lady O and Jensen were already seated in the dining room with Barton Matthews, Windermere's secretary and constant companion, when Jassie and Fran entered. Both had a healthy glow from their exertions in the tilt yard and then the leisurely baths they had indulged in before dressing in exquisitely genteel morning gowns as befitted Ladies of the ton who'd been doing nothing more strenuous than walking in the gardens. It was a game the pair had long played and enjoyed, a game both knew was only possible while they lived in the seclusion of a country estate.

Bart instantly came to his feet to greet them and assist them into their chairs. Jassie could scarcely wait for him to resume his seat before scanning the other faces at the table and then asking outright, 'Windermere is not with you?'

'No, my Lady. I'm afraid not.'

Jassie's chest swelled with indignation and then she bit down on her lip, looked at Lady O and said brightly, 'And how are you this morning, Mama? Did you sleep well?'

'Very well thank you, Jassie-love,' Lady O answered, her eyes shining with tears Jassie suspected were on her account. Then she began to wonder if Bart had brought news that had upset her mother-in-law.

'Is something upsetting you, Mama? Has Windermere sent a communication?'

'I'm just upset at my son's—recalcitrance,' she, said sadly. 'However I do believe Barton has something for you.'

'F—From Windermere?'

Jassie couldn't keep the pathetic hope from quivering in her voice. Struggle as she might to be strong and resilient she was just pathetic, needy.

At Bart's nod, Jassie leapt to her feet.

'Where is it? Why have you not given it to me?'

'Jassie,' the Dowager, said gently. 'Settle down. Barton has had a long, hard ride this morning and is in need of his luncheon.'

'Oh! Of course. I'm sorry,' Jassie muttered, and subsided back into her chair like a limp rag.

'Perhaps you could meet me in Windermere's study after luncheon,' the secretary said, looking distinctly uncomfortable.

'Yes, certainly.'

The food on the table had lost all appeal. Her stomach was tied in a knot of Gordian proportions and she simply couldn't sit still and wait.

'Please excuse me. I don't feel hungry. I'll meet you in the study in half an hour.'

Thus wresting back at least some small amount of control over the situation, she rose and hurried out of the room. Fran rose to follow her but the Dowager raised her hand and, to Jassie's relief, Fran subsided with a troubled frown.

Never had time moved so slowly. Jassie paced up and down the ancient cloisters, supposedly a place of quiet contemplation for the monks of long ago. But nothing quieted the riot of her thoughts, the racing of her blood, the surging of anticipation. What did Windermere have to say to her?

Unable to wait the entire half hour, Jassie was already ensconced in the huge leather chair to one side of the unlit fireplace in the Earl's study when Bart entered. His face was grave and Jassie had the sinking realization he didn't relish the task his cousin had set him. What was Windermere about?

With only a nod of acknowledgement, he opened a drawer of the huge mahogany desk and withdrew a bulky packet of papers, which he handed to Jassie.

'Windermere said if you had any questions about any of the enclosed you should apply to me. I will be gone from here again at sunrise tomorrow so perhaps you should study the information carefully so I can help with anything you want to know before I leave.'

Confusion slowed Jassie's trembling fingers as she began to untie the wide ribbon holding everything together. Bart's words implied the packet contained more than just a personal missive, which was really borne out by the bulk of the papers.

'Would you like me to leave you alone to read, my Lady?'

There was a terrible pain in her heart for somehow she just knew Windermere was about to deliver the cruelest blow yet, but in the depth of her distraction she couldn't imagine what it might be.

'Thank you. I'd like that.'

Her voice was little more than a whisper and on some vague level she registered the deeply concerned frown on the man's face but her only real focus was the packet of papers she held in her hand—that felt as if it were something that might explode in her face the moment the ribbon came loose.

Rising slowly to her feet, she crossed to a chair offering a view of the rose gardens, one of the many treasures of Windermere Abbey. Barton Matthews forgotten, she let the packet fall open on her lap. The top sheet was indeed a missive from Windermere, his writing a little less carefully formed than usual.

My Dear Jassie,

There are no adequate words to express my deep sorrow at what has occurred between us. I am not the man you deserve to have for husband. I am honored by your love and that you now bear my name. But you must understand that is all I can give you. I will not subject you to the beast that lives within me and which—at certain times—I am unable to control.

I have sent you the marriage settlements. I trust you will find them satisfactory. If you have any queries at all, apply to Bart. He knows as much as I about Windermere affairs.

By the time you receive this package from me I will be back in Europe assisting the war effort as best I can. There will be a big and hopefully defining, battle fought in the very near future. I must do my part to ensure the victory is ours and the monster Bonaparte is banished forever.

If I should not return I ask you remember me as we were before that fateful day on Neave Tor and that sometime in the future you will find a man who will truly care for you and love you as you deserve to be loved.

Forever yours,
Windermere.

How long she sat staring at the words Jassie could not have said. She'd certainly read and re-read them several times but no amount of reading or re-reading could change the message contained therein.

Windermere intended to get himself killed in the line of duty.

After some time she unfolded the sheaf of papers comprising the marriage settlements and perused the dry contents. That her portion included Brantleigh Manor and all monies she'd had in her own right before marriage was no surprise. But Windermere had added a further £20,000—which could only mean he was trying to ensure she did indeed find another husband! There was also, gifted to her outright from the date of their marriage, the topaz and diamond wedding ring and the topaz and diamond parure from the Windermere jewels comprising pendant necklace, tiara, combs, brooch, earbobs and a pair of bracelets.

She wanted none of it. She just wanted Rogan.

The papers fell from her lifeless fingers and for a long time she stared blankly at the window before her. Then slowly all the blood that seemed to have leached from her veins flowed back and with it came a surging rage like she'd never known. Suddenly she was running, the papers forgotten where they'd fallen on the floor. Up the stairs she raced as if pursued by the Furies of Hell. In her room she ripped at her clothes impatiently until Ruby appeared and began scolding.

'Miss Jassie, you'll ruin that gown with your impatience.'

'Then hurry and get me out of it Ruby. I have to ride before I do something exceedingly foolish.'

'Miss Jassie! You need to calm down.'

'What I need Ruby, is my Lord Windermere's head so I can smash it, smash it—*smash it*!'

'Oh Miss Jassie! Please don't talk like that. It might not be wise to ride in this state—'

'It would be much less wise to stay here where there is so much that reminds one of Windermere one could smash!'

Ruby made a funny little squeaking sound and snapped her mouth into silence. As soon as she was dressed in buckskin trousers once again exactly as she had been early that morning, Jassie raced down the back stairs to the stable, dashing in the door and calling for Dobbie.

'I'm here Miss Jass—my Lady,' Dobbie responded from the cool dim interior of the vast stable block. 'You be wanting to ride—again? You gave Chester a pretty wild ride this morning.'

'Don't-argue-with-me-today-Dobbie,' Jassie growled between her teeth. 'If you don't get me on that horse and away from this place in the next five minutes I will probably tear the whole goddamn edifice apart with my bare hands!'

Her voice rose on every word so she was practically shouting at an astonished Dobbie by the time she'd uttered the last. His eyebrows climbed into his hair as the unladylike epithet issued from her taut lips, but it seemed he had enough sense not to comment—on the language at least.

'Yes, Miss Jassie. Keep yer hair on, lass. T'ain't like ye to go up in the boughs like this,' he muttered as he strode off to fetch Chester. 'I'll call young Jem to ride with ye. Ye're like to break yer pretty neck, the mood ye're in.'

'I'll ride alone thank you, Dobbie, just as I always do. I think sometimes you forget who issues the orders here!'

The old man swiveled back to cast her a searing scowl, then stalked off muttering about people who allowed themselves to become a slave to their ill-temper.

Jassie knew she was out of control but hadn't a clue how to address that problem except in the way she'd handled every emotional trauma since childhood. She needed the strength and power of a good horse beneath her, the wind burning her eyes and rushing down her throat, and the wild thrill of riding to the edge of danger. If her future was not to contain Windermere then she was damned if she wanted a future! If Windermere could opt out, so could she!

Dobbie led Chester out and Jassie threw herself up into the saddle before the old man could even think of helping her.

'Thanks, Dobbie,' she growled as she turned the animal, put him to the first fence and the next until they'd leapt out of the stable yards and onto Home Park where she gave him his head. They rode in a mad dash through the great trees of the park, scattering the deer that had been quietly grazing, jumping logs and streams, Jassie urging the big red horse ever faster. When they came to a point where Neave Tor was directly before them, she suddenly knew where she had to be and set Chester on a direct course for the distant stone-crowned peak.

With every thud into the hard ground she imagined Windermere beneath Chester's hooves, pounded into a pulp by her fury. How dare he go off to die just to avoid her! Body lying low along the animal's sweating neck, Jassie yelled into the wind.

'Go Chester! Go!'

The big animal was nothing loath. If his mistress wanted speed then she should have it. His hooves pounded with a satisfying rhythm against the hard earth of the track spiraling up the Tor and in minutes they'd arrived at the top, both breathing hard and fast. Almost before he'd come to a halt Jassie threw herself from the saddle and dropped into the crater, the place where the madness had started nearly three weeks ago.

She punched her gloved fist into the ground, just as Windermere had done and welcomed the jarring pain that streaked through her body with each violent impact.

'Damn you, Windermere!' she yelled. 'You're a craven coward! How dare you? How dare you go off and leave me here without you! Damn you!'

Jerking to her feet she closed her eyes and screamed into the wind, 'You're a goddamn craven coward, Windermere. If I were a man I'd call you out and fight until you agreed to face me, talk to me! D'you hear me, Windermere? I'll not live without you! That was never how it was meant to be!—Windermere, I don't want anybody else. How could you even suggest it—?'

Her voice wobbling to a watery whisper on this last, Jassie sank back to the ground and hid her face in her arms on her knees and let the despair take over her body in big heaving sobs.

Barton Matthews had never had cause to regret his work for the Earl of Windermere; until three weeks ago when his always controlled, slightly aloof cousin had become someone torn, driven, irrational. In all the years they'd worked as a team Windermere had never asked anything of him he'd felt more unfit for and less inclined towards, than bringing what amounted to his last will and testament to Jassinda Carlisle, now the Countess of Windermere.

He'd admired her ever since he'd known her. She was everything Windermere needed in a Countess and their friendship with each other was legendary. No one had been able to understand why Windermere hadn't offered marriage as soon as she was of age, for it was obvious the lady would have acquiesced in a heartbeat. Bart understood a lot more now after he'd forced that confession from him, but believed his cousin was wrong—wrong to discount his Lady's ability to listen and understand his problem and to work with him on a solution that would allow them to pursue the marriage and the deep abiding friendship that had sustained them both throughout their lives.

Never had he known Windermere so bull-headed as he was about this. He'd not even given Jassinda the choice to try and help him. He'd acted with a stubborn arbitrariness Bart had never seen in him before. He couldn't see past the shame and humiliation to anything approaching hope for their future.

Bart had scarcely been able to look at Jassie when he'd entered the office, so intense was the hope and anticipation in her warm golden eyes. When she realized the packet contained only a short missive from Windermere and had probably guessed something of what the rest contained, he'd been unable to watch while the glow, the hope faded from those eyes and an insidious trembling began to invade her body.

Abandoning her as she'd agreed she wanted, he'd left the house faster than a rat deserting a burning ship and taken refuge in the large tack room off the stables. He needed to talk with Buckton, Windermere's head groom to ascertain there had been no problems integrating the stock and staff from Brantleigh Manor into the Windermere Stables. It was the ideal opportunity.

The sound of Her Ladyship's voice, abnormally pitched and on the edge of control, took him to the door where he could watch without being seen. It was quite obvious Windermere's communication had not been to her liking. When she threw herself into the saddle with the ease of a seasoned cavalryman and put her horse to the fences about the stable instead of using the gates, he knew old Dobbie was right in his troubled mutterings.

The mistress should not be riding alone in that state of mind.

'Buckton, I think you'd better saddle a horse for me. That grey of Windermere's. I don't think Mayfair is fresh enough to stay in sight of that big red fellow after the long run he had this morning.'

The grey was not Mayfair but he was a fair ride nevertheless. When he entered the vast expanse of the Home Park in a much more sedate fashion than Jassie had a few minutes earlier, he set the horse to an easy canter. Not wanting to catch the flying red horse, just keep it in sight, he headed into the shadow of the trees. The new Countess wouldn't appreciate knowing she was being shadowed, but Windermere's only hope of salvation would be useless with a broken neck.

When the red horse emerged from the trees at the south end of Home Park and galloped at breakneck pace towards the stone wall and the fields lying between the Park and Neave Tor, Bart nudged the grey in that direction and picked up the pace so he wouldn't lose sight of his quarry. As the red rose up and over the dry stone wall he couldn't suppress a mutter of appreciation—for horse and rider. The animal was beautiful to watch, art in motion, flowing and rhythmic, while his rider was possibly the most efficient female equestrian he'd ever watched. Thank God, she was not too proper to dress for the style of riding she obviously preferred.

By the time he and Grey Cloud leapt the stone wall at the south end of the Park, Jassie and her horse were a flying speck in the distance, lifting and soaring over the stone wall at the base of Neave Tor. Realizing now the Tor was her likely goal, he relaxed his pace a little. He wasn't crass enough to intrude when the woman wanted to be alone, but he did want to keep her in sight.

He put the grey to the stone fence beneath the Tor, trotted along the base of the hill and into the patch of woodland on the western toe. From the shadow of the trees he watched the red horse appear from behind the Tor again, still galloping tirelessly up the spiral track. He would remain where he was and hopefully she'd find some solace up there that would ease the fury riding her so relentlessly. Dismounting and with reins in hand, he leant against a sturdy oak and closed his eyes for a moment.

He'd had little sleep last night after failing to convince Windermere he should be heading to Neave to do something about his marriage instead of firing himself like cannon fodder into a war that just seemed as if it would go on into eternity. And he'd definitely gone with the intention of not coming back. Windermere's estate business and political concerns had also become his. He didn't like to think what he'd do if Windermere was successful in getting himself killed. He could only focus on the fact his cousin had not cared for his own existence for some years now and despite the risks he took in a very risky occupation, he had always escaped unharmed.

He was not going to start panicking.—The thought was broken off by a distant, long drawn-out yelling that floated down the hillside on the wind. What the hell? Throwing himself back up into the saddle, he rode out from the trees and put the grey to an oblique though reasonably direct route up the face of Neave Tor. Leaving the horse lipping grass alongside the big red, he climbed a little higher to find Lady Jassinda sitting in a small indentation in the ground, sobbing as if her heart would break.

She didn't appear to be hurt as the yelling had suggested she might be. And what the hell did a man do with a woman in tears? Perhaps he could just sneak away.

'Why are you here?'

Obviously she was more aware of her surroundings than he'd thought.

With a sigh of inevitability, Bart said, 'Making sure you stayed safe. I was keeping my distance—until I heard you yelling. Are you all right, Jass?'

Neither of them noticed he'd slipped into the familiar use of the name he'd known her by since childhood.

Those topaz eyes sparkling with tears just widened with incredulity as she gazed up at him.

'Oh—yes thank you, Bart, I'm in absolutely *fine fettle!*'

Her pseudo-polite, lady-like speech was spoiled by a hiccup of abject misery at the end.

'Ah, Jassie, we both know that for the Banbury tale it is.'

She swiped a hand across her eyes and dragged a kerchief out of her breeches pocket to blow her nose.

'Do you know what was in that packet, Bart?'

He held her gaze, all the while wondering whether he could get away with denying any such knowledge and then decided she deserved better from him.

'I knew about the marriage settlements and I know he enclosed a personal missive. I don't know what was in that, though I could probably make a good guess.'

She nipped at her bottom lip then released it and stared down the hillside to where the horses grazed contentedly.

'Do you know he has gone to the Continent with the express purpose of getting himself killed?'

'I wouldn't put it as strongly as that, my dear,' he tried to remonstrate.

'Wouldn't you? Well how would you interpret a request I remember him as we were before—well—before—I forced him to marry me, and then hoped that sometime in the future I would find a man to love me *as I deserve*?—Sounds like—a death intention, to me.'

Realizing leaving her to her cogitations now would be nothing short of churlish, he sank to his haunches beside her and began pulling idly at the grass.

'Jass, Rogue has been—doing what he does—towards the war effort for many years now. From the very first mission he had no care for the danger or risk involved. Generally the more risky and dangerous the mission, the more likely Windermere would be asked to undertake it—and accept. There's nothing different in the mission he has set out on now. Same level of risk and danger.

'But whether he knows it or not, he has a very highly developed instinct for survival. It's what makes him so good at what he does. Ultimately his goal is to gather the information required and see it finds its way to where it will do the most good—for England. For us. If he's killed and the information doesn't get through he will have failed;

himself, his over-developed sense of honor, and his country. That's what has kept him alive all these years—and will continue to do so now. Windermere will be back. He just won't be happy about it.'

He was deeply conscious of those topaz eyes fixed on him now, hope shining in their depths, like diamonds, pure and indestructible. God alone knew how Windermere could walk away from a woman who cared this deeply.

'You give me hope—just when I had lost all shred of it. For a terrible moment I had lost sight of the fact I must always—*always*—trust and believe he will come home safely. He always has before. This time will be no different. Thank you.'

Her eyes dropped to where he pulled abstractedly at the grass, building a tiny stack between his boots. Then she continued, her voice more steady.

'What will I do? How can I persuade him just to talk to me?—Bart, do you know why Rogan is—as he is?'

He swallowed, hard.

'Yes I do. But it's Windermere's tale to tell, if you can persuade him to it.'

'Obviously you did.' She said flatly. 'When? How?'

Her questions came at him like pistol shots. He never thought of not answering her.

'The night after your wedding I was to wait for him at the stables while he saw you upstairs and told you he was leaving. I thought he was being an absolute ass—in fact he'd been behaving very strangely from the day he first told me of your betrothal—and as he came towards me out of the darkness I twitted him, asked if you'd got the better of him because I couldn't imagine his plans were going to please you any! He punched me in the teeth and I replied in kind. Sat him on his backside. He was cursing like I'd never heard him. So I taunted him a bit about— stuff—and he got up and hit me again. So I flattened him again and told him if he wanted a damn good fight I was happy to give it to him. But he just sat there, calling himself all sorts of names and saying how he'd just proved he was right to resist marrying you all those years. How you'd still cared for him but he'd taken care of that now.

'There was a tone in his voice I'd never heard before and I began to get a real bad feeling. I yanked his head up by the hair and demanded to know what he'd done to you. And he told me—in a flat, dead voice that made the hair stand up on my arms.'

A groan of embarrassment escaped her but he continued.

'We had some pretty harsh words then, but I began to realize something was seriously wrong and I threatened to thrash him senseless and leave his employ if he didn't tell me what it was. It's not a pretty tale—'

'I need to know,' Jassie ground out. 'Tell me!'

'—and it's not my story to tell and I really only have a sketchy outline. Bear in mind also he threatened to punch *me* senseless, even kill me if I uttered a word of it to anyone. I gave him my word. If you are ever to know, Jass, it must come from Windermere. I just hope you have the stomach for it.'

'And that you can count on, if I can ever get the stubborn man to talk to me!'

'It's not a tale a man is likely to tell a woman—*any* woman—much less one raised as genteelly as yourself.'

She all but snorted in her impatience.

'Not all that genteel, as it happens because Rogan and my brother had quite a hand in my raising, thankfully! I'd like to ask you to inform me when my husband comes home again please. As soon as he sets foot in the country. Before, if you happen to have prior notice of his arrival.'

There was a long silence while Bart considered where his loyalty lay. But it didn't take him long to realize loyalty to Rogue meant securing his happiness in any way he could. Jassie was the sum total of that happiness and he slowly came to his feet and held out a hand to help her up also.

'I'll send you word whenever I hear from him. It can be a long time when you're waiting to hear if someone is alive or not. You're not alone in wanting what's best for Windermere.—Will you allow me to escort you home now, Jass? The clouds are beginning to look threatening. No point in getting drenched.'

She looked about her, as if suddenly aware of the world around her. The clouds were indeed massing and darkening to the southwest and they would probably be very lucky if they did reach the Abbey before the weather broke.

'Thanks, Bart.'

With relief he proffered his arm and led her down the hill to the horses.

Weeks dragged by, dismally wet, sometimes for days on end. To add to her misery, regardless of the two times Windermere had succumbed to her desire for him, she was not with child. An heir for the Windermere title and estates would have pleased everyone. Jassie wouldn't have cared whether it was a son or a daughter, she would just have been happy to have something else to focus on except the desperate hunger that tore at her body.

Hunger for the love she longed to share with Rogan; hunger for the sound of his voice, the solid bulk of his presence; hunger just for a sight of his dark, windblown hair, midnight blue eyes, and lithe, muscular figure. Some days the pain within her heart almost kept her in bed. Only the vague memory of her mother, pale and languid amid heaped pillows on a high bed, goaded her into action each day—and Fran. She was not some pitiful, spineless thing to give in to the darkness assailing her from within.

Self-pity was not allowed around Fran, nor any vapid moping and staring longingly out rain-streaked windows. Every morning, if it was too wet for Jassie to ride, Fran insisted they take their exercise with the swords in the old tilt-yard or she challenged Jassie into competing against her at the archery butts set up in the ancient refectory. The afternoons when there were no school lessons were more difficult. They were both accomplished needlewomen but Jassie found it very hard to be still, to focus on setting the tiny stitches required for the delicate embroidery she'd decided to undertake on a waistcoat for her husband in a shade of blue as dark as his eyes.

It was all too easy for her mind to wander and her fingers to fall still and often she'd jolt back to awareness to find herself staring blankly at whatever was in front of her. Usually it was Fran or the Dowager who'd pull her out of her thoughts and worries of Windermere with a loud question or demand for an opinion on some discussion or other. None of it seemed important to Jassie.

The only bright days were those when a brief note would arrive from Bart telling her he'd heard from Windermere—which meant the wretched torment of her heart still lived. For a few hours on those days she could maintain a lightness of spirit that pleased those around her. She knew they worried for her but she couldn't pull herself out of her maunderings long enough to really make an effort.

It was the second week after Bart's brief visit that Fran suggested now might be a good time to undertake the redecoration of Brantleigh Manor. It was a project Jassie had been mulling over for some time but had kept putting off because of the disruption it would cause to the household. But now they were not actually living there would be the perfect time to embark on such a project. At first Jassie had struggled to find her previous enthusiasm for the undertaking, but Fran had kept returning to the idea, sending to London for pattern books and samples until Jassie was inevitably drawn into involvement.

Though she couldn't help wondering whether her real interest lay in the fact it was the perfect excuse to spend many dismal afternoons back in her old home. Whatever the reason she was glad to feel an interest for something to help fill the long, dull days.

When word came of the Duke of Wellington's victory at Waterloo and the welcome end to a war that had dragged on for nigh on twenty years, it brought a feeling of festivity to the Abbey for a few days and a flurry of visitors. The wet weather and the polite society habit of waiting a month before calling on a newly married couple had spared Jassie this ordeal until now.

But in the excitement of victory in Europe, people took to their carriages, braved the weather and called on their neighbors in order to share the joy of it. Any surprise at the absence of Windermere was quickly dispersed by the brief intimation he was assisting the War Office in some secret capacity in Europe. While some appeared a little startled by this information, several nodded their heads sagely, as if to imply they'd known Windermere would be up to something of the kind—even though it was the first anyone had heard of it.

Thus Windermere's absence was accepted, even applauded and none needed to know he'd been gone since the evening of their marriage. Both Jassie and the Dowager became quite adept at turning the conversation to other topics at this point. Nevertheless the constant need to project the aura of a happy bride awaiting the return of her husband was wearing and as the weeks of celebration drifted by, Jassie simply refused all invitations to the endless soirées, fêtes, and dance evenings, citing her husband's absence and his mother's health as her excuse.

Windermere had to return from the continent soon. Even Bart admitted there were business matters piling up that needed his urgent attention and he couldn't put off coming home to deal with his affairs for much longer.

But it was still at least four tedious weeks after the victory at Waterloo before Bart's note arrived, advising her Windermere was back in London and aware he must visit the Abbey in the very near future. Jassie thought she might faint from the violent leap of her heart as she read the brief missive. Bart was never one to waste words.

But then no more words were needed, unless it was to tell her of the state of her husband's mind. Knowing Windermere however, it was very likely Bart was not being given any opportunity to assess it. If patience was her lesson in life then she was getting plenty of practice.

The only communication from her husband was a formal note advising of his planned arrival at the Abbey four days hence in time for luncheon on July 24th.

Jassie knew she was foolish to hope but regardless of what she told herself that emotion took a strong hold of her mind. Perhaps Windermere had done some deep thinking while in Brussels and was ready to talk about their marriage at least. A deep inner voice rose up to mock within her and she ruthlessly tamped it down. Hope was all that kept her going and she would not relinquish it.

The morning of the 24th dawned clear and sunny, a rare day in a summer that had felt more like a milder version of winter. Almost whooping with joy at the sight of clear skies, Jassie was out and riding as the birds began their first chirrups. Heeding Dobbie's advice, she skirted the low-lying flat ground of the Park where water still lay in the hollows and headed up onto the Downs, roaming far over both Brantleigh and Windermere lands and dreaming of how she and Rogan would talk, patch their differences and live happily ever after.

Sighing over her naive stupidity, she finally acknowledged the sun was now quite high in the sky and it was time to head for home. She would be better setting her mind to working out what she would say to Windermere and how she would comport herself in his presence. Foolish dreams would not help her decide whether she should act cold and aloof, wickedly seductive, calm and friendly, or simply fall into his arms and declare she would be whatever kind of wife he desired her to be if only they could return to their old friendship.

She still hadn't decided what stance she was going to take when she came downstairs just before the luncheon hour to find Rogan ensconced in the sunny front parlor talking to his mother. Pausing in the doorway to drink in the welcome sight of him, she found her eyes suddenly filled with tears and the decision of how she would comport herself was taken completely out of her hands. She was simply going to fall into his embrace and rain tears of relief and gratitude for his return all over his perfectly arranged neck cloth.

One step into the room and she knew it would not be so simple and faltered to a halt. Even through the blur of tears she could see the stern cast of his features, the dark warning in his eyes and the hands clenched at his sides as he rose to his feet to greet her.

What if she threw herself into his arms and he didn't open them to receive her? What if he stepped back, pushed her away? How could she face that? Knowing she would simply die if he rejected her, she turned on her heel and dashed back past Fran who had followed her into the room, along the hall and into the warm comfort of the Abbey library. A fire burned in the grate there year round and Jassie dropped bonelessly to the rug before it and sat staring wide-eyed into the flames, hoping the heat would dry her foolish tears. She had been quite determined Rogan should not see her cry, that she would be strong, calm and dignified.

A small hiccup of mockery escaped her at thinking she could ever act dignified. It simply wasn't in her make-up, but strong and calm should have been possible. She had cried so much these last weeks in the solitude of her empty bed there should have been no tears left to cry. Oh damn you, Windermere.

CHAPTER SEVEN

She was sitting on the rug before the fire, sage green skirts fluffed around her like she'd simply deflated there. Her eyes were wide open to the flames, no doubt to burn away the horror of seeing him again.

'Would you prefer I return to London?'

She turned towards him, cheeks pale, eyes huge and shadowed—and swimming with tears. He'd done that to her. He was a gutless, selfish bastard who should have severed their friendship years ago once he realized he could never allow it to develop as it should—as he and she had both dreamed it would. Had he turned his back then she would probably have been married to some other more deserving bastard now. Wolverton most likely.

And he'd have had to kill him, because Jassinda Carlisle was his. She'd been born for him.

Nothing more could be said about him than he was a selfish, cowardly, brutalizing bastard.

'Please—don't leave.'

Her voice was a watery whisper but the words rang in his heart as if sung by a chorus of angels. Miserable sap that he was, he could only feel joy and relief she would not banish him from her sight. That he didn't deserve such consideration was a given; that he would accept every moment in her presence she would grant him, was also. He'd been such a fool to think he could stay away from her.

'No matter how I courted it, death evaded me. I thought of ending my life myself, but I seem to be too much the coward for that. So I've returned, Jass, with the realization that somehow I have to talk to you.'

How the hell did he interpret that wide open, shocked look on her face? Disbelief? Hope? Horror?

'Now?' she managed to squeak.

'Well, perhaps a little later. Mama is holding luncheon and it would probably set her mind at ease if we could at least show we can be in the same room together.' It was a poor attempt at lightening the air between them, not helped by the fact he couldn't seem to form any semblance of a smile to accompany it. 'Will you come and eat?'

She rubbed at her wet cheeks with the unselfconsciousness of a child and he longed to fold her in his arms and kiss the tears away. They'd always been totally natural with one another, interacting with the ease and comfort of lifelong friends. Thank God that did not seem to have changed, at least on her part.

'Um—in a minute. I just need to—get over—seeing you again.'

Her words were a knife slicing deep into a heart already utterly shredded.

'I'm sorry. Jass, I know this must be hard for you—after—after—that night. You can't know how sorry I am about that—but you also have to know I can't guarantee it won't happen again.—It's what I've been trying to avoid all these years.—I'll leave you then to—'

'No! Oh please don't go away again—you've only just arrived and you haven't even kissed me or—or said 'hello'—or anything!'

'K—kissed you?' he repeated stupidly. 'But—aren't you—I thought you'd be disgusted with me; never want to see me again.'

'Oh Rogan,' she whispered. 'I couldn't bear that.'

His heart pounded a dull heavy beat in his chest and his brain throbbed in concert. Damn but he wanted to kiss her, wanted—needed her. But before he touched her again they had to talk. How was he to keep his hands still, and keep himself from condemning all talk to hell and just taking her—right there on the rug before the fire?

'I—missed you, Jass.' The words were not what he'd intended to say but now they were said he knew them for the profound truth they were. He pressed his clenched hands deep into the pockets of his coat. 'Do you realize this is the longest we have ever gone without seeing each other?'

A faint hiss escaped her lips and her soft hazel orbs suddenly blazed like the fireworks at Vauxhall Gardens. He'd forgotten how quickly her mood could change when she was under stress.

'*You* ask *me* that? It has been exactly sixty-five days, Windermere,' she snarled, 'and I've endured every second of every minute in an agony of worry, anger, sorrow, *anger*, desire, *anger*, frustration, *anger*—'

She scrambled to her feet, propelled by her intense emotions. Any minute now she was going to attack him and then—No!

'I get the picture, Jass.—I'm sorry. I can't say anything other than that. There are no other words.' He stepped back quickly and interrupted the flow of her invective. He must not allow her to get her hands on him. 'But if I had it to do again I would probably react in the same way. By far my greatest instinct right now is to run, flee to where I will never have to expose what I am to you—or confront it—but no matter how far I go, how deeply I try to mire myself in other people's lives and problems, mine don't go away. *You* don't go away! You're constantly in my mind whether I'm awake or asleep. And now that we're wed, and having known one another in the way of husband and wife, however crassly done or maybe because of it, it's so much worse. You're like a haunting; torturing me day and night until I can't rest.'

She stood so still staring at him, eyes now wide with a terrible longing to believe what she was hearing. It would appear he had done a reasonable job of concealing the depths of his feelings over the years, to the point she could still undermine her own belief in their love with self-doubts. He was a low, callous bastard. She should know his heart at least; know she held it, chained to her own for always. If he could give her nothing else today he would give her that.

But it would be somewhere safe, where touching one another was not an option. He offered her his arm.

'Let's go to lunch then perhaps you would consent to ride with me.'

Ignoring his arm, she looked up at him with a sulky pout.

'I will have my kiss, Windermere.'

One delicate finger prodded her cheek where he usually bussed her when they met. He bent forward and touched his lips to her brow and he thought he felt her trembling.

'You've lost weight. Mama says you've been fretting.'

'I'm fine,' she averred so tensely and fiercely there was no doubt she was anything but. Now was probably not the moment to press that issue.

He extended his arm and after a second's hesitation she laid her hand on it and they proceeded back to the dining room.

Luncheon was an endurance trial. Instead of seating her at the opposite end of the table from his lordly chair, he'd led her to his end and seated her at his right. Close enough to touch him, if she dared. Close enough he would notice her inability to eat. She'd scarcely managed to get a drop of the delicious mock turtle soup past her lips and had spent the entire course mashing the croutons to a porridge-like substance in the bottom of her bowl, making her think nostalgically of meals in the nursery at Brantleigh, and Nanny's frown when she 'played with her food.'

She managed a little better with the main of chicken and rice gratin flavored with bacon, onions and tomato puree served with carrots, asparagus and white haricot beans with a port wine sauce. Flaubert, the Abbey's elderly French chef produced amazing meals, but Jassie was afraid she was able to do it no more justice than she had over the last few weeks.

When Melton brought round the almond cream ices to finish, Jassie waved him away. If she tried to eat anything more her stomach was going to revolt, it was such a churning mess of anticipation. Windermere, his thigh only inches from hers, had completely stolen her senses. She'd barely managed to acknowledge Bart Matthews sitting a little further along the table opposite Fran nor made any effort to follow or add to the conversation around the table. The others had been all agog to hear what the Earl had to say about the victory at Waterloo and the surrender of the French, and in particular, the Corsican martinet who had held Europe to ransom for the best part of twenty years.

Although Rogan had not managed to eat much more than Jassie had, he'd certainly kept up his end of the conversational obligations. Perhaps it was his way of not dwelling on the 'talk' he had promised her. When he also waved away the dessert course, her heart started to flutter more wildly in her chest.

Patience had never been one of her strengths. Regardless it would have been polite to remain sitting until the Dowager rose, Jassie was almost to the point of excusing herself and asking Windermere to leave the table with her when he took matters into his own hands.

Pushing his chair back and standing with a hand outstretched to Jassie, he said, 'I beg you all to excuse us. Lady Windermere and I have—a riding engagement.'

Jassie was on her feet before he'd finished speaking, her hand engulfed in his large, warm one and almost leading the way out of the room. His mother lifted her gaze anxiously to them both as they passed her chair and he bent to place a kiss on her forehead before they continued on out the door, leaving a room of arrested silence behind them.

But anything other than their own concerns was forgotten once the door closed.

'You'll need to change,' he began, but Jassie interrupted him.

'It won't take me long, Rogan. I'll see you at the stables in ten minutes.'

'Ten? Really?' he raised an eyebrow teasingly at her. They both knew she could do it in less, but that small precious exchange had righted something between them; reminded them of the strength of the bonds forged in childhood.

With a toss of her head, Jassie ran lightly up the stairs, trying to still her crazy heart that would insist on quivering with hope.

They took an easy path along the lower slopes, circled the entire Brantleigh estate, riding back round the south side of Neave Tor. They'd talked of the affairs of both estates. Jassie had allowed herself to be cozened into describing the redecorations she had planned for Brantleigh. He'd asked her what she intended to do with it and her answer was not well received.

'If my presence at the Abbey is going to keep you from home I shall probably return to Brantleigh, so in the meantime I'll retain a small staff and leave it empty.'

'As my wife your place is at Windermere.'

'As my husband, so is yours!' Jassie couldn't help but snap straight back.

A dull color burned along his cheekbones and a muscle jumped in his clenched jaw.

'Mama would be very disappointed if you did that, Jass. She's so delighted to have your company at the Abbey. And as the Countess of Windermere it is inconceivable you would live anywhere else. It would create just as much of a scandal as—anything else.'

'Mama will not enjoy my company for long if it means she is deprived of yours. You are her son after all.'

'Damn it, Jass,' Rogan exploded in a rare spasm of temper. 'You will obey me in this!'

Incredulity flooded through Jassie and she brought Chester to a standstill to sit and stare at her husband. Then, as her brain kicked into gear, she exhaled softly and gave him the benefit of a wickedly assessing frown.

'I will *obey* you, *husband*, when you accord me *all* that is due to me as your *wife*.—You said you wanted to talk. So far we've not covered any topic that comes anywhere near what I expected you to talk about. Or satisfies me as to why you will not share my bed.—And here we are almost back at the stables!'

The color deepened in his cheeks and she was sure she heard him mutter, 'Bloody hell!' under his breath. Had he hoped she'd forgotten? He knew her better than that.

Rogan cursed himself for a fool. He'd meant to tell Jassie what she wanted to know as they rode so he wasn't able to reach for her, touch her in any way. He'd not even noticed the passing of time or where they'd ridden. He'd simply been immersed in her company. He could scarcely suggest they turn the horses about and ride out again.

Putting it off was no longer an option. In fact there was a growing yearning within him to lay the whole sordid tale before Jassie and let her make of it what she would. Nothing could be worse than how things stood between them at present.

Without giving himself a chance to think better of his decision he dismounted, handed Raven's reins to a stable hand and walked to Jassie's side to help her dismount also. Once her feet were on the ground and Dobbie had taken the horse, Rogan quickly disengaged her hands from his shoulders, held out his arm and said, 'Will you walk with me? It will be private down by the lake and—I'll tell you all you wish to know.'

Her relief was palpable and they maintained a tense silence as they walked through the neatly kept Capability Brown-designed landscape. Rogan tried not to consider the imprudence of being alone with Jassie far from the house and any likelihood of being disturbed. It seemed inevitable their feet would take them to the Greek Folly, which was the main feature at the southwest end of the lake.

As he handed her up the wide marble steps and noted the neatly swept interior with its gaily colored cushions on the wide benches, he grimly reminded himself he'd been able to keep his control round her for the last nine years. Just because he had succumbed a couple of times did not mean he no longer had the strength to deny her that which he knew she desired of him, should indeed expect of him as her husband. Heat and passion were a palpable energy in the air about them.

She settled on the striped cushions with all the elegance of a woman gowned in silk and satins instead of a practical dark green velvet riding habit. Untying the silk scarf securing her jaunty riding hat and tossing both aside, she settled back and looked expectantly up at him.

Her eyes had the same deep knowing that had snared him in her babyhood, her gold-tipped, sable lashes thick and gleaming against her fair skin. There was no one he trusted more, he reminded himself so why did the thought of telling her his story cause the sensation of a large feral animal tearing at his guts?

She patted the seat beside her, jolting him back into an awareness of the necessity for keeping distance between them. He shook his head and turned to gaze out the doorway, his back to her. Perhaps it would be easier if he couldn't see her eyes.

'You were always to have been mine, Jass. From the moment I looked into your incredibly knowing eyes as a baby I think I knew we were bound to one another in a way that was precious and I innocently believed could never be sullied or destroyed. At twenty I learned life is never so simple, so clean-cut or straightforward. At twenty any innocence I might still have had—for I was no saint as Philip would cheerfully have warned you had he lived—was ripped to shreds and forever debauched by a woman whose depravity haunts me to this day.'

The soft fall of her boots was the only warning of her approach, then her hand slid through his, drawing him back inside.

'If you will not sit beside me, sit at my feet, Rogan. Then I can knead your head in the way I used to do when you would carry me on your shoulders. You always found that soothing. Unlike Philip who threatened to toss me into whatever handy water that offered if I did it to him. He said it was ticklish.'

She tossed one of the cushions between her feet and for a moment he stared at it, bemused. This is how it could have been between them if he'd been able to allow himself to truly be her husband. He was so miserably lacking in willpower where she was concerned. His legs buckled and he sank to the cushion, his shoulders framed by her velvet-clad knees and her fingers immediately crept into his hair and began gently kneading, massaging. It had been years since she'd done this for him and a glorious peace seeped through his being.

'Talk to me, Rogan. Please? I have to know what I'm dealing with here.'

'Bart said I should tell you too. He said I just needed to off-load the horror of it to *someone* and in his book that someone had to be you. You are the one who has the most to lose or gain by it. It's not the kind of story your genteel ears should be sullied by, Jass. I have never breathed a word of it to anyone, until Bart threatened to beat me senseless and leave my employ if I didn't. Even to him I couldn't reveal the whole of it.'

'Has there ever been anything we couldn't discuss with each other?' she asked softly.

'No. But we have never tried to discuss anything like this, anything with the depth of depravity inherent in this.'

Jassie's hands dropped to his shoulders for a moment. They were warm, soft. God, he wanted her. Her lips pressed to the top of his head and he had to clench his hands round his knees to keep from grasping for everything she offered.

'Don't,' he whispered. 'You—distract me and I-will-not-be-distracted in that way.'

Gently he closed his hands over hers and returned them to his head. The massaging was soothing. He could handle that.

'I'll tell you what happened, Jass. But you must promise—no interruptions. No distractions. Let me just tell it and then—let's see if we can talk. You see, one of the things that has kept my lips sealed all these years is the deep down conviction anyone knowing about—this— will have an abiding abhorrence of me thereafter. I don't think I would survive you reacting that way.'

Her fingers clenched reflexively in his hair.

'Rogan Wyldefell,' she hissed between clenched teeth, 'how dare you doubt the strength and depth and endurance of my love for you!'

'Easily, Jass. I have such a deep abiding abhorrence for myself.'

'Oh Rogan,' she whispered, slipping her hands from his head. Sliding them around his neck, she held him with all her strength, her face pressed against his hair. 'I love you—unconditionally.'

The words were a balm to his lacerated soul—but still a craven part of him feared to believe.

'We'll see, hmm?'

The sensation of her holding him was almost too precious to endure, especially when his mind kept reminding him the more sensual memories he allowed her to make the more he would have to regret and yearn for when she turned from him in disgust, as he knew she must.

He threaded his fingers through hers and held her hands against his throat. She had small, strong hands. He'd often imagined them—*don't go there Windermere. Just tell the goddamn story.*

'When you were twenty, Rogan, what happened?'

Her breath ruffled his hair and he rather imagined she was deeply content to be sitting so with him—as was he. *Enjoy it while you may,* his inner voice snarled. *Once she knows what you have to tell her she will simply be—repelled.*

I love you unconditionally, she'd said. It would be his talisman. There was nothing else to cling to. He'd told this story once to Bart. It should be easier a second time though somehow he had to find the courage to tell Jassie all of it.

He closed his eyes and once again he was in the large terrace house in Oxford where he'd boarded with a half dozen other young men.

'I boarded in the house of a professor when I went to university. He was probably in his late forties but he had a young wife, much younger. She was something out of every young man's dreams. Idiot that I was, I thought life had been very good to me.'

Jassie pressed her lips to his hair.

'Go on,' she whispered.

'The professor was often out in the evenings, tutoring or at meetings. One would've thought he might have known better than to leave such a—hot, hungry bitch alone in a house full of testosterone ridden young men.'

He stopped and wiped a hand across his sweating brow.

'I'm sorry, Jass. I shouldn't have said that but—I think the only way I *can* tell it, is like that. Can you bear with me? It's an ugly tale and the only language that seems to suit it is the profane.'

'Rogan, just tell it. Forget I'm sitting here listening to you. Just get every ugly detail out of your heart, off your conscience and to *hell* with how you have to tell it! You and Philip didn't raise me to be a prissy-mouthed prude.'

'No, but I'm sure my mother tried.'

She snorted. Nothing lady-like in that. He clutched her fingers a little more tightly. Forgetting her presence was impossible when finally her small hands were caressing him as he'd so often dreamed. He shuddered in a breath and continued.

'I think now I wasn't the only one she so entranced, though that didn't occur to me at the time—probably wouldn't have worried me either. I was ignorant and arrogant enough—to think I was doing *her* a favor. But she—wanted more than I was prepared to give. She began harassing me to—let her tie me up, promising I'd love it, especially if she were to—stimulate me with whip and belt.'

He managed to ignore Jassie's inrush of breath and continue.

'She also wanted me to tie her up and use a riding crop on her—or my bare hand. Apparently she found that kind of stimulation very exciting. If I would let her show me, maybe I'd—accept her domination as well. God! I was a stupid, horny young bastard but I was not into deviant stuff. The thought of—doing any of the stuff she talked about actually—nauseated me.'

He couldn't restrain a groan at the memory.

'But I was so arrogant. I thought I could control the situation. Sex was—pretty much all I thought about at that age.—It's all most young men think about at that age,' he added bitterly, his mind spiraling down into that place where guilt rode him relentlessly.

'What happened?'

What hadn't happened?

'I think she must've laced my ale at dinner with laudanum. Then she slipped me a note to say she'd come by my room later and suggested I should be naked and ready for her.—So as soon as dinner was over I went upstairs, stripped and lay down to wait. I felt strangely tired and the next thing I knew was waking up gagged and with my wrists bound and secured to the head board. She'd obviously been working at arousing me before she decided to wake me—in a very painful way.'

Hell! He couldn't tell her that!

'How?'

The word was a whisper against his hair. He swallowed.

'I think she bit my balls—hard.'

Jassie jerked involuntarily against his back and he muttered another apology.

'Don't apologize,' she hissed. 'Just talk. It's way past time you told someone instead of trying to hold it all in. It's destroying you, Rogan. It's destroying us.'

Fingers still entwined with his, she slid her hands a little lower to cover his heart. It felt as if she channeled her own strength into him.

'Yeah.—Um—She waved a small, deadly looking dagger before my eyes and threatened to cut out my balls so I'd never—be able to function as a man—if I didn't do exactly as she ordered. She actually made a small nick—'

Jassie's fingers flexed against his heart. Breathe, he reminded himself. Just—breathe and keep talking.

'She prodded me over and up onto my knees, which she then secured to the head of the bed as well, so my butt was—embarrassingly exposed. I was trussed on my knees like a f—goddamn Christmas goose! I was so angry I tried to rip the headboard from the bed. I finally reasoned maybe if I just let her have her way she'd set me free—and *then* I'd make her f—s—sorry.—Do you know anything about—um—hell! Do you have any idea what a—a cock ring is?'

'N—no. Not really. Though I guess—it's what it says it is.'

'Yeah—this one was like a split ring and—she put it on me. Then she set about arousing me in every deviant way imaginable—and unimaginable; she fastened some sort of clamps to my nipples that were so painful I was yelling. I tried to slide them off against the mattress but my knees were pulled up so tight I wasn't able to get my chest low enough. And even though I was whimpering like—like a puling babe with the pain, my—I became very painfully aroused. The blood rushed in to my—penis—but the ring wouldn't let it out again. Then she began—'

How could he tell this beautiful woman of the ugly things the bitch had done to him? There was no language he could use to make it in any way acceptable for her to hear.

He rolled his head back on his shoulders and closed his eyes.

'I can't—'

'You can.'

'It's ugly, sickening—'

Her hands caressed up his neck, over his ears and back into his hair. The magic of her fingers against his scalp eased the panic swelling in his chest.

'That's why you have to say it. All of it. It's festering inside of you like a great, poisonous canker. What-did-she-do-to-you?'

'She m—massaged my butt with oil, and shoved her fingers into me—there—and finally jammed in something cold and metallic that felt as big as—felt huge. I think she enjoyed me yelling in pain. The gag and the pillows must have muffled it because no one came to see what was wrong. Then she stroked more oil over my b—balls and penis until I was so hard I thought I'd burst. But I couldn't come because of the f—damn cock ring. My—cock—penis—felt like it was going to explode.

'I knew the bitch was enjoying hearing me scream so I tried to think of something to take my mind off it. I recited mathematical equations, Shakespeare and Latin declensions but nothing would close out that torturous fire building behind my c—penis. At that point, when I thought I couldn't take any more, she began flogging me with a leather flail, the tails of which nipped and stung with a deadly precision. She'd obviously had a lot of practice with that infernal piece of torture. I was moaning constantly against the gag by this stage, unable to distinguish whether I was feeling exquisite pain or the most intense pleasure. I think I lost my mind about then. If I was finding any pleasure in this fucking torture I was a sick bastard.'

He'd been trying not to let the coarser profanities creep into his tale but the memories of that night were so profane it was inevitable.

'I'm sorry Jassie. So sorry. I didn't mean to say that—'

'Will you stop damn well apologizing!'

Leaping to his feet he stalked back to the doorway, braced his hands high against either side of the frame and dragged in gulps of refreshing air.

Jassie was immediately behind him, rubbing her hands rhythmically up and down his back.

'It's all right, Rogan. You can do it. What happened next?'

'She released my knees though she left my wrists bound together and still leashed to the headboard. When she told me to roll over I complied with alacrity, thinking she was about to untie my hands. But she was still a long way from granting me any kind of release. She straddled me, impaling herself on—on my p—penis, so distended and painful I couldn't stop myself from just moaning and moaning—and begging her to let me come.

'The bitch pleasured herself to oblivion—and *then* she untied me. I still hadn't come because of the damned cock ring and it was as if all the remaining blood in my body rushed to my brain.—Oh God!'

His legs were shaking. He had no choice but to fold where he was, sinking down to sit on the step. Jassie came down beside him, her arm across his shoulders.

'Go on,' she whispered.

He dropped his head onto his hands and continued, talking to his boots.

'Quicker than the bitch could blink, and regardless of how hard she fought—though I suspect that was just for the pleasure of it—God she was perverted!—Anyway I very quickly had her secured exactly as she'd had me, gagged, manacled and on her knees with her ar—butt in the air. I was so far gone I didn't even think to remove the cock ring and I rammed straight into her backside and fucked and fucked until her muffled cries were silenced and I began to wonder whether she'd passed out. Finally I thought to rip off the cock ring and my release was so violent and explosive it was a dreadful kind of pleasure pain—that to this day, I—long to feel again.'

The last few words were a mere whisper, but he'd had to say them, admit out loud the depth of his depravity.

'Bloody hell!'

He wrapped his hands round his head and groaned.

'Rogan! None of this is your fault! Stop flaying yourself. What did you do then?'

'I collapsed beside her wondering if I might be going to cry but thinking at least I'd showed her how—wrong—her actions were—how painful. Then I became worried because she'd gone silent, so I ripped off her gag—and the first words out of her mouth were, —'*God, Wyldefell, you were magnificent!*

'I can't describe how that made me feel—like—impotent with fury because no matter what I did to her, it would never—*could*—never be punishment because she enjoyed it!—It sent me a little insane, I think. I untied her wrists—only her wrists—and made her remove the thing she'd shoved in my—butt.'

He stopped to draw several fortifying breaths, squeezed his eyes shut and said, '*Then* I bound and gagged her again and flogged her until there were welts on her backside and then I fucked her until I exploded again, so violently, so stupendously, I can't ever seem to forget it.—Finally I shoved her out of my room, and threatened her with death if she came anywhere near me again. I left that house the very next day.'

He didn't tell her he believed Adelaide Barratt may have used Philip in the same way or at least had been threatening to. He could spare her that.

Jassie's head rested on his shoulder and her hand continued to rub rhythmically up and down his spine.

'So—when you make—love to me, what happens? Have you developed the need for more of that kind—of—sex?'

'Not really—it's more like a compulsion,' Rogan muttered, dimly aware there was moisture on his cheeks and he swiped at it absently. 'When I make love to a woman there inevitably comes a point when the man I always believed I was, disappears and some ravening monster takes his place and it's no longer anything to do with making love. It's about the same time all women merge and become that one in my mind; that one, who so deeply humiliated me and denied me the satisfaction of revenge by thoroughly enjoying everything I dished out. Every woman becomes that perverted bitch I have to—*succeed*—in punishing.'

Convulsively he turned and folded Jassie in his arms, pressing her precious head against his chest.

'That's why I've tried so hard to keep our relationship to— friendship. I love you Jass. I can't deny it and I never should have tried. I should have told you all this long since so you understood why I could never make you mine. I cannot bear to drag you into my darkness. I— ache with a terrible agony whenever I think of what I did to you on our wedding night. And I can't get the memory of it out of my mind—or the look in your eyes afterwards. I love you, Jassie, but I cannot be a true husband to you. I'll not risk hurting you like that again.'

Jassie reached up and cupped his face in her hands.

'I understand. Kiss me, Rogan. I love you so much.'

'God, Jass, don't,' he pleaded, his voice scarcely more than a raspy whisper. 'You un-man me with your love. I don't deserve it. I don't deserve *you*. I'll not put you at risk again. I realize if I don't come home, at least as much as I used to, we might as well not have bothered to get married. But don't tempt me to make love to you. I can't resist because you are everything I've ever wanted. But I love you too much to subject you to—the—animal I become. The only way I can do this is to go back to how we were—before—Neave Tor.'

Her eyes were like bruised golden pansies, gazing up at him and as he watched they filled with tears that welled and rolled down her cheeks.

'I'll try, Rogan,' she muttered at last, swiping impatiently at the moisture on her face. 'But—I'm not sure I can go back to how I was—before Neave Tor. I—will try though, if that's what you really want.'

'I do,' he said gently, and thumbed the rest of the tears from her pale skin. 'Why don't you go in and get Ruby to make you a tisane or something. I think I'll walk for a while, if you don't mind.—I feel kind of—stripped.'

She started to protest but he laid his finger across her lips.

'T'is best this way.'

Her mouth tightened, the last spark of hope died from her eyes and she turned from him to walk down the steps. She glanced back once, and then stuffing her fist in her mouth, turned and ran back along the lake edge and under the trees towards the Abbey.

He watched until she disappeared from view then sank back to the step once again to sit staring into nothing—nowhere—never at all—and wondered how he would bear it.

Her first instinct was to run to the stables and demand Dobbie saddle Chester again but though she knew the faithful animal would carry her wherever she needed to go, she'd asked enough of him today. The place she wanted most to be was in her own suite of rooms at Brantleigh Manor, but it really was time she started behaving like the Countess she'd become. She'd brought all of this on her own head with her wanton desire to know how it was to be loved by a man—no—loved by the Earl of Windermere.

Would it have been better to have left well alone, to have continued simply as best friends? Would she put the clock back if she could? Could she even wish to go back to being that untouched, innocent virgin in danger of sinking further into bitterness with each passing year?

She didn't think so and yet—when compared to the life she could be forced to live now, there was a certain wistful appeal to that innocence.

With her mind so busy her feet took her where they would and suddenly she found herself striding through the cloisters with enough raging energy to rouse the spirits of the monks who'd walked here in ancient times. She slowed her steps, but continued moving towards the arched portico of the chapel where she and Rogan had pledged their vows to one another a few short weeks ago.

Maybe if she sat for a while in the hallowed space where the pale stone walls and high clerestory windows created an atmosphere of light wherein negativity was difficult to maintain, she could bring some of that light into her ravaged heart. If there was any place that would lift her spirits and empower her to be the woman she had to be as the wife of the 8th Earl of Windermere, it was this beautiful little chapel whose only adornment was the light within.

Lifting the heavy iron latch, she opened the oak door, stepped into the sun-shafted sanctuary and closed the door gently again at her back. A natural wood cross, believed to be a relic from when the Abbey had been a thriving religious community back in medieval times, stood on the unadorned wooden altar, flanked by two equally ancient heavy silver candlesticks.

Fixing her eyes on these Jassie stood with her back to the door and allowed her memory to transport her back to the day of their wedding. Scarcely aware the clothes she wore in no way resembled the beautiful gown Rogan had later destroyed or the handsome, broad-shouldered Earl who walked at her side was a love-wrought projection of her own imagination, she began a slow walk up the aisle.

Every step accented a memory from that day: the intense welling of relief when the horses pounded up the Elm Drive and she knew Windermere was safe—and had kept to his word; the sudden terror that had assailed her as they'd entered the chapel, that she was doing the wrong thing, closely followed by the knowledge she would not turn back unless God sent her an indisputable sign—like a bolt of lightning; the sensation of everything becoming so light as to fade into nothingness and thinking she might fall on her face at Rogan's feet— and the welcome support of his hand at her back.

She could still feel the heat, the strength he'd willingly shared with her—when, even though the vows fell clearly from his lips, he'd intended to keep the rest of himself from her. Her vows had been spoken too. She could hear their voices.

Her thoughts brought her to the chancel steps and she sank to her knees and listened to the words echoing in her head again.

I do. One voice deep, clear, as if the two words were deliberately and loudly spoken to eradicate all the terrible doubts he must have been suffering. One voice squeaky with nerves and guilt for forcing Windermere into revoking a vow he clearly wouldn't have made without some profound and awful reason.

And now she knew what that reason was.

She clasped her hands at her breast, closed her eyes and raised her face to the light shafting in through the high arched windows.

Well God, was this Your plan all along? I thought I'd managed all this on my own, but perhaps—I should acknowledge Your Divine Hand in bringing Windermere to me as husband. In a way, I feel as if arriving at this point in our lives was pre-ordained, inevitable from the start. But where do we go from here?

God, You gave me that which I've longed for all my life; marriage to Windermere. Please grant me also the wisdom and the strength I need to heal the deep and ugly wounds he carries; to be the wife he needs to bring him the happiness he deserves; the happiness we both deserve.

Because they did! Why should the vice of one depraved human being be allowed to impact their lives to the extent they couldn't love one another as a husband and wife should? To the extent they might never have children? Never know true happiness?

They could be friends. They'd proved that over all the years of their lives. But they'd be denied the richness, the ultimate shared ecstasy of being lovers.

Parents.

The shafting sunlight seemed to enter the top of her head, flow down her spine with a tingling sensation of empowerment. Slowly she came to her feet again and allowed herself to feel fully energized by the charge of light—and the sense of a Divine Presence.

She would give Windermere space, time to adjust, but she would *not* give up her dream. They *were* husband and wife. They *would* be lovers.

CHAPTER EIGHT

Sitting at the opposite end of the dinner table from Jassie was as insufferable as he'd thought it would be. Several leaves had been removed and the table reduced in size so that six people could sit around it and converse without having to shout at one another. Jassie was too close. It was too easy to lose himself in the hungry depths of her gaze when their eyes met down the length of the table. She was too far away. If he'd seated her at his side he could have touched her—safely surely—and allowed himself to draw her into conversation.

He wanted all he was entitled to as her husband and yet—he wanted none of it.

How could he face himself—or her—if he allowed himself to indulge in the fullness of their marriage and thereby destroyed that which he held most dear in all his life?

No. She had to understand it could never be more than it now was. He would return to London. The fighting might be over but the War Office would still have need of him—or he could take his place in the House of Lords.

So tomorrow, he would once again tear himself away from her, seek to lose himself in service to King and country. At least he had that. Deep in thoughts of keeping himself occupied and away from Jassie, he was interrupted by his mother, clearly intent on rousing him from the brown study into which he'd fallen.

'Don't you think, Windermere?—Rogan!'

The sound of his given name in a tone of voice unusually sharp for his mother, successfully snagged his attention. At his ascension to the title she'd taken to according him the respect due his exalted status and now rarely used his given name.

'I'm sorry, Mama,' he responded. 'I didn't catch what you said.'

'That was perfectly obvious, my son. I said I have decided we should celebrate your marriage and the defeat of Bonaparte by having a house party here at the Abbey for the opening of the grouse season and a ball—as we used to when your father was alive. It would allay the gossip about the haste with which you were wed not to mention your absence since.'

A response was beyond him. He wanted to howl at her—his beautiful, gentle mother—and ask her what the hell she was trying to do to him? But of course he couldn't ask that for she wouldn't understand to what he was referring. She continued in the face of his silence.

'I know the Duke of Wolverton has asked repeatedly when you're going to reinstate the annual Abbey House Party at opening weekend. He'll attend which will ensure that everyone else you invite will come also. The gentlemen will come for the shooting of course and every mama with an eligible daughter will come hunting a dukedom with a handsome and wealthy Duke thrown in.'

Rogan grimaced. At least his marriage would protect him from that sad mêlée. But would it protect his wife from Wolverton? The Duke was his closest friend but the bastard had offered for Jassie in her first season and again later although she'd turned him down. But he'd offered for none other since, and readily admitted he still carried a torch for her.

His wife. Jassie was his and the thought that she might turn to Wolverton for the satisfaction her husband refused her burned like bile in his gut. He lifted his eyes to the end of the table and she was waiting for him, smiling brightly at the thought of the house party. Or was it the possibility of Wolverton spending a week at the Abbey; a week during which opportunities would abound for clandestine meetings?

Wolverton's status, experience and reputation had increased during the years since Jassie's first season, along with his looks, which were divinely enhanced (in women's eyes, so it seemed) by a scar down his right cheek from a sabre cut incurred at the battle of Talavera. As the third son his chances of inheriting the title should have been minimal but his eldest brother had died of pneumonia in 1811 and his second brother had been killed at the battle of Toulouse in 1814. Thus, Lord Dominic Beresford had become His Grace, the Duke of Wolverton and arguably the most eligible bachelor in Britain.

Rogan swung his gaze back to his mother.

'I'll be returning to London tomorrow. I do not have time for pointless days of idle amusement. I'm needed at the War Office and I also intend to put in an appearance at Parliament. I'll shoot on opening day with a few close friends as I always do.'

The Dowager sank back into her chair as if he'd slapped her and when he looked back at Jassie her face was white, her gaze shocked. He could easily tell she was wondering when he'd intended telling her of his plans. As for Bart, his eyebrows had risen but he'd immediately dipped his head so none should notice his surprise. No doubt his secretary would berate him later for the coward and fool he undoubtedly was.

Suddenly Jassie looked about the table then said in a strained voice, 'If everyone is agreeable, ladies, we'll retire to the salon and leave the gentlemen to their port.'

Without another glance in his direction she rose and swept out of the room, his mother and Mrs. Lyndon following close behind.

At the door, his mother turned and fixed him with a straight, piercing gaze he remembered well from childhood.

'Attend me in my rooms in an hour, Windermere, if you will.'

He knew those last three words were not a request he could choose to disregard or not. They were only tacked on for politeness.

Mama was everything that was polite but he knew he could not ignore the steely tone of her voice or avoid a discussion he was naive in thinking he'd never have to face.

'What the devil are you doing, Windermere?' Bart exploded the moment they were alone.

For the first time in their association Rogan regretted that Bart was his cousin and therefore not intimidated by either his title or status as his employer. He felt the heat burn in his face and he clamped his jaw against the spate of angry invective that wanted to spew out of his mouth.

When he said nothing, just downed one glass of port then poured another, Bart placed his elbows on the table and leant towards Rogan with an expression calculated to slice him open.

'Did you tell Jassie why you won't bed her?'

Rogan flinched at the directness of Bart's question and had difficulty keeping his expression neutral.

'Yes.'

'And?'

'And what?' he stalled, taking another swallow of port.

'And what was her reaction?'

That she loved me unconditionally.

'She allowed me to send her away. She accepted that things are best left as they are.'

Bart stared at him long and hard then sat back in his chair with his arms folded across his chest.

'You think?' he asked softly.

When Rogan continued to sit glaring into his already half empty second glass of port, Bart needled deeper.

'She's a married woman now. How long before she realizes the protection that affords her and decides to satisfy her urges else-where? How many *gentlemen* do you know who'd be honorable enough to turn her down if she offered?'

'She's never shown any inclination towards another.'

The words were out before he could think better of them.

Bart's eyes widened with incredulity.

'One thing I've always admired about you, Windermere, is that you were the least selfish person I knew. You've just shot that belief to smithereens. Will you also stay celibate?'

He'd had enough. Storming to his feet, he downed the dregs of his port, poured another and carrying it with him, growled, 'Go drink tea with the ladies. I'm going to my study and I don't want to be disturbed.'

He left the room without a backward glance. He didn't need to look back to know Bart was regarding him as if he'd turned into some kind of gargoyle.

Truth to tell it wasn't far from how he was feeling.

Ugly. Angry ugly. Ashamed ugly. Frustrated ugly.

She could only be lying when she said she loved him. There was nothing about him for a woman to love. And if she didn't really love him there was nothing to stop her from doing exactly as Bart had suggested; exactly as many elegant, dissatisfied wives of the ton did. Found their satisfaction outside of their marriage.

Fuck! He downed the rest of the port he'd carried into the study, then aimed the crystal glass viciously at the hearth. It shattered into the grate and he stood staring as the flames licked impotently at the gleaming shards.

His love for Jassie was like that. No matter how broken, how shattered, how destroyed, it lived within him still, defying any effort on his part to burn it out.

And it always would. He'd kill any man who came anywhere near her. Dropping into a deep leather armchair, he sat glaring into the flames.

A brief knock on the door followed by Melton's long, solemn countenance interrupted his ugly inner raging.

'I'm sorry to disturb you, my Lord, but the Dowager Lady Windermere requests your presence in her rooms.'

'Thank you, Melton,' he muttered, wondering where that hour had gone. Dragging both hands down his face in an attempt at wiping away the fog of fury that had overtaken him, he said, 'I'll attend her presently.'

The butler bowed and withdrew and Rogan tried to work out what he was to say to his mother; how to explain; how to put her off without explaining; how to just slink away somewhere and put a bullet in his worthless head. Only the thought of the pain such an action would cause her, who had suffered enough loss in the last few years, and Jassie—

Fuck! He'd spent years trying to think his way out of the imbroglio that was his life. Why would he think a solution was suddenly going to appear now?

Wearily he rose and left the study, slamming the door at his back.

Childish, Windermere, he chided himself as he strode along the hallway to his mother's suite of rooms.

Her door was slightly ajar and he entered without knocking to find her settled in her favorite powder blue wingchair before a glowing fire. A matching chair was pulled up alongside. Perfect for a cozy chat, he thought, the sarcasm feeling good as he shut her door with an equally childish but satisfying thunk before crossing to drop heavily into the chair at her side.

He couldn't look at her, couldn't confront the displeasure or unhappiness he would see in her gentle blue eyes. He hated when he fell short of her ideal of him and knew in the darkest places in his soul that it was a long time since he'd truly lived up to that ideal—if ever.

For several moments he sat with his head pressed back against the chair and his eyes tightly closed, aghast at the sudden awareness that it wouldn't take much to have him at her knees, bawling in her lap.

The feather-like touch of her cool fingers on his hand preceded her softly spoken words.

'Talk to me, son. If you think you're succeeding at outrunning this thing that has pursued you for years, I have to tell you, you're failing. It's catching up to you, consuming you and all around you. You cannot believe it doesn't affect all of us. Talk to me. Tell me what drives you—before it—kills you—and Jassie both.'

'I cannot—to you of all people, Mama—I cannot!'

His voice had little more substance than a whisper but there was nothing wrong with his mother's hearing. She emitted a soft sigh then sat forward in her chair to suddenly wrap her fragile fingers around his huge hands with a strength that surprised him.

'Then I will talk and you—will listen.'

There was no response in him, just a sighing gratitude that he didn't have to find the words that would form the pictures for her. He should've withheld on that gratitude, he decided a moment later as her words brought him out in a cold sweat.

'I've long been aware that something happened the second year you were at Oxford, Rogan. You changed. No matter how hard you tried you couldn't disguise the darkness that lurked in your eyes—that heretofore had always been filled with light and laughter; not from your mother. At first I thought it might have been that your heart was broken but in time I came to see that no matter what it was, your heart was still Jassie's. Just as it had always been. Then I hoped that when she became of an age to wed, you'd make her your wife and all would be well. But year followed year until it became all too plain you never intended to offer for her, regardless that you kept her heart tied to yours so that she sought no other.

'Jassie is a remarkable woman and no mother could wish for a better wife for her son. But you've not been fair to her, Windermere. I'm sure I don't need to tell you that. Do you think I haven't seen how you've ached and yearned for her, while denying yourself—denying both of you—the happiness marriage could bring? I know my questioning almost drove you away from home in those early years and so I learnt to keep my mouth shut for I couldn't bear it if you did not come. It's long past time this canker in your soul was brought out into the open. I'm done with silence, my son.'

'I don't have to listen to this, Mama,' he growled, starting to struggle to his feet. Horror filled the whole of his being at the thought of exposing the ugliness he carried in his soul to this gentle, loving woman.

'No, son, you don't. But I beg that you will.'

The grip of her tiny hands softened but she didn't relinquish him. Somehow he couldn't rise out of his chair. He dropped his head back and closed his eyes again. Perhaps that way he could shield her from the ugliness within. Quentin's untimely and senseless death followed four years later by that of their father had stolen all the strength and animation from her and he'd had to watch her fade to a pale shade of her former vitality in the years since. How could he add to the grief she carried?

By staying—or by going.

A painful sigh shuddered through his chest and he waited, feeling a definite empathy with a convicted man waiting for the moment the hangman's noose stole his breath with its ugly bite.

'Jassie told me of your encounter on Neave Tor—and of your—wedding night.'

'Oh—God!' His body jerked forward in the chair as if his feet had indeed fallen out from under him and he swung at the end of a rope. 'Why—in God's name—Fuck!'

And to his shame a deep raking sob erupted out of him. Again he went to rise but this time she pushed him quite hard and the surprise of it was enough to collapse him back into the chair.

'Just listen to me, son! You don't have to say anything. All you have to do is listen! Jassie loves you. I love you. This discussion was between her and I—just the two of us—did you expect her to carry it all on her own? Has that tactic served you all these years? And she didn't come running to me. In fact she tried just as hard as you have to shield me from whatever the unpleasantness you both considered me too frail to face. You need to forget I'm your mother, Rogan. I'm simply a woman—like any other. I too have loved and—*fucked*—and lived.'

Rogan jolted again at the crass term that fell with such—relish—off his mother's sainted tongue, but she didn't stop speaking.

'I was pretty certain it was something to do with a woman, or something sexual. I even considered you'd discovered a preference for men. I'm grateful to find that's not the case. Although it would have made no difference to my love for you if it was.

'But what Jassie told me of your wedding night tells me something is dreadfully amiss. Violence to women is definitely not something you learned in this house. And the way Jassie explained it, it seems you have no control over what happens. That tells me why you've avoided marriage to Jassie. You know this happens and you, quite honorably, chose not to subject her to it.—Am I right, son?'

Incapable of any other response, he simply squeezed her hand.

'Because of something that happened back when you were about twenty?'

He tried nodding his head though it felt like more of a flinch.

'Oh Rogan, my love, have you never in all these years talked to anyone of this?'

'Too ashamed,' he whispered.

'It'll only grow and fester until it sucks all the life out of you if you don't speak of it. It's eating you alive, from the inside out. Can you not talk of it—maybe not the details if that is too horrific to put into words, but at least enough that we who love you can understand—and maybe help?'

'How can you help? How can anyone help? It's—' Suddenly he sat up, groped in his jacket pocket for a handkerchief and wiped roughly at his face. Something inside him seemed to break open and he knew there was no holding back any more. But he'd temper what he said, sanitize it if it killed him. 'Bart has an understanding of it. I—

He forced me to talk of it on—the wedding night. He made me see I had to tell Jassie, that it was unfair not to. I told her today—the whole of it—and—now she knows what she's married to.'

Words ran out and he sat with his head in his hands, just concentrating on drawing breath—and not crying like a small bereaved child.

'And what is she married to, son?'

Her words were so soft, so filled with love he knew he had to find her an answer.

'She's married to a man who—needs—to punish—to—hell, Mama! A woman did something to me that—that no matter how hard I tried, I couldn't punish her for it because—because—she was so perverted that she enjoyed every goddamn ugly thing she had done to me—and that I could do to her. I nearly lost my sanity. It's like something burst in my brain and every time I'm—with a woman there comes a point when that—that—implosion happens again. I lose all control of myself. All I know is I must restrain her so she can't get away, gag her so she can't scream, and punish, punish, punish—' He clutched at his hair, struggling to keep from giving in to the agony that wanted to burst from him in howls of fury. 'The worst was knowing I could never marry Jassie, never subject her to the beast I'd become.'

In the silence that followed his mother slipped to the floor and knelt before him, clasping her hands gently round his and finally he gave in and let the ghastly unmanly tears flow freely down his face to mingle with hers.

The fire in the grate had died down to glowing embers by the time he had enough control of himself to raise his mother to her chair and throw more wood among the ashes and encourage it to burn again. Dropping back into his seat, he laid his head back and stared up at the ceiling trying to think of what he should say next.

'Nothing can ever be mended if you keep running away.'

Soft, gentle words delivered in a voice like velvet over steel.

'You've told Jassie. You've told me. The worst is over. Did either of us run screaming from you?'

Wearily he shook his head.

'Did she perchance simply reiterate that she loves you?'

He breathed deep and closed his eyes for a moment, remembering the incredible depth of the love that had shone from her topaz eyes.

'Unconditionally,' he whispered.

His mother nodded silently for a moment. Then she slipped her hand into his again.

'As do I.—Jassie is your salvation, Rogan. You have to know there's nothing weak or insubstantial about the woman you've married, however well-bred she might be. She has strength enough for both of you and if her strength fails her you can be certain her love won't.—But you have to stay. You have to give her a chance; give *love* a chance!—Will you?'

Oh God!

'What if—'

'Talk to Jassie, my son. Ask her what she wants to do. At least allow her some sort of choice here. So far *you* have decided how it shall be—for both of you. Marriage is a partnership. I know that's not a generally held belief but all the best marriages I know of have succeeded because they are *equal partnerships*—welded together with love. At least allow her to tell you how she would like your marriage to proceed.'

Had he just been a selfish bastard rather than a gentleman of honor by sheltering Jassie all these years, never giving her a chance to accept or reject what he was? Had he simply been too cowardly to face the fact there was an even chance he would lose her altogether?

'You've everything to gain, son. Nothing to lose. For nothing is exactly what you have now.'

At last he allowed himself to look into the love that shone for him from this amazing woman who'd borne him—who'd *fucked.*— The gutsiest woman he knew.

Although—he might just have a wife with a similar strength of character—and depth of love.

'You're right—as always. I'll go and talk to her now.' Rising, he bent to kiss her brow then said, 'Thanks.'

He couldn't leave the room however without turning back one more time and sharing a crooked smile with her.

'I need to tell you that I'm singularly blessed in having you for a mother—though I'm not absolutely sure I really needed to know you had—*fucked!*'

Color stormed into her cheeks and she flapped her hand at him.

'Get out! I suppose that was the only word you heard in all that I said!'

He grinned openly back at her. It felt good to lighten up a little, to let her know he was okay.

'Not at all. I heard all the rest but I wanted to let you know I heard that word fall from your saintly lips. I clearly recall being severely reprimanded for using it in your hearing once!'

'And you will be just as severely reprimanded if I hear it again!' she rattled back at him, her blue eyes dancing with merriment.

Satisfied that she was now in a lighter frame of mind than he'd found her, he stepped into the hallway.

'Oh. And Windermere?' she called after him. 'I meant what I said about the opening day and the ball. The occasion of your marriage should be brought to the notice of the ton, not allowed to slip by unheralded as if it was something to be ashamed of!—You will not return to London—please. The War Office will manage fine without you —and so will Parliament. It has up to now. No more excuses!'

Forcing himself not to think what that would mean for him and Jassie, he nodded. Then realizing she couldn't see him, he called back, 'All right, Mama. I'll stay and—I'll try it your way. But from here-on it'll be as Jassie and I decide.'

'Of course, Windermere!'

Her airy agreement followed him down the hallway but he didn't miss the note of satisfaction in the musical voice.

Aware that Fran and the Dowager were observing her with concern as she led the way out of the dining room and were both about to launch into a discussion of Windermere's declaration of intent to return to London on the morrow, Jassie turned to her mother-in-law as she settled in to pour tea.

'So Mama, have you decided on the colors and patterns for your rooms—or have you changed your mind again?' she asked brightly.

To her surprise the Dowager allowed her deflection from the topic that had to be uppermost in all their minds and entered into a happy discussion of the different color combinations and pattern styles she was considering. The Egyptian mode was still her favorite.

In the middle of their discussion Bart Matthews entered the room, asking if there was any tea left in the pot. Lady O looked up sharply and asked, 'Is Windermere not joining us, Barton?'

'I don't believe so, Aunt Olwynne. He headed for his study saying he didn't want to be disturbed.'

Her mouth twisted with annoyance. Jassie almost snorted in disgust. Windermere seemed to have lost any semblance of gentlemanly behavior since their marriage—no, since their memorable contretemps on Neave Tor. She desperately needed another conversational gambit to divert everyone's minds, but to her relief the Dowager claimed to be weary and made her excuses to retire a little earlier than usual.

As soon as she was gone, Jassie turned to Fran and said, 'I'm going up too if you don't mind, Fran. You might as well make use of the fire and the good reading candles in the library, if you want.'

Fran smiled and said, 'Thanks Jassie. I'm dying to start on that novel by that new author, Emma Parker, so now would be a good time.'

Their eyes met and Jassie knew Fran understood that what she really wanted was just to be alone—in case Windermere came to his senses and to an awareness of his obligations to his wife.

'It would,' Jassie agreed. 'Let me know what you think of it.'

'Good night, Bart.'

'Good night, Lady Jassie. I hope it wasn't something I did! I never meant to interrupt your evening.'

Jassie sent him a wan grin.

'Of course not. Anyway, Mrs. Lyndon probably wouldn't mind some company in the library.'

'I was rather hoping she wouldn't mind if I accompanied her there. Windermere has some excellent tomes on the Far East and I rarely have the leisure to study them. Tonight would be a good time to indulge—if Mrs. Lyndon doesn't object.'

'No objection at all, sir,' Fran responded, eyes downcast and cheeks slightly flushed.

Jassie hurried out of the room, leaving them to settle the affair between themselves. If she were to say any more Fran would accuse her of match-making. And she'd have had to lie!

Her feet dragged as she climbed the wide oak staircase to the upper floors. A part of her wanted to confront Windermere in his study and tell him she had no intention of being abandoned here at the Abbey while he did—whatever gentlemen did—in the capital. But pride would not allow her. The next move was up to him.

'Thanks, Ruby, I can manage now,' Jassie said as soon as her maid had unlaced her gown and stays. 'I won't need you any more to-night.'

After building the fire up a little more, Ruby glided happily out of the room, no doubt looking forward to a quiet coze with Randall the footman, who seemed to have taken her eye since they'd settled into the Abbey.

Jassie stripped out of her clothes and laid them over a chair in the dressing room, achingly aware that only a couple of doors stood between her naked self and her husband's bedroom. Entertaining and swiftly discarding thoughts of settling into his bed instead of her own, she turned back into her room and pulled on a sheer lawn nightgown and matching peignoir embroidered around the borders with dainty pink rosebuds. Settling herself at her duchess with just one candle and the glow from the fire for illumination she unpinned her hair and began pulling the brush through it. Usually Ruby brushed out her hair but tonight she just needed to be alone.

Ruby didn't need to know her mistress was in the mood to attack her husband. She wouldn't sit meekly back and allow him to reject, neglect or ignore her. From him of all people she deserved better. Her fury grew, along with the realization that he'd denied her the whole of himself for years and condemned them both to a kind of purgatory without even giving her a say in the matter. She hadn't even really understood just what he'd done to them.

Until now. It would not be allowed to continue. Scenarios began to play through her mind; herself storming downstairs and flinging the study door open and yelling at him—or throwing herself into his arms and demanding he take her to London with him; walking calmly through the connecting door to his room and settling in among the quilts on the Earl's high tester bed; Rogan finding her there and being unable to resist—Pshaw!

She was no better than a dreamy-eyed miss just out of the schoolroom. She would do none of those things. If Windermere didn't deign to come and talk to her of his plans she'd simply follow him to London and install herself in Windermere House.

Leaping up she began pacing restlessly around the room adjusting a chair here, straightening a rug there. All the while telling herself to simply get into bed, so that maybe she could just go to sleep and forget the whole sorry mess. But she knew there was no way her eyes were going to stay closed even if she could convince her body to lie down and relax. Putting out the single candle, she snatched a quilt off the bed, wrapped it around herself and settled into the window-seat, her knees drawn up under her chin.

The room was now only lit by the intermittent leaping flames of the fire and the soft almost-darkness surrounded her with a piercing solitude. She could've stayed downstairs with Fran but in her contrary state of mind she knew she'd rather suffer the deepest pangs of loneliness than be with anyone other than Windermere. Beyond the windows the moonlit gardens of the Abbey were a mysterious patchwork of white light and deep shadow and as she stared down into the magical scene she began visualizing scenarios whereby she made Windermere jealous. If she went to London there would be no shortage of soirées and social events she could attend even at this end of the season—with or without the frustrating man.

Such behavior had never occurred to her before and in truth it didn't appeal to her now. But what else was she to do? How was she to make him see what they could have—together? Besides, did he not deserve to suffer for what he'd put her through? What he'd denied her?

A soft knock sounded at the door and it opened before she'd gathered her thoughts to respond. Rogan stepped into the room, his dark bulk easily recognizable against the glow of the fire.

'Jass? Are you awake?'

'Of course not! Why would you think I'd not be asleep? I'm a perfect model of happiness and contentment! What could possibly keep me awake?'

Unerringly he followed her voice to the window-seat and settled beside her, almost sitting on her toes.

'Sarcasm doesn't suit, you, Jass. I would've come sooner but Mama summonsed me. I don't think I've ever appreciated how blest I am to be her son. You know what she told me? That she'd loved, *fucked,* lived. How many women of our class do you know who could use such language to put her profoundly fucked-up son at ease?'

Awe colored his voice but it scarcely registered with Jassie. Fury fountained in her breast and she felt a terrible desire to launch herself bodily at him, attack and scratch. Dear God, she'd thought she was in control but there was no way she could withhold the words that wanted to spew out of her mouth.

'You expect to just sit down here and talk about your wonderful *mother?* Lady O has always been the most amazing woman I know! Nothing's changed there. And I do know one other woman like her. Me! How could you not have known that you could talk to me about *fucking* and such? God! We've shared rotten egg and spew; talked of mating horses and dogs; dealt with maids gotten pregnant both here and at Brantleigh.

'Not only *could* you have talked to me of fucking but you *should* have! And we should have *been fucking* way before this! Do you have any conception of what you've denied us? Denied *me*? And now you intend to just swan off to London again tomorrow without alerting anyone—not even your secretary if I interpreted Bart's shocked expression when you mentioned it—*oh so casually over dinner!*'

She pulled her foot back and kicked his thigh, hard.

'Well you needn't think I'm going to sit tamely here in the country twiddling my genteel Countess's toes while you—do whatever you do in the city! I *will* be coming to London too!'

Jassie ran out of breath and words at the same time, suddenly realizing she'd leaned right forward and was shouting into Rogan's face. Before she could calm her breathing and huddle back into her corner of the seat Rogan had possessed himself of her hands and raised them to his lips where he proceeded to cover them with hard, burning kisses.

Then gently he pulled her onto his lap and no matter how filled with hurt and anger she was, there was no way she could deny herself the joy of being that close to the man she'd loved from the cradle.

'I'm so sorry, Jassie,' he murmured against her hair as he clasped her close against his chest. 'I know I deserve everything you could possibly throw at me. I thought I was doing the right thing by holding myself away from you—even though I wasn't able to remain entirely aloof, as I should have. But Mama has made me see how selfish and inconsiderate I've been all these years, how—autocratic. That at least has to change. You have a right to some say in how our lives are to be lived.'

Jassie lifted her head and squinted against the darkness trying to see into his eyes but they were just shiny pools of blackness.

'You'll talk to me? *Ask me* what I want? *Because your sainted Mama said you should*? I get to have a say in our marriage? Is that what you're saying?—And would you even have listened if *I* had told you that was how it was going to be? Because I'm informing you here and now, Windermere, that's exactly how it's going to be. There'll be no more secrets however awful, however shameful or heinous. We will be open with one another and make our decisions *together.*'

'I freely admit I might not have listened to you. But Mama didn't lose control and start throwing orders about.'

He had the gall to smile, his teeth white in the moonlight.

Jassie felt the fury building within her again.

'I'll not be toyed with, Windermere! I've a lot of catching up to do in the decision-making stakes and I don't intend to be led astray by your ever so charming smile.'

His head tilted a little to one side, he considered her for a moment. Jassie wished desperately for more light to read the thoughts she knew were flashing through his eyes.

'Um—I thought that was exactly what you were wanting.—
Me to toy with you.'

Damn if he wasn't laughing at her again. Who was this man
who'd suddenly found the ability to talk to her, touch her, tease her?
Please God let him be real.

She leaned back, trying to read his face in the moonlight.

'Who are you? Where have you been hiding?'

The teasing light faded from his eyes and suddenly the serious, almost stern, Rogan was back. His mouth firmed and his chin,
always chiseled and square, jutted belligerently. She'd also swear that
his hands, wrapped firmly about her body, were trembling.

'This isn't easy, Jass. I long quite desperately to discard that
repressed—restrained Windermere you've become used to over the
years but I'm absolutely terrified of what could ensue if he relaxes his
guard and—allows his true self to be revealed.'

His jaw worked for a moment as if he ground his teeth.

'I'll not allow anyone to hurt you, Jass. I'll not allow *me* to
hurt you,' he growled, his voice harsh and intense.

Jassie sat for a moment watching the fierce scowl on his face,
then couldn't resist reaching up to try and smooth it away.

'Rogan, what's the worst you might do to me? Where on the
scale of severity would our wedding night fall? Could it get worse?
And if so, how much worse?'

Suddenly he screwed his eyes tight and pulled her close in to
his chest and the trembling in his hands became markedly more no-
ticeable.

'Rogan talk to me. I need to know! If I know and am prepared
for it, I'm sure I can handle it. What you did that night—I cried because it hurt and I was simply not expecting anything like that! Don't
you see? I can cope if I understand what the possibilities are.'

'Why should you cope?' he snarled. 'No woman should have
to *cope* with such abuse! Unless she freely offers herself—and is paid.
Christ, Jassie, I made you cry! I thrashed you as if—as if you were the

worst miscreant imaginable. I won't subject you to that. I love you. How could I hurt you?'

His voice had become a broken whisper but Jassie heard those three precious words. *I love you.* He'd told her that in the folly that afternoon and she would never tire of hearing those words from his lips. She reached up and held his head down to hers, their foreheads resting against one another.

'Those words are very precious to me, Rogan. Your love is all I've ever wanted.—So please explain to me—on a scale of one to ten—no, tell me have you ever really hurt a woman? I mean hurt as in—damaged in any way.'

His body jerked in reaction to her question.

'No, thank God,' he muttered. 'I've never damaged anyone. Though I always make them cry.'

She *would not* allow herself to dwell for even one second on the thought of Rogan with another woman.

'So what you did, tying me up, gagging me and thrashing me? That's all that you do?'

'All! Isn't that enough?'

'Hush,' she murmured, pressing her lips to his forehead. 'What I'm trying to say to you, Rogan, is that if that is the extent of the abuse, it—was not so bad. Yes, it made me cry because it did hurt. Punishment is meant to hurt and meant to make one cry. But—but if I understand it's not really me you're punishing then—then it's all right. And if I know it doesn't get much worse than that, I won't panic—and scream—and—'

'And hate me,' he finished for her, the words flat and angry. His head dropped back on his shoulders and his eyes were scrunched tight.

'Rogan.' When he didn't relax she grabbed his shoulders and shook him. 'Rogan! What part of 'unconditional love' don't you understand? I—love—you. There's nothing you can do or say to me that can change that. I—love—you—unconditionally.—Please—take me to bed.'

At last his whole body relaxed and he wrapped his arms about her once more, holding her against his heart in such a way as to make her feel precious, treasured. Jassie had never felt more blessed than in that moment, never more hopeful or at peace.

'I don't deserve you,' he murmured.

'Yes you do. And I deserve you. Please stop denying us to each other.'

She climbed off his lap and tugged him to his feet. He towered over her and she slid her arms around his waist and laid her head against his chest. The freedom to finally be able to do this almost stole her senses for a moment but then she became aware of the hardness of muscle beneath her fingertips, the breadth and strength of him that she'd never been free to experience since she'd been sixteen.

'Want to know something funny?'

'What?' he asked, his lips nuzzling into her hair.

'I've never seen a naked man. Except in books. Do you know there are some very—informative books in your library, Lord Windermere?'

'You mean those ones hidden behind a row of others on the very top shelf, Lady Windermere?'

'Oh! So you do know!' she pounced.

'Philip and I found them when we were about twelve I think.'

'I was fifteen. It was not long after Quentin died. I spent more time here than at Brantleigh once Phil joined the army and I was here then. You were somewhere in Europe—'

'Austria. I didn't know about Quent's death until weeks afterwards.'

Jassie nodded.

'That just added to everyone's misery of course; your mother's in particular. It was a very dreary time once all the visitors had stopped coming. I rather think your parents forgot I was here half the time and I spent hours hiding and reading on the window-seat in the library. There was no one to monitor what I read and I knew exactly where to look because I had found a couple in exactly the same place at Brantleigh—on the highest shelf and hidden behind a row of other very boring tomes. I considered that I was educating myself for you. But you shattered that particular pipe dream on my sixteenth birthday—along with my heart. It has lain, smashed, at your feet ever since.'

Jassie felt that organ swell painfully in her chest, even now, remembering the bleakness of those days of grief. She'd sustained herself with dreams of Rogan and how much more grown up she'd be when he finally returned, how he'd recognize the woman she'd become and start to treat her as his love instead of a pesky kid-sister as he always had before.

The pain strengthened when she thought of how innocently she'd looked forward to that momentous birthday. At sixteen she'd decided she was definitely a woman grown, and had blithely believed all her fantasies about Rogan Wyldefell would then be realized.

Jassie leaned back in his arms and looked up at his face, stern and deeply shadowed against the moonlight.

'I dreamed a lot of wasted dreams back then, Rogan. About the only one that has come to fruition is the one where you became my husband. Even that didn't much resemble the romantic fantasy I made of it. And if I thought I was frustrated before it's nothing to how I feel now. I burn and ache for you in places a true lady doesn't ever mention. But I think your mother gave up on the idea of turning me out as a true lady years ago.—Rogan, please make love to me.'

His arms tightened, clasping her roughly back against his chest.

'I want to, Jass. More than you can ever understand but—'

Stretching up onto her toes, Jassie closed her mouth over his.

'No more 'buts',' she murmured. 'Kiss me.'

His beautiful mouth softened over hers. A deep moan of surrender vibrated through his body and his tongue slipped between her lips and Jassie thought her crazy heart would leap right out of her chest. Rogan was kissing her, deeply, lovingly, just as he'd done on the night of her sixteenth birthday before his deeply ingrained sense of honor had forced him to step back—and deliver the cruelest words he'd ever spoken to her.

Her tongue danced delightedly to meet his, their lips melding, clinging. His hands cupped the back of her head, fingers spearing into the mass of her hair. It was as if shafts of wildfire left his fingertips and coursed through her body.

It was happening, it was really happening.

Her hands slid round to the back of his neck, hanging on, dragging him closer until her breasts were mashed against his chest, the nipples hard and burning.

'Oh Rogan please!' she breathed into his mouth.

He stilled, removed his mouth from hers and raised his head. When she looked up, ready to plead yet more, his mouth was a taut line, his nostrils flared and his eyes closed.

'Don't beg. Please, Jassie, don't beg. I promise to try and make love to you, as you should be made love to. But—there are triggers—and begging is one of them.'

'But—I want—'

'What do you want?'

'You—you showing me—loving me—'

'That's what I want too. Just let me show you.'

He slipped the peignoir off her shoulders then whispered harshly, 'Take your gown off. I want to see you.'

Jassie stepped back from him, shaking her head.

'Only if you'll remove your clothes also, Windermere! I'm not going to be the only one in the buff here! And I have absolutely no doubt you know exactly how the female body looks where as I—'

'Yeah, I know. You've only seen pictures! Let's get naked together. But I'm telling you, Jassie, if I hurt you again, it'll be the last time.'

Jassie sucked in a ragged breath then almost sobbed on the exhale. She didn't know what affected her most, the realization she was about to see Rogan without his clothes for the first time or the thought that it might also be the last.

And if it was the only time she might ever see him then she really wanted to see.

'Do you mind if I light a candle?'

A rough chuckle escaped him.

'Why would I ever have thought you'd be a shy bride? Most virgins, especially the more gently bred ones, would cringe at the thought of exposing themselves for the first time. It was that which terrified me most about you all these years. I'd half expected that confrontation on Neave Tor years ago. Let's light all the candles. We've both waited too long for this moment.'

Jassie couldn't keep the grin from her face and she set about creating as much illumination as she could.

'I'd been thinking of approaching you about it for a long time but you see—maybe your Mama did succeed in teaching me a little—for I had a really hard time talking myself into actually doing it.'

His chuckle was the most beautiful sound she'd heard in a long time.

With the last candle lit, they came together again beside the bed and Rogan sat on it to pull his boots off. As they hit the floor he came back to his feet and looked down at Jassie with a quizzical smile.

'Are you going to take that gown off or are you just going to stand there and watch me?'

'The latter. You've way more to remove than I do. And I don't want to miss a thing! I've only ever seen a gentleman immaculately turned out, proper from head to toe. The salacious mystery of how he came to appear like that and how he divests himself of all his finery at the end of the day in the privacy of his bedroom has completely escaped me. I intend for that gap in my education to be filled this night.'

His eyes were glowing oceans of darkness as he considered her, then with a small shake of his head, he ripped off his neck cloth and hunched out of his dark blue superfine jacket and dropped them on the ottoman. Shirt, breeches, stockings all swiftly followed until he stood before her in only his drawers, the front standing out like a tent.

'Let me,' she whispered and stepped close to pull his hands away from the laces. He let his arms fall to his sides and looked down at her with an indulgent smile.

It was going to be all right, she thought. If he can smile at me like that surely it is going to be all right. She wanted to touch the smooth skin overlaying the sides of his muscular stomach and ribs, the vee of soft dark hair across his chest, the hard flat nipples peeking through. Laying her hands on the smooth skin at his waist, she slid them slowly up to cover his nipples then further upwards to splay across his upper chest.

'You are very—impressive, Windermere.'

Now she felt oddly shy but couldn't resist leaning in and placing a teasing kiss first on one nipple and then the other. A faint hiss of air passed his lips and she darted a glance up at him.

'Am I doing something wrong? Don't you want me to touch you?'

'Nothing wrong, Jass. It's just that—finally having you before me like this, your hands on me like this—my brain is having trouble adjusting. I've denied any thought of this for so long that it's hard convincing myself it's all right. And then there's the wild sensations that race through my blood and flood into that one place that is so desirous of—knowing you, filling you, f—'

'F—fucking me?'

'Yeah.' His chest heaved. 'Are you going to untie those laces? Because I'm starting to feel quite—urgent about the fucking part.'

CHAPTER NINE

Tentatively she reached for the ends of the laces and tugged them undone and the garment slid easily down his legs. Kicking them off, he reached down and tossed them on top of the rest of his clothes. When he came upright again she was standing, wide-eyed and still.

'It looks bigger than in the books.'

'Mmm. He's not usually that big. He's excited.—May I now remove your nightgown?'

Wild color flooded her cheeks and he realized the shy virgin was there after all, though of course he'd taken care of the virgin part on Neave Tor. She could only maintain the bravado for a little while. Please God, he could finally show her the bliss of coming together in love.

He plucked at the shoulders of her gown and lifted it up over her head to fall away from the ends of his fingers, forgotten in the glory that was Jassie.

His wife. Fingers of panic clawed into his heart but he swiftly thrust them aside.

'You, Jassinda Wyldefell, are a beautiful work of art,' he whispered.

And she was. Rich, sovereign gold waves of hair drifted down her back and across her shoulders. There was a warm blush on the honeyed satin of her skin. But she stood proudly, beautiful full breasts with taut rosy nipples begging for his attention; the deeply curving indentation of her waist and the toned flatness of her belly tempting his caress; the darker gold of the soft curls hiding her woman's secrets from him; her long, lightly muscled horse-rider's legs that would wrap so strong and lithe about his body.

But when he looked back up at her eyes he was captured by the wide open, topaz stare as she took in all of him. Though he rather thought her attention was firmly fixed on one part of his anatomy.

'You look—worried.'

'I'd like to touch—it.'

Her cheeks bloomed with color and her eyes glowed with excitement.

'I'd like nothing better than for you to touch—him.'

He forced himself to smile encouragingly at her when what he really wanted was to lay her on the bed and ravage her with his mouth, hands and body. But he could be patient. He *would* be patient. She was adorable in her ambivalence of desire and anxiety.

'What are you afraid of?'

Her tongue slipped out and nervously wet her lips that now glistened like ripe cherries in the candlelight. She had no idea how she tempted him. There was no artifice about his Jassie. She was as honest and forthright in this as she was in all things.

'It—he—looks too big.'

He shook his head.

'Fitted just fine the other day—on Neave Tor.'

Damn, he wished he hadn't thought of that day and how he'd taken her without a thought for her virginity or her finer feelings.

His blood was beginning to surge in a disconcerting way. He must stay in control, not allow himself to become immersed in the passion of the moment. Maintaining mental clarity was imperative; as was redeeming himself in her eyes—and his own.

He reached for her hand before he could dwell on her expression that had fleetingly looked like fear. He'd hurt her that day and again on their wedding night and if he did it again now he'd want to slit his own throat. And he certainly would not be tempted to try making love to her again.

Please God, he could behave like the gentleman he'd been raised to be.

Drawing her closer, he placed her hand against his swollen cock and watched as her eyes glowed with wonder. Her fingers felt like velvet against his straining flesh, cool and tantalizing.

'Don't be afraid to hold him firmly, to stroke him, caress him. He'll be deeply responsive to such treatment.'

His voice sounded like something from the bottom of a tin of rusty nails, his throat tense with anticipation. Incredibly, he registered nothing had ever felt more arousing than her tentative, curious—loving—touch.

'Jassie!'

Her name was a groan torn from his throat and she snatched her hand back and stared up at him.

'What?'

'What? You don't know what that does to a man?'

She shook her head, her gaze never leaving his. His innocent Jassie—and he'd had the utter gall to thrash her and practically rape her. She'd bring him to his knees yet.

Irresistible Jassie.

Cupping her head, he held her for his kiss and almost immediately her arms slid up his body to clasp at the back of his neck. He was lost. If there'd ever been a moment when he could turn back the tide of his need for her it was long gone. Her mouth was a sweet moist cavern of temptation, and he delved hungrily, tasting, savoring the sweetness and intense flavor of her desire—for him. Gently he turned and laid her back on the bed, their mouths still clinging, their hands roaming, seeking, discovering. He wanted to bless her, everywhere, with his mouth. He drifted kisses across the top of her lip, along the bridge of her beautiful straight little nose, and up onto her forehead.

'Oh Rogan,' she moaned, her fingers spearing into his hair and gripping his scalp. She was so deeply responsive and he'd scarcely begun searching out the erogenous zones of her body. Sweat popped out on his forehead but he was determined tonight should be all about Jassie. His own needs were of no import.

Pressing her back onto the bed, he trailed his mouth and tongue down her neck and onto the soft plane of her chest. He aimed straight for a straining breast, and closed his mouth over it, suckling firmly. Jassie cried out, her shoulders coming up off the mattress as she thrust her breasts urgently upwards, needing more. Nothing loath, Rogan intensified the suckling until Jassie was moaning incoherently and writhing beneath him in a manner guaranteed to boil his blood.

'God Jassie. You're so hot! Do you like that? Do you?'

'Ooohh! Oohhhh!'

Rogan lifted his head and immediately she was dragging at his hair in an effort to get him to return to his ministrations. She was so sexy.

'Answer me my darling. Do you like me suckling you?'

'Yes! Rogan, I love it! Can't you tell?'

He couldn't hold back a chuckle.

'I just need for you to tell me what you like—and what you don't. If I do something you don't like, please tell me and I'll stop—I hope.'

'I like everything you do. I want you to do everything a man can do to a woman. I need to know how it feels, how everything feels, Rogan! Please show me.'

'God, Jass, you're so beautiful.'

He lowered his head, circled each nipple with his tongue then suckled deeply one more time on each before licking and tasting his way down to her belly-button. Here he stopped and rimmed the indent repeatedly with his tongue until she was breathless with giggling. It was a beautiful sound. He wasn't used to laughter during sex. Perhaps this could make the difference. He had to stay in the moment, stay conscious this was Jassie—whom he loved more than life itself.

'Rogan, that tickles!'

Laughing, he kissed across her belly and then trailed moisture down and into the dark golden curls at the apex of her thighs. Her hands grasped his hair and he could feel her rising up to watch him.

'R—Rogan, what are you doing?' she whispered hoarsely.

'I'm loving you, Jass,' he said gently, looking up and pushing her back down onto the pillows. Her face was flushed and her hair a glorious tangle about her head and knowing he'd done that for her filled him with intense joy. 'You want to know. I want to show you. Just as your touch on my cock excites me, so does my touch here in your quim excite you. Let me show you.'

'But—but—you're going to put your mouth—there?'

'I am, my love.'

'But—'

'Relax, Jassie. One day you might try putting your mouth on my cock. I guarantee we will both enjoy the experience. Just as I intend to enjoy the taste and texture of you and the glory of bringing you to a climax with my ministrations.'

'Climax?'

'Like on Neave Tor, when I made you feel good after—after.'

'Oh! And you—you like doing that with your mouth?'

'God, yes!'

Jassie finally dropped her head back onto the pillows.

'I really liked what you did on the Tor—after. I'd like to cl—climax again.'

'Good. Then relax and open for me.'

Gently he urged her heels up towards her buttocks and pressed her knees down to the mattress and kneeling before her he stopped to fully appreciate the picture she made, laid open for his delectation—at last. He bent his head to taste of her nectar. Opening her folds with his thumbs, he slid one into her moist channel and began swirling within her, relishing her moans and trembles, reveling in the vibration of her passion through his body. With his tongue he continued to stimulate the bud that would drive her over the edge to ecstasy, his own body poised in anticipation.

She couldn't lay still, she couldn't be silent and she couldn't stop her body from arching up towards his mouth, pleading, begging for more. She was everything he'd known she would be.

'Rogan, Rogan please don't stop! I feel—I feel—Oh God, I feel as if I'm going to blow apart! Rogan!'

'Hush, my darling,' he growled against her quim. 'Relax and just let it happen. Enjoy.'

Dear God! I want you—with me! Please—please Rogan, I need you—inside me—please—I *need* you to—'

It was as if the blood stopped flowing in her veins—and his. His whole body stilled, shuddered, and he slowly raised his head to glare unseeingly at her. When her blood started pumping again it was pure panic. Oh God, his eyes. They were leached of all color, silvery mirrors of white fury. His mouth that but a moment before had visited such pleasure on her, had thinned and twisted in raging ugliness and he rose unsteadily to his feet, casting about, looking for something.

Suddenly he reached down, gripped her arm and hauled her over to the ottoman where he'd tossed his clothes.

'R—R—'

She wanted to tell him she loved him; that it would be all right, even though she wasn't sure it would be, but her throat was closed with terror. No words would form. He whipped his neck cloth out from under the pile of clothing and swiftly and expertly bound her wrists together then wrapping the rest of the cloth round her head he tied off the ends so her hands were flattened against her mouth. What if she couldn't breathe?

She tried to yell his name against her hands, but only a garbled high pitched moaning came out. Should she fight? Before she could decide one way or the other he'd tipped her across the edge of the bed again and landed the first heavy slap across her naked buttocks.

It's not me he's punishing, she cried in her head. It's not me. It's nothing I did—at least—oh God! She'd begged. He'd stolen her sanity with his sensual onslaught on her body and she'd become pure instinct, pure ecstatic response—and she'd begged.

The slaps on her skin were getting heavier, the sting unbearable, and tears spurted from her eyes. She tried to twist away from him but he grabbed her hair and held her in place and thrashed her until she wondered if she'd even be able to stand afterwards, let alone sit.

'Fucking slut!' he suddenly yelled. 'I'll teach you to respect a man's decision. I *will* teach you respect if it's the last thing I do! Fucking bitch!'

Just when Jassie was fearing she might black out, the wild flailing of his hand stopped and he roughly spread her legs and thrust his cock deep. She thought she'd die of the ugliness of it, of the terrible grief ripping through her body for this man who, by his own words, would never make love to her again after this. The pain of that knowledge was far greater than any he'd inflicted. His body stiffened in orgasm, straining and spasming deep within her as he groaned out his release.

For a moment the only sound was her own ugly deep sobbing, the only movement her convulsive gasps for breath. Rogan held himself deep within her, his body rigid and straining. Then slowly she felt him soften and sink away from her. She wanted to listen, to hear the moment he returned to himself but she couldn't stop the moaning gasps wracking her being. She wanted to tell him she loved him—loved him still—unconditionally—and she would the moment he released her.

He didn't yell as she'd thought he would. But he did swear. At least she presumed he was swearing. The string of words that left his mouth in a dreadful hiss, were words she'd never heard before. Then he was tearing at the cloth binding her hands against her face and dropping to his backside on the bed he hauled her into his arms and rocked them both. Gradually she realized the tears running down her face were no longer just her own.

'Dear God, Jassie. I should be hung for this. What manner of beast have I become? Oh Jassie, Jassie, Jassie.'

His voice faded into a soft moan as his hands ran caressingly over her body, massaging her wrists, her hair, her backside.

'Not ever again, Jass. Never.'

Every word sank into her gut as if she swallowed balls of lead. Anything she might've said was swallowed in the devastation of it. How was she going to bear it? How could they ever show their love for one another? How would they ever have children? An heir for Windermere? Her sobs became silent shudders through her body and forming words was still nigh impossible. But she had to tell him, make him understand—

Slowly she unfurled her body within his arms and reached up to clasp her hands about his neck and hold his cheek against hers.

'It wasn't your fault, Rogan.—You told me not to—not to beg, but I did.—It wasn't your fault! I love you. It changes nothing!—I love you!'

She could hear the desperation in her voice, feel the rigidity of his body and the futility of it all sapped away the last of her energy.

'Oh Rogan! Please don't leave me.'

'I must, my love. This can never happen again.'

Gently he laid her back in the bed and covered her.

'Wait here,' he whispered.

As if she could go anywhere! She was naked, so weak and hurt she didn't think she could even walk. What in God's name was she to do? She couldn't let him go. How could the dream she'd cherished almost half her life have become such a horrendous reality?

She tried to tell herself she wished she'd left things as they were, but nothing could make her wish she could go back to being Miss Jassie Carlisle. She was now who she'd always been meant to be, Rogan Wyldefell's wife. Nothing he could do would make her wish anything different.

He was back, pulling the bedding away from her body.

'Turn over,' he murmured.

When she did as he bid, he began rubbing lavender infused oil into her buttocks and every now and then she felt the hot splash of a tear falling on the backs of her legs. Perhaps even if she couldn't have left things as they were for herself, she really should have for Rogan's sake.

She'd had no idea her willfulness and wantonness would cause him such suffering.

'Sit up and drink this,' he murmured. 'It's a very weak dose of laudanum. It'll help you sleep. As I said at dinner this evening, I'll return to London tomorrow.'

'No!' Jassie swung over to glare up at him. 'Don't leave me! There's talk enough already. We need to be seen together, at least in public, Rogan. Please stay. I won't tease you further. I begin to understand that by so doing I've hurt you unbearably. I love you. I love you, Rogan.'

The tears spurted from her eyes again and her attempt at being stern or immovable dissolved in another woeful fit of weeping.

'I need you.'

He just shook his head at her, and began inching away until he was on his feet and covering her body with the blankets again.

'No Jassie. I'm not what you need. I'm not what any woman needs and it is *because* I love you that I must stay away from you.'

Rogan tapped lightly at his mother's door and entered at her call. Closing the door at his back, he stood and allowed his gaze to lock with that of the frail woman framed by the jonquil silk pillow shams. Her hair, once as dark as his was almost white but her eyes still glowed as brightly blue as his own.

'Rogan?'

'Morning Mama,' he murmured. 'I hope I didn't wake you?'

'No, son. Lucy has just gone to get my hot chocolate. Do you want a cup also?'

'No thank you, Mama. I'll have breakfast shortly and be on my way.'

As she started to struggle to sit more upright, he strode across to help, plumping the pillows behind her. She smiled her thanks and patted the edge of the bed. He sat, hoping the tension thrumming through his body was not transferring itself to her.

'You're still going to London? But you promised! And what about opening day and the ball? What about Jassie?'

Feeling sweat beading his forehead, he swiped a hand across it and closed his eyes for a moment. Then knowing he couldn't fool his mother even if he wanted to try, he said, 'It's because of Jassie, I'm going.'

She reached out and urgently gripped his arm.

'Windermere?'

He squeezed his eyes closed against her piercing anxiety and dropped his head back, seeking relief from the constriction that bound his chest as he thought of Jassie.

'It's no good, Mama. I'll only hurt her more if I stay. Go ahead and organize the opening day shoot and the ball. I know you don't need me here for the organizing part. I'll arrive back on the evening of the 11th with some friends. I'll invite anyone I can think of and let you know the numbers. Will that be all right?'

She nodded and continued to anxiously scan his countenance.

'Is Jassie all right?'

'I guess. But I hurt her again last night—and still she tells me she loves me. I can't do this to her, Mama. It's not right. It's like I revert, become someone else entirely and I've no control over it—no control over *him.*'

Her hand slid down his arm and her fragile fingers entwined with his.

'There must be something you can do. Somewhere you can go for help?'

'Where, Mama? Just tell me where and I'll go there.'

'I don't know,' she whispered and the hopelessness in her voice was almost his undoing.

'I have to go. I—need to get away. I'll send word, and I'll see you on the 11th.'

He stood, bent to briefly salute her forehead and left the room before he lost control and cried more of the helpless bloody tears that had flowed from him last night. It wasn't right. None of it. And thinking to end his worthless life wasn't right either. Surely he had more strength of character than that.

Bart found him at the breakfast table pushing kippers round his plate trying to pretend he might eat them.

'So we're off then?'

'I was thinking it might be best if you stayed and helped Jassie and Mama organize the house party. I think they'll have more need of you than I, at this point.'

'You think?' Bart asked, loading his plate with kippers and potato hollandaise and adding a side of hot bread slices. 'What are you planning to do in London?'

'Stay away from Jassie. It's easier if I'm there and she's here.'

'Nothing's changed then?'

Rogan's fist suddenly slammed the table, making the cutlery and condiments dance and earning him a shocked frown from his secretary.

In grim silence, Bart rounded the table and sat down beside Rogan.

'There must be somebody who can help you,' Bart muttered. 'What about that new physician everyone's talking about in the city. Dr. Pen— Penwarden, I think? Hasn't he had some success?'

'With women in a state of depression, I believe. Hardly the same situation,' Rogan snarled. 'Who can help a thirty-six-year-old man who reverts to a single night in time fifteen years before? It's—sick! It's crazy! It's unheard of!—Damn it. I need to get going. I'll be back on the evening of the 11ᵗʰ—with a party of shooters, I have no doubt. Can I leave everything else in your hands?'

'That's what you pay me for,' Bart muttered, round a forkful of kippers.

With a sigh, Rogan left the room and headed for the study. He'd ride to London where surely there would be some distraction that'd take his mind off the pain looking out of Jassie's eyes through her tears last night—and her broken words, 'I love you.'

When Jassie didn't go down for breakfast, Fran came up and knocked on her door.

'Can I come in, Jass?'

'Of course.'

Fran entered, a worried frown creasing her brow as she crossed the room and peered at Jassie, still snuggling into her pillows.

'Are you all right? It's not like you to miss breakfast unless you're out riding.'

'The weather isn't really conducive to riding this morning,' Jassie defended her unusual sloth.

'You've ridden in worse weather than this before,' Fran commented almost acidly as she settled on the end of the bed. 'Where's Windermere?'

'I—haven't seen him this morning.'

'So you saw him last night?'

Jassie couldn't help it. Her stupid weak eyes started leaking the moment she thought of last night—and Windermere. *Never again.* She nodded.

Fran didn't speak. Just waited, head a little to one side, like a blackbird listening for a worm. Even that quirky analogy couldn't lift her spirits.

'He said if he hurt me then he'd never make love to me again.'

'And?'

'Never again.'

'Sweet Jesus, Jassie! He's right! He can't go about abusing you like that. He knows it. Why don't you see it?'

Jassie swallowed, dragged herself upright with the sheet round her shoulders and raised watery eyes to Fran.

'Because I love him. I've loved him and longed for his love since as long as I can remember. It was to be so perfect. But nothing could be less perfect than this.—I won't give up, Fran!'

'Are you—all right, Jass? He hasn't hurt you really badly?'

'No, Fran dear. Don't fuss. I'll survive. I just had to keep reminding myself it wasn't me he was punishing—and in a way that helps. But what I can't bear is for us to have a—a sexless marriage!'

Jassie looked at her friend and gave thanks for her sanguinity, her experience and her willingness to discuss pretty much anything.

'Warning! Forbidden discussion approaching.'

Fran's face broke into the silly grin those words always evoked and Jassie struggled to mirror it. She *would* smile and force herself to simulate happiness.

'Did—did Abingdon ever give you—a 'climax'?'

Fran's cheeks brightened and she looked as if it was only determination keeping her chin up.

'Don't answer that if you'd rather not,' Jassie whispered.

'It's all right,' Fran said firmly. 'It's just—you might have to explain what a 'climax' is. Which probably means Abingdon *didn't* give me one!'

Her cheeks were now a fiery red, and Jassie suspected it was as much from fury in thinking about her erstwhile husband, as from embarrassment.

'Abingdon was usually in his cups when he—when he came to me. He would just—put it in—and buck and thrust a bit—and that was it. I hated it. But if I tried to deny him he would become violent. It was easier to—just—submit. From what I've been able to glean from Addy it can be much better than that but—I really wouldn't know.'

'Do you think you might ever marry again?'

Fran twisted the stuff of her gown between agitated fingers, then muttered under her breath and smoothed the cloth over her knees.

'I never used to but—recently—'

'Recently—you've been thinking about it? Who?'

Jassie sat upright and pulled the sheet up under her chin.

'B—Bart Matthews kissed me last night.'

'And?'

She'd been right to push them towards each other!

'And—I liked it! Now you know my *most terrible* secret so you have to tell me yours. Did Windermere give you a *climax*?'

Jassie covered her hot cheeks with her hands but grinned openly at Fran.

'He did that. A few times now. So you see it's not all bad. In fact that part is—I can't describe it! But it's amazing. I couldn't bear it if that's all I'm to have. It'd be so unfair.—Oh Fran, what am I to do?'

'Why don't you go up to London and talk to Addy? Or better still, talk to Madame Lady Bouvier.'

'*Madame* Lady Bouvier. T—talk to a—*Madame?*'

Jassie felt her eyes growing wider at the thought.

'Yes. Addy says Lady Bouvier is a true lady. I only met her once, but I would have to agree. She seemed really—*nice*. Addy says she really cares about her girls and their clients and if any of the—clients—have issues or problems—like Windermere, I guess—she will talk with them and help them. Maybe she can help Windermere?'

Jassie felt something inside her shift; something dark and obscured was suddenly flooded with light.

'I'm so glad you came to live with me, Fran. You have often shown me the way when I've been hopelessly mired in ignorance and fear. Maybe Madame Lady Bouvier can help *me*! We've seen those books in the library, but still they don't really tell us what to do—how to p— pleasure a man—how to *love him*—physically. If you wanted to seduce Bart Matthews, would you know how?'

Fran stared back at her, blue eyes bright with laughter and cheeks as rosy as apples.

'Good heavens no! Such subjects did not feature in the curriculum taught by Miss Golding, our governess at Abingdon—nor at Mrs. Rabone's either!'

Jassie laughed outright.

'Even trying to imagine that is beyond me!—But I really think it is too bad we're expected to go into marriage knowing *nothing!* I just know Windermere meant what he said. He'll do all in his power to stay away from me after last night. But I also know if I knew *what to do* he wouldn't be able to refuse me. That's what happened on Neave Tor. But I more or less fell off the horse and into his arms then and he was still recovering from the shock of what I'd just asked him. If I were to slip into his bed when he was asleep—what would I do then?'

'Addy would help you with that, I'm sure. But it's really Lady Bouvier you should talk to about Windermere's problem. She's totally discreet.'

'Thank you, Fran! You're wonderful. I'll need a new gown for the ball so I shall go to London and visit La Callista to order the finest she has to offer—and while I'm there I shall pay a visit to a very exclusive *bawdy house*!'

'What about all the planning for the ball and the opening day?'

'I'll spend this afternoon planning everything with Lady O and travel up to London tomorrow. I can take all the lists with me and can write invitations and deliver them much easier there than here.'

At last Fran's brow cleared and she allowed herself to be cajoled.

'Would you mind very much staying and helping Lady O?' Jassie asked.

Fran nodded.

'I've no love for London. I admit I'd far rather remain here at the Abbey. But will you be all right on your own?'

'I'll have Ruby with me—and Windermere.'

Fran made a comical moue.

'You think?'

'I intend to make my visit to Lady Bouvier my first priority and then I intend to seduce Windermere. The less people in the house the better. And I shall ensure the footman, Randall, accompanies us so he will occupy Ruby! She seems to enjoy his company.'

'Then you'd better get up,' Fran said in her best school ma'am imitation. 'Shall I send Ruby to you? The sooner she starts packing the better.'

'Yes,' Jassie agreed, bouncing out of bed. 'Before you came in I was thinking I'd just hibernate here all day. Everything seemed so hopeless. Now—I can't wait to be in London! Write down your measurements for me and I'll bring back a ball gown for you too. What color do you want?'

Fran's eyes went dreamy then she said, 'Deep rose pink. I had a gown in that color once and I always felt—beautiful—when I wore it.'

Jassie smiled.

'I can just imagine it with your dark hair and soft coloring. Barton Matthews won't be able to resist you!'

Fran flushed deeply and hurried from the room.

It was late afternoon of 26th July when Jassie stepped down from the carriage into Berkeley Square in London and sighed with relief for the end of the journey.

'Here at last, my Lady,' Ruby said, surreptitiously stretching the kinks from her back. Relief was stark in her maid's voice and Jassie felt much the same. But any relief she felt was deeply overlaid by the anxiety gnawing at her stomach as she wondered whether Windermere was at home and how he'd react to her arrival.

Randall appeared at the door and let the steps down, offering Jassie his hand to alight. As her feet met the pavement she drew a letter from her reticule.

'As soon as you've brought in all the luggage, would you deliver this for me please, Randall, and wait for a reply?'

'Certainly, my Lady,' Randall responded, with a nod of his head.

Deacon, Windermere's long serving town butler, met her at the top of the steps.

'Welcome home, my Lady. We're all very happy to finally be able to call you Lady Windermere.'

Jassie smiled up at the very correct and formal appearing butler.

'Please don't go all formal on me, Deacon. I'm still the same Miss Jassie you caught sliding down the banister during my first season. And I might just do it again. It was fun!'

Deacon's stern dark brows twitched.

'I really would prefer not to have to explain to his Lordship how you came to break your neck in the hall, my Lady.'

Jassie grinned openly and tapped his arm with the glove she'd just removed.

'Don't be so stuffy, Deacon. I'm sorry I didn't send word of my arrival, but there was no time. So please don't throw the staff into a fanfare. Any room that is ready will suit me just fine.'

'Your Ladyship's rooms have been readied since your engagement was announced. Mrs. Beecham will show you up. If you'll just wait a moment while I fetch her.'

Randall and another footman had gone ahead with the luggage, Ruby accompanying them. Her skirts had just disappeared into the hallway above when Deacon returned with Mrs. Beecham.

'My Lady!' the plump housekeeper cried. 'We're so pleased to have you here. And may I congratulate you on your marriage.'

'Thank you Mrs. Beecham. I pray I've not put you out by arriving unexpectedly.'

'We've awaited your arrival on a daily basis ever since the wedding,' the housekeeper responded with a sunny smile. 'It'll be ever so good to have some life in the old place.'

Jassie turned back to Deacon.

'Is my husband at home, Deacon?'

'No, my Lady. He went out after luncheon as is his habit and we do not expect him home until quite late. Though if he knows you're here—'

'He doesn't,' Jassie quickly intercepted. 'And I'd prefer you not enlighten him on that point.'

Deacon's stance stiffened and his eyebrows rose. Her gaze flitting from one to the other of these trusted retainers, she said, 'Please. I'm sure there is very little you're unaware of that concerns your master and so you'll probably know marriage was not really in his plans. He'll not be best pleased to find me here and I'd rather apprise him of that fact in my own time—and my own way. I intend for us to have a real marriage and we won't if it's left up to him.'

Neither retainer batted an eyelid at her very personal disclosure. They'd become used to her outspoken nature and grown very fond of her during her first season spent in Windermere House under the old countess's sponsorship. Nor had Jassie ever doubted their loyalty and affection for their master and his mother. They'd do anything to promote the happiness of either.

'The master has been deeply troubled for many years,' Mrs. Beecham opined softly as they mounted the wide marble staircase. 'And if anyone can help him overcome that trouble, it be you, Miss Jassie— my Lady.'

'Thank you Mrs. Beecham. It's kind of you to say so. I certainly hope I may live up to your belief in me. I certainly intend to try.'

'You will, my Lady, you will,' said the housekeeper as she ushered Jassie into the Countess's suite. 'This is your private sitting room and your bedroom is through there. There is a door from your dressing room that connects with the Earl's rooms.'

Jassie looked into the bedroom to find Ruby already sorting through the trunks and hanging her clothes.

'Thank you Mrs. Beecham. I would so love a bath if it could be arranged. And if Windermere is not expected home for dinner perhaps Ruby and I could just have a tray up here? No fuss. Just something simple followed by a pot of tea.'

'Certainly, my Lady.'

Having donned a soft violet dressing robe over her ivory silk nightgown, Jassie was partaking of a solitary breakfast at the small table in the bow window of her sitting room next morning and happily perusing the invitation from Lady Bouvier to a private luncheon with her at Half Moon Street the following day, when her sitting room door crashed open and Windermere strode in.

'What the devil are you trying to do to me, Jassie? Do I have to leave the country to keep my distance from you? You know what I'm capable of now. Why do you do this to me? To you?—To us?'

With the last two words his voice had lowered, the dark angry slash of his brows softened and he was almost pleading.

Jassie came abruptly to her feet, not yet used to confronting Windermere in a temper. That she had the awareness to slip the letter into the pocket of her robe she'd marvel at later, for by his very presence she was thrown into a fever of conflicting emotions. There was fear and that she knew and understood, but there was also excitement, a wild carousing of her blood that surged through her veins in an agony of anticipation although she couldn't have said precisely what it was she anticipated.

But she did know what she wanted and she must ruthlessly suppress that wanting if she was to have any hope of reconciling her husband to her presence in London for at least a few days without him haring off back to Windermere or to another of his estates entirely.

She busied her hands drawing her robe more closely about her body to keep from reaching out to caress the black frown from his forehead, coax laughter into the deep blue eyes, press her lips to that chiseled mouth and feel it move against hers. She wanted, in the worst way, to feel his arms about her, his body pressing urgently into hers, showing how much he desired her—as she desired him.

Smoothing her hands down the all-enveloping robe and then folding them firmly across her abdomen, she tilted her chin and fixed him with a steady glare. Perhaps if she could convince him she was unaffected by his presence he would be also.

'Both Fran and I are in need of new gowns for the ball and there are very few days in which to accomplish that. I have invitations to the house party which I intend to deliver personally. It'd also be a very good thing if we were to be seen at an event or two while I'm here to allay the gossip that will surely have us estranged as soon as we're wed. To that end perhaps we could attend the theatre or the opera this evening. That would serve to show people we're in town and garner some calls and invitations. There'll be no shortage, I should imagine, as the best hostesses will be falling over each other to be the first to have us attend their affairs since we're probably the latest *on dit*. We need only accept a couple, just so we're seen about together.'

Jassie snapped her mouth shut, astonished at her own inventive thinking. She hadn't expected Windermere so early in the day nor really thought through what she'd say to him. Her mind had been too taken up with the discussion she meant to have with Madame Lady Bouvier.

Windermere had come to a halt just inside her door and was staring at her as if she'd suddenly sprouted an extra head.

'You want to go to the theatre? Or the opera?'

'Well, yes! That surely is not so horrifying? Your mother still keeps her box at the theatre. The season is almost over so there shouldn't be too much of a crush. It'd look very odd, Rogan, if it became known we were both in town but were never seen together—anywhere.'

As she watched, he seemed to consciously calm himself, flexing his shoulders, sliding his hands into his trouser pockets and rocking back and forth on his heels. Turning abruptly for the door, he said, 'Very well then. We shall attend the theatre tonight. I'll see you at dinner.'

He left almost as precipitately as he'd arrived and Jassie found herself staring at the empty doorway and wishing Fran had come with her after all, so she could share her moment of triumph. She was going to the theatre with Windermere, her husband. She could only hope she would be able to focus on the play, whatever it might be. Edmund Keane was sure to be acting and she longed to see what all the fuss over the actor was about.

Hugging herself to keep from flinging her arms out and dancing about the room, she returned to the table and settled herself on the chair. She couldn't afford to lose her focus now. She must steady her nerves and concentrate on her visit to Madame Lady Bouvier. If there was to be any hope of a normal marriage with Windermere she had to keep her mind on the goal, not on the immediate gratification of all her desires. Desires that were so much more defined and urgent, now she'd finally broken through her husband's carefully shored up walls of resistance. For while there were aspects of being a wife to Windermere she definitely didn't want to perpetuate, there were others her body hummed to experience again.

Her thoughts roamed back to their encounter of a few minutes before. Where had he been going? In typical understated Windermere fashion, he'd been dressed for the city. Slate grey pantaloons and waistcoat, snowy white linen and a blue superfine cutaway jacket should have softened the hard masculinity of his body, the harsh angularity of his cheekbones and jaw, and the searing blue of his gaze; the woman-clenching impact of his total maleness.

But it didn't. Jassie felt again the magnetism as he'd stood just inside the door, every fiber of her being yearning towards him. While her eyes drank in the height, the breadth, the burning glitter of his luminous blue eyes, her heart had stuttered at the obvious tension holding him rigid.

She understood that terrible tension all too well; understood his desire for her was as deeply entrenched as her own for him. Also, she now understood what her presence did to him; her determination to overstep the bounds he'd set for them, all those years ago. The torment she'd unleashed on Rogan she'd visited equally on herself.

The wonder of it was she'd managed not to launch herself at the cruelly tempting masculine feast that was her husband.

Her husband! Dear God, such exquisite torture after all the years of hiding and suppressing her feelings for him, to finally know the intense gratification of shared sexual freedom and release. She couldn't countenance the agony of trying to return to that repressed self, of trying to stuff all the Pandora-like ecstasies and horrors back into the darkness and confinement Windermere begged of her.

But she would—for a while longer at least—until she'd talked to Madame Lady Bouvier. Fran had painted the woman as some kind of counsellor in the realms of bedroom activities and she was pinning her hopes on Fran having it right. Today must be put aside for a visit to the modiste, La Callista, for there was little more than a week until they needed the gowns for the ball. But Madame Lady Bouvier had agreed to see her tomorrow.

And she must send a note round to invite Sheri and Aunt Gussy to dinner and the theatre thereafter. She could only hope they weren't irrevocably promised for somewhere else tonight. They'd provide the perfect distraction for her and Windermere and maybe they'd be able to get through the evening without destroying one another completely.

Where had his demure Jassie gone? In all the years since she'd emerged from the schoolroom, she'd never been one to flaunt her feminine charms. In fact he'd been intensely grateful for the fact she'd never worn the style of evening gown to display more than it concealed or succumbed to the foolish fad for wearing dampened muslin gowns that clearly exposed the feminine form within. But she was now his wife and, apparently, no longer felt constrained by the need for maidenly modesty. The expanse of ivory skin with the satin sheen of rose petals shown off by the low décolletage of the bronze silk gown the exact shade of her eyes, was alluring.

More than alluring. Mesmerizing. Notwithstanding they were seated in a box at the theatre with more eyes trained on them than he cared to contemplate, he wanted to touch that skin, experience the silkiness of it, not only with his fingers but with his mouth. He wanted, in the worst way, to expose the soft peach-rose nipples he knew lurked just below the neckline of the gown reflecting the light of a thousand candles in the delicate crystal beading.

Devil take it! Where was Wolverton? And Baxendene? They'd both maintained they'd attend the theatre tonight for the express purpose of making their bow to his wife. He leant forward to scan the milling patrons below, wishing himself anywhere but trapped in this box with Jassie. Or so he told himself. Parts of him were very pleased indeed and he couldn't help wondering how long his mind could hold out over the demands of his body.

At least they weren't alone. Aunt Gussy and Lady Sherida had joined them for dinner and ridden in the carriage with them to the theatre. Was Jassie just as anxious not to be alone with him? He wished he could believe that, but was more inclined to think she but bided her time, confident in discarding the fichu that would once have modestly filled the neckline of her gown she was tempting him to abandon his plans to steer clear of their bed.

And she was!

He turned his attention to Lady Augusta, her patrician nose quivering as she commented on that 'hussy, Harriette Wilson, parading about on the arm of the Prince Regent as if she were a lady of the highest connections instead of the cast-off paramour of any number of titled gentlemen'. Any distraction would do and he followed her disdainful gaze to where indeed the two promenaded with all the aplomb of the righteous.

Rogan felt his lips twitch a little but thought it best to restrain his smile. Aunt Gussy would no doubt be openly scathing should he appear to condone such scandalous behavior, regardless that she was, to all intents, his guest. Glancing back at his companions he found Jassie watching him with eyes glowing and reflecting back to him the light from the brilliant chandeliers. He had the distinct impression she could scarcely contain her excitement. Worse, he was having trouble disengaging from the shimmering desire blazing beneath the dancing reflections of light. He was being drawn into the heart of the flame, into the inferno of his desire for Jassie.

A knock on the door of their box was followed by the entry of his second cousins, Dominic Beresford, the Duke of Wolverton with Hades Delacourte, the Earl of Baxendene hard on his heels.

Rogan leapt to his feet, relief flowing through him like a tide and set about convincing his friends they should remain through the duration of the play. It wasn't difficult. Bax's smoky grey orbs glowed with a typical satanic gleam as they settled on the ethereal and remote perfection of Lady Sherida Dearing. Almost of an age with Jassie, she could definitely be considered 'on the shelf', was rumored to have turned away more than a dozen hopeful swains and had thus acquired for herself the title of 'the Heavenly Iceberg'. The wonder of it was the Great Bax, as the ton had dubbed him, hadn't decided to consider the challenge long before this. That Sheri was unimpressed or possibly even unaware the Great Bax had settled in beside her with a very predatory gleam in his eye boded for an interesting evening.

Interesting enough, Rogan hoped, to keep his mind off his wife. Except, Wolverton chose to arrange his elegance in the seat at Jassie's other side after possessing himself of her hand and lightly touching her fingertips with his lips, thereby assuring Rogan's attention stayed very firmly on his wife throughout the entire three acts of the play.

He knew he was building her expectations for later but he couldn't keep his arm from the back of her chair or his fingers from caressing the warm skin of her back and shoulders. Never in all the years he'd longed for her had he allowed himself such liberties with her person, but forced into close proximity, emboldened by the darkness during the acts and goaded by the presence of a hungering Wolverton on her other side, he'd succumbed.

To the allure of Jassie. To the lash of jealousy. She was his; had always been his and he was beyond knowing what he'd do if now, after having known her as his wife, he lost her to Wolverton or some other man who could love her as she should be loved.

Because it was pointless deluding himself. Now Jassie had experienced the physical act of love her body would crave more and if he could not, would not, give it to her how could he condemn her if she sought that satisfaction elsewhere? How could he condemn Wolverton if he followed where his heart surely tempted him?

As soon as the lights came up for the last time, Rogan was on his feet and ushering his companions out of the theatre. He had to get Jassie home and himself away from the house before he gave in to the ugly jumble of his needs and desires; before he could instigate a pathetic argument by asking Jassie whether Wolverton had pressed his thigh against hers or dared to lay his hand on her knee in the darkness during the play.

As he handed Jassie up into the carriage after Lady Augusta and Sheri, he turned to Wolverton and Baxendene.

'Where are you headed now?'

Bax just shrugged but Wolverton's mouth tensed and he muttered, 'Eagle Street. Good night, Rogue.'

Feeling the heat rising up his neck and his fists clenching, Rogan turned abruptly and leapt up into the carriage, slamming the door and rapping on the roof with his cane as soon as he was seated beside Jassie.

Wolverton kept a mistress in Eagle Street whom he patronized far too infrequently for her liking. That he felt the need to visit her now told Rogan more than he needed to know about how his friend had been affected by sitting alongside his wife through the interminable and gloomy rendition of Hamlet.

He could barely find civil, let alone intelligent comments to add to those offered by his aunt, who was quite outspoken in her praise for Keane's acting abilities and criticism of the rumored eccentricities of his personal life. Little caring to offer an opinion on either, he was very relieved to see the ladies to their door in Grosvenor Square although that meant he was now alone with Jassie in the carriage.

His brain told him to sit on the opposite seat just vacated by their guests, but his body, with a will of its own, returned to the space beside Jassie. His feeling of victory for having left a gap between them was short-lived for his beautiful wife immediately slid along the smooth leather so her thigh fit snugly against his. As if pulled by a puppeteer's strings, his arm slid behind her shoulders and she turned to snuggle against his chest with a purring sigh that stole the last shred of his sanity.

He lowered his head, breathing in the scent of violets from her silken curls, then cupping her face he lifted it for his kiss, a harsh groan of surrender vibrating through his being.

'Jassie.'

Her name was a prayer on his lips as he lifted away for a breath then sank back into her honeyed softness. This was where she should always have been; in his arms as she was in his heart.

Her arms stole round his neck, a soft little moan sounded from the back of her throat and Rogan felt the blood draining from all points of his body to coalesce in his groin. It was a long time since he'd tried making love to a woman in a carriage and memory said it was difficult and uncomfortable but the only memory retained by the body cells located in his groin was the ecstasy of the release. And, that Jassie was the woman in his arms ensured no other cells in his body were any longer functioning.

Tilting her head, he traced kisses down the heated velvet of her neck, sinking into the hollow at her collar bone and tasting her with his tongue.

'God, Jass, you taste like ambrosia.'

Her head fell back on her shoulders and she surrendered the creamy expanse of skin to his ravening mouth. Nipping and laving, he tasted his way to the glittering edge of her bodice, aware his breathing had become choppy, and his hands were trembling.

But not enough to keep him from sliding his fingers beneath the cloth to find the nipples that had so tormented his imagination earlier in the evening.

'Oh Rogan,' Jassie murmured, her voice a husky cry in the darkness, strumming across his nerves as if she'd physically touched him. 'Yesss—'

Reverently he freed one perfect globe and then the other and lowered his head to feast with a noisy greed he was beyond controlling. This woman was his everything, the very air he breathed. Her body melted in his arms and he gently began easing her back onto the seat and groping for the hem of her silken skirts.

His only awareness other than Jassie abandoned to his loving was the burning, swollen ache in his trousers. He was going to have to open his falls soon or the buttons would pop. But not yet.

'Rogan!' she gasped as his fingers found her heat. 'Oh Rogan—oh God!'

He covered her quivering lips with his, thrusting his tongue into her moist mouth just as his cock was planning to plunge between her nether lips. Damn, he wanted inside her. Now.

It took a long minute to realize the carriage had stopped. Bloody hell!

Coming upright, he hauled Jassie up after him, dragging her cloak up around her shoulders from where it had fallen behind her.

'Hold it together,' he whispered fiercely as it seemed she was still lost in the haze of sensual longing that had engulfed them both and was unaware of the imminent exposure they faced. She'd scarcely come upright when the door opened and Deacon's face filled the aperture.

'Jassie!' Rogan rasped again. 'Have you got hold of your cloak?'

Lord knows what the very proper butler's reaction would be if he got a glimpse of the Countess's beautiful breasts propped wickedly atop the edge of her bodice.

'Oh—um—oh yes,' Jassie managed at last and Rogan stepped down from the carriage, blocking Deacon's view of the interior and hopefully giving Jassie a few more precious seconds to pull her senses together. He turned to offer her his hand and she took a moment to fumble the edges of her cloak tightly together with one hand before carefully extending the other to clasp his as she stepped from the carriage. When she reached the pavement her body sagged against him as if she'd lost all stiffening in her limbs. Keeping a wary eye on the silken gloved fingers clenched on the edges of the cloak he nodded his thanks to Deacon and with his arm firmly about Jassie's waist, he almost carried her up the stairs and into the blazing light from the chandelier in the ornate marble floored entry of Windermere House.

With a curt word of thanks, he dismissed the butler the moment he closed the door at their backs.

'We'll see ourselves upstairs.'

Thankfully Deacon understood better than to linger and the moment they were alone, Rogan turned Jassie to face him. Her eyes, as she glanced up at him, shone with the dancing light of a thousand candles and her mouth quivered, lips red and glistening from his kisses. It was all he could do not to lower his hand to his groin to try and ease the agony that was going to seriously impair his ability to walk for some time.

But walk he would. Out of that door. Away from Windermere House. Away from the gut-wrenching temptation that was the Countess of Windermere.

His Countess. His wife.

She'd read his intention in his eyes and her own began to darken, blaze with a shimmering, stormy fire. Her hand shot out to grasp his wrist, the velvet cloak falling with a soft swish to the marble floor, exposing her in all her bare-breasted glory.

'Don't-do-this-to-me-Rogan,' she hissed. 'Don't—'

'I have to, Jass. Can't you see? I have to!'

'No! You don't! I want you to make love to me, Rogan! I—I *need* you!'

Oh God! Wrenching his wrist from her clutching fingers he ran for the door.

'I'll not hurt you again. *I will not!*'

Slamming the door at his back, he ran headlong down the stairs to yell at the coachman who had the carriage almost to the corner of Charles Street ready to turn for the Mews at the back of the house. Rather than wait for the equipage to back up and risk Jassie chasing after him, for he had no doubt she was capable of it in her present state, he ran down the street, opened the door of the carriage and hauled himself in, calling, 'Chapel Street.'

The Matrix Club was the only place he would find surcease for the terrible need riding him, to prevent him from going back into the house and taking everything Jassie was offering; to lose himself in her unconditional love; to use her—abuse her. Not ever again. Please God, his determination wouldn't weaken whatever provocation his beautiful wife posed for him.

He would save her from what he was.

Her head would explode with trying to hold in the dreadful invective she wanted to hurl after Windermere as the door slammed on his fleeing form. How dare he leave her like this, her whole body on fire for him, her knees shaking with desire, her mind filled with visions, hopes—desperation. Slowly she brought her hands up to cover her naked breasts, the nipples throbbing and hard, still remembering the pull of his lips, the rasp of his teeth.

'Damn you, Rogan Wyldefell,' she whispered into the clanging silence of the elegant hall as she slowly bent and groped for her cloak. What did she have to do, she wondered, as she dragged the voluminous velvet garment around her. What could she do to make him understand she could cope with most anything he might do to her—*so long as he loved her?*

Walking unsteadily to the base of the broad sweeping staircase, she gripped the balustrade and with slow dragging steps pulled herself upwards, still clutching at the edges of her cloak. She traversed the echoing hallway to their rooms at the end, her feet slowing as she passed the door to Windermere's room. Briefly she thought of throwing herself onto his bed and awaiting him there, begging him to continue from where they'd left off in the carriage. But she still retained a modicum of the lady-like strictures his mother had striven to instill in her and she continued past, finally having the presence of mind to make an effort towards pressing her aching breasts back into the confines of her bodice.

By the time she reached her own room she wanted nothing more than to curl into a fetal ball in her bed and seek shelter beneath the covers; hide from this needy, craving mess she'd become. If she'd understood it could be like this she might have made a different decision about seducing Rogan into making love to her—perhaps. Though truth was, she still felt her life had more purpose than it had held in all her previous twenty-five years.

Dismissing Ruby as soon as the maid had unlaced her gown and corset, Jassie threw her clothes over the ottoman, pulled on a creamy lace and satin night rail and crawled into her bed. Her hands crept down her body and in an effort to cool the throbbing heat she cupped her mons while she rocked and alternately cursed Windermere and the unknown woman who'd made him as he was.

Rogan handed his cane, hat and gloves to Knightsborough's butler before passing into the Red Salon where the patrons of the Matrix Club gathered to socialize, play hazard or whist, and set up their liaisons for the evening. There was an accepted format to the procedure by way of an ironic nod to polite society. One accepted a drink from a waiter who appeared at the moment of arrival. One surveyed the gathering, assessing the proclivities of those present and selecting those who would best suit one's needs. After a few moments, in which those already in the room also had the chance to consider one's person and appeal, it was then acceptable to engage the selected ones in conversation and by an exquisitely polite exchange of ambiguous questions which were likely to garner equally ambiguous answers, a language all members understood perfectly, a mutual agreement to engage was reached—by two or more parties depending on the needs expressed.

Rogan was not in a mood to be polite or patient. Tossing back a brandy and slamming the glass down on the startled waiter's tray, he swept the room with a glance, giving a grunt of satisfaction when he saw Mrs. Marcia Grey, sitting quietly in her usual dim corner, playing patience. The demure, almost puritanical air she contrived to portray was a complete solecism. They had partnered one another on a few occasions and she would suit his purpose admirably. She craved pain as an alcoholic craves strong drink.

She was also a stickler for the protocols but tonight he had no patience for such. If she baulked he was likely to begin her punishment right here in the public room. Not that any member of the Club would be unduly shocked by such an event, but he was not into putting his alter ego on display as many other members did. For even after all the years he'd suffered the affliction, he still viewed it as shameful, something to be hidden, even denied if he'd thought he could manage it.

Reaching her table, he gripped her wrist, arresting her dealing of the cards.

'I need you now,' he growled. 'Don't argue or I'll start your punishment right here.'

Something almost feral flashed in the pale eyes before she dropped her gaze and let the cards fall from her fingers. He was dimly aware of his cousin rising to his feet from where he'd been deep in conversation with the aging Lord Basingstoke and an elegant, bold-looking woman he'd not seen before. The Earl of Knightsborough watched over his patrons like a broody hen and he'd be keenly aware the Earl of Windermere was not his usual urbane self tonight, if only for the fact he'd neither greeted nor acknowledged anyone, least of all his kinsman and host, before homing in on his quarry. Knightsborough took pride in the fact his was a house where high society's misfits could safely indulge their damaged psyches, the perfect cover for his hidden identity as Chief of a clandestine courier service. Tonight he could probably be forgiven for considering Windermere a threat to that general safety.

Curling his fingers like a manacle around Marcia Grey's wrist, Rogan turned his back on Knightsborough and marched his willing victim out of the room and along the hallway until he found a vacant room. He slammed the door at his back and dragged her round to face him.

'Beg,' he snarled. Someone had to pay for what he'd lost, what he'd become.

What he couldn't have with Jassie.

Heat flared in her eyes, fleeting, glittering, before her lashes drooped, hiding her excitement from him. Slowly she sagged to her knees.

'Please, Master, please, please punish me. Please—'

She'd started in a whisper but ended in a desperate husky cry.

Starting somewhere in the center of his brain, a shudder ripped through his body leaving his hands tingling, trembling; the familiar onset of the madness. Not even trying to hold it at bay, he wrenched her to her feet and pushed her over a long padded stool, roughly but loosely wrapping the attached ropes around her wrists.

The miasma that had threatened at the edges of his consciousness when Jassie had cried out her need of him finally flooded the whole of his being.

'Oh I will punish you, you fucking whore,' he growled and threw her skirts up over her head, exposing the perfect satiny cheeks of her backside.

Thwack! A whimper.

Thwack! Another whimper.

Thwack! More of a cry this time.

As the volume of her cries increased so did the power of his arm. He lost track of time, had made the bitch come several times and punished her for it, had thrashed her till his arm ached and still she sobbed and begged for more. Something suddenly snapped in his brain and between one thwack and the next, he stopped, reeled across the room, wrenched the door open and almost fell into Knightsborough's arms.

'What the fuck?'

Knightsborough staggered a little, but made no effort to disengage. In fact his fists clenched round Rogan's triceps and for a moment they stood, eyeball to eyeball. To lash out was his first instinct, but the fleeting thought he'd thrashed all the strength out of his arm, stopped him acting on it.

He closed his eyes and dragged in air through his nostrils, then shook himself free of Knightsborough's grip just as the man loosened it.

'Brandy. In my rooms. Now.'

The habit of obedience to his seniors was ingrained and tight-lipped, Rogan followed the Knight, as he was often called, down a side hall and into the sumptuous apartment that gave no hint of the high office its owner held in the War Ministry and yet was more often than not the room from which many a secret mission was begun.

Back stiff and jaw clenched, Rogan stood just inside the door and watched while his cousin poured a generous measure of brandy into two crystal snifters and took a slow sip of one before handing the other to Rogan.

'Do I need to go back and release Mrs. Grey?'

Rogan concentrated on the movement of the liquor as he swirled the glass, then closed his eyes and tossed the entire nip down his throat. While he savored the burn and the warm serenity of it pervading his brain he allowed his memory to roam back to the room he'd just left. The peculiar thing was, while he had no control over what he did when the madness took him, he could always remember his actions in vivid and bitter detail afterwards. Slowly he shook his head.

'She wasn't tied.'

The Knight just nodded, his dark auburn hair gleaming like polished copper in the lamplight. Then he fetched the decanter and refilled Rogan's glass.

'Sit,' he said, waving his snifter towards the pair of leather wing chairs by the hearth.

The brandy was doing its work, filtering through Rogan's veins and nerve by nerve easing the tension that had held him in its grip. He sank gratefully into the chair as the familiar weakness that always followed one of his mindless tangents seeped through his body. Resting his head against the back of the chair he closed his eyes and simply concentrated on breathing. It was that or confront the sickening reality of who he was.

'What was that about?' the Knight demanded, sinking into the other chair. 'You didn't even fuck her. Just thrashed her—like some demented demon of vengeance.'

Demon of vengeance. Exactly.

'That's what it felt like. What it always feels like. I have to punish the fucking bitch. I'll never be free of it until I can—'

'What?'

'—break her.'

'*Break* her? Who? The *lady* you've just taken to wife?'

The pain when he thought of treating Jassie that way was like a giant fist wrenching at his intestines.

'God no,' he growled. 'I *will not* visit this festering toxicity on her. That's why I'm here—and she's at home—needing a husband in her bed—and laying some very choice epithets at my door.—What a bloody mess!'

The Knight was five years his senior and revered by all members of the Club as a fount of wise counsel in all matters pertaining to life. He was the one person Rogan knew who would understand the demons that drove him. He had to wonder why he'd never thought of baring his soul to his cousin before.

Knightsborough leant forward and threw a shovelful of coal onto the fire then downed the rest of his brandy and set the glass aside. For several moments they sat in silence watching the sparks lift and vanish up the chimney.

Finally the Knight tilted his head sideways and rested his cheek on his hand while he surveyed Rogan thoughtfully, his black eyes reflecting the dancing light of the fire.

'You know Rogue, I've seen some seriously fucked up people in my time, through my job and this place. They probably don't come much more fucked up than me. But I've always taken the view that every man—and woman—carries his own baggage, his own secrets and lives with them as best he can. T'is not my place to condemn, or even question who they are, or why they are as they are. But something about you has always struck me as—perverse. Most men who become involved at Matrix are comfortable with who they are and how they are; some of them outright enjoy it. I've never felt that about you. There's no real satisfaction for you in the scenarios you act out here. If anything, the scowl you wear is deeper and darker when you leave than it is when you arrive. In fact I would say you hate yourself and what you do. Would I be right?'

'Of course you're right!' The words exploded out of Rogan before he could think to monitor them. 'Would you be happy if you could never marry the woman you love because every time you make love to her you're going to end up thrashing her to within an inch of her life?'

He was shouting, breathing heavy, and his hands were curling into fists ready to hit something.

Knightsborough didn't even flinch. In fact he nodded as if finally understanding the answer to a puzzle, but he just kept observing Rogan through those almost mesmerizing black eyes.

'But you have married her.'

Rogan stared back at the Knight for a moment then leant forward and dropped his head onto his hands. There was no answer to that accusation except the obvious.

'I'm guessing you weren't always this way, Rogue, that something happened? Who is the woman you're trying to punish?'

A shudder pulsed through Rogan's body as he thought of the answer to that question, thought of telling the story again.

'Have you ever talked to anyone about this?' Knightsborough persisted when Rogan still didn't answer.

'Never, until the day I married Jassie. Since then—Bloody hell, Knight!'

'Another brandy, I think,' Knightsborough said calmly, rising to his feet.

Settled back in his chair once he'd refreshed both snifters, he said, 'In my position as your superior in the War Office, if we were in the military, I'd have the authority of your Commanding Officer and I'm invoking that authority now. Tell me who you need to punish—and why.'

Dropping his hands, Rogan just stared into the flames as he tried to breathe away the familiar panic that rose whenever he thought of exposing this ugliness that had somehow come to define what he was. It was a good sign—perhaps—he hadn't already left the room running, or maybe just a reflection of the respect he felt for Ajax Beresford, Earl of Knightsborough.

'Over the years, Rogue, I've counselled many men for many reasons and I've never revealed to another living soul one word of those discussions. Whatever is said in this room never leaves it.'

Jassie Carlisle had a lot to answer for. For sixteen years he'd held the secret of that humiliating night close, deep and dark, but since that day on Neave Tor he'd already exposed the filthy depravity of it three times and here he was, backed yet again into a corner from which the only way out meant telling it again. If there was any truth to the old saying 'a problem shared is a problem halved' his should be miniscule by now. Hah!

'She was the wife of a professor when I was up at Oxford—'

Once started, the story flowed and he found he no longer worried about censoring it. None of it would have shocked the Knight anyway. His cousin just sat watching and listening in silence, one perfectly manicured finger tapping absently on the arm of his chair.

When he'd finished, having explained enough his listener could not fail to understand what had transpired in the carriage on the way home from the theatre and in what state he'd left Jassie, Knightsborough silently reached for the decanter and filled Rogan's snifter again.

'This brandy is from the Bonaparte's personal cellar. It's good stuff. You should probably savor it instead of swilling it down like cheap gin.'

Rogan's fingers tightened on the stem of the glass. He'd been about to do exactly that, craving the distraction of the burn as the neat liquor poured down his throat. He cupped his hand round the bowl of the snifter and gently swirled it instead. With a nod and a smile, Knightsborough appreciated the aroma of his own brandy then raised his glass.

'I'd like to propose a toast to a rare and courageous woman.—To your wife, Windermere.'

Slowly Rogan raised his own glass and murmured, 'To Jassie.'

They both drank then the Earl wrestled his big body into a more comfortable position and fixed Rogan with a steady gaze.

'Has Lady Jassinda ever given you reason to doubt her word?'

Rogan shook his head.

'Then why do you not take her at her word. Love her. Trust her?'

'Because I don't trust myself,' Rogan snarled. 'What if I really hurt her? Actually damaged her. I have no control over my actions when I'm like that. Haven't you heard anything I've said, Knight?'

'Every word—and nowhere have I heard you've done anything other than subject a lady to a thrashing. It's not life-threatening.—And some women actually enjoy it. The Countess may prove to be just such a one.'

Unable to stay still any longer, Rogan surged to his feet and began pacing.

212 · JEN YATESnz

'That's the problem, Knight! I cannot abide a woman who *enjoys* being thrashed. The more she enjoys it the more I have to punish her to try and make her see the error of her ways! Can you not see? And if Jassie allows me to treat her in that way she may come to enjoy it and then I shall hate the woman I love!'

'Calm down, Rogue. I do see. You're making a crazy kind of sense. Have you considered involving a third party?'

'What do you mean?'

'Having someone stationed outside the room to—intervene—at the appropriate moment.'

Rogan felt his whole being clench and his breathing shallow out.

'Do you seriously consider that to be a solution, some pervert outside the door while I make love to my *wife*, a *lady*?'

'Perhaps not,' Knightsborough conceded, rubbing a hand across his forehead. 'Though I'm still inclined to think you should trust the Countess, Windermere. It's the only way you're going to get an heir.'

Rogan stopped pacing and turned to face the Earl. A heavy sense of despair settled round the region of his heart, a dead hopelessness the more draining because for just a moment he'd allowed himself to believe Knightsborough might have a solution. There was no way he would consider humiliating Jassie by having some voyeur listening outside their bedroom door, much less primed to intervene. Damn it all to hell!

'I need to get out of London for a few days but I have to be back at Windermere for Grouse Shooting. My dear mama has decided it's time the Abbey put on her glad rags and hosted an Opening Day Shoot and a ball as we used to do. You're invited of course.—And now—the Ministry must need something couriered to Paris. I could be there and back before opening day.'

Anything to keep him away from Jassie.

Dark auburn hooked brows clashed above Knightsborough's nose and he unfolded his long body to stand with one elbow on the mantelpiece and his severe gaze pinning Rogan to the spot.

'I thought Hadleigh would have told you. You're married. You have made your last run for the War office.'

At eleven of the clock next day, Jassie stepped from a hackney onto the cobbles at the corner of Half Moon Street. With the hood of her cloak drawn closely about her face she walked briskly along to number nineteen, a discreetly elegant house with nothing but the number above the lintel to differentiate it from any other in the street. Mounting the few steps she banged the highly polished brass knocker. Ruby had been scandalized her mistress meant to venture out into London on her own but Jassie had no intention of divulging the details of this excursion to anyone—except Windermere or Fran.

Her heart beat a wild tattoo in her chest as she waited for someone to answer her knock and she was again assailed by the fierce wish she'd insisted Fran accompany her to London. But before total panic could take over and set her to scurrying away from the door, it was opened by a bent and wizened old woman gowned in black silk and Brussels lace who glared up at her from under bristling white brows without saying a word.

Jassie swallowed, thought of invoking her status as the Countess of Windermere and just as quickly discarded the idea. It would be quite foolhardy to bring unwanted attention to herself after having gone to such trouble to appear unexceptional and anonymous.

'Good morning. I am Miss B—Brown and I have an appointment with Lady Bouvier for eleven of the clock.'

The old woman inclined her head and said, 'You're expected. Come this way.'

The house was preternaturally quiet apart from the distant clatter of utensils somewhere in the back regions. Jassie supposed, because of the nature of the place, most of the residents slept late. There was also an air of quiet luxury about the house, a thick piled carpet on the floor, silk wall panels and a collection of exquisite Sèvres urns in niches along the walls.

Up a curving marble staircase, they traversed another long hallway past several reception rooms to a set of double doors at the end. The old woman knocked and pushed the doors open, ushering Jassie through ahead of her.

'Miss Brown has arrived, my Lady,' she said and stepped back into the hallway, closing the door.

What had she been expecting? If she was honest with herself she'd envisioned an exotic creature, voluptuous, statuesque maybe, with a cloud of artificially enhanced black hair, smoldering black eyes and lips painted a vibrant and provocative shade of red. She had not expected this exquisite creature who, notwithstanding her natural beauty, could have been Jassie's own mother.

Reclining on a chaise longue in the window bay overlooking a small but entrancing garden courtyard was a woman with eyes more gold than hazel and hair almost the shade of Jassie's own. The soft hint of grey at her temples added a touch of elegance rather than detracting from the picture she made. As the regal creature rose from the chaise in welcome, golden eyes liquid with emotion and curved unpainted lips trembling just a little, Jassie had the strange sensation of gazing into a mirror that reflected back to her the woman she would be a quarter of a century on.

Her shock must have shown clearly on her face, Jassie thought, as Lady Bouvier's mouth twitched and compressed and in the blink of an eye her soft welcoming expression had hardened and Jassie caught a glimpse of the type of woman she'd expected to see—a woman tempered to blue steel by the vicissitudes of her life.

'Lady Bouvier?' Jassie all but stuttered.

'You've found me.'

The response was coldly accusatory to Jassie's ears and the feeling of teetering on the edge of an unstable cliff shivered across her nerve endings.

'What do you mean? Oh! Maybe it was wrong of me to come! I'm sorry but my friend, Lady Francine Abingdon was—was certain you'd be able to help me—'

'Help? You've come for my help?'

Was that uncertainty she heard in the woman's voice?

'Yes.—Oh!' Jassie felt heat pour into her cheeks. 'You thought I was—looking for—w—employment?'

A golden brow cocked in definite challenge.

'What is your real name?'

'M—my real name?' Jassie parroted, stalling for time, hoping some clever and plausible response would occur to her.

The mobile mouth twitched into a knowing smile.

'You see, I would swear that you would have to be the daughter of my—of Lady Mary Swinbourne, as became Mrs. Robert Carlisle. And if that is the case you have recently become the Countess of Windermere.'

Jassie's jaw dropped, knowing it was pointless to try and maintain her masquerade as the modest Miss Brown.

'You—you knew my mother?'

'She never spoke of me, I presume?'

'Well—no! At least—I don't think so.'

The Madame sighed and her mouth drooped a little but then she straightened her shoulders and tightened her lips.

'I don't know why that should hurt me. It's no more than I expected, no more than I deserved by making the decision I did. She would've been foolish to do anything other than sweep all taint of me from her life—as you should.'

Jassie opened her mouth to speak then closed it again. For what could she say? She tried again.

'Who are you?'

The words shot out of her mouth before she could rethink them, because really, she needed to know if she was to make any sense of the conversation.

'I'm Mary's twin sister, Isabelle.'

Jassie's legs suddenly lost all strength and she groped towards a chair pulled up to a small table to the side of the chaise. Her heart was pounding in her chest like a runaway horse and she had the momentary feeling her head was going to shatter.

'You're my mother's *twin sister?*'

'Yes.'

'But—I thought there was no one. When Philip died—I thought I was—alone.'

Lady Bouvier sat back on the chaise and gazed at Jassie for a moment and then she said, 'It probably would have been fairer for me to leave you in ignorance for you can never claim me as a relative. No, your mother had the right of it. I've been unforgivably selfish in revealing myself to you.'

Jassie came suddenly to her feet, all effects of the shock overcome by the swelling of delight in her breast. She had *someone*. She had family.

'You could not have hidden it from me I think, for I already felt as if I were looking into a mirror showing the future and how I would look—twenty or so years from now. You are so like me. But more than that, you cannot know what it means to me to find I have—family. I have felt so alone since—since Philip died.'

'Philip?'

'Philip. My brother—half-brother actually. He was killed at the Battle of Vitoria.'

Suddenly the older woman surged upward with her arms outstretched.

'Come,' she begged huskily and Jassie rose and went willingly into her embrace.

They clung for long moments while Jassie fought to make sense of the cascade of her feelings. Shock. Sadness. Joy.

Isabelle Bouvier sat her back gently on the chair and settled herself once again on the chaise.

'Did you really only come to me seeking help?'

'Yes! Oh—what I really came for has gone right out of my head—and that's saying something,' Jassie added ruefully. 'Does anyone else know about you? The Dowager Countess of Windermere for instance?'

Isabelle's smile was bright and appreciative.

'You're not slow, are you my dear? Yes, Olwynne and I keep in regular contact. Have done ever since Mary died. There was little I could do that wouldn't bring scandal on your head and so I settled for watching over you from afar—through Olwynne. She's been a loyal friend to you all these years.'

'I know that,' Jassie answered with a warm smile. 'I remember little of my own mother except she always seemed to be sickly and in bed. If I had any mothering at all it came from Lady O—and Morrie, Miss Morrison my governess. And I had the best big brother a girl could have and—I had Rogan. I've always had Rogan—until I went and spoiled it. He was my—everything—after Philip was killed and still—I—risked that most precious of friendships because I wanted—more. But—Lady Bouvier—'

'Call me Belle—please. And may I call you Jassinda?'

'Jassie,' Jassie breathed, her heart swelling with the realization she'd found someone who shared the same ancestry that she did. It was quite startling how important she suddenly understood that was; how it gave her a sense of having an anchor. 'I want to know all about you, about my mother, your family—my family! Why—why did you become a—a Madame? I always understood the comfort with which we lived was due entirely to Mama's 'portion' as it were. You must have had the same?'

Isabelle regarded her with a level gaze then drew in a breath as if trying to settle her nerves.

'I'm sorry! I shouldn't have asked that—', Jassie began but Isabelle smiled resolutely.

'You have every right to know my story, Jassie, just as I'm going to demand yours shortly. Mary was the quiet one. I—was not. Our mother died when we were in our early teens and our father's spinster aunt came to live with us. Aunt Elisabet was a martinet and I hated her with a vengeance. Mary had no trouble for she was ever happy to be organized and guided by someone else. I was not! The only useful thing that woman ever said to me was said under extreme duress after I'd turned away yet another suitor for my hand. I was destined for scandal, she said. She wanted nothing more than to get us off her hands and collect the stipend and cottage at Brighton my father had promised her.

'I had no desire to marry and hand my life and fortune, modest as it was, to a man who then had the right to use it, and myself, as he saw fit. And so I told the old besom and she lost all semblance of the well-bred manners she'd been trying to instill in us. I was an ungrateful little bitch and spoilt for choice, apparently. I had no appreciation of the chances I had by being well-dowered and fair of face and figure as well. I would end up alone and a law unto myself and therefore the butt of cruel innuendo if I didn't accept someone soon. Already twenty-one, I was in danger of finding myself on the shelf and ignored by any but the most ineligible. Worse I was influencing Mary to follow my example.

'Truth was, we were having too much fun and had no inclination to bring it to an end. Then Father died—in the card room at White's. He left Aunt Elisabet exactly what she wanted, the cottage in Brighton and an income. As soon as all was settled and with Father barely cold in his grave she left for Brighton, leaving us to fend for ourselves. We deserved no better for we were totally ungrateful for what she had sacrificed these last few years.

'Mary was appalled and accepted the next suitor who offered for her hand, for of course we were now in possession of a comfortable fortune each. We argued terribly for I thought her very foolish. Your father was no great catch, though he was nice enough. But Mary was suddenly terrified she'd be left on the shelf and this, to her, was the worst outcome she could envisage for her life. Whereas the opposite was true for me. My resolve hardened once Mary was gone and the gossip began. I was accounted a diamond of the first water in those days, as was Mary. But immediately I signified my intention to live alone and take charge of my own household a subtle change came over how I was received in society. In fact, it became obvious in a very short time I was no longer *being* received in society!

'Mary begged me to come and live with her, but I could imagine nothing worse than being buried alive in that rustic little village where you grew up. I'd never lived anywhere but London. I will not deny I made some foolish decisions and was as naive and foolish as Aunt Elisabet had often told me I was. But when my best friend accused me of making cow's eyes at her husband and told me several other of our friends were also concerned, I decided I would *be* what they were painting me. And I started with my friend's husband. He was a very handsome and unscrupulous rake. There were a couple more and of course I found myself totally ostracized by the female half of the beau monde—but extremely popular with the other half. And so the idea was born. I became a courtesan—available only to the wealthy. When that palled, I set up this place. Mary never forgave me and that is really my only regret—and that I could not be the comfort to you I should've been on her death. I've lived my life on my own terms and if I had the chance to relive it I'd probably do the same again. So there you have the story of your only living relative, Jassie. I'm unashamedly beyond the pale and you may never be seen in public with me or ever let it be known you even know me, much less acknowledge the relationship, but I shall be very honored if we can continue our association as we have begun it—quietly over a cup of tea from time to time, if you will it.'

'I will definitely be back. You'll probably get sick of me!'

Isabelle laughed outright; a beautiful bell-like sound with husky undertones Jassie knew must drive men mad.

'Now,' she continued hurriedly before Jassie could comment further, 'I'm going to call for a fresh pot of tea and some of Cook's fruit tartlets and you are going to tell me how you thought I might be of help to you.'

It was well into the afternoon when Jassie pulled her cloak about her once more and stepped into the hackney cab a footman had called to the house for her. She and Windermere were attending a dinner and musical evening at Lady Augusta's that night and Jassie couldn't help but wonder if she was capable of containing this secret or the incredible happiness filling her because of it.

Windermere was waiting in the hall when Jassie came downstairs, the light from the chandelier highlighting strands of silver in the dark sheen of his hair. He was reading the cards and invitations left by callers during the day and as she watched his jaw clenched, a frown settled on his brow and agitated fingers suddenly ploughed through the perfect arrangement of his hair. Now he looked like her Rogan and less like the perfect example of an Earl.

'What is bothering you?' Jassie asked as she crossed the expanse of floor to where he stood at the hallstand. The subtle hint of a spicy cologne and an underlying scent that was essentially Windermere teased Jassie's senses, tempting her to reach out and touch the tensing jaw-line. She clasped one hand firmly within the other. They were going out together. She would be content with that.

'Are you expecting we'll attend all of these affairs?'

He sounded as if she was asking him to step into a den of hungry lions. Though there were times such a description would apply to society events, she thought wryly.

'Not at all,' Jassie responded, taking the pile of cards from him and quickly sifting through them. 'Pick a couple you think you might be able to tolerate and I'll send apologies to the rest. I intend to return to Windermere as soon as I have things properly in train with La Callista. I feel bad about leaving all the arrangements for the house party to Mama and Fran. Our gowns can be posted down to Windermere when they're ready.'

The dark frown cleared from Windermere's brow and his features relaxed into an almost smile. Jassie wished she knew whether that was because she'd let him off the social hook or because she was returning to Windermere. She very much feared it was the latter.

'Are we ready then?' he asked.

'Yes.'

Deacon appeared to open the door and see them down the stairs and into the carriage. Rogan's gloved hand was firm beneath her elbow as she stepped up and slid onto the leather seat. The heated imprint of it remained long after she'd arranged her skirts and he'd settled himself across from her—as far away from her as the confines of the carriage would allow.

Jassie tightened her lips, but couldn't maintain her displeasure for long. She was still shimmering internally with delight from the disclosures of the day and now, as they travelled confined alone together, was the perfect time to relate them to her husband.

He was only a dark outline in the gloom of the interior but she could feel the tension flowing from him as no doubt, he was remembering the last time they were alone together in the carriage. Her cheeks burned and she was grateful for the concealment of the darkness. He was sitting so straight and rigid, every inch the haughty aristocrat he was. Did he think he could hold her at bay by pretending a cold, autocratic demeanor?

A smile curved her lips, the same smile she'd been trying to suppress since leaving Half Moon Street, as she considered how best to shock him out of his determinedly stiff aloofness.

'I visited a house of ill repute today, a very exclusive house of ill repute but—a brothel nevertheless.'

If anything, Windermere's posture became even more rigid, but his eyes glittered through the darkness at her.

'Why?'

If she were not so filled with happiness and outright delight she might have felt the harsh staccato question like a gunshot to her chest. But she was inured to all shafts and arrows tonight. Her smile widened

as it had wanted to ever since leaving her aunt's house that afternoon—
her *aunt's* house.

'I went to seek help for—us.'

Ignoring the choked sound from the opposite seat, she continued,
'and I found *so much more than I was looking for!* Rogan, did you know
my mother had a twin sister?'

His mouth, which had hung open for a moment, snapped shut then
opened again to utter one syllable.

'No.'

'Well, she did—and the reason we've never heard of her is because
she's the Madame of a brothel, Madame Lady Bouvier to be exact.'

Windermere suddenly sat forward with his arms across his knees,
his gaze intent.

'Madame Lady Bouvier? Good God! I should've seen that for
myself. The likeness is uncanny. I'd even wondered at it when I met her
once.—So that's why happiness is shimmering around you like
starlight? You've found a relative!'

Only Rogan, who knew her so well, would glide effortlessly over
the potential drama of finding *such* a relative to the essential heart of
the matter for Jassie. Whoever the woman was, she was family and to
one without family it was like stumbling upon a rich vein of gold.

She just nodded—and beamed.

Windermere's teeth gleamed white as he grinned back at her for a
brief moment then all too soon his happiness for her was gone and he
was pressing his shoulders back against the seat and glaring at her
through the gloom.

'You know you can never acknowledge her or be seen with her. The
likeness is quite obvious now you point it out. And—'

Suddenly his whole body stiffened and she could feel the waves of
tension flowing off him.

'—what the devil were you thinking to visit such a place?'

'Clearly you have visited or you'd not know the lady I speak of! She told me she rarely goes out socially anymore.—Dear God, Rogan! Have you—slept—with my *aunt*?'

It struck her as odd the thought had the power to chill her bones when the lurid story Rogan had revealed to her in the Greek Folly at Windermere had merely made her heart ache for him.

'Your aunt is a little old for me and has not plied her trade in a good while, I believe. She leaves that to her 'ladies'. But you haven't answered my question as to *why* you went if you didn't already know she was your aunt?'

'Why did *you* visit her *if you didn't know she was my aunt?*'

She wished she could see him more clearly to gauge his reactions. But his voice, when it snapped back at her, was indication enough.

'I'm a man. I need no other reason to visit a brothel.—*Why*?'

Feeling her temper rising, Jassie sucked down a few breaths.

'I told you. I hoped she might have some advice for me—for us. Apparently she has a reputation for helping people with problems of a—um—intimate—nature.'

'I see.—And did she?'

She wasn't about to tell him Belle had advised that her most likely asset in luring Windermere was her innocence; that a man enjoyed knowing he was the one to teach her how to please him—and she was very conscious she was not pleasing him at all at this moment. Waves of cold fury were rolling towards her from the other side of the carriage.

'Rogan, Aunt Isabelle knows a lot about such things and is happy to share her knowledge with those in need. If you would just go and talk with her she said she may be able to offer some suggestions.'

Silence. The air in the carriage was almost at freezing point and Jassie knew pulling her velvet evening cloak closer about her shoulders would make little difference. She'd never felt so distanced from Windermere and the chill was causing her heart to stutter in panic.

'You-told-her-about-me?'

She couldn't deny it, no matter the terror induced by the ugly, alien tone of his voice.

'Yes.'

There was no response. His silhouette seemed to darken and become one with the shadows that filled the carriage. Jassie had run out of bravado. She'd hurt him beyond redemption this time, betrayed his trust in her. Maybe she'd not actually promised to keep his story safe in her heart, but in trusting her with it she knew that had been implied. But she couldn't see how suppressing it was going to help either of them. And her decision to take control of her life—their lives—had not wavered. In fact, once she'd taken that first irrevocable step it was as if the changes had taken on a momentum of their own.

She could not, would not, go back to being that unawakened, miserable woman she'd been for the last nine years. *They* could not go back so they must go forward. And allowing the present impasse to stand was unthinkable. She would face whatever he threw at her but she had to keep seeking a way forward.

He didn't speak as he helped her from the carriage, nor as they sat opposite one another at Lady Augusta's table, although he chatted quite readily with Miss Cobden-Smythe who sat to his right and Lord Presterton on his left. Nor did he speak as they left the house and re-entered the carriage at the end of the evening, except to issue terse orders to the coachman to drop himself at White's and to 'see Her Ladyship home.'

She didn't see him again until the night of the 10th of August at Windermere Abbey.

Life had blown up in his face. Spectacularly—like a science experiment botched on a cosmic scale. In the space of a little more than three months he'd broken his vow never to marry; he'd broken his vow never to talk of the shameful liaison of his youth that had made him the man he was; and he'd broken his vow never to subject Jassie to his brand of loving, which could more properly be called abuse. Add to that the Ministry's refusal to send him on any more missions where he might die an honorable death and what did he have left?

A bloody mess!

And if he wanted to be picky he could lay the blame for all of it at Jassie's feet; at the dainty, sexy feet of his wife.

And in trying to escape from the ugly, emotional tangle of it all and trying to escape from her, he'd been spending day after day, night after night in gambling dens and flash houses, losing an unconscionable amount of money and risking a very dishonorable sort of death indeed.

He'd finally, as he'd often feared he would, given in to the kind of desperation that could steal a man's sanity—and his soul. Wolverton had tracked him down once again last night and hauled him out of the back room of some dingy gin parlor where he was on the verge of throwing a punch at the dodgy cove who'd come late into the game, swept the pot clean and then had the gall to leave the table without giving the rest of them the chance to win it back.

Dom had practically tossed him in the front door of Windermere House with instructions to his butler not to let him out again. He'd passed out in his study where he'd sat and sullenly drowned what was left of his consciousness in very expensive brandy.

And he felt like shit. He wished he'd brought Bart up to London after all so he'd have someone to abuse, or someone to abuse him, which was probably what he really required.

He took inventory. Sprawled on the leather couch in his study, he was still fully dressed, even to his boots. The only thing he'd removed was his neck cloth which was still draped around his neck, its ends dangling like a scarf.

The crystal brandy decanter lay on its side on the carpet, empty, though there didn't seem to be any spillage. Where was his glass? Had he been drinking straight from the bottle? Come to think of it, he smelled like brandy. Probably accounted for the dark stain down the front of his sadly wrinkled shirt.

Disgusted with himself, he struggled to sit upright and fell back, groaning with the agony of the hammers in his head.

A knock on the door heralded Deacon, his long face expressionless as always. Rogan couldn't help wondering what it would take to make his stoic butler lose his reserve and show emotion. The man would be formidable at poker!

'You are awake, my Lord.'

'I am, Deacon. Though I wish I weren't!'

'I took the liberty of bringing a—er—pick-me-up—as was recommended to me by Lord Biggleston's man. He swears it sets his Lordship up right and bright every morning—,' Deacon stopped to cough '—er—afternoon.'

'Biggleston's man?'

What had he become? Biggleston's name was a byword for sottishness.

'Well—I thought for sure the man would have a recipe and he assures me it's right efficacious—if not exactly palatable, my Lord. The trick is to down it in one.'

Deacon had gone to this trouble for him? How many nights now had he slept in his clothes on this damnable couch, insensible from excess of hard liquor?

And in a mood not one whit the better for it.

Silently Rogan held out his hand for the tumbler of cloudy liquid and tossed it back, not allowing himself to breathe until the last drop had slid down his throat. Handing the empty glass back to Deacon, he pushed himself heavily to his feet and stood for a moment to allow his spinning head to settle.

'Send Brixton to me upstairs—make that in ten minutes. I have a note to write first. I'll need someone to deliver it for me and to wait for a reply.'

'Very good, my Lord. Allen will be waiting in the hall when you're done writing and I'll send Brixton to await you upstairs.'

'Thanks, Deacon. Your—ah—consideration is appreciated. I apologize for causing concern.'

The man's habitual lugubrious expression almost softened and the head bowed infinitesimally.

'T'is my job, but if you don't mind me presuming on my long service to the Windermere's, my Lord, I'd just say there's no shame in seeking counsel when one is bedeviled and seeing no way forward.'

Rogan offered the older man a rueful smile. Deacon had served his father and had in fact entered service with his grandfather.

'You're right, Deacon. Pride is a damnably lonely bedfellow.'

'Indeed, my Lord. Will that be all?'

'Send a maid to clear up in here. Thank you, Deacon.'

'Of course, my Lord.'

Rogan sat at his desk and stared at the sheet of crested letter paper on the blotter. He'd written 'Madame Lady Bouvier' as the salutation but how to proceed? With a sigh, he scrawled a brief request for an interview as soon as possible, preferably this afternoon, signed, sealed and handed it to Allen, who waited in the hall, with instructions to await a reply and bring it to him immediately.

It was time for some changes—more changes—in his life. If there was anything he could do to ensure those changes included a happy marriage—any sort of marriage—with Jassie, then he had no choice but to pursue it.

Turning for the stairs, he had the startling realization his head was almost clear—and hope was sprouting like spring in his heart.

'Brixton,' he said as he strode into his rooms, 'are you still of a mind to be my full-time valet?'

'Yes, my Lord.' The ex-army major who limped from a leg wound sustained at Ciudad Rodrigo, drew himself up to his considerable height and for a moment Rogan thought the man would salute him. He was always impeccably turned out and acted in the capacity of a valet whenever Rogan resided in the capital long enough for it to matter.

'Good. There will be an increase in wages of course but I'll expect you to take complete responsibility for my appearance. Marriage has changed a few things. I'll be taking my seat in the House next session and will largely be dividing my time between here and Windermere. No more tripping out of the country. We travel down to the Abbey for Opening day. My mother, in her infinite wisdom, has decided we should host a house party, like in times past—with a ball. I should probably visit my tailor while I'm here and update my wardrobe somewhat. It never used to matter but it appears I may have to become a little more of a society animal.'

'Very good, my Lord.'

The man was hard pressed to keep his smile from becoming an out and out grin. Rogan knew he'd long wanted to take his master seriously in hand and now he had his wish.

'Right. A bath and a shave are my requirements right now.'

His new valet became a whirlwind of action, ordering up the bath, laying out soap and towels, shaving apparatus, and a clean suit of clothes.

Rogan was relaxing under the man's skilled hands, his face half shaved when a knock came at the door.

'Enter.'

'The reply to your note, my Lord.'

Allen crossed the room and handed him a dainty sheet of paper folded, sealed with pink wax and bearing the sweet scent of violets.

'Thanks, Allen. I'll call you if I need any further assistance.'

The man bowed out the door and Rogan realized with dismay his hand was almost trembling and although he tried to tell himself it was the result of too much alcohol last night, the truth of the matter was, he was filled with a tremulous hope Madame Lady Bouvier would have some miraculous wisdom that would help him overcome his obsession with punishment so he could truly make love to his wife.

'Hold the razor for a minute, Brixton.'

The man held the blade aloft while Rogan broke the seal and read the brief message within. She would see him at two o'clock that very afternoon. Crushing the note in his hand he laid his head back and closed his eyes.

With a sigh of satisfaction, he said, 'Proceed.'

Precisely at two Rogan was shown into a small, luxuriously appointed salon, the focus of which was a doll-like creature clothed entirely in lilac and seated near the window reading—a book of Byron's poems if he wasn't mistaken. Her likeness to Jassie was uncanny though she appeared to be of a more dainty build. It was like looking in one of those trick mirrors that distorted familiar features to look the same— but not.

'Lord Windermere,' she said, starting to rise.

'Please don't get up, Lady Bouvier,' he said after retrieving his sagging jaw. 'And since I believe I'm married to your niece you should more properly call me Rogan. The likeness is stunning—to Jassie and her late mother.'

He took the hand she raised to him and lifted it to his lips and she smiled—and he became aware her eyes were light, almost yellow, and suddenly she was nothing like his beautiful golden Jassie at all—more like a slightly faded counterfeit. Now able to block the mental distraction of the woman's appearance, he could focus again on the purpose of his visit.

And with that focus the claws of tension were back in his gut.

'Mary and I were identical twins. She was quieter and would never have done what I did. Not that I regret my choices, for I don't, except in so much as she never spoke to me again. We weren't as close as some twins for our personalities were so opposite—but I miss her. It was a great joy to receive a visit from Jassinda last week.'

'The pleasure was mutual. She feels the lack of family very keenly.'

Silver glinted in the immaculate golden coiffure as she dipped her head in acknowledgement.

'Please be seated, Rogan. You don't intend to keep her from me, then?'

'Of course not. It would be like trying to keep bees from nectar. Though in the interests of Jassie's standing in society I would request you to be excessively discreet. Besides, I love her too much to do anything so cruel. Her happiness is very important to me, which is why I'm here now. Nothing else would've dragged me through your door.'

'Nothing?' she asked archly, and for the first time he glimpsed the courtesan behind the sweet, ladylike facade.

Rogan returned her direct gaze with one of his own.

'You'd have soon turned me away, I think, if I'd sought relief for my—proclivities—here, which Jassie tells me she has disclosed to you.'

To his chagrin, heat raced along his cheekbones and he clenched his jaw in irritation.

The smile died from her eyes to be replaced by a more solemn expression.

'After hearing Jassie's explanation of your—'condition' I'd call it— I'd have to agree. But let's start right there. The term 'proclivity' implies it's a condition you're inclined towards and I gather that's not the case. It's more like something has been implanted in your psyche against your will. Would my assessment be correct?'

Rogan was impressed and, for a moment, even forgot the swords of tension slicing into his belly.

'You seem to have grasped the picture very accurately.'

Her smile flashed again and then she glanced down at the book still open on her lap. Carefully arranging the ribbon marker between the pages she set it on the small table at her elbow and clasped her hands loosely together.

Raising her gaze to his again, she said, 'And you've come to see whether I could help in this matter?'

'Truthfully? It was Jassie who came seeking help. When she suggested I visit you and admitted she'd disclosed my ugly story to you—I—suffice it to say I've not spoken to her since.'

The carefully shaped brows rose.

'Something changed your mind?'

'Other than being dragged out of one hell-hole or another by my friends night after night—and waking on the couch in my study with the devil's bells ringing in my head and the study reeking of spilt brandy, you mean?'

She nodded, sympathy shining in her eyes.

He didn't need sympathy, dammit. He needed help. He ground his teeth and tried to rein back his impatience.

'It became clear to me this morning when I found my butler had been so concerned he'd gone to the trouble of seeking out a remedy for hangovers, that something must change. Much already has and can never be undone. Therefore I have to find a way to live with those changes. I have to find a way to make new changes, to change the fundamental—beast—I have become so Jassie and I can have the kind of marriage I had once dreamed we would.'

'I guess producing an heir is of paramount importance?'

'To a degree. There are a couple of male cousins down the Windermere side of the family tree who could step into that role if I fail in that respect.'

'You could—,' she began then stopped and lowered her eyes to briefly examine the perfection of her manicure, though Rogan had the impression she wasn't really seeing it. 'Had you thought of asking someone else to sire your heir?'

'Someone else?' he asked, confused. Then as he studied her watchful expression he felt a terrible heat build inside him.

'You mean—ask someone else, a cousin perhaps, to sire the next heir to Windermere—on Jassie?'

A flicker of golden lashes indicated that was exactly what she'd been inferring. The heat flared into his brain and he started to push himself up out of the chair. He'd been wasting his time!

A cool, delicate hand clamped around his wrist.

'Clearly not. Please stay.'

She waited until he relaxed back onto the seat, though 'relaxed' was something he despaired of ever feeling again.

'I just need to know what's really important to you. Would I be right in thinking producing an heir is not your top priority then?'

Rogan took a moment to tamp down the murderous rage that had risen within him at the thought of some other bastard lying with Jassie, siring a child on her to be raised as his, Rogan's, son. It took another few deep breaths before he could unclench his jaw in order to speak.

'Producing an heir is important—of course.' He could admit to that much. 'But if my wife is to produce that heir then I will be its father!'

'And quite rightly so, Rogan,' Belle agreed soothingly. 'Perhaps you could enlighten me a little more as to what happens. Jassie says it's as if you change, become someone else and you don't really know what you're doing once you enter that state.'

Unable to stem the tide of agitation that flowed through him at the thought of exposing the depths of his depravity yet again, and this time to a stranger, Rogan surged to his feet and began prowling the perimeters of the room. He felt a deep sympathy for the big cats caged in the Royal Menagerie and reminded himself there were no bars here restraining him. He could leave if he wanted, if his shame was greater than his love for Jassie. He stopped before a window at the far end of the room and gripped his hands firmly behind his back.

'There are triggers. The worst one is when she starts to beg.' He swallowed. 'Dammit, it's not right. The only way I could make love to her without becoming that punitive beast is to take her without arousing her at all. I can't do that to her! But if I take the time to—arouse her, to *make love to her*—inevitably there comes a point when she will beg. Beg me to take her, beg me to enter her, beg me to love her. What does it matter! The moment that happens I lose control and the woman beneath my hands becomes that whoring bitch and I have to bind her and punish her. I have to make her understand what she did was so *wrong*! I cannot stop myself!'

'A word from Jassie wouldn't stop you?'

Rogan came to a standstill in the middle of the room, startled to find he'd been pacing in time to his feverish words and his heart was thundering in his chest. His arms were now rigid at his sides and he slowly unclenched his fists and moved back to the chair opposite Lady Bouvier.

'There is no thought in my mind but punishment, no sound penetrates the haze of rage that fills me. All I hear is that fucking bitch urging me on, moaning and whimpering her delight in every foul action I can perform on her body—and when I thought I had thrashed her to submission, in fact feared I might have actually killed her, she told me I was—magnificent. What do I have to do to make her understand?'

He stopped, appalled to feel the ugly miasma tearing at the edges of his mind. His legs and hands had begun to tremble and even though he knew he should take himself out of this room, out of the house immediately he also knew if he tried to stand he'd probably fall and lie trembling on the floor like some poor idiot who should be confined at Bedlam.

Vaguely he was aware of Lady Bouvier moving as he dragged unsteady hands over his sweating face.

'Brandy, Windermere. Drink.'

Gratefully he took the glass and downed the generous tot it held.

The darkness threatening his mind receded and he sank back in the chair, relieved to feel a calmness flowing through his nerves after the fiery burn of the liquor.

'I shall leave—'

'No, Windermere, you will not.'

The words were crisp, the tone in which they were spoken deeply authoritative. It was shock as much as anything else that kept him where he was. She rang a small hand bell and ordered tea and cakes to be brought immediately.

As the maid hurried to do her bidding, Lady Bouvier turned back to him and asked, 'And how is Olwynne? I know she doesn't keep well but she never tells me much in her letters.'

'Letters? You correspond with my mother?'

'Yes.' The sleek golden head nodded. 'Ever since Mary died. I could never play a part in Jassie's life, but with Olwynne's connivance I've watched over her as best I could. Quentin's death broke your mother's spirit, but your father's death broke her heart. She would be pleased by your marriage, I think.'

'Yes. It's given her a new lease of life. But she's very frail and I— we—worry. But I think if I were ever to talk seriously to her about it she'd say she'll be happy to go—to be with my father.'

'And that's as it should be.'

A maid arrived with the tea trolley and parked it at Lady Bouvier's side. She busied herself pouring tea into fine china cups and offering him a plate of small, elegantly iced cakes. Adding a sugar lump to her own cup, she stirred ruminatively, took a sip and set the cup carefully on its saucer at her side.

'It would seem some sort of intervention is needed, a third party, if you will.'

Rogan felt his chest swell with the anger that had filled him while talking to Knightsborough.

'That's already been suggested and I refuse to employ some— pervert to loiter outside our bedroom door. I could possibly countenance it for myself but I won't subject Jassie to such humiliation.'

'I was thinking something a little more intimate than that.'

'More intimate?'

'A ménage a trois, perhaps?'

Rogan set the delicate teacup aside before he crushed it between his fingers. He began to push himself up from his chair, his teeth grinding with impotent despair.

'For Jassie's sake, Windermere, I must insist you at least talk about this.'

'Talk about inviting some other bastard right into our bedroom? Invite him to—make love to my wife, *right alongside me?*'

'That is what I'm suggesting. Because if he were to stand inside the room instead of outside the door, he would still be—er—loitering—like a pervert, as you say. But this is all conjecture. We are just trying to think what might work. Please hold the emotion for a bit and try to focus on the problem—as if it concerned someone else. Not you.'

Rogan almost rolled his eyes, but he stayed in the chair, suddenly conscious that while there might be ways to forestall his descent into madness while making love to his wife, they were likely to involve scenarios neither he nor Jassie would countenance. It was much like tying a starving man to his chair and then placing food just beyond his reach.

'I have great difficulty in imagining as you suggest.'

'I'm sure you do, but try. Remember what's at stake.'

He nodded.

'We've established the only way you could be distracted from the—change of personality—is by a third party, have we not?'

Surely there was some other answer, but he knew it for the futile hope it was. How could Jassie stop him when she was bound or gagged—or both? He nodded again, not trusting himself to speak.

'And from what you tell me, some sort of intervention is probably needed to break the cycle of your behavior. Your mind learnt such a terrible and deeply ingrained lesson, it can't respond any other way when the remembered stimuli are applied. So it needs someone strong enough to overpower you should you become physically violent or try to oppose them. It needs someone both you and Jassie would trust implicitly—with your lives, your happiness. It needs someone who would treat Jassie with the same deep love and respect—and discretion—you would yourself. And speaking as a woman—not a courtesan—the only way I wouldn't find the introduction of a third party humiliating, is if they were as deeply involved emotionally and sexually as you and she are.'

Unable to sit still any longer, Rogan leapt once more to his feet and began pacing, his mind a raging mess of thoughts. She was right. But he couldn't countenance it. Who on earth did a man ask to play such a role for him? How would he not want to murder the bastard afterwards? What if he demanded always to—share? How could he even broach such a scenario to his innocent wife, much less subject her to it?

He couldn't. He loved her too much.

'I imagine you're no stranger to such arrangements? In establishments like this they are relatively common—and with proclivities like yours you would have to be familiar with establishments like this—unless you've lived your life like a monk.'

He'd never blushed so much in his damned life and certainly couldn't understand why he was now, in the presence of a woman who'd sold her body for the pleasure of others, times without number.

'Of course you haven't,' she went on when he didn't answer. 'But you're selfish enough to inflict such a life on Jassie because you can't countenance sharing her with another in order to make a happy marriage between the two of you possible.'

Enough!

'Dammit! Do you have nothing else to offer?' he snarled, coming abruptly to his feet.

'The only thing I can see that would help is some sort of physical intervention—'

'Thank you, ma'am.'

Dropping a small purse of gold on the table at her side he strode out of the room, snatched his hat and gloves from the stand inside the front door and let himself out into the street.

Anger fueled his momentum down Half Moon Street. If he let go of anger there was nothing but desperation left and he wasn't yet ready to deliver himself back into the black and destructive pit of hopelessness where he'd spent the last week. On Piccadilly he hailed a cab and directed it to Knightsborough's house, the Matrix Club on Chapel Street.

As he fumbled in his pocket for coin to pay the jarvey, he looked up at the house and a wave of revulsion washed over him. There was nothing he wanted within those walls, nothing that could fill the empty places in his soul or hide those places from his consciousness any more.

Nothing could do that but Jassie. Jassie was in Neave and if she'd been in London he'd not seek her out anyway. But he had to do something to assuage the storm of fury, frustration and despair that wanted nothing so much as to avenge itself—somewhere—on someone.

'To hell with it,' he muttered then dropped several coins into the jarvey's out-stretched palm. 'Take me back to the corner of Piccadilly and St. James Street.'

Maybe by the time he got there he'd have decided where to go.

Gentleman Jackson's? He could pummel it out of some poor unsuspecting bastard and probably kill him in the white heat of his aberration. In fact, he was pretty certain the kind of fight he felt inclined towards could best be found in a dark alleyway and had nothing to do with anything gentlemanly.

Night had fallen by the time they'd maneuvered through the traffic on Piccadilly and as he alighted he thought he might just get his wish for real. Only a fool walked the streets at night, especially when everything about him from his dress to his mien screamed wealth and privilege. The fact he carried a knife in his boot and a hunger for violence in his heart would not be immediately apparent.

Let them try. The thought was a snarl that almost erupted into words as he passed a rough looking cove whose shifty gaze followed him from beneath a grimy slouch cap. The scowl on his own face must have been deterrent enough for he made no move and Rogan came at last to St James Street. Since he was probably not in a suitable frame of mind for the boxing saloon it would have to be White's.

And alcohol. It was all that was left. As he approached the Club a carriage pulled up and a man alighted and when he stepped into the light shining from the bay window Rogan recognized his cousin, the Duke of Wolverton.

'Wolf!'

He turned and immediately a white smile slashed across his dark good looks.

'Windermere. What the devil are you doing risking your life to the footpads of London?'

'Taunting them to do their worst.'

He let an evil grin twist his mouth and hoped he'd fool Dom he was just talking up air.

Wolverton's brows twitched and his grin flashed again.

'Come on then. Let's go and find a game. I plan to fleece you blind tonight.'

'You'll have to get me drunk first,' Rogan drawled back.

Wolverton clapped him on the shoulder.

'Oh I'm sure *that* could be arranged,' he laughed, and they entered the Club together, Rogan welcoming the distraction and the sense of being able to distance himself from the ugly churnings of his mind.

They'd settled into a game with Lord Cholmondeley and Viscount Stapleton. The brandy flowed and Lady Luck had been as fickle as in fable, settling on the shoulder of first one and then another among them. But as the night grew late Wolverton began gaining the upper hand as he'd threatened right at the start and Rogan was sinking into a pleasantly numb place where nothing much mattered and he could forget most anything that did.

A buffet on his shoulder and a loud drunken voice abruptly shattered his expensive-brandy-induced nirvana.

'Windermere! Heard you finally got leg-shackled to the delectable Carlisle chit. What have you done with her? If you don't want to be home tupping her after all perhaps I should go calling? She at Windermere House?'

In a blinding instant Rogan erupted to his feet and gripped the offensive Lord Cockington by his neck cloth, pulling it tight until the man's eyes bulged.

'I say, Windermere,' he croaked. 'Only funning, old chap!'

Wolverton rose, a little unsteadily to his feet, and carefully unclasped Rogan's fingers from Cockington's neck cloth.

'He'll apologize tomorrow. And so will you. If that don't settle it prepare to meet us both on the field of honor.'

He then turned to the two men still at the table.

'That'll be it for tonight, gentlemen. Windermere and I are leaving now.'

Rogan struggled out of Dominic's grip, turned his back on Cockington and waited like a stone statue while he settled with Cholmondeley and Stapleton. Then he followed his cousin out of the Club, feeling as if he walked in the center of a dark smothering cloud.

With the assistance of the footman and the doorman from the Club they climbed into Wolverton's carriage. Neither spoke until they were settled before the fire in Dominic's study in Wolverton House on Bruton Street, a large pot of coffee between them.

They'd downed a cup each of the rich brew when Dominic said, 'Time to open the budget, Rogue. We've known each other all our lives and I'd have thought we knew pretty much all there is to know about one another. But there's a dark part of you that you hold close to yourself; a dark place within where you shut yourself off, even from your friends; from those who love you. Like your wife. You know my deepest ugliest secret. It's probably even quite widely known I'm hopelessly in love with your wife and would have made her mine long since—if she'd have had me—regardless that her heart is irrevocably yours.

'I can deduce whatever drives you to fuck up your life and the lives of those you love, has something to do with Jassie, or women in general, or a woman in particular.—For God's sake, Rogue, what the devil goes on with you? You're finally married to that woman and what are you doing?

'It would seem you strive to be where she is not! When I saw you together at the theatre that night the wall of resistance around yourself was almost tangible and no matter how bright her smile, how gay her laughter, the pain, the apprehension, the longing in her eyes when she looked at you was cruelly obvious. Probably not to anyone else, but to someone who loves her and only wants to see her happy, it was agony to watch.'

'I ought to call you out.'

Rogan stared moodily into the fire, trying to find the anger he should be feeling at Dominic's declaration of his love for Jassie. But the ugly fire of jealousy that had fueled his actions since leaving Half Moon Street, seemed to have sputtered out, leaving only cold, dead ashes.

'Is that all you can say? If you doubted my honor in the matter we would've fought long since.'

Wolverton fell back in his chair with a huff of exasperation.

'God knows,' he added, dropping his head back further to stare up at the ceiling, 'I'd probably relish the chance to go a few rounds with you and hopefully punch some sense into you—or finish you off so I could have your wife. Much good it'd do me when it's you she wants, you she loves. So—as there's nothing else I can give her to make her happy I have to try and give her—you!'

Rogan continued to stare at the fire, hatred for himself burning deeper, gnawing at his guts—like maggots on rotten meat. The analogy was particularly apt, he thought hazily. He was rotten—no other word for it.

Damn the coffee.—It was allowing him to think and feel again just when he'd reached a state of numbness that had been quite restful. Half an hour ago he'd not have registered the pain in Wolverton's voice or felt the depths of his own shame for inflicting it. But what could he say? What could he change?

He was as he was.

'You need more coffee,' Dominic stated. 'Drink up and answer me some questions.'

He watched closely while Rogan drank down more of the coffee then unsteadily set the cup back on its saucer.

'Whaddya want ta know.'

'I want to know why you allowed Jassie to reach the age of twenty-five before taking her to wife when you've loved her all your life. I want to know what changed and finally brought about that marriage so precipitately. And I want to know why you're not with her now; why you're drinking yourself into a stupor night after night and adding fuel to the gossip mill that is already grinding exceedingly fine without you feeding it yet more grist. I want to know *what the fuck* is wrong with you, Windermere!'

That again? Was this where he had to tell his story yet again? Expose the truth of who he was to his cousin and best friend and risk that friendship? Who would pick him up out of the gutter if not His Grace, the Duke of Wolverton? Who had more right to know the answer to the questions he posed than Dominic who'd loved Jassie so honorably and so hopelessly for so long?

'I'm damned,' he growled at last.

'Why? How?' Dominic demanded.

Rogan gulped the rest of his coffee, replaced his cup then sat forward in his chair with elbows on his knees and head in his hands. It should be easy now. He'd told the damned story so many times in the last few weeks but still the words wouldn't form in his brain, let alone pass his lips.

'Answer me one question then,' Dominic said patiently. 'What stopped you from offering for Jassie all those years?'

And so the story began to pour from him once again, encouraged by questions from Dominic, until Rogan lost himself in the telling and spared nothing. In the end it was easy, his tendency to over-think and censor as he talked was completely obliterated by the excessive amount of alcohol floating in his blood, the warmth of the fire and the realization there was nothing he couldn't tell Wolverton and no one he trusted more unless it was Jassie herself. He only stumbled into silence when he arrived at the point of his visit to Madame Lady Bouvier.

Dominic waited while Rogan collected himself, his green eyes watchful and filled with shadows. What the hell was he thinking? He'd said little enough while Rogan had spewed his guts like some puling little fool still in the nursery. He didn't want to say any more. The futility of it, the utter despair that had sent him reeling back into the street from Madame Lady Bouvier's house was lurking, waiting to engulf him once again.

'And did the Madame have any words of wisdom for you?'

Dominic's words were quiet, almost gentle, as if he knew the pain inherent in the answer.

Rogan caught back a snarl, turning it into a growl of assent, then watched as a log fell apart in the grate, its center glowing with a fiery echo of the fury in his heart.

'What?'

'First she suggested I could ask someone else to sire my son—on Jassie.'

'I take it that met with a brick wall of resistance?'

Too restless to stay sitting any longer, Rogan surged, albeit unsteadily, to his feet and began prowling about the room, fingering the curios that every Duke since the first had collected on their world travels and perched in peculiar places about the room.

'What else did she suggest?' Dominic persisted, his words slow and careful as if coaxing a reluctant child.

Rogan scowled at him then came back to lean on the mantel and kick at the grate with his boot.

'Rogue? You might as well spill this. It's only a tiny crumb after all the rest.'

'You never did know how to leave a man any pride, did you, *your Grace*?'

'Resorting to *name-calling* never worked either,' Dominic bit straight back, a wry twist to his mouth.

Rogan dragged a hand through his hair then collapsed back into his chair.

'She thought the cycle of my behavior needed to be broken and for that to happen a third party is needed. The idea of someone listening outside our door while I make love to my wife was—is anathema to me. Then she had an even better idea,' he finished bitterly and fell to staring moodily into the smoldering embers of the fire again.

'Which was?'

'That I—we—should ask someone we trust to join us,—ménage à trois, no less. It needs to be a man who is capable of overpowering me should I become physically agitated and she thought it would be more acceptable to Jassie if that man was to make love to her also, rather than just watch. It would seem less—more—Damn it!'

The jagged scar down the side of Dominic's face gleamed livid white against the darker hue of his skin.

'It could work,' he said quietly.

'You think?' The words erupted out of Rogan as he felt the fury gathering in his chest again, like a terrible festering bubo at the point of rupture.

Dominic sighed, twisted his long fingers about the scrollwork on the arms of his chair then stood slowly and stretched like a large lazy beast.

'Enough, I think,' he said as his arms dropped back to his sides. 'Our brains are too fuddled to think clearly tonight. Thank you for trusting me with—your story, Rogue. My head is now filled with a thousand thoughts and questions, but any more is best left for tomorrow when we're both a little more—lucid. I'll get Grigg to show you to a room and we'll leave any further discussion for the morning. We'll think better then.' For a moment his hand rested affectionately on Rogan's shoulder then he added, 'I have a much better understanding now of what drives you, Rogue. Thank you again for trusting me.'

The day was well advanced when they met again over the breakfast table. Patchett, the Duke's valet had attended Rogan and had come bearing a glass of cloudy liquid very similar to that which Deacon had prepared for him yesterday morning. He'd downed it without a peep and gratefully submitted to his other ministrations and if he still felt like a hunted fox who'd run into a blind dene and was all out of options at least he was clean-shaved and his neck cloth had been washed, ironed and expertly tied. He felt marginally back in control of his faculties.

Dominic already sat at the table, the morning paper in his hands. He peered at Rogan over its tops.

'Morning, Rogue. You're looking remarkably chipper for someone who imbibed as much of the hard stuff as you did last night.'

Rogan grimaced and surveyed the array of dishes on the sideboard. The aromas of bacon, hot toast and coffee made his mouth water and his stomach groan. When had he eaten last?

'Well, Boney is finally on his way to St. Helena where he should have been put in the first place. Apparently the harbors at Brixham and Plymouth have been crowded with boats full of sightseers hoping to catch a glimpse of the infamous one-time Emperor. Amazing how quickly some can forget the thousands of good men of many nationalities whose lives were cut short because the Allies didn't have the sense to incarcerate him safely the first time around. Pray we are not so careless this time.'

Rogan settled at the table with a plate of bacon, eggs and fried potato cakes.

'The little upstart should be stood against a wall and shot. No other man in history has caused more loss of life. He should be treated no better than a damned murderer.'

Dominic folded the paper and laid it aside and they continued to discuss the brutal effects of the twenty years of constant warfare on the countries involved and how Britain in particular was left with her economy in ruins.

'It's where you should focus your energy now, Rogue,' Dominic said, as they took their cups of coffee along the hall to the Duke's study.

Ensconced once again in the chairs where they'd sat last night, Rogan responded, 'I agree. It's time to take my seat in the House and accept my responsibilities—as my father did. But I have to do something about my marriage first or the gossip-mill will effectively scuttle anything worthwhile I might try to do.—I'm at the end of my rope, Dom. There's nowhere left to turn.'

'Except perhaps to trust your wife—who loves you unconditionally.'

Rogan swirled the last of his coffee relentlessly round in his cup, then he looked up and directly into Wolverton's dark green gaze.

'And have you call me out every time you see me because you know how I'm using her? Abusing her? I can't do it. To her, to me—or even to you. She shouldn't have to live like that.'

'Rogue, do you trust me?'

There was an odd note in Wolverton's voice and the scar on his cheek seemed to whiten. Rogan laid his cup aside and frowned across at his friend.

'What sort of question is that? I trust you with my life!'

Dominic continued to hold his gaze and the very room seemed to hold its breath.

'Would you trust me with your wife?'

Rogan reared back, each word feeling like a stab wound to his chest.

'What—do you mean?'

'I know you said you'd have to kill any bastard who touched Jassie but—if there truly is no other way, and if there really is a possibility a third party intervention could work—I could be that third party. None better. I love Jassie for a start and deeply desire her happiness. She said she'd have accepted my suit and been happy to do so if she hadn't loved you so desperately—or if something happened to you and there was no longer any hope.'

Dominic was eyeing him a little warily as Rogan fought to control the red surge of anger that threatened to cloud his brain. When he couldn't form any sort of an answer, Dom continued, his voice rough and strained.

'I'd not make love to her fully. That can only be for you. But—I could be in the bed with you, holding Jassie, arousing her perhaps; ready to act should you need it. It certainly wouldn't work if I was just standing to one side, watching—'

There was a huge knot in his belly trying to unravel. Rogan folded his arms tightly across his chest in an effort to hold himself together. Still watching him, his brave—or was that foolhardy—cousin forged on.

'Just try and think of the outcome, Rogue. Think of being able to love Jassie—truly love her—and all that would mean to both of you. Focus on that—being able to give Jassie what she's risked all to achieve for herself.'

'You think your control is that good?' Rogan snarled at last. 'And why? Why would you put yourself through such—pain?'

Dominic raked his hands through his black locks in a rare burst of vulnerability, completely destroying Patchett's stylish arrangement.

'I can't deny it would be fulfilling my deepest desire to make—hold Jassie in that way—and if that scenario could actually work I'm the only man you could ask to fill the vacant third. Precisely *because* I love her. I'm the only man Jassie might accept in that role. I'm someone you trust and I rather think Jassie would trust me also.—As for being able to control myself? That's a given.'

Wolverton had risen while he was talking and now leant against the window-frame staring down into Bruton Street.

'I will control myself because I love Jassie and because—and you will forget I ever said this—I have a deep regard for you. And maybe for Philip, who loved her more than either of us. Her happiness and her safety was all he cared about. There is little else we can do for him now.'

To someone who didn't know him he might appear relaxed. Rogan knew the Duke too well and the fine waves of tension radiating from the lithe, whipcord tough body posing with such spurious nonchalance against the filtered sunlight, were almost visible; certainly tangible.

And not much different to those Rogan felt spiraling around himself. His whole body seemed to be on alert.

As if waiting for just one more word from Wolverton before Rogan body-slammed him and rammed his oft-professed love for Jassie down his throat. The thought had no sooner formed than he realized that was not the source of the peculiar tension that had every hair on his body standing rigid and every muscle quivering.

He was not rigid with jealousy. He was frozen with hope. And as he realized hope was the strongest emotion driving him, it burgeoned forth like an exotic bloom in the succession houses at the Abbey. If he could overcome his possessiveness towards Jassie, enough to allow Wolverton, his best friend, to touch her, hold her as he would himself, then he might also hope the scheme would succeed.

For his ultimate goal, his sole raison d'être now, was to be able to love Jassie, slowly, erotically, and with all the love in his heart.

So she could finally love him in the way she'd wanted, needed, longed to do for so long. He might just be trembling with hope.

'Well—say something! Land me a facer. But for God's sake stop sitting there like you've been struck by lightning or something! I can't even tell whether that's good or bad.'

'Good—I think,' Rogan rasped. 'I should be pummeling your lecherous face into the carpet, but—the only thoughts in my head are 'when', 'how', 'how soon'? It's finally happened. I've gone insane like I always feared I would.'

'Hell, Windermere! I thought I'd have to talk and talk, wheedle, cajole, threaten—I never thought you'd agree—just like that!'

'Nor did I,' Rogan said, suddenly aware they both had stupid, scared grins on their faces. 'But—what if it fails?'

The question fell out of his mouth as soon as it formed in his brain.

Dominic's tall frame tensed and he fixed Rogan with the aristocratic stare he did so well, even though he still jibbed against the ducal role almost two years after inheriting it.

'Shooting yourself in the foot before we've even dared to try?'

Fetching up at the next window, Rogan stared unseeingly down onto Bruton Street where Wolverton's neighbors, Lady Archibald and her mousey twin daughters walked with their maid towards Berkeley Square where they liked to take the air. It was a fine sunny day outdoors, perfect for a stroll through the colorful gardens. The tableau faded from his consciousness to be replaced by a vision of Jassie on his arm, her golden curls peeping from beneath her bonnet, her topaz eyes dancing and her mouth curved deliciously in laughter.

Warm. Vibrant. Happy. In love with one another and—free to indulge that love when the doors of Windermere House closed behind them.

The scene was so vivid, felt so real he could feel the imprint of her fingers on his arm and hear the music of her laughter in the air all around him; compelling him to step forward, not retreat back into the horror and darkness of that place where he'd lived for the last sixteen years.

There was only one way now.

Forward.

He straightened away from the window, strode down the room with his hand out-stretched to Dominic.

'There's no way back. We have some careful planning to do—after I've convinced Jassie.'

'Have faith in your wife, Rogue. Jassie Carlisle is the strongest female I know. Did she not vow she loves you—unconditionally? Do you not think she'll see as you see, hope as you hope?'

A peculiar ache, more of a suffering, flowered in his chest; a wistful kind of sadness.

'I'd rather face a score of Fouché's goons in a dark alley than face Jassie with this scenario. She may not be a total innocent but no gently bred young woman should expect her husband to invite a third into their bed.'

'That last is true, but again I say you underestimate your wife. Was it not she who visited the Madame in the first place? Was it not she who sent you there?'

'Yes. But I'm certain this outcome is not one she'd thought of!'

'Probably not,' Wolverton agreed, 'but if we devise a plan whereby privacy and discretion are guaranteed, she might be more readily convinced. I'm thinking of the hunting lodge up in Cumbria. You could take a honeymoon trip and I could meet you there.'

'And meantime there's this damned house party to get through.— Or—could you be ready to leave for the Abbey tomorrow? That way we'd be a couple of days ahead of everyone else who have all been invited for Thursday. It'd give us a couple of days to—'

'Court Jassie?'

Rogan looked at his friend and saw the same wistful expression that must have graced his own rugged features a few minutes before. For the first time in sixteen years he felt a wide and genuine smile stretch his face.

CHAPTER THIRTEEN

After a dreary wet morning, which Jassie had spent with her steward in the study at Brantleigh Manor, the sun had come out and the wind had completely dropped. Since the Abbey smith had fixed wheels to the sedan chair it was the perfect afternoon to wheel Lady O round the cinder paths of the Garden Walk and allow Jensen the afternoon off to visit with her sister, the Cook at Brantleigh.

They'd just entered the cloisters of the medieval Cistercian chapel when the thud of hooves coming up the Elm Drive brought the small cavalcade to a halt.

'Surely we're not expecting anyone today?' The Dowager looked puzzled.

'No, but—,'

Before Jassie could say more the riders broke from the cover of the elms.

'It's Windermere!' Fran said.

An eerie sense of déjà vu settled over Jassie as she recognized the other rider.

'And Wolverton, if I'm not mistaken.'

She held her breath for a moment, half expecting the reckless thud of the horses across the front of the Abbey, kicking up divots from the lawns the gardeners had not long repaired from the last time.

But today they weren't late. Early, if anything. Gradually she eased air into her lungs and continued pushing Lady O's chair from the cloisters into the stone-flagged hallway at the back of the Abbey as the echo of the hooves carried on past to the stables beyond.

There would be two more for tea in the small parlor Lady O favored and she had a few more minutes to steady her racing heart and school her features and emotions into something bland and socially acceptable.

By the time her husband stood before her, she would be armored against his scowl and continued determination to keep her at arm's length. She would have banal, polite pleasantries ready at the tip of her tongue and would be able to suppress all emotion as she lifted her cheek for his chaste and perfunctory duty kiss of greeting.

She would, in short, project the image of the perfect society hostess, regal Countess, happy bride. And if she did not fool her husband she would, hopefully, conceal the worst of her inner panic from these two closest companions whose concern for her ran deep.

But the man who arrived in the small parlor at almost the same time as themselves was a Rogan Wyldefell she'd not seen for many years. His dark hair was ruffled as if he'd run his fingers through it after removing his hat, and his riding attire, while of the latest cut and fashion, was dusty and a little rumpled from the ride. None of that was out of the ordinary but the wide smile, the wicked deep blue sparkle in his eyes and the general air of suppressed excitement emanating from him caused Jassie to stand like a statue in the middle of the room while he descended on her with a promise in his gaze that stole her ability to think or move. Stern and solemn, Rogan Wyldefell was a handsome man. Smiling and with devilment (Devilment? Rogan?) in his eyes, he stole what little composure she'd managed to gather.

As if no one else was present in the room, he held out his hands for hers, drew her close and raised her fingers for a lingering kiss. Then he leaned back to survey her startled countenance, smiled into her glazed eyes, and said, 'Wolverton and I decided to come down a couple of days ahead of time to—help.'

Jassie followed his glance back over his shoulder to where the Duke, his head almost brushing the lintel of the door, coal black locks a little long as always, observed them with a pirate's wickedly scarred grin.

And his eyes beneath thick dark lashes glowed with the same anticipatory gleam she'd just seen in Rogan's.

What were the two of them up to? A fleeting stab of grief assailed her with the thought that only a couple of years ago, Philip would have been shouldering Wolverton through the door with the three of them tossing friendly abuse at one another as only friends from boyhood could. As Rogan turned aside to greet his mother and Fran, Wolverton took his place before her, raising her hand to his lips and kissing her fingertips with all the rakish grace for which he was famous.

Jassie had the strangest sensation she'd been spun several times in a circle and the real world had shifted a little sideways allowing a glimpse through to a different reality.

A reality that seemed to promise to substantiate dreams and grant wishes; a reality where the impossible became eminently possible and fairies appeared at the bottom of the garden.

Lady Windermere sent the hovering maid for the tea trolley and Rogan steered Jassie towards the love seat and sat himself beside her—so close their thighs were touching and she could feel his heat through their clothing.

Wolverton declined a seat, electing instead to drape his elegant form from the mantelpiece, specifically it seemed, so he had a clear view of the two on the loveseat.

Jassie had never been so thankful for the perspicacity of her mother-in-law or her ability to maintain polite conversation in the face of the most unusual circumstances. For Jassie could not fool herself Lady Olwynne was unaware of the air of suppressed excitement emanating from the men or her own complete inability to hold two coherent thoughts in her head, let alone converse intelligently.

They both accepted tea, drinking thirstily and holding out their cups for more. They appeared to relish the small meat pies Cook had thought to provide in their honor as well as the dainty sandwiches and fairy cakes, the usual fare for afternoon tea.

Jassie mashed a fairy cake to crumbs on her saucer, sipped once or twice at her tea and listened to Rogan telling his mother, to her obvious delight, now he was married he intended taking his seat in the House of Lords. He also said he'd promoted Brixton to be his full-time valet and that he and Patchett, Wolverton's valet, should be arriving soon in the ducal carriage with their luggage.

Participating in the conversation herself was impossible. Each new snippet of information twitched the knot of tension that had formed in her belly the moment Rogan strode across the room to her with the light of desire—she could only call it that—and anticipation in his beautiful eyes. She felt as if she confronted the ghost of the old, happy, devil-may-care Rogan from her childhood.

The tension had spread to her fingers and she scarcely dared lift her cup to her lips for fear of sloshing the tea on her gown. She wondered why his presence made her nervous then realized it was excitement fizzing through her veins and all she wanted was to be alone with her husband so she could test the theory he was done with running from her and somehow Wolverton had had a hand in that.

How soon could they politely withdraw?

'Your gowns arrived and we've brought them with us,' Rogan said, turning to address her directly.

'Oh—good!'

She'd forgotten about the gowns, the ball, the house party, everything she'd been worrying over earlier that afternoon as they'd walked in the gardens. Whatever importance she'd attached to those problems had faded to nothingness in the space of the half hour since Windermere's arrival.

'Is that all you can say? I thought you'd be pacing the drive looking for them by now!' he teased.

He teased? When had he last teased her with that devilish twinkle making his eyes shine like stars in a midnight sky?

When she didn't answer, just stared at him with questions whirling in her brain, he gently took the cup and saucer from her hands, set it on the tea trolley and rose to his feet.

'Come walk in the gardens with me,' he commanded.

Jassie immediately looked to Lady O, who was rarely without her trusty Jensen, but she waved an airy hand at her.

'Go on,' she said. 'I shall go up and have a nap and I'm sure Fran won't mind assisting me.'

'And I,' Wolverton put in quickly as if forestalling any concern for him, 'shall catch a few winks on that very comfortable daybed you keep in the conservatory.'

The men shared what Jassie thought was a decidedly conspiratorial smile before Rogan extended his arm and led her out of the room. She had the distinct impression if it were not for the comment it would provoke, he'd have been running and dragging her after him, feet and skirts flying—like a boy with a kite.

In silence he hurried her through the galleries and hallways, back the way she'd wheeled Lady Olwynne less than an hour before, across the partly cloistered quadrangle of lawn to the chapel.

'It'll be quiet in here and we won't be disturbed. I have much to tell you.'

Jassie made no demur, allowing him to lead her into the sanctuary of the sacred place and close the door at their backs. Looking up at him as he turned back to her, Jassie thought she'd never seen a more beautiful man. The wide brow topped with unruly, dark mahogany hair; a straight, elegant but very masculine nose; a square harshly carved jaw-line and a mouth chiseled by a master artisan.

A mouth she desperately wanted on hers, on her body, everywhere.

'Don't look at me like that!'

'Like what?'

They were whispering, as if they could keep God from hearing their words. Rogan smiled, slow and dark.

'Like you want to devour me.'

'I do,' she said simply. 'But this is scarcely the place for it.'

'No,' he said, suddenly solemn. 'And that's why we're here. To talk. Nothing else—yet.'

Taking her hand, he led her up the aisle and urged her to sit on the chancel steps then dropped down beside her to take her face in his hands and kiss her swiftly and deeply, all in one movement.

Setting her from him and shuffling away so a few inches separated their bodies, he said, 'That's just to hold us for now.'

Instinctively she reached to pull him back to her. The kiss was wonderful but it was too little.

'No!' he said sharply and her hands fell to her lap. 'Nothing has changed and yet—perhaps—a lot has.'

Jassie knew her confusion was evident in her eyes for he offered her a wry smile.

'You're not making sense,' she whispered when he said no more.

'I will explain.'

Suddenly he was on his feet, pacing across the stone-flagged floor before her.

A shaft of sunlight from the clerestory windows outlined his form, the shoulders broad and strong beneath the perfectly fitted blue jacket, and his long muscular legs show-cased in the buff riding breeches and close fitting hessians. Her eyes were remembering that form sans clothing and her body was having much trouble staying where he'd put her, where he clearly wanted her to stay while he talked. Really? Was talking all he wanted at this minute?

He turned to face her and stood still in the shaft of sunlight.

'I love you, Jassie. You know that, don't you?'

The tone of his voice sent echoes of anxiety rippling through her body.

'Yes,' she whispered.

'And did you really mean it when you said you loved me—unconditionally?'

How could he doubt her?

'Yes.'

Her voice was a little stronger but even she could hear the note of apprehension in it.

He seemed to exhale in relief then resumed striding back and forth across the small space.

'I went to see—your aunt.'

'Madame Lady Bouvier? You—you went? Did she—help?'

Suddenly breathing was the hardest thing she'd ever had to do and hope and longing tangled in her chest with painful intensity.

'She made me extremely angry!'

'Oh!'

She couldn't think what else to say and felt as if she would choke on hope and longing. If her aunt had not been able to help then what was the source of the suppressed excitement she'd felt emanating from Rogan since the moment he'd stepped into the small parlor?

'First she suggested we should ask one of my cousins to sire an heir for Windermere—on you.'

Jassie felt her eyebrows fly up into her hair. Her mouth dropped open, but no words would issue forth.

'If she'd been a man I'd have called her out! I think she was just testing me, trying to see what was really important. So then she asked more about my—condition and what exactly happens—and then she said it was clear the only thing that could work was a third party intervention.'

His jaw tensed and fire flashed blue and furious in his eyes.

'The thought of someone lurking beyond our bedroom door or watching while I made love to you, standing ready to intervene when I lost control, was beyond horrific. She saw my point and agreed and then she said—Fuck!'

His pacing became little short of manic and Jassie couldn't think of one thing to say to stop him or intervene in any way even though she didn't really think that word was what her aunt would have said. At last he dropped to his haunches before her and took her hands in his.

'She thought the only way it would work would be to have the third party in the bed with us—making love to you too.—A ménage a trois, if you know what I mean?'

Wordlessly, Jassie nodded. She just kept her eyes on Rogan's mouth, that was uttering words way beyond any fantasy she could ever have imagined because she was too afraid to examine the real reason her own mouth was suddenly dry and her heart was pounding like a runaway horse with the Devil on its back.

'She said it should be someone I trusted; someone you trusted, and who would fully understand their role. It would not be so embarrassing that way.'

'It—wouldn't?'

Jassie managed to squeak the words out and then her mind made the lightning leap of awareness.

'And you thought of Wolverton—and here the pair of you are—like roving bucks in the mating season! That's why you both look—as if—
,

Unable to continue she just stared wordlessly into his eyes.

'No—I—didn't,' Rogan snarled, arresting the breath in her throat once more. He rose abruptly to his feet, pulling her with him to stand gripping her hands and glaring back at her.

'I stormed out of there with murder on my mind. I'd have picked a fight with anyone who crossed my path and I walked the length of St. James Street looking for just that. It gave me a chance to cool down and realize I'd get myself banned from Gentleman Jack's if I went there and I ended up at White's. Swilling brandy and playing deep. But the brandy didn't really help because when Cockington stopped by with a snide question as to why I wasn't with my new bride I almost throttled him with his own neck cloth, right there in the card room at White's. Dom dragged me out before I got myself banned from there too and took me home to his place and the whole sorry tale come out—again. It wasn't till next morning when we were both sober, he dared to offer himself. My first gut reaction was to flatten him there in his own house, but then

I realized it was the only chance left. If I couldn't countenance the presence of another in our marriage bed—for long enough to break the cycle of my behavior at least—then we would never—effectively— have a marriage.'

They were still standing facing one another, their hands clasped tight enough to whiten their knuckles and their eyes locked in a mirror image of horrific hope.

Jassie couldn't get her tongue off the roof of her mouth or even blink her eyes. She wasn't sure she hadn't morphed into a marble statue right where she stood.

'Say something,' he whispered.

She opened her mouth and closed it again, then shook her head in desperate little movements that felt oddly out of control.

'Breathe!' he commanded suddenly, hauling her into his arms and giving her a quick thump between the shoulder blades. Perhaps he was right and she'd been starving for oxygen for her legs had the sudden tendency to collapse as if they were fashioned from limp knitting yarn.

Clinging to his shoulders, she buried her face in his neck and breathed in the familiar manly scent of him, soaked his strength and physical power into her bones to steady herself. As her body relaxed against him, he lifted her easily into his arms and sank down onto the steps again with her nestled in his lap and her head pressed against his shoulder.

For a moment his hand stroked soothingly over the crown of her head and Jassie thought she'd never felt so cherished.

'Talk to me,' he murmured. 'Tell me what you're thinking.'

'I'm not sure I can—think. It's—my mind is a mess of—questions mostly.'

'Fire them at me. Let me hear all of them. Dom and I have had a whole night and a day to talk through our thoughts and worries about it. The one thing we're agreed on is, it feels the right thing to do. It feels as if it could work. And—you know Dom loves you and would dearly have loved to make you his wife. Though he admits there's an element of total selfishness in his desire for this, he maintains he can control himself—that is, be with us, loving you but not actually—'

'—loving me.'

'Yes,' Rogan breathed against her skin. 'He also just wants to see you happy. And me? I can't believe how fast my psyche turned the tables on me—from wanting to kill him where he stood to perceiving him as our chance at a miracle. Something in me strongly believes this could work because—perhaps because most everyone who truly matters in my life now knows the ugliest depths of my depravity—and they are still my dearest friends. Not one of them has turned their backs or run screaming from me in righteous horror. It's as if—holding it in, protecting it from exposure all those years, fed it, empowered it and by letting the light in, it has lost the hold on me it once had. I can now believe I can change.—So—let me hear those questions.'

'Oh God, Rogan!' Jassie whispered. 'I—what if—where—when—*how?* How could I do this? How could I allow—*both of you*—to hold me, touch me—to—love me at the same time? What if—someone found out? How long are we talking about? Just once? A night or two? Forever? What if—oh God—what if I *liked* it!'

Her whole body was trembling and she was helpless to stop it, but the horror of that last thought blurting from her mouth stopped her lips from uttering more.

Now—*now*—he would throw her from him, look at her with the horror and disgust he'd saved for himself all these years. She wasn't sure she wouldn't look at herself that way.

His lips pressed, warm and soothing, against her brow.

'I love you, Jassie, and all I know for a certainty is I want to *make love* to you and I've discovered I will do whatever is required to realize that dream—for both of us. There are many ways a man can pleasure a woman without committing the ultimate act. So that way is for you and I alone. We want to keep this as uncomplicated as possible. The only real goal is to allow me to make love to you without descending into that pit of vengeance that claims me and turns me into a monster. I believe *he* can do that for me, for us.'

She fiddled with the buttons on his shirt, longing to simply undo them and slip her hand inside to find the warm skin and muscle beneath and as if he divined her thoughts his large, strong hand came over hers, lacing their fingers together and keeping them from temptation.

'I—don't know what to do!' Jassie blurted then. 'I hardly know what to do with you. How does one make love to two men at once?'

His breath was hot on her skin as he pressed his cheek against her hair.

'Jass, you're an innocent. We've discussed that. I know you've read books and looked at pictures but the fact is, your only experience is a few disastrous encounters with me, which did little to teach you anything. It's a wonder it didn't simply give you a disgust of the whole business.'

'I love you, Rogan. Nothing you could do would change that. How many times do I have to tell you?'

'I don't deserve you, Jassie.'

'You do!' she snapped, coming upright and glaring into his concerned eyes. 'You do deserve me and you do deserve to be loved! What you didn't deserve was to have your whole life, your psyche, so cruelly damaged by that wicked, brutalizing woman. You *deserve* to be loved. You *deserve* my love!'

Unable to desist any longer, Jassie reached up, cupped his rigid jaw and pulled his face down for her kiss. Their lips came together in a fierce melding that wrenched little moans of need from deep within them to meet on their lips. Boldly Jassie probed the seam of his mouth with her tongue then he opened for her and stole the initiative back and kissed her just as he'd done in her dreams forever.

They were both breathing deeply when he finally lifted his head to look down at her and she could only gaze back at him with a soft, happy smile stretching her face.

'You'll do it then?' he asked, his eyes so dark she thought she would drown in them.

'Yes,' she whispered, 'but—I still don't know what to do!'

His smile was slow and now wickedness lurked in the cobalt orbs making them sparkle again.

'Dom and I do. All you really have to do is surrender—to us both.'

'When?'

'Tonight. That's really why we came down early.'

Panic flared through her whole being. So soon?

'What room had you planned for Dom?'

'Well—he's a Duke, out-ranking everyone else, so he obviously gets the best. The Blue and Gold Suite, I thought.'

'Put him in the valet's suite next door to me.'

'But didn't you say you brought Brixton with you? I had thought to leave that room empty—so no one would hear—'

'When I beat you?'

She stared mutely at him.

'God willing, I'll never do that again. Brixton and Grigg can share a room up on the servant's floor. We won't need them later anyway and by morning all will appear as it should—with Dom back in his own bed.'

'You've thought of everything,' she accused, feeling just a little—manipulated.

He grinned unrepentantly down at her.

'I told you, Dom and I have talked of little else since yesterday. We've thought of your every possible objection and worked out arguments to overcome them. I'm telling you, Jass, I feel very hopeful for the outcome of this—as I never have.'

Jassie stilled as she realized there was one thing she must make clear to Rogan if, God forbid, he was wrong. She placed her hands on his chest, fingers slipping beneath the folds of his neck cloth and looked up at him, seriously, openly, so he could not doubt her determination.

'And if perchance it doesn't work, Rogan, I will not accept your absence from my bed. I'll follow you wherever you go. I will be your wife—for better *and* for worse! I meant that vow when I made it—before God and our closest friends and family. We're married. It's what we both wanted and I'll accept nothing less than a *full* marriage—whatever form that takes for us.—And I make that vow to you again, here, now, before God in this sacred place.'

The love and hope shining from Rogan's eyes was Jassie's undoing. With tears welling in her own, she clasped his face and sealed her vow with a kiss.

Their mouths were heated, hungry, suckling and probing accompanied by soft moans of need and urgency. Of their own volition their hands started seeking buttons, openings, bare skin. Rogan lay back, taking Jassie with him then stopped with a muttered oath as the hard ridge of the step behind him dug into his back, reminding him where they were and what they were risking.

'Damn,' he muttered against her mouth. 'Not here. Not yet!'

Gently he held her away from him and searched her face.

'Not here. Not yet!' he growled again. 'I'll not risk thrashing you in God's own house!'

Putting her gently aside he leapt to his feet and extended his hand to help her up.

'The carriage should have arrived by now and Dom and I can have baths and get changed—and I can see to the arrangement of the rooms. Tonight you'll retire early. No one will see anything odd in that! Dom will wander off to the library to get a book after we've had our port and I'll follow you upstairs. With no one else about to entertain him it'll be no strange thing if he takes the book to his room and then—'

He bent and kissed her startled mouth, grabbed her hand and began pulling her out of the chapel to find the sun had already faded from the day.

'You really have thought of everything, haven't you?'

'Yes!' he said and Jassie hugged to her soul this vision of Rogan exuding a confident, buoyant happiness so reminiscent of her old childhood hero. The light might have leached from the day, but the brightness of it illuminating her heart was blinding.

Just as well his grasp of her hand was firm and he led the way for she was so enveloped by happiness she saw nothing but him.

Ruby was laying out her nightdress and turning back the bed covers when Jassie arrived in her room directly after the ladies had risen from the dining table, leaving the men to their port.

'My Lady! I wasn't expecting you yet!'

'Why not, Ruby? My husband is home and we *are* newly married. I can't imagine why you'd be surprised we'd wish to retire early,' she said, hoping she sounded quite nonchalant and Ruby didn't notice the bright color in her cheeks.

She needn't have worried, she realized as she watched a dull tide of color flood Ruby's cheeks and her pale blue eyes suddenly blazed quite ferociously.

'Oh my Lady! If he's going to hurt you again—'

'Say no more, Ruby.' Jassie said sternly. 'Lord Windermere is my husband and whatever happens between us stays between us. You can do nothing—and even though I know you will think a lot, I ask you to say nothing. Not even if my body is beaten black and blue. Do you understand, Ruby?'

The maid looked inclined to argue.

'Please,' Jassie added a little more gently. Ruby scrunched her face into a grimace.

'All right, Miss Jass—my Lady,' she muttered. 'I'll say naught, but it won't stop me thinking!'

'I know Ruby, but truly, I think things will be much better now.'

'I hope so, my Lady.'

'You may have the rest of the night off, Ruby—and don't be too early in the morning!'

The maid went off muttering and Jassie dropped to the chair before her mirror and lifted trembling hands to remove the pins from her hair. Her eyes were very bright and her cheeks a little pale. Not surprising, she decided when she considered the evening before her. Rogan's whispered instructions just before she left the dining room were still echoing in her head.

'Get rid of Ruby. We'll be your maids and undress you tonight. I expect to find you sitting at your duchess brushing this beautiful hair—waiting for us.' Then dropping a kiss on her brow, he'd added, 'We'll be up soon.'

And throughout the short exchange she'd been supremely conscious of Wolverton's smoldering emerald gaze burning into her shoulder blades. Just as each time she'd looked up during dinner he was watching her, his eyes warm and just a little hungry. It had felt strange knowing later he would come to her along with Windermere—and they would all get naked together and—

Lord, her mind was fragmented, wanting to dart in several directions at once, and none of it was productive. Her thoughts only seemed to agitate her more and it was likely by the time the men arrived she'd be a quivering mess of nerves.

In an effort to divert the channels of her mind she began counting the strokes of the brush through her hair and thought of the nurse she'd had when young, Old Mallie, who'd insisted she give her hair one hundred strokes each night and count them out loud.

She'd reached two hundred and sixty one and her arm was getting tired by the time Rogan entered through the dressing rooms. Dressed only in a dark blue brocade dressing robe tied loosely at his waist, his strong muscular legs were bare and the sight was somehow shocking and exciting all at once.

He crossed the room to turn the key in her door and then came to stand behind her with his hands on her shoulders. Jassie's had dropped to her lap.

'How are you feeling?'

Their eyes met in the mirror and Jassie saw concern for her behind the excitement glittering in his.

'I'm not sure. I don't know what I feel or what to think! I was simply counting brush strokes trying not to do either.'

'Ah, Jassie,' he murmured, his eyes dropping to where her fingers twisted restlessly round the handle of her brush. Slowly he reached down and plucked it away to begin drawing it through her hair with sure, languid strokes. She loved having her hair brushed. Her eyelids wanted to drop so she could drift away on the beauty of the sensation, but she forced them to stay wide so she could watch Rogan's every movement in the mirror.

Her husband; brushing her hair. Her heart wept for the joy of it.

'You can't know how I've longed to be able to see your hair out like this. It was always coming loose from your ribbons as a child and dancing round your head like whorls of fairy gold. But once you grew up it must always be confined, quite ruthlessly. It has been deeply painful believing I would never have the right to do this; to see this; feel it.'

Laying aside the brush he simply drew his fingers through the thick silken strands and Jassie felt her heart trembling for what she saw on his face.

'Rogan?' she whispered.

'I have so longed to love and pleasure you as you deserve, Jass. Making love can be, should be, such a beautiful thing and I want you to know that. It's my driving force, allowing me to remain sanguine about Dom loving you. When he told me he was going to ask you to marry him, after I'd assured him I wasn't going to, I thought at best it would mean the end of our friendship or I would have to kill him and then put an end to my own miserable existence. I couldn't face the thought of him having you as his wife. I ask myself what has changed and I think it has to do with the fact back then I couldn't see past myself and what I couldn't have, what I'd been denied. Now I'm able to see that the most important issue is you—and your happiness.

'And the wondrous thing about that is, if we achieve your happiness then we also achieve mine.—And in the process we bring a modicum of happiness to Dom who, for so long, has had to watch the woman he loves suffer after another.'

A huge lump in Jassie's throat made speaking difficult and as if he knew, his fingers glided up the column of her neck, trailing satin fire, which also made it difficult to think. But at least it released the words she'd wanted to say.

'We owe Dom so much. Perhaps we can help him find a wife—someone of his own to love.'

'Perhaps,' Rogan allowed, fanning his fingers across her cheeks and following every languid movement with his eyes, 'but love is a capricious emotion. If there had been another he could love, surely he would have found her by now.'

Jassie's gaze danced between the midnight glow of Rogan's eyes and his hands, the same hands that had thrashed her to the point of bruising. They were so large, so strong, and now—so gentle. What were they talking of?—Dom—

'Maybe he wasn't really looking. Like me, maybe he just kept hoping—while there was still reason to hope.'

'That you'd change your mind, you mean?'

Jassie nodded, reaching up to cover Rogan's hands and pull them down to cup her throat.

'Possibly. But that's something for us to think about later. I think you're procrastinating now, keeping me talking because you're so unsure about what comes next. And poor old Dom is sitting next door probably just as anxious!'

'That I don't believe,' Jassie muttered. 'I don't believe the Duke of Wolverton would ever have felt anxiety about making love to a woman! I'm the one who is all anxiety!'

Rogan chuckled.

'You're probably right. Come.'

He turned her on the stool until she faced him and then drew her up into his arms and Jassie reveled in the simplicity of the act. Most couples took such intimacies as normal and yet that had never been so between her and Rogan. For so many years he'd not dared to touch her at all.

Gliding his hands up her arms, he thumbed the hollows beneath her clavicle then cupped her face with fingers splayed across her cheeks.

His eyes made her think of drowning, blissfully, in a midnight ocean, as he gazed steadily at her and said, 'I love you Jassie, and my promise to you is, tonight will be about your pleasure and if my alter ego arrives to foul that promise then Dom will be there to sort it out. And I think he has his own promises to make to you.—So, are you ready?'

He leant back, their gazes still locked and it felt as if she could see to the innermost sanctuaries of his soul. Love shone back at her.

Love—and hope.

Wordlessly she nodded and slipped her hand into his.

CHAPTER FOURTEEN

A fire burned merrily in the grate in the Earl's bedroom even though it was late summer and not yet really cold. Branches of candles glowed from the mantel and the tall dressers either side of the huge and ancient ancestral tester bed. Wolverton, also garbed in some sort of male dressing robe, his in a heavy bronze silk, lounged in the large leather chair before the fire, a book on his knees.

That he was staring into the fire rather than reading could have been because the book was boring but Jassie had the impression his thoughts were deep and complicated as he dragged himself back from some distant place when Rogan spoke to him.

This man had promised to change his rakish ways for her if she would only consent to become his wife—not once but twice. It would be his greatest joy, he'd said, for if he had her he would need no other. Lost in her own desperate dreams, Jassie had had little thought to spare then for the Duke's pain. But the full force of it struck her now as he looked up at her and she saw that pain shimmering behind the desire in his incredibly green eyes.

She was struck also by the beauty of the man, the perfect symmetry and autocratic strength of his long dark features, brought to life by the glowing emerald orbs that expressed so much and yet hid so much more. Framed by coal black curls just a tad longer than was fashionable, and with the wicked sabre slash down his cheek, Jassie had often thought he had the look of an aristocratic pirate.

Her Rogan was darkly, ruggedly handsome, the epitome of male beauty in her eyes, but she could not deny it was deeply flattering to be the object of desire to such a man as the Duke of Wolverton.

'We're all agreed then?' he asked, the tone of his voice saying he was unconcerned either way but the white-knuckled clench of his hand on the spine of the book spoke otherwise as did the wide, slow smile lighting his austere features at their twin nods of assent.

He took a moment to draw breath, lay the book aside and rise slowly from the chair. Jassie had never been more aware of his singular height as he took her hands in his and raised them both to his lips. Then he raised his head to hold her gaze.

'I had a speech,' he said, the scar distorting his cheek as he grinned ruefully down at her. 'But—in the reality of this moment I seem to have lost it. I wanted you to know, Jass, what an honor I deem this night to be; what an honor you do me, accepting my presence in—this way. I pledge to—do what I may to bring about the happiness of two of my dearest friends.'

Jassie blinked back the prickle of tears, bit down hard on her lip and curled her fingers tightly around Dom's. Words were impossible. She could only hope somewhere, someday, the Duke of Wolverton would find that perfect woman who would appreciate the true man rarely seen behind the carefully schooled cynical façade.

'May I kiss you, Jassinda?' he asked huskily.

Her gaze flew to Rogan's. There was nothing she wanted more at that moment than to grant the Duke's wish, but suddenly she felt as if she walked a tight rope and one misstep could mean the annihilation of all she'd gained so far. She could not deny Dominic Beresford stirred her responses, had the power to make her desire him. She'd known that even as she'd turned down his offers of marriage. He'd made certain she was aware of that.

But what she was uncertain of was how Rogan would react should he see her respond to Dominic. She didn't want to lose what little she already had with him nor did she wish to jeopardize the close friendship the two men shared.

There was a sternness about Rogan's mouth as if a part of him did indeed object, but his gaze was steady on hers, his understanding of her concern clear.

'It's all right, Jass. If you cannot respond to Dom just as openly as you respond to me this scenario really won't work. You've admitted you could've had a satisfactory and happy marriage with him if it weren't for what you feel for me, what I can't question you have always felt for me, and the fact you *can* respond to him is what makes him the perfect man to help us. Just relax and do what comes naturally. Our common goal is your happiness, your—deeply carnal satisfaction.'

Jassie blinked and Rogan smiled and for a moment she was lost in the wonder of him appearing as he'd used to be, blue eyes bright and almost dancing in anticipation, and with a long-absent air of ease about him. Could she dare believe the darkness was lifting?

'Kiss the man,' he murmured, leaning in close to press his lips to her ear. 'I intend to indulge myself with other parts of you while he has your attention.'

Dear God! Could she really do this? Her blood had heated several degrees since entering this room. Her mind had vanished completely and her body felt as if it were about to dissolve. If they both touched her at once—

Rogan's glance connected with Dom's and suddenly Jassie realized these two had probably planned how this encounter would go and they meant to enjoy themselves, just as they were determined she would. That realization only swelled the excitement already churning through her bloodstream.

With a soft caress of her fingers through Rogan's rumpled hair, Jassie finally allowed her hands to move and spread across Dom's broad and lightly furred chest inside the gaping lapels of his robe. When he stayed absolutely still, she looked up at him and her mouth dropped open at the dark storm of desire she saw gathering in his eyes. Slowly, he settled his hands at her shoulders, caressed up the column of her neck and buried his long, tensile fingers in the mass of her hair. As his head dropped lower and the sensual mouth aimed for hers, Rogan's hands slid beneath her arms to cover her breasts and begin a sensual kneading through her gown.

Dom captured her soft gasp in his mouth and Rogan's teeth nipped gently at the tender skin between neck and shoulder and all thought was suspended. Their heated, mobile mouths were organs of exquisite torture and her body, disconnected totally from her mind, became a humming instrument responding only to the expert guidance of two maestros. The duet they played over her skin was beautiful beyond description.

Dom's hands molded lovingly along the curves of her jaw, angling her head and holding her captive for an onslaught of lips and tongue not only stealing her breath but dragging small whimpers of need from her throat. These he devoured from her mouth transmuting them into deep purring growls that vibrated from his mouth back into hers, creating paths of lightning fire, each one leading straight to her feminine core that ached and writhed in an agony of wanting.

Rogan, his lips hot and murmuring love and encouragement by her ear, slipped his hands inside the top of her gown and corset. Threads of flaming need arrowed to that place already burning for them both as he released her breasts so her nipples pouted between his fingertips. Her body lost all ability or desire to stay upright and her legs began to simply melt beneath her.

'Oh Jass,' Rogan murmured by her ear. 'This is what I wanted for you. This is what I want you to feel.'

'Rogan? Rogan! I don't know—Dom!'

Her incoherent attempts at responding were lost in a wild breath of ecstasy as Dom's hands slid down to grasp her waist and he lowered his head to suckle greedily at one wickedly straining nipple held for his attention by Rogan's gently kneading fingers.

'Dear God!' she whispered and her head fell back on Rogan's shoulder. Instantly he angled for her mouth until their lips were sealed in a mutual blending of souls. At last Rogan was kissing her as she'd always wanted; his mouth, the torment of her dreams for so long, was devouring hers; his tongue—

Dom's noisy suckling brought the thought crashing into her passion-dazed mind her dreams had never reached these heights.

Rogan's fingers were now working at the fasteners down the back of her gown as his lips nipped and sucked at hers and his wicked tongue delved to find hers and stir her already boiling blood to flash point.

The only thought dancing lustily through her mind was 'May this ecstasy never end' and yet her body hungered and yearned for more, for the conquering of some unnamable pinnacle.

As Rogan's lips left hers and he concentrated on stripping her gown down her arms and off her body, Jassie found her voice.

'Oh please,' she whimpered. 'I can't bear it!—Don't stop!—I can't—'

Her body threatened to sag to the floor in the wake of the dress and all that would issue from her trembling lips was, 'Please, please, please!'

So focused on her desperation to vocalize her needs, Jassie hadn't registered Rogan's body stiffening at her back and the removal of his support from hers. But when Dom's mouth lifted abruptly away from her breast her eyes flew open to see him straightening and all his attention focused beyond her. Before either of them could move, Rogan shoved her forward into Dom and landed a resounding smack on her buttocks.

'Fucking bitch! I'll teach you—'

In an instant Dom's support was also withdrawn and shocked from a total nirvana of the senses, and now clad only in her corset and chemise, Jassie slumped bonelessly to sit amidst the crumpled pile of silk and lace on the floor.

A loud slap reverberated through the room.

The ensuing silence had an eerie, suspended quality, as if all three had stopped breathing, or even thinking—and simply waited.

Several heartbeats passed before anyone moved.

278 · JEN YATESNZ

'Bloody hell!'

The soft expletive came from Rogan as he dropped abruptly to his haunches beside Jassie.

'Are you all right, sweetheart?'

Silently she reached out to caress his cheek where Dom had slapped him.

'I'm fine,' she whispered, managing to dredge up a smile to accompany the assurance. With Rogan's cheek resting against hers, she looked up at Dom, who stood rigid with horror, staring down at them both.

Instinctively Jassie reached her other hand up to him and as his long legs, bare beneath his robe, folded and he came down to kneel at her other side, the look of glazed horror faded from his eyes.

'I'm sorry,' he growled, 'that I took so long to react! I thought there'd be more of a warning—and I hadn't realized how difficult it might be to stay focused when I have the reality of you in my hands—my mouth!'

Jassie looked from one to the other and saw a rare vulnerability in both faces and with that came the realization of her own power and responsibility. None of this would have happened if she hadn't importuned Rogan on Neave Tor all those weeks ago. They were all three here because she was determined to have a marriage with Rogan, who'd been forced to expose his dark and bitter secret over and over, finally to this best of friends.

And Dom had committed to helping them and though he maintained it was worth it for his chance to make love to her, she knew there'd be an emotional toll for him none of them could truly envisage. If only because, for all his rakish tendencies, he was an honorable rake.

It was time *she* actively committed to their tripartite liaison rather than passively submitting to their efforts to achieve a goal she herself had set. It was time she again found the determination and strength that had funded her proposition on Neave Tor.

Because if she didn't she had an uneasy feeling these two were going to weaken in their resolve just when she perceived the first hint they would succeed. They were staring at her, both of them looking so contrite and apologetic, like small boys who'd failed yet again to please their governess. She wanted to grin and share her silly thoughts with them, but shaped her face into a slight frown instead.

'It worked, didn't it?' she demanded, glaring from one to the other.

'Yes,' Dom agreed, 'but I should've stopped him before he hit you!'

'This is supposed to prevent me from hurting you, Jass!' Rogan exploded.

'I'm not made of spun glass,' she growled at them fiercely. 'You've never damaged me, Rogan. You've never done more than give me a thorough thrashing. You only got one smack in this time before Dom stopped you. It worked! Are we to stop now because you two have turned lily-livered on me? Or are you both actually going to deliver on your promises to show me how a woman should be loved?'

'You still want to continue?' Dom asked, the shadows receding from his eyes.

'But what if—' Rogan began, the pall of dark despair threatening once again.

'Dom smacks you again!' Jassie interrupted. 'And we start again. Dear God, I want you too much to allow you to stop now. I want—quite ferociously—to be naked and at the mercy of your mouths and hands and—other parts.'

'Cocks,' Rogan supplied for her. 'As a kid you always wanted to use the correct term for things, regardless of how unsuitable it sounded on your childish lips. Remember the bull's penis that day when we stumbled on Mr. Bracewell from Neave Farm mating one of his cows?'

Blood rushed into Jassie's cheeks. She'd been all of seven years old and to her young eyes the appendage had been quite startling. And as always she'd expected Philip and Rogan to explain to her what it was and why it was hanging out of the bull's belly. Nothing loath, for by that stage they'd both been used to incessant questions and demands for all kinds of information, they'd explained the thing was called a penis and the bull would stick it into the cow's bottom and that's how a calf was made. Of course there had been other questions about how the calf could live inside the cow where there was no air and more puzzling still, how it was going to get out. They had been so patient with her.

'Penises then,' she muttered, trying very hard to maintain the appearance of nonchalance and not panic as to how forward her admission of need had seemed.

'Uh-uh,' Rogan said, laughing at her and leaning forward to kiss the end of her nose. 'That was the proper term appropriate to a very inquisitive seven year old. You're a woman now and the more appropriate term would be 'cocks'.'

Suddenly Dom stood up and held out his hand to Jassie with a smile she suspected was only ever seen in a bedroom behind closed doors. When Rogan came to his feet beside them his eyes too were blazing with the blue heat from the heart of the fire.

Jassie began to tremble, as if she would melt all over again in the blaze of their combined regard.

'Naked,' Dom demanded. 'Let's get her naked and then we'll show her how we keep our promises and what you can do for her with your cock. I really appreciate a woman who knows what she wants.'

'That's my Jass,' Rogan said softly, leaning in to press another burning kiss just below her ear, as if he simply couldn't keep his mouth away from her. 'Keep us focused on the goal.'

His fingers immediately began loosening the laces of her corset while Dom attacked the ties at the front of her chemise. There was scarcely time to draw breath before she stood naked between them.

'Now you two,' she said imperiously, determined to show no shame at her nudity. 'It's your turn.'

They needed no second bidding and before she could properly appreciate the beauty of their fit muscular bodies, one whipcord lean and strong, the other broadly muscular and powerful, Rogan swept her into his arms and carried her across to the huge tester bed where several successions of Earls of Windermere had been sired.

None so unconventionally as the next could well be, Jassie surmised, as Dom circled the bed and landed at her other side.

Rogan kept waiting for the deeply ingrained possessiveness he'd always felt towards Jassie to overtake him. He expected the ugly burn of jealousy to curl his fists when Dom looked his fill of Jassie's naked bounty.

Instead, he was oddly shaken by his inordinate pride in the elegant perfection of her, from her beautifully rounded tip-tilted breasts, slender waist, femininely curving hips and her strong horse-woman's legs, lithe and shapely.

She was perfection and he wanted Dom to appreciate that too. But more than these strange and confusing thoughts, he just wanted to cherish her, make love to her delectable body and clever mind. Dom's presence and participation in all of this just seemed right in some odd and unaccountable way, especially when he considered it wouldn't be happening if it weren't for his cousin.

Holding her naked form in his arms was like something from a dream. He'd always known Jassie would be as honest and open in her loving as in everything else. This knowledge had added an extra edge to the purgatory that had been his life for the last sixteen years. As he laid her on the bed, he was aware of Dom moving round and climbing up beside her from the other side. For a moment they just sat and stared at the perfection of her then their eyes met across her and Rogan saw his own excitement mirrored in the deep smoky green of Dom's eyes.

'Ours to pleasure,' Dom said, stretching out a hand to cup her breast and roll the beading nipple between thumb and finger.

'Ours to love,' Rogan countered, bending to her other breast and taking it deeply into his mouth. For it was true. They both loved her even though Dom was obviously monitoring his own natural responses.

'Oh God!'

Her words were a tortured whisper and her body arched upwards as she tried to thrust her breasts closer to them. Dom obliged by lowering his head and suckling right alongside him and Jassie began clawing at the sheets and moaning as her head thrashed from side to side. Damn, he wanted her; longed to just sink his flesh deep into her. She was so responsive, so open about what she wanted.

But not yet. They would take her soaring again first.

Dom snagged his gaze briefly and said, 'North.'

Rogan surprised himself by winking at him. It was years since he'd felt this light-hearted, this excited.

If ever.

Trailing kisses down over her ribcage, he left her breast and moved south. Jassie had found his hair and her fingers threaded through it in a gesture as trusting as it was demanding. The sense of freedom to love this beautiful woman was downright intoxicating.

Down he roamed to the softness of her belly and its neat indentation, laving it with his tongue until she giggled in an oddly muffled way and squirmed as if he'd tickled her. Rogan wondered if his heart would burst with the joy of it. Glancing up he saw Dom's mouth tangled with hers, plundering hungrily. Dom would swallow her pleas. She'd only be able to whimper and moan into his mouth, unable to utter anything coherent, no pleading.

He crawled lower down her body, his tongue trailing liquid heat that would rapidly cool on her blushing skin. He savored the ability to kiss and nibble at her flesh and feel her minute responses and he focused on the moment when he'd close his mouth over the burning core of her and she'd jerk into him and cry out straight into Dom's mouth.

Kneeling between her legs, he caressed the well-formed calves and stroked up her thighs with long silken sweeps of his hands. Then spreading her nether lips with his thumbs he lowered his head and took her into his mouth.

Her reaction was everything he'd just been imagining. Her legs and body writhed frantically and she began crying out and threshing her arms across the bed. Dom caught her hands and pinned them above her head, glanced briefly at Rogan feasting like a starving man, then lowered his head back to Jassie's breast. Her cries were no longer muffled and Rogan drove her relentlessly with his tongue rasping over her clitoris and delving deep into her hot, wet channel.

Then as her body exploded around him and she tried to arch completely off the bed, she began calling to him.

'Rogan! Rogan! For God's sake—please—love me! Oh pleee-ase!'

The darkness tore at the edges of his psyche with grasping tentacles and he reared back. Fucking slut! He'd teach her!

'Rogue! No!' Dom's voice, harsh and peremptory, slashed aside the ugly veil that had almost engulfed him, rending it, letting in the light. He felt his nostrils distend with the effort to drag clean air into his lungs. Then he opened his eyes and looked directly at Dom.

'Fuck her!' Dom ordered.

A smile of pure joy broke through the whole of his being and he rose up and thrust into Jassie just as she'd been begging him to.

'Yesss!' he hissed and Dom grinned at him then bent his head to suckle at Jassie's breast again.

Death by ecstasy. Was it possible? Jassie didn't know but in that moment it definitely felt likely. Rogan's body was joined with hers, loving hers, after he'd brought her to such a peak of need she'd lost all sense of anything else. Her only awareness was what he'd taught her to crave, with no reticence in demanding it. Now he was thrusting deep into the core of her, his eyes alight with love and triumph while Dom wrought such sweet torture on her breasts she could no longer utter words, only cry out deep rasping sobs of need.

A fiery ball had formed deep in her belly, fluorescing, building, until her moans and gasps became one prolonged plea for release. Dom covered her other breast with his hand and rolled the nipple between thumb and finger as he bit sharply down on the one in his mouth.

With his blue gaze riveted to hers, Rogan slammed his hips into the cradle of her thighs, his cock thrusting right to the mouth of her womb and the fiery ball within her shattered in spectacular starbursts throughout her body, like the fireworks display she'd seen once at Vauxhall Gardens.

Every muscle in her body clenched, gripping Rogan's cock within her and triggering his own violent expulsion of seed deep in her body.

Dom suckled harder and Jassie's body jerked against Rogan's in a series of aftershocks rocking them both and dragging groans and gasps of elation from deep in their bellies as Rogan continued to arch his body, holding himself deep inside her, absorbing every nuance of her climax until he felt her subsiding beneath him. Gradually he relaxed and rolling to lie beside her, cupped her face in his hands and fastened his mouth to hers in a kiss that clearly transmitted his joy at making love to her without metamorphosing into a sadistic monster.

As he lifted his head Jassie looked into his eyes and felt tears of joy searing the backs of her own. It was a precious moment and all due to the intervention of Dom. Languidly she turned her head to see what he was doing. Kneeling at her side with his brilliant green gaze fastened on hers, the Duke smiled a slow, glittering smile, warning Jassie he was about to make more demands on her.

Instantly, her nerve endings were tingling again, dancing in anticipation and she had the fleeting thought she might be enjoying this too much. But all thought was banished as he leaned closer and said, 'I'm burning up here, Jassinda. That was the most beautiful thing to watch, to share. Could you take me in your hand?'

She couldn't stop her gaze from jerking down his body to where his organ jutted from its nest of black curls, a little slimmer than Rogan's but—probably longer. Hesitantly she raised her hand.

'She's not done that before,' Rogan spoke for her, when it became obvious she was incapable of answering. 'Dom has to be hurting in the worst possible way, Jass. Do you think you could help him with that?'

She swallowed then managed to rasp out, 'I think so but how—what do I do?'

Rogan snuggled in against her neck.

'Give Dom your hand. He'll show you,' he whispered, nibbling at the lobe of her ear then lipping his way gently down her heated skin to her breast. 'You are so beautiful, Jassie. I always knew you would be, despaired of ever really knowing—'

His mouth closed over a nipple again and Jassie felt the fire of it all the way to her core. She simply hadn't understood the simple power of that act, the all-consuming joy of Rogan loving her.

Nor had it occurred to her how silky and delicate a penis would feel and yet how rigid.

With one hand braced beside her head Dom had taken her hand and curled her fingers about his thrusting organ. Now he moved her hand gently up and down the satiny length and Jassie began to understand the deep satisfaction to be had from giving another the kind of pleasure and release the two men had given her. Dom's eyes were closed, his head straining back so the sinews in his throat stood out in stark relief.

Her mind was a crazy jumble of thoughts and feelings; heated pleasure, intense gratitude, and an irresistible need to close her eyes, to turn her face into Rogan's neck, to drag in huge lungfuls of the unique scent that was his alone—as if that moment Dom surrendered to the ultimate physical ecstasy was not hers to watch. It should, eventually, belong to some other woman, someone who would love the Duke of Wolverton as he deserved to be loved; as she loved Rogan.

Liquid, hot and viscous sprayed across her belly and slowly Dom's rigid posture eased and he relaxed down to her side and began massaging the fluid into her skin.

She'd never felt so cherished, she thought, as the two men nestled against her, arms cradling and hands caressing.

They slept, their arms and legs intertwined about her body, their faces buried against her neck. Jassie lay for a long time, eyes closed, relishing the feeling of absolute trust that filled her, absolute love. She

couldn't but marvel they'd been able to put all prejudices and pre-
conceived notions of acceptable behavior aside to enable her and Rogan
to have a normal loving relationship.

She had Rogan Wyldefell for her husband at last and in achieving
that dream she'd gained so much more. She'd been able to open herself
to receive the love of Dominic Beresford also, to give him a little of
herself. Rogan would always be the mate of her soul but there would
now also be a small place reserved for the man who'd made the fullness
of her love for Rogan possible.

As sleep claimed her she wondered if she'd ever be able to hide the
glorious smile that was rooted in her heart and simply glowed through
every particle of her being.

The dream woke him and Rogan lay staring into the dark shadows
of the room. It was a long time since he'd suffered from the nightmare
where he was naked and at the mercy of several women, all built like
prize fighters. Always they pursued him through the gloomy stone
hallways of an ancient castle or fortress, trapping and chaining him in a
dungeon where blazing torches illuminated the scene of his shame and
downfall—and the stark but evil beauty of the Dominant Flagellant
whose long flowing ropes of dark auburn hair and snapping green eyes
were those of Adelaide Barratt.

It was usually the lash of the whip across his genitals that woke him.

Unable to stay still, he slipped quietly out of the bed and crossed to
the window, pulling aside one drape, allowing moonlight to shaft across
the floor. He looked back at the bed, but its two sleeping occupants were
hidden in the dark shadows beneath the canopy. Working silently, he
tied back the drapes so the moonlight allowed him to discern their
outlines, Dom spooned protectively around Jassie's back.

Though he couldn't see their faces clearly, he imagined Dom's dark
austerity softened by the satisfaction he must feel to be at last holding
Jassie's naked body in his arms, for having loved her and been loved by
her. It was a small enough gift when he considered the pain his friend

would have to live with from here on, the pain of watching Jassie happy in her marriage to Rogan.

He turned to gaze out onto the vista over the lake and the Greek Folly where he'd made his confession to her. Moonlight gleamed white across the open spaces, accentuating the shadows and bathing the whole into an eerily magical penumbra. It took his thoughts back to the dream.

Tonight, for the first time, he'd run in a different direction through the castle, a direction he'd never noticed before and instead of feeling as if his legs and feet were weighted with lead, he'd moved with the surefooted lightness of a gazelle. He'd easily outrun the women and their evil clutching hands and had burst through the heavy castle door that had always been barred to him before.

Almost blinded by sunlight, he'd gulped in great breaths of the sparkling fresh air and turned to look back at the castle that had imprisoned his soul for so many years. There was no edifice, only fountains and gardens, all shimmering in the early morning brilliance. A great shout of laughter had burst upwards from deep inside his chest and it was this that had woken him. He thought he'd actually laughed out loud in his sleep but obviously it had not been loud enough to awaken Jassie or Dom. But the sensation of stepping into the light from a dungeon of eternal darkness was still with him.

Could it be that simple? Was he free? Free to be the husband to Jassie he'd always been meant to be? And if it was that simple, he owed Wolverton more than he could ever repay him. In all honesty, one night in the arms of the woman he loved seemed a paltry recompense. He could not see how he could refuse Dom if he wanted to be a regular part of their lives—a constant third in their marriage.

Pray God, he hadn't simply created another desperate situation through the means by which he'd overcome the first! Jassie had responded so openly to their joint ministrations. How would he feel if she wanted that to continue?

Would time dim his gratitude to Dom and his old possessiveness return, his need to have Jassie for himself alone? Would he become jealous and suspicious and ruin with bitterness everything they'd achieved?

Gazing at the two sleeping so closely entwined he could find no hint of jealousy in his heart—as yet—just the thought that Jassie deserved her pleasure. She'd waited long enough for it. He could not deny either of them.

Dom stirred and suddenly his eyes were open, gleaming in the moonlight and looking straight at Rogan.

'Rogue? You all right?'

Dom's murmured words seemed loud in the stillness of the room, but Jassie didn't stir.

He considered the answer to that question for a moment then he allowed the smile lighting up his insides to light up his face.

'I don't think I've been better in a long time. Thank you. I also want to make love to that beautiful woman again. Think we should wake her up?'

'Wake who up?' Jassie demanded, albeit a little sleepily. 'Who can sleep with you two having a midnight palaver?—What are you doing over there, Rogan?'

'Just thinking about coming back to bed and waking you.'

'And why would you do that?'

The sleepiness was rapidly fading from her voice. In fact, he rather thought he could detect a hint of laughter in her words.

'Because,' he said, climbing back under the covers and pressing his chilled body against her warmth so she yelped in protest, 'having discovered I can make *love* to my wife I want to do it again. Would she welcome me, do you think?'

'Probably not. You're as cold as a frog!'

The laughter felt good, so right, and he kissed her nose.

'You'll soon warm me up. In fact parts of me are steaming already. What about you, Dom?'

Dom's chuckle resonated in the darkness around them, rich with sensual innuendo.

'I'd always be ready for this woman.'

As if they'd worked in tandem many times before, he and Dom settled in to giving Jassie the kind of loving that might come somewhere towards making up for all she'd been missing. Rogan kissed her eyelids shut and nibbled down the length of her straight little nose while Dom took her lips in a kiss more in the nature of a blessing than an arousal.

As he began to kiss his way down her throat, Rogan leaned in and slipped his tongue between her soft trembling lips to tease along the sharp edges of her teeth and dance with her tongue. Her sweetness burst into his mouth and they shared the deep sigh of his breath.

'I love you, Jass. So much. Being with you like this is the manifestation of my every desire. Thank you for making me confront what I am—was. Thank you for accepting this totally unorthodox way of resolving things.'

Jassie's small strong hands cupped his face and she leant back, trying to read his eyes in the shadows from the moonlight. Dom's head lowered and his mouth closed over her breast and he smiled to watch her struggle to remain in charge of her mind.

'Oh Rogan—Dom! Oh my God that's—'

'Good?' Dom rasped.

'Yes! Dear God, I never knew—yes—it's good!'

His richly wicked chuckle hummed in the air around them.

'Enjoy my love.'

Watching Jassie's eyes drift shut and her body respond so naturally to Dom's attentions unfurled a coil of aching heaviness Rogan had carried in his heart for years. God, she was precious.

'Rogan?' Her arm curled up round his neck and her voice was breathy with arousal, but also tinged with determination to get out what she wanted to say. 'I love you so much. I'd do anything required for us to be together like this!'

Darting her head forward she dabbed a swift, hard kiss to his mouth before arching back again. Then she almost entirely undid him.

'Are you going to love me again?'

'Lord, yes,' he whispered, pressing her back into the pillows and taking her mouth. 'I want tonight to make up for all I've denied you all these years—and inflicted on you since we married. I also hope it's a promise of all we will have together in the years to come.'

Jassie's finger pressed against Rogan's lips.

'Hush. I understand it all now—and I keep telling you, the joy of finally being your wife and able to make love with you far outweighs any pain you inflicted.'

He opened his lips and sucked her finger deeply into his mouth. She smiled and her eyes dilated. He wished he could see the sparks of topaz fire he knew would be lighting their golden depths.

With a soft sucking pop, he released her finger and nuzzled his way down her neck until he found the thrusting peak of her other breast. Sliding a hand down over the smooth planes of her belly he delved through the nest of curls to find the nub he knew would be aching and throbbing for his attention. She'd always had a fearless need to experience all life had to offer, which had sometimes made things difficult for his mother and Jassie's governess.

Philip and he, on the other hand, had indulged her whenever they could, ensuring her adventurous spirit had not been squelched. She'd been able to climb a tree with the same agility and skill as either of them had achieved and could ride bareback by the time she was six years old. Archery, fencing and marksmanship had all come a little later—though not much, as he recalled. She could swim like a fish and easily darted away from their wicked teasing—unless she'd wanted to be caught and tossed high in the air to land with a resounding splash in the water. Her rowing skills were second to theirs only because of her femininity and lesser years. If they could do it she'd believed she could also.

It had led to some lively lectures from his mother as Jassie outgrew childhood.

It struck him, as Dom moved in to nuzzle deeply at the back of her neck, she was used to having two males at her beck and call. All her life, until Philip went and got himself killed at Vitoria, she'd known they would aid and abet her tomboyish schemes. Philip was gone, and could never have figured in this scenario anyway. Her easy acceptance of Dom's presence was not to be wondered at. It probably felt perfectly natural to her.

The oddest thing was, it felt that way to him as well.

CHAPTER FIFTEEN

She'd certainly dispensed with that innocence, which at twenty-five had begun to irk her so! Accepting the attention of two men at once had to be thoroughly wicked, but as Rogan took one breast into his mouth in a deeply sensual suckling and engulfed her other in his large strong hand and teased and pulled at her nipple, any thought of protest vanished. She'd known, at least since she was sixteen, she wanted this kind of attention from this man. Her body had hungered and ached in strange heated ways that had always left her frustrated and often irritable. She'd wanted this even though she'd not understood what 'this' was. And she'd wanted it with him.

The sensation of coming alive from the core of her being outwards would not be denied. Now she understood what she'd been craving, and it was being served to her with such love, it was like finally arriving at the Promised Land. It felt no more wicked than taking tea with the vicar and his wife—although she didn't let herself dwell on that thought too long—how could she when Rogan—and Dom—were playing her body like the finest of musical harps.

Rogan grazed his teeth down over her belly in a sensual glide that sent every nerve ending dancing then almost lifted her into flight as he slid his tongue down through her curls and into her hot wet core. It was impossible to control the wrenching moans generated deep in her belly and torn out of her by the exquisite sensuality of his touch. Her legs would not stay still, her body alternately clenched and arched, responding to all the stimuli at once—Rogan's mouth at her quim and Dom suckling at her breasts with a hunger definitely not childlike.

The wildness was growing in her again, the incredible feeling of evanescence, of exploding and being out of control all at once.

'Please, Rogan!—Dom!—Please—'

Biting off the words was the hardest thing Jassie had ever tried to do. Rogan couldn't expect to arouse her to this level of desire and she not beg, cry for the completion her body craved.

More aware this time, Dom nipped at her nipple, as if to warn her, then lifted his head to watch Rogan, who had stilled and was starting upright. Immediately Dom placed a firm hand on his shoulder. Jassie saw their eyes meet, knew that was all it took to keep her husband focused on her, in this place and this time.

He drew in a harsh breath, then crawled back up her body to take her mouth with his and she tasted herself on his lips.

'Come ride me, Jass. Take what you want from me.'

With his arms strong about her shoulders, he rolled to his back and lifted her to lie along the hard planes of his body, his rigid erection pressing up into her belly.

'Kneel,' he ordered hoarsely. 'Take my cock inside you. Ride me.'

As she struggled to make her trembling body obey, Rogan gripped her hips and helped her to straddle him until she was poised above his rigid organ.

'Hold me. Guide me into you,' he rasped.

In the dim light of the moon his eyes shone like silver, his love bright and open to her at last, and his mouth worked as if he was in pain.

'Take me, Jass. Slide your hot, wet quim down onto me.'

He gripped her hand and wrapped her fingers around his thrusting shaft. The feel of his straining flesh in her hand was Jassie's undoing and the sensual delight of it dragged a soft moan up through her throat. Raising her hips, she positioned the head of Rogan's cock at her opening then eased herself down on him, savoring his moan of satisfaction as she took him deep into her body.

'Up and down,' Dom murmured, nipping the back of her neck and she was instantly put in mind of the time she'd watched a stallion serving a mare. She wasn't supposed to have been anywhere near the stables that day but because everyone had been so adamant in keeping her away, she'd slipped up into the loft so as not to be the only one to miss out on whatever was going forward. She'd been twelve years old but when they led Rogan's stallion in to where one of the Brantleigh mares was tethered she had understood immediately why they'd banned her. The big grey had been very excited, nipping joyfully at the mare's neck while she swished her tail and tried to back herself into him. Jassie had lain very quiet in the straw and dimness of the loft but it had been difficult when her own body had wanted to squirm and thrust in a similar manner.

Now she truly understood what the mare had been feeling and she finally had the stallion—not one but two!

Dom pressed his hand to the back of her head, pushing her down to Rogan.

'Give Rogue your mouth and—I'll just hold you from behind.'

His hands settled at her hips, showing her the rhythm as she began rising and dropping back down, reveling in the wonder of being able to make love with her husband at last. Rogan's hand slid down between their bodies to find the tiny nubbin, which seemed to have the power to send her spiraling into an ecstatic fever. Dom's mouth played a symphony of kisses up and down her spine while his hands slid rhythmically from her hips to her breasts as she rose and fell on Rogan. Then with a deep groan of desperation Dom pressed his rigid cock between the globes of her buttocks, and held her soft flesh tightly about its steeliness.

That also was a sensitive area it seemed and the intense friction of Dom's powerful body coupled with Rogue's deep throbbing penetration catapulted her into a stunning starburst of ecstasy that threatened to overwhelm her.

Dom rode the rhythm from behind, pressing her down onto Rogan who was trapped by their combined weight. The sudden rigidity of his body was not enough to pierce the intensity of her orgasm but his maddened shout did.

'Get off me, you slut! Get off—'

'Rogan!' Jassie yelled back, focused only on her own pleasure. 'Rogan! Stop it! Love me!—It's me, Jassie and I need you to *love* me! *Love me*, Rogan!'

Dom said nothing, but he had stilled at her back as if waiting to see if Rogan would respond to her, she guessed.

There was a moment of complete stillness when their three bodies seemed to hang in the silence, waiting. The first sound was air hissing out between Rogan's teeth, then the rigidity slowly left his body and he whispered, 'I love you, Jassie.—Love me.—It's all right, Dom. I'm all right.—Let's take her up again.'

Dropping down to the pillows, Dom rasped out, 'You take her up again, Rogue. Show your wife what it means when you say you love her.'

For a second or two there was no sound or movement beyond the combined thudding of their hearts. Jassie watched Rogan's lashes fall briefly to form dark crescents above his cheekbones, then they lifted and his smile blazed up at her, as hot and demanding as she'd always known it could be.

With an easy twist of his powerful body, he rolled Jassie beneath him. Bracing himself above her, their lower bodies still deeply joined, he demanded, 'What do you want, Jass? Tell me what you want.'

This! Yes, this was what she'd needed so desperately in her life.

'I want you to—f—'

'Fuck you?'

'Mmm. That.'

'Say it.'

'I—I can't! It's not—'

'You can. I won't do it until you say it.'

Dom traced her mouth with his finger, stopping to press gently into the dip in her lower lip.

'Tell him what you want, Jass. You won't be sorry,' he murmured against her ear before slowly rimming its curve with his tongue.

Dear God! Jassie raised her hands to where Rogan's jaw was grinding with the tension of holding still.

'F—fuck me, Rogan,' she whispered, as she dragged his mouth to hers in an effort to muffle the words.

With a deep groan of surrender, Rogan began to move, fusing his mouth to hers while lifting his buttocks until their bodies almost separated, then thrusting back deep and hard.

Together they built an exquisite tension she couldn't have imagined or described. All she knew was any greater excitement than this could stop her heart forever. As Jassie felt the fountaining of the incredible heat and ecstasy from her deepest core yet again she thought her heart would burst as Rogan quickly followed with a harsh, prolonged groan of release. Rolling to his side he gathered her against his chest, his arms straining with joy. It was some moments before either of them noticed Dom had pulled away.

It was Rogue who finally lifted his head to gaze across Jassie to the Duke.

'Dom? Did you—? Fiend seize it—!'

'Settle, my friend. This is not about me. It was only ever about you and Jass. How do you two feel about things now?'

There was a flat, expressionless tone to his voice as if he were simply asking what they thought about the weather. Jassie turned to kiss his hand and Rogan pulled himself up against the pillows on her other side.

'You responded to Jassie, Rogue, when she reminded you it was her and she loved you.'

'You did,' Jassie averred, gripping Rogan's hand and Dom's at the same time. Bringing them together at her breast she held them tight within her own. 'I feel sure you'll hear me now. I know I have to be quick—and loud—and speak my name and my love. That's what got through to you, I think. Failing that, I'll just have to find the presence of mind to slap you!'

She reached up and pulled Rogan's head down so she could claim his mouth and affirm such a slapping would be administered with love.

She felt his smile against her lips and a sudden wave of emotion swept through her. Clambering higher up in the bed, she flung her arms around Dom and with tears clogging her voice, exclaimed, 'How can we ever thank you?'

For a moment his grip was fierce and tight about her shoulders and his lips pressed fervently to the top of her head.

'You have, Jassie. You have. Both of you. This night has been the most amazing gift I could ever have asked for.—And I'd be greatly honored to be named god-father to your first born, for I shall always cherish the precious secret I just may have been present at his—or her—conception.'

He reached a hand across Jassie and gripped Rogan's, holding tight and obviously struggling for words, an unusual occurrence for the deeply assured Duke of Wolverton.

That Rogan was similarly affected meant the two men just stared mutely at one another for a moment until at last Rogan managed to say huskily, 'We'd be honored also, Dom.'

'Then perhaps it's time I returned to my room. Don't want to be found here come morning! If you should need me again I'll always be available to you—but—otherwise we shall be as we were before, the best of friends.'

With a final squeeze of Rogan's hand and another quick kiss to Jassie's upturned mouth, he left the bed and vanished through the dressing room to the door leading to the valet's apartments.

Silence descended with his leaving, disturbed a moment later by an abrupt hiccup of a sob from Jassie.

'You're crying, Jass?'

Like a chicken burrowing beneath its mother's feathers, Jassie turned and buried her face against the soft thicket of dark hair on Rogan's chest and wrapped her arms tightly around his body.

'I can't help it. I feel so sad for him. He's everything any woman could ask for in a husband—and so much more. I could've loved him, married him and been happy with him if—if I hadn't loved you!'

Reaching up she traced the long, hard bones of his face and gazed lovingly at him through her tears.

'You were always to be mine,' she went on. 'I believe we knew that before we were ever born. I'd swear we made a pact.'

'Ah, Jassie,' he whispered. 'If I could've made such a pact I certainly would have. You're the only woman I've ever truly wanted and you will never know how close I came to choosing death as the preferable option when I thought I could never have you. I understand your grief for Dom. He's a good man, a friend without price and there'll be someone out there for him. He'll find her one day—especially now he has to finally relinquish any hope of making you his Duchess.—But, I have to ask, Jass. Are you sure you can be happy with just me after— well, it's not just Dom. All your life you've had two males at your beck and call.'

Jassie stilled his lips with her finger.

'This night was total erotic fantasy. It'll be a treasure we can bring out and reminisce over from time to time. And yes, I miss Philip. How can I not? But as I've already said, *you* are all I've ever wanted and I'll prove that to you every time we make love.—Starting now if you have the stamina for it, Windermere!'

His laughter was free and untrammeled as Jassie had not heard from him for many years. It sang and chimed through her heart with all the promise and cheer of Christmas bells.

'We've got years of loving to reclaim and my stamina feels damned amazing at this moment!'

Sliding them both down in the bed, he pressed his burgeoning erection against her thigh to prove his point.

'I'm unconditionally yours, Jass. I even have the feeling one day I could allow you to bind me to your bed and have your passionate way with me!'

Jassie leaned back to search his eyes in the dim light of the dawn. They were blue, the vibrant, startling hue of bluebells in the woods. No hint of the stark, colorless horror that had invaded them the first time she'd mentioned such a scenario.

Her own smile was wide and came from some place warm and deep inside her heart.

'That idea does have a certain appeal, but I don't think we'll try it yet awhile,' she murmured, leaning in to trail her tongue through the hair on his chest until she located the tight flat nub of his male nipple. Sucking it hard into her mouth caused a very satisfactory groan to rumble through his chest and immediately had him rearing up to take control of the situation, just as she wanted.

He knelt between her knees, nudging her legs wide and opening her for the press of his thigh hard up into her core. Jassie thrust her hips off the bed, seeking to deepen the friction and Rogan bent his head to trail his tongue from her navel up to her left breast. Circling the raspy tip of his tongue around the rigid nipple, he suddenly dropped his head a little lower and sucked it deeply into the hot, moist cavern of his mouth.

Liquid fire arced straight to her groin where already his hair-roughened thigh had set her clitoris alight. It burned and throbbed with a rampant urgency beyond Jassie's limited experience. Her newly sensitized body was aroused way beyond the reasoning of her mind. Desperate for Rogan to fill her with his rigid flesh, Jassie had no thought to control what she was feeling. She was on the verge of implosion and when that happened she wanted, with all her being, to have Rogan thrusting and pulsing deep and hard inside her.

His hot and ravenous mouth dragged across the valley between her breasts and drew in her other nipple, suckling with an urgency that sent more trails of fire straight to her groin.

'Oh God, Rogan!' she begged, the raspy wail bordering on a scream. 'Rogan, please! I need you—inside me—now! Damn you, Rogan, please love me!'

She ground her clitoris hard against his thigh and writhed violently in an attempt to reach the unyielding thrust of his cock.

'Please—'

Rearing back, he glowered down at her, his eyes losing their deep, dark hue and beginning to glow with an eerie pale fire.

'Fucking bitch!' he snarled, leaping off the bed and heading to where his neck cloth hung over the back of the chair.

He'd turned back towards her with it in his hand before Jassie's mind had cleared enough for her to realize what was happening. Staring back into his blazing light eyes, she was hit with a sudden epiphany.

Before he'd taken a step back towards the bed she'd forced her trembling body to calm enough she could slide off the mattress and stand upright, meeting him halfway across the floor.

His eyes flared like torches in the dark. 'You never learn do you, bitch? You're a fucking—'

'I'm sorry! Rogan! I'm sorry!' Jassie cried.

She reached her hands out to him and he took them in a punishing grip.

'—damaging whore and I *will* make you sorry—'

He began wrapping the neck cloth around her wrists. Jassie let her body sag against Rogan's instead of going rigid and resistant. Startled by this departure from her normal behavior, he let her hands slide through the cloth and she fell to her knees before him, wrapping her arms around his knees.

'I *am* sorry, Rogan! I'm *deeply* sorry—truly—so *sorry*—'

Jassie clung tightly to his naked legs and pressed kisses to his knees, then slowly kissed down one shin until she knelt with her mouth pressed fervently against the top of his foot.

'I'm *sorry*, Rogan and—I love you. Please forgive me.'

For several seconds he hung, motionless above her, then with a deep, dragging breath he began to sag and fold until he knelt before her. Clasping her shoulders, he lifted her until they knelt, facing one another.

Then he leant forward and kissed her forehead, her nose, her mouth. Each touch of his lips was a benediction, a blessing, a touch of grace.

'Thank you,' he whispered against her skin after a few more deep breaths. 'I love you, Jassie. I love you in ways I can never explain.'

Jassie thought her heart would swell right out of her chest as he slid his arms around her body and held her close, rocking their bodies and continuing to press soft kisses across her cheeks, nose and forehead.

'Forgiveness,' he murmured at last, pulling back to look deeply into her eyes. 'I know it wasn't your sin, my love, but hearing you ask, hearing you speak that word, was like soothing balm on a livid, searing burn. It was like—in that moment before sanity returned—I felt a satisfying, deeply fulfilling peace flow through the whole of my body from somewhere deep in my core.'

Jassie couldn't keep her mouth and hands from him any longer. She cupped his face, drew it down to her and sealed their lips together. It was gentle, reverent at first. But when her tongue slipped into his mouth a soft groan rumbled up from his belly and she finally knew her Rogan was back.

When an answering moan vibrated from the back of her throat, Rogan lifted his head and whispered, 'Shall we take this back to the bed?'

Smiling against his mouth, she murmured, 'Yes.'

Nine months later almost to the day, Jonathan Dominic Wyldefell, heir to the Windermere title and estates was born at the Abbey—in the very bed where he'd been conceived. His dark hair and sunny blue eyes were all Wyldefell but the dimple in his chin was generally held to be a Carlisle trait.

On the day of his christening in the Cistercian Chapel at Windermere, the Duke of Wolverton held his godson in his arms—and remembered. He looked across at the boy's parents, and found himself struggling with a surge of emotion that would not be so easily buried beneath his cultured aloof façade as usual. Since that night just before the opening of the grouse season at Windermere, he'd watched his cousin emerge from the shadows, like a portrait taking on a sharper, clearer focus under the skilled brush of an artist. Rogue had finally stepped fully into the sunlight—and that sunlight was Jassie.

They both glowed with happiness and the joy and gratitude Dom saw in their eyes as they smiled across at him was almost his undoing.

He glanced back down at the baby, whose blue Wyldefell eyes were watching him, as if committing his face to memory. Disconcerted to feel tears stinging the backs of his own eyes, he was devoutly grateful he'd already said whatever was required of him for he could not have spoken if life itself had depended on it.

Surely there was a reward for being honorable and heroic, but any reward for him could never include Jassie—nor the kind of happiness that radiated from her and Windermere. And if it was to include children of his own it was time to cast aside impossible dreams and dredge up honor and heroism once more to do his duty by a title he'd neither wanted nor ever thought to inherit.

Time to choose an acceptable duchess from among the highly suitable families of the ton, a young woman with the breeding and consequence to honor the role when there were none so golden, so bright or alluring as Lady Jassinda Windermere.

Time to acknowledge it was Windermere's presence at Jassie's side fueling that glow from within, not the Duke of Wolverton's.

Time to put his foolish heart aside and focus on duty.

What was going through Dom's mind? Jassie watched him with her son and knew him affected by deep emotion. It was not hard to guess what his heart ached for. He had changed in the last year; become a little more austere and cynical and yet less inclined to his old rakish pursuits, if rumor was to be believed. Surely there was a woman somewhere among all the diamonds of the ton who could put the wicked buccaneering glint back into the Duke's somber green eyes.

If only Sheri—

So tall, so regally blonde and serene at Dom's side, she was the perfect foil for the dark piratical Wolf of Wolverton. Perhaps she and Dominic could—

Her husband leaned close and proved how close their thoughts always were.

'Not our place to interfere, my love,' he murmured. 'Dom will find his happiness now he knows we've found ours.'

She smiled up into her husband's dark blue eyes. It was because she'd never ceased to believe in their love they stood here today with this child as testament. If belief was what it took then she would concentrate on believing hard enough that the Duke found his love also.

She and Rogan and the future generations of Wyldefells of Windermere Abbey owed it to him.

Sneak Peek at Book 2 in
'Lords of the Matrix Club' Series

'The Perfect Duchess'

As a third son Dominic Beresford should not have been the next Duke of Wolverton, but like it or not, he's inherited the titles and the estates, and the pressing obligations to find a wife and provide a ducal heir. His first choice of Duchess recently married his best friend so now he seeks marriage with the next most suitable candidate, longtime family friend, Lady Sherida Dearing. He has also been commissioned to locate a missing heiress as a favor to his erstwhile commander, a woman with a birthmark one cannot ask to see in polite circles. Lady Sherida Dearing would make the perfect Duchess. She is exquisitely fair, icily regal and with an unfashionable tendency to wear high-necked gowns, she's been dubbed the 'Heavenly Iceberg'. Only Sheri's maid knows the depth of her sinful imperfections and although Sheri has loved Dom since her first ball, can she marry him and keep her heart intact—and her secrets?
What the Duke of Wolverton hasn't envisioned is exposing his own secret life as the Master of Virgins at the Matrix Club. Or that beneath the icy façade of his wife he will discover that one who will cause him to forsake all others; that one who is indelibly marked for the Duke of Wolverton—that one he's been searching for.

Chapter 1.

He was like a bloody moth to a flame.

Dominic Beresford, Duke of Wolverton, dragged his eyes from the compelling allure of Lady Jassinda Windermere—yet again. It was a year since the night he'd shared with Rogue and Jassie, a night in which he'd been given so much, yet nowhere near enough, of the woman he loved. The woman who loved his best friend, Windermere, more. Sharing their marriage bed that night had enabled them to overcome Rogue's obsession with punishment, enabled them to have a normal marriage and now a son.

Today that son, Lord Jonathan Wyldefell, had been christened and endowed with god-parents, himself and Lady Sherida Dearing. The guests promenaded about the gardens or stood in groups chatting in the afternoon sunshine.

Radiant in a rose and cream striped afternoon gown with a rose-trimmed cream straw bonnet on her golden curls, Jassie stole his senses, as always.

It was almost a year since that night when he'd come so close, and yet achingly nowhere near close enough, to having with Jassie all he'd dared to hope for with a woman. Somehow he had to get himself in hand and the only way he could think of to do that was to find another to take her place in his mind. He had no illusions about anyone taking her place in his heart. That organ had been tortured and denied once too often and he'd not expose it for more of the same.

And protecting it with discreet liaisons with beautiful widows or his occasional duties as Master of Virgins at the Matrix Club would not beget him an heir.

He needed a wife. It was three years since he'd inherited the bloody title with all its duties and responsibilities, including the siring of the next generation. Last night he'd realized he was ready, more than ready, to be a father.

And that had been Jassie's doing. After dinner, she'd insisted he accompany her upstairs to the nursery, at Windermere's instigation apparently. Then she'd torn his stupid heart from his chest by settling in to feed her son in his presence—albeit with the perfectly modest covering of a linen cloth.

'Jass! Don't do this to me!' What was meant to be a roar was little more than a harsh whisper. 'I can't sit here and watch you—you can't—I can't—'

'I can! And—you—will!'

His whole body had stiffened. He'd never heard that tone in her voice before.

'It's been a year, Dom!' she'd said, her voice suddenly deeper, softer. '*We* need to move on, but we can't because we know you're suffering and we know what we owe you—and we don't know how to fix it. You should've moved on. And *you* are the only one who can make that happen.'

He'd stared at her for long moments, the Madonna-like picture of mother and child another privilege that should've been exclusive to her husband she'd gifted to him. Jonathan could have been his son, and his heart had almost burst with the need for the reality of his own child.

'We were meant for one another, Windermere and I, and can never thank you enough for your part in making it possible for us to be together. You and I could've been happy, for a time—but long term? I think in time you'd weary of—what Papa used to call my 'hoydenism'. I'd wear on your nerves. It's neither here nor there anyway for it can never be. But until you move on, marry, we're all stuck in this kind of—vortex—watching and waiting. It's time you relegated me to—last year's cast-offs. Please Dom, cast *me* out of your dreams and make room for someone else.'

Was she right about her effect on him long term? She wasn't serene, cool, poised—like her best friend, Lady Sherida Dearing, who'd never irritated him in any way and he couldn't imagine ever would. In fact,

Lady Sheri had all the requirements for the perfect duchess; breeding, beauty, poise, serenity, intelligence—

But the picture of Jassie nurturing her child was emblazoned on his mind. How could he concentrate on courting anyone else? Move on, she'd said, but he was still caught in the web of her allure, an allure that now included a babe.

But he'd had to agree.

'I hear what you're saying, Jass. I'll go forth and find a wife! It's a wonder Aunt Georgiana hasn't started on me.'

He'd stood and winked at her, hoping to lighten the moment. There must be no more deep emotion between the three of them, just an abiding friendship.

Jassie had breathed an audible sigh of relief then said, 'I think Lady Baxendene has a challenge enough with her own son without worrying about you.'

...

Still focused on Jassie across the lawn, he was jolted back to his senses by a warm hand slipping into the crook of his arm.

'Walk with me, Dominic.'

'Aunt Gussy! Well—certainly! Where shall we walk?'

'Towards the lake will do fine. I want to talk to you!'

'Sounds ominous,' Dom quipped, still struggling to get his mind off Jassie. Focus returned with the thought Aunt Gussy might be ready to talk of her family scandal.

Lord Hadleigh, Chief of Intelligence under whom he'd worked from time to time in that other life before he'd inherited a dukedom, had coerced him back into service to find the missing Walsingham heiress. Born twenty-three years ago in America. Sylvaine Walsingham had vanished without trace before the age of two and the only clue he had to work with was that she bore an ugly birth mark across her chest. He'd called on Augusta and her daughter, Lady Sherida, because the girl would have been Augusta's great niece. He'd been stymied by Aunt Gussy's distress when informed that Maynard Walsingham, the child's father and Augusta's nephew, had died some sixteen years ago.

The man would have been a similar age to Gussy, given his father was her much older brother, and had absconded to America in the wake of a terrible scandal. He'd eloped with the Duke of Halcombe's youngest daughter and refused to fire when he faced the Duke on the field of honor. Nevertheless the Duke had collapsed and died of a heart attack.

The babe's mother had died in childbirth and Augusta had claimed no knowledge of any child.

'What's on your mind?'

'You, my boy,' she said in her forthright way, immediately dashing his hopes of new information. 'I was very close to your Mama. I'm going to talk to you as I think she'd want me to.'

Damn. She was Windermere's aunt, not his, but he'd always accorded her the courtesy title. He knew he wasn't going to like what she had to say, but because of his deep respect for her he'd listen. Nevertheless, his response when it came was a little stiff.

'And what do you think she'd want you to say?'

'It's not healthy—for you or Jassinda—the way your eyes follow her all the time. You must find another focus, another woman. Jassie was never for you. You have to accept that and look elsewhere!'

Just what Jassie had said; what he told himself several times a day. But the chasm between knowing and doing seemed too vast to bridge. Especially when he was anywhere in Lady Windermere's vicinity.

'What woman would want me? My obsession with Jassie is no secret. Given that fact, it's unfair to even court another woman.'

Augusta made that inelegant sound he'd heard her make before and he wondered if she knew she snorted when she was annoyed. And she was just getting into her stride!

'You have wealth and a prestigious title. Few in the ton would expect to marry for more! For goodness sake, Dominic! You could have the pick of the season! The first woman you ask will fall at your feet with delight.'

Dom shuddered.

'Would you want that for Sheri? A title and wealth and a cold, loveless marriage?'

Augusta came to a halt by a seat facing the lake and the amazing sculpture of Zeus and his chariot appearing to skim across the surface of the water that Windermere had commissioned for his wife shortly after their marriage. She plopped down and by dint of a gentle but firm hand on his sleeve, urged him down beside her.

'Of course I don't want that for Sheri! She doesn't want it for herself! It's why she's still unwed at almost twenty-four! But she's running out of options. Holding out for love is not getting her anywhere. Now, *she* would make the perfect duchess.' Augusta said, turning urgently towards him as if the idea had just struck her.

He'd lay a monkey it'd been her agenda all along.

'You look stunning together, you so dark and her so fair. The Pirate and the Princess!'

'Now you're getting carried away, Aunt,' he said drily, then fell silent.

'Think about it, Dominic. You need a wife. An heir. You need to move on from this unhealthy obsession you have for Windermere's wife.'

'You would encourage the match, knowing the lay of my heart?'

'Sheri needs a husband.'

As they walked back towards the house he couldn't help wondering what Sheri would make of the conversation. It also struck him Augusta was the third or fourth person lately who'd pointed out what a perfect duchess Lady Sherida would make. She would. If he were to make a list of the eligible women available to him, her name would be first on that list.

He'd already thought he should get serious about courting her.

But—and his eyes drifted across the lawns, seeking the flash of a rose gown or the dance of gold ringlets.

...

For the rest of the afternoon and all through dinner, Dom tried to focus on the icy perfection of Sherida Dearing. He'd been partly successful, he supposed. The third child in a family of four, he'd never been one to follow the herd or fall meekly into line. But with the number of his friends who'd been at pains to wake him up to the duchess-potential of Lady Sheri, he was beginning to think even the Universe was conspiring to bring him into line.

His natural inclination was to tell them all to let him go to the devil in his own way. Then he thought of Windermere and how he'd still be wallowing in his dark pit of despair if a friend hadn't cared enough to interfere; *really* interfere. He'd been that friend for Windermere. He'd spoken and acted because he cared, not just wanted to interfere. Perhaps he should allow his friends the possibility they too only spoke because they cared.

Currently his older cousin, Ajax Beresford, Earl of Knightsborough, stood first in the line of succession. Knight was not, and had no intention of becoming, that which a Duke was made of. Nor was he likely to breed an heir for the succession. That, Knight was inclined to remind him frequently and forcefully, was his job.

Thus he needed an heir and therefore a wife, and there was none more suited to the role than Sherida Dearing. As a daughter of an Earl she had breeding, wealth, beauty and the regal bearing required of a duchess. Best of all she was intelligent, easy to talk to and comfortable to be around.

Could he bed her? She wasn't Jassie, but she was beautiful, shapely. A man would have to be dead not to desire her. Perhaps he should've tried kissing her during their ride down to Windermere on Saturday. It might've done what he hadn't been able to do for himself, take his mind off Jassie.

Hopefully the weather held for the ride back to London tomorrow and an opportunity might present itself. Though he'd have to find some way of ditching the groom! Old Carter was excessively diligent in the care of his mistress.

The gentlemen had returned to the salon after their port and the ladies were being entertained by his and one of Bax's sisters singing a duet to Sheri's accompaniment. Lord Baxendene immediately ambled over to perch on the stool at Sheri's side and turn the pages for her. It was exactly where his rakish lordship had been when Dom had returned to the salon after talking with Jassie last night. What the hell was his cousin up to?

'You're very quiet this evening, Wolf,' Rogue said at his elbow as they took their stance against the mantelpiece to survey the room. 'You're not upset with Jassie and me, are you? After your chat last night?'

Dragging his hand down the scar on his cheek, which tonight was aching like a bastard, he said calmly, 'Everything she said was valid and only reiterated by several others who've taken it upon themselves to advise me on the direction they perceive my life should proceed. And they're right, dammit! It *is* time I moved on—and—what the fuck is Hades playing at?' It had finally registered Bax was sitting close enough his body touched Lady Sherida's from shoulder to knee and she had an unusual and very becoming flush in her cheeks. 'Sherida Dearing's not some barque of frailty for him to dally with!'

Rogue observed the pair on the stool more closely then said, 'She's just the sort of challenge he'd enjoy. I'm surprised the Great Bax hasn't set out to thaw the Iceberg before now.'

'He'll set Sheri up for ruin over my dead body!' he snarled, surprised at the vehemence of his feelings on the matter.

'She's managed to look after herself very well until now,' Rogue noted, turning a lively gaze on his cousin. 'Bax is honorable enough not to risk his handsome hide by hunting on another's preserves—or dally-ing with family. It's to be expected he'd seek her out. She's the only single, unattached female present who's not directly related. What did you think of the portraits she did of Jassie and me?' he asked, patently trying to divert Dom's attention from their cousin and his amorous pur-suits.

As a ploy it was well judged. He appreciated good art and was im-pressed with Lady Sherida's skill. Dom turned to where the two portraits which Sheri had given the Windermere's yesterday now hung over the fireplace, The Earl and Countess of Windermere posed in the ancient and partially crumbled stone archway, all that remained of the original Abbey church at Windermere.

'She's good, don't you think?'

'Better than good,' Dom muttered, leaning forward to examine the one of Jassie more closely. Something about the style, the brush strokes, the layering of the color reminded him of the set of three smaller ex-quisite semi-nudes he had on the wall in his study. They weren't nudes in the classical sense, being back views only. Entitled 'Innocence', 'Awakening' and 'Awareness', they were a delightful portrayal of a young woman growing in confidence in her own sensuality. He'd come across them at an exclusive little gallery on Bond Street.

He studied the delicately executed signature in the corner of the painting.

S. R. Dearing.

Nothing like the spidery *S. P. R. Woods* in the corner of each of the nudes. Thinking the 'Heavenly Iceberg', as the ton had dubbed her, might paint anything as sensually appealing, as blatantly sexual as the three pieces of *art érotique* brought a smile to his lips.

'I was aware Sheri painted, but I had no idea of the level of her abil-ity. Every bit as impressive as the *S. P. R. Woods* trio of nudes I discovered at Puttick's Gallery.'

Rogue nodded.

'Did you ever discover who he is?'

'No, but I live in hope—and that he paints more!'

...

It was easier to keep his focus on Sheri after that. When the evening ended he made a point of raising her hand to his lips, looking deeply into her eyes and enjoying the confusion he saw there and the hint of color in her cheeks. He could ruffle her demeanor. It was a start.

Bax's room was next to his. As they climbed the stairs, Dom said, 'A cigar on the balcony before bed?'

Bax, his eyes on Sheri's silken skirts disappearing at the bend in the stairs, murmured, 'Yeah. Probably better if I don't know which room she's in.'

The punch of fury to his gut almost brought Dom to a standstill, but he forced his legs to keep climbing. No need to alert the out-sized Lothario his comment had struck him in any way.

'If she didn't tell you which was her room she didn't invite you to call.'

Bax chuckled.

'It'd never be that easy with the 'Heavenly! It'd have to be seduction pure and simple! A real test for my skills. Is that a little—antipathy I hear, cousin?'

'Sheri's a lady,' Dom all but hissed. 'Not some light-skirt you can toss behind the arras! She's the kind of woman you marry—not—'

'—just fuck for the fun of it?' Bax happily finished for him.

'I might not have put it so crudely,' Dom growled back, his voice stiff with anger.

'Of course you wouldn't,' Bax soothed. 'You're the Duke and Lady Sheri has all the hallmarks of the perfect Duchess. But dammit, Wolf, she's what—twenty-three?—and never been fucked. Imagine the frustration! Women need it, ache for it, just as much as we do, you know. It's just that they've been taught to suppress their urges. But think what pleasure I could give her. Think how it'd be, awakening the frozen princess beneath all that ice.'

They'd reached the balcony. Dom had snagged a couple of cigars as they'd passed through his room. There was a short silence while they lit up and stared out towards the distant lake.

'You damage that woman's reputation and I'll call you out,' he snarled, not allowing himself the chance to rethink. The notion sat right with his honor. He *would* call his cousin out. In fact he'd kill the cocky bastard, if he damaged Sheri in any way.

'I'm your cousin,' Bax said easily. 'Besides, I'm bigger than you and if you call me out I get to choose the weapons—fists, at Jackson's!'

'Hurt Sheri and I'll take you apart however and wherever I have to do it!'

'Hell, Wolf, if you're hung up on the Iceberg yourself you only had to say!—Tell you what—'

Dom sucked hungrily on the cigar to calm himself. It was somewhat alarming just how volatile his cousin's casual intent towards a woman of Sheri's caliber, made him.

'—I'll make you a little wager—'

'You'll keep your lecherous paws off Sherida Dearing. End of discussion. And just so I don't lose my temper completely and toss you over the balcony, tell me about the new hunter you bought at Newmarket last week.'

He definitely didn't want to hear him crow one more time about the fat purse he'd won at the Derby by betting on the Duke of York's Prince Leopold who'd edged the favorite out by half a length.

...

They should've left for London that morning, but a soft rain was falling and in the gentlemen's opinion it was setting in for the day. The ride back to London therefore was out of the question and if Dom and Sheri both rode in the coach it would be crowded and uncomfortable.

'So if you think Aunt Gussy will be agreeable we'll hope for a better day tomorrow,' he'd suggested.

'Of course Mama will agree. Another day with Aunt Olwynne will delight her.'

Sheri would happily wait a week rather than forfeit a day riding in his company. On the way down to Windermere they'd visited his old family estate in Canborough to check out the new colt sired by her Golden Boy on his Silver Lady. It had been an idyllic day, with Mama travelling by road in the ducal carriage and she and Dom with her groom as chaperone, riding cross country.

The ladies were gathered in the morning room, their hands busy with various handwork projects while chatting about domestic issues. Sheri settled herself at a low table with sketchpad and pencils.

Jassie had placed Jonathan on a thick quilt on the floor where he gurgled happily at Dom's nieces crowded about him in fascination. Sheri's fingers were busy capturing images of the child, but her mind was worrying again at the problem of Dom and Jassie.

Like most of his peers, she imagined he saw no reason to remain celibate because he loved another man's wife. Being the private sort, he was probably just discreet.

Now Jassie was married would she become one of those discreet liaisons? Sheri wished that thought hadn't occurred to her. She sketched the curve of Jassie's cheek and the caress of a curl as she leant over the baby. Marriage suited her. Health and well-being glowed about her and couldn't fail to draw a man who loved her.

She and Lady Windermere were close friends. What if Jassie confided in her about such a liaison? Jealousy, ugly and painful welled in her breast. She had no right to feel that way—he'd certainly never given her any reason to do so. Male voices interrupted her thoughts.

'Lordy! It's like a chicken house in here,' Bax grumbled striding across the room to arrange his big body on a chair at her side. 'Looks like you've given yourself a crick in the neck leaning over that low table,' he scolded. 'You should be working at a proper angle.'

Reaching for her pad, he flicked through the sketches.

'These are good. How about doing my portrait—you know, private sittings?'

He grinned disarmingly at her and Sheri could only laugh back and comment lightly that at six foot five and built like a national monument, she didn't think she could find a canvas big enough to do him justice.

Should she feel flattered, she wondered, as she considered his particular attention over the last couple of days, but reasoned she should read nothing into it. She was the only unattached and unrelated female present.

'Ladies don't usually complain about my size.'

He grinned again, giving her a rakishly sidelong glance.

Recognizing the innuendo, she knew by the rules of polite society she should pretend to misunderstand or give him a severe set-down, but she was tired of being so proper. In fact at twenty-three she should even try a little male-female dalliance to see if some gentleman other than the Duke of Wolverton could attract her. The Great Bax had everything going for him. Well-endowed with the dark Beresford looks, he was an impressively built man. Big—not fat. She imagined his naked person would steal a woman's senses, a fact he traded on shamelessly.

'I imagine not. I've heard it mentioned a time or two,' she answered lightly.

'Ouch! Should I be blushing?'

'I doubt that face has seen a blush in many a year!'

He'd made her laugh openly at him, and he was giving her the full benefit of his heated grey gaze, but she felt nothing, not even the urge to further their dalliance in the interest of light entertainment. Perhaps the popular assessment was right and she *was* frigid!

'Let's escape this menagerie! Come walk with me in the conservatory. We could discuss—blushing—a little more fully.'

'No thank you,' she said, loading her voice with mock primness. 'Give me my pad and I'll sketch you. I could put it up for auction. It'd probably go for a mint as all your besotted admirers tried to outbid one another!'

'You'd not keep it for yourself?'

'Whatever for?'

'To put under your pillow—so you'd dream of me.'

'Nightmares tend to keep me awake.'

His eyes danced back at her, obviously well pleased with their repartee.

Dom settled on the window seat behind their chairs.

'Morning, Lady Sheri,' he said, the mellow timbre of his voice quivering a nerve in her chest, when Bax's voice though deeper still, had no effect at all.

'Morning, Your Grace,' she responded in a more formal vein then bent her head to the sketch she'd started of Bax.

'Sheri's doing a sketch of me—to keep under her pillow.'

She shook her head then gave him a teasing smile.

'I'm going to do several and make my fortune selling them to the ladies of the ton. Then you'll find one under every pillow—'

She stopped, color flooding her cheeks. What was she doing, allowing the rake to loosen her tongue like that? Might as well loosen your stays—and she could just imagine him suggesting it!

'She's got your measure, old chap,' Dom interjected smoothly.

Abruptly, Sheri rose and said, 'I—um—need to go and see if Mama is coming down to luncheon. Excuse me.'

It was easy to see how Bax charmed women, she thought as she crossed the room. He'd had her eating out of his hand, so to speak, even though she wasn't in the least attracted to him. Why couldn't she relax like that around Dom?

Probably because she was too dashed attracted to *him*.'

. . .

Bax followed her progress through the room, then turned back to confront Dom.

'Well, damn you, Wolf! You chased her off just as the thaw was setting in! She was just about to agree to a private *tête à tête* with me.'

'You think?' Dom gave his big, brash cousin a skeptical grin. 'I'd say she left to avoid that very thing. I doubt she'd have allowed me to chase her away if she'd been in the least interested.'

'I was getting further than you've ever got!'

'I've never tried.'

'And like we said, she'd make a perfect Duchess,' Bax needled.

'I'm not interested in your leavings!' Dom snarled, wondering why he was reacting so intensely to what should have been mere banter.

'Beat me to the prize then!'

A stab of excitement quickened his blood. A challenge! That could be just the spur he needed to cast his lure somewhere other than at Jassie.

'A small wager—like I was going to suggest last night.'

The perfect distraction! It was a while since they'd played off against one another.

'What did you have in mind?'

His grin felt feral, even to himself.

'That's more like the big bad Wolf I know!' Bax said with satisfaction. 'We've both just acquired some new bloodstock. Prime pieces. First to claim the cherry wins the hunter from the other's stable.'

Dom winced. He'd finally talked Briersley, his brother-in-law, into selling him a big chestnut mare he'd wanted for ages—at an exorbitant price. She was a prime goer, poetry to watch at the fences and he planned to breed from her a little later on. Then again, Bax's golden palomino stallion, Zeus, was just as valuable. He'd reached that point in his internal argument when Bax laughed outright as if he'd been privy to his every thought.

'Doubting yourself already?' he taunted, 'or is your horse more important than Lady Sheri's favors?'

He didn't intend to lose.

Available from Amazon
http://www.amazon.com/dp/B01MSBW42C

~~~

AUTHOR'S NOTE

Clubs of varied natures abounded in Regency London. And I can readily imagine one such as the Matrix Club might have existed. It was interesting trying to devise 'help' for Windermere's problem in an age before there were therapists or any understanding of such disorders and I hope you were able to read past his traumas to his HEA.

I sincerely hope you enjoyed the Earl of Windermere's story, the first in 'Lords of the Matrix Club' series and will leave a review at www.amazon.com/dp/B01ENSMA2A

NEWSLETTER

If you want to join JEN YATES$_{NZ}$'s email list to be informed when a new book is due out, send your details to:
jenyatesnz@mail.com
You will receive a free short sequel to the series,
'The Townville Legacy – A Darkness in the Blood'.

To find other books I have written please visit my website -
http://www.jenyatesnz.com

Happy reading.
Jen YatesNZ.

ABOUT THE AUTHOR

Jen YatesNZ is a Great-Gran privileged to live in beautiful New Zealand with her 'somewhat younger' 2nd husband. She found her very own hero and knows romance really exists.

The stories were in her head from as early as she can remember, and they were always romance. For years writing took 2nd place to her 'real work', which was 33 years as a teacher and 6 years as an antiques dealer. Now, writing is what she does and romance, preferably historical, is her genre. The characters in her head are finally getting their stories told.

ACKNOWLEDGEMENTS

My eternal thanks to Jean Drew for the vision to found Romance Writers of New Zealand over 20 years ago. This organisation has nurtured so many talented New Zealand authors and helped us gain the skills necessary to become better writers and to succeed in realizing our dreams.

Thank you also to YOU, my readers. YOU complete my stories.

~~~~~~

39468322R00188

Made in the USA
Lexington, KY
18 May 2019